C000177170

DICK LOCHTE

Sleeping Dog

PENGUIN BOOKS

PENGUIN CLASSICS

UK | USA | Canada | Ireland | Australia
India | New Zealand | South Africa

Penguin Books is part of the Penguin Random House group of companies
whose addresses can be found at global.penguinrandomhouse.com.

First published 1985, updated 2011
This edition published 2023
001

This is a work of fiction. The author acknowledges that there is a not-quite-mythical state
known as California, but any similarity to existing people, places, and situations is 100 percent
coincidental and unintended.

Set in 11.25/14pt Dante MT Std
Typeset by Jouve (UK), Milton Keynes
Printed and bound in Great Britain by Clays Ltd, Elcograf S.p.A.

The authorized representative in the EEA is Penguin Random House Ireland,
Morrison Chambers, 32 Nassau Street, Dublin D02 YH68

ISBN: 978–0–241–65692–1

www.greenpenguin.co.uk

MIX
Paper | Supporting
responsible forestry
FSC® C018179
www.fsc.org

Penguin Random House is committed to a
sustainable future for our business, our readers
and our planet. This book is made from Forest
Stewardship Council® certified paper.

*For Nick, who liked the idea,
and for my mother, who likes
all of my ideas.*

Preface

It is no longer a rare occurrence in contemporary publishing for several books to cover the same subject matter – the scandalous behavior of a deceased film star, perhaps, or a voguish diet plan, or a method for combatting some well-publicized health scare. In this instance we are dealing with the events surrounding a series of brutal murders committed in California during the summer of 1982.

Two involved parties penned separate first-person accounts of the mass murders. Ordinarily these manuscripts would have resulted in two competing volumes. Publishing, however, can be as surprising and deadly as the business of murder. Because of a sudden, if not totally unanticipated, merger, both *Dog Days* by Serendipity Renn Dahlquist and *Die Like a Dog* by Leo G. Bloodworth became the joint properties of the same publishing house.

Obviously, they could not be released individually. The decision was made to combine them into one volume, with excessive repetition deleted. The authors were not pleased by this decision. They viewed the result as 'excessive and repressive editorial meddling' (Dahlquist) and 'a first-class hatchet job' (Bloodworth).

Regardless, both were eager to see their maiden efforts in print, and finally they came to understand that first novelists should never expect to find things going entirely their way.

DICK LOCHTE

Sleeping Dog

I

(Beginning: **DOG DAYS: A Personal Account of the Kaspar-Helmdale Slayings**. By Serendipity Renn Dahlquist)

The following appeared in somewhat different form in the pages of the Bay High Guardian, *considered by many to be the leading high-school newspaper in the Greater Los Angeles area. And yet, regardless of the* Guardian's *heralded integrity, its faculty advisers went soft as grapes when it came to the story's more ghoulish aspects – descriptions of the corpses and the like – as well as the admittedly gross little detours the case took. The dogfight atrocities, for example, and the brush with the Mexican Mafia and the really depraved stuff that the noble and gallant Mr Leo Bloodworth, master detective, endured on my behalf.*

On one hand, I am most proud to be the only sophomore woman – no, make that the only sophomore, period – to have had anything printed in the Guardian *this past year. On the other, having been hugely influenced by Mrs Ida Sperling's lecture, 'Journalism: The Truth Shall Make Us Free,' and then having witnessed that same Mrs Sperling edit significant passages from my original manuscript, every word as true as gospel, all I can say is that this writing business must be filled with continuous heartbreak. In any case, I dedicate this, my first book, to my beloved grandmother, known to her many fans as Aunt Lil Fairchild.*

S.R.D.
Bay Heights, California

3

1. My last day as a hopeless junior-high-school worm was marked with *merde*. Veritably mottled with *merde*. Someone stole my slam book. (Even now, nearly a year and a half later, I remain unconvinced that I simply misplaced it!) Then, Sylvia Leonidas, my supposedly best friend, with whom and with whose parents I had planned on motoring through the great Northwest, dropped the bomb that she had managed to get herself with child, thanks to some George person. Not a Bay Heights boy, more's the pity, for I have it on good authority that their narcotic consumption has rendered them 99 44/100 percent impotent. In any case, it's difficult to imagine a woman in her mid-teens, even one as admittedly backward as Sylvia, failing to take steps to avoid the possibility of conception. And George was almost college age, for heaven's sake. Because of their sexual ignorance and lack of self-control, the trip through the great Northwest was off.

Piling grief upon grief, Mr Madill, whom I cannot abide as either a teacher or a representative of the human race, gave me a C+ in 'Functions and Limits' and would not budge on it, though I humbled myself before his table in the faculty lounge, begging for a B-. And then – would it never end? – Greg Stillman, a Pacifica High senior with serious blue eyes who'd asked me to a junior–senior thing at Carbon Beach, got so stoned after his physics final that he fell into the Pacifica swimming pool while it was drained and broke his leg in two places.

Accepting the fact that this was destined to be my *dies irae*, I skated home as quickly and carefully as possible to discover that the door to the apartment had been left open and that my beloved little bullterrier, Groucho, was missing. Not only was he my lifelong companion, he had been a gift from my father, the only link to a man who had gone away thirteen years before to meet his fate in a seemingly senseless war. Frantically, I rushed through the apartment – my bedroom; grandmother's;

the guest room, where mother stayed when she was in town without male companionship (which was seldom); the bathrooms; the living room, where Groucho often hid under the tufted couch; the dining area and the kitchen.

It took the usual ten or fifteen minutes to get through the UBC switchboard to grandmother. She was and always will be an actress. If you don't immediately respond to her name, Edith Van Dine, you would surely recognize her as Aunt Lil Fairchild, the voice of reason and morality on the top-rated soap, 'Look to Tomorrow'. Grandmother hates me to phone her at work, but this was an emergency.

'Groucho was in his box when I left this morning,' she told me rather peevishly. 'And I certainly shut the front door when I left.'

'It was wide open.'

'Well, I don't understand that at all, dear,' she said, and I could tell her mind was occupied with other things – lies, adultery, deceit, abortion, murder, the junk her television life is so full of.

'Sehr, we'll have to get into this Groucho business a bit later. Gene's waving at me and there's blood in his eyes. Look around the apartment. I'm sure he's just being playful.'

Grandmother is sweet but not what you'd call dependable. Groucho, who was much too old to be playful any longer, was gone. And I knew that I had to take matters into my own hands.

2. According to the post office on the corner, the Bay City Police Department was responsible for crimes perpetrated in Bay Heights, where we lived. It was located at the rear of the white art-deco City Hall Building on Main Street that you've probably seen on all those TV crime shows that so often lack authenticity. The interior was quite different from the TV versions, however, dark and dank and depressing and painted a sickly green. It was filled with different activity, too. As I roller-skated

in, two clean-cut policemen were supporting a badly mauled black fellow whose right eye was hanging out of its socket. The poor man glared at me with his one good eye and asked, 'Are you a Baptist?'

I shook my head and one of the officers informed him, 'You're shit out of luck, Willy, looking for a Baptist in this neighborhood.' And they dragged him away, past a wire cage door and on to God knows where. I was staring after him when a very stern uniformed policeman with a sand-colored crew cut and moustache asked me if I was looking for the Motor Vehicle Division.

'I am not,' I told him. 'I'm here to report a stolen dog.'

He sighed. 'Well, take those skates off, then. No skating in here.'

That *extremely* important task having been disposed of to his satisfaction, he sighed again and dug through papers beneath a long counter. He handed me one and said, 'Fill it out, please.'

It was labeled 'Petty Theft Report'.

'There's nothing petty about the theft, officer,' I told him. 'Groucho is descended from the white bullterriers of England and has the papers to prove it. He was a gift from my late father. So excuse me if I do not consider him petty.'

'It's just a classification, miss. Fill out the form, or don't fill it out. Your call.'

It was a foolish document, designed for a thing and not a living creature. I was doing what I could with it when an aging Chicano in a coffee-pastel suit (the lightweight, three-piece kind with tacky subdued piping on the lapels) entered the waiting area from what was apparently the squad room. He stared at me, frowning as if he were trying to remember something. Then he strolled over and picked up my half-completed report. He glanced at it and asked with a cocky grin, 'So you got a missing mutt?'

'My dog is missing, yes.'

'Well, honey,' he said, 'we got eighty-seven murders on the books, sixty-eight muggings and rapes, upwards of one hundred and thirty b-and-e's. So I wanna be straight with you. Unless your dog happens to bite some traffic cop in the butt, he's gonna stay missing.'

'My Groucho has better manners than to bite some cop on the butt, or even to respond to that kind of impolite language,' I told him, wadding the sheet into a ball and tossing it into a wire basket. 'Sorry to have taken up so much of your valuable time, which, of course, our taxes pay for.'

'You a big taxpayer, honey?'

'My grandmother is.'

'What about mom and pop?'

'My pop, as you call him, is deceased. My mother . . . well, I don't see much of her. Now, if you've no other questions about my family, may I go?'

'Hey, don't be so tough,' he said, grinning. 'Maybe I got an idea for you. There's this friend of mine, one no-nonsense son of a bitch – excuse my French. He's got the reputation for finding anything – men, women, runaway kids on dope. That's how he got his nickname, the Bloodhound. Maybe he could find your mu– dog.'

I stared at him, trying to ascertain how much confidence I should place in a smirking Latin dandy.

'Where is this Bloodhound?'

'Downtown L.A.,' he said, slipping a card from his smooth leather wallet and scribbling a name and address on its blank side with an imitation gold Cartier pen. 'Here you go, honey.'

I looked at the name he had written: Leo Bloodworth. The other side of the card read: Lt. Rudy Cugat, BCPD, in embossed letters.

'No relation to the bandleader,' he said.

'Who?'

'Xavier Cugat? Little guy with a moustache and a restaurant on La Cienega. No? Before your time, I guess, honey. Never mind. You give the Hound my card and tell him his friend Cugie recommended him highly.' Lt. Cugat was almost giggling now.

'Is this going to cost me a bundle?' I asked.

'Oh,' he replied airily, 'a few bucks. But it'll be worth it, I guarantee, to experience the Bloodhound in action.'

3. I do very little traveling beyond the West Side area. In all of my fourteen and three-quarter years, I had been to downtown Los Angeles only twice. The first time was when my mother was staying at the Bonaventure with her lover of the moment, a really rancid personality who was singing dreary old Frank Sinatra stuff in a cocktail lounge there. The other time, Gran took me to the Music Center to see one of her cronies, a nice woman named Beverly Smythe, in a new play imported from England in which the F-word was used repeatedly, much to Gran's chagrin. (The way the world is headed, she says, they'll be asking her to use those kinds of words on her soap, and that's when she fully expects to pack it in. 'Just pack it in,' she promises.)

Anyway, though I was as careful as possible that afternoon, I caught the wrong bus and wound up several miles north of the address on Lieutenant Cugat's card. Luckily, I'd brought my Rollerballs.

It was nearing 4: 30 P.M. when I skated up to find – in the midst of a bunch of discount stores, pawnshops, and a porno movie house that looked like one giant rats' nest – a dark, brooding building. A directory informed me that Mr Leo Bloodworth and his associate, Mr Roy Kaspar, were officed in suite 403.

Since there were no signs prohibiting it, I skated into the gloomy building.

It was not a busy place. Lots of wood and some of it polished. A rather unsound cage elevator in the center of an open skywell lobby was readying for takeoff. Two nuns were boarding it and I skated on behind them. They were discussing a bargain in plain white underwear they expected to find on the third floor, chattering away like chirping penguins.

The elevator operator, another birdlike creature, a molting chicken, seemed very relieved when the nuns left us. So much so that he slipped a pint bottle of whisky from the inside pocket of his shiny orange jacket with yellow piping, and drank freely from it. He turned to me, wiped his lips on his sleeve, and, grinning most obscenely and toothlessly, offered me the bottle. I declined politely, wondering what sort of mess that smiling Latin had gotten me into.

Naturally, Bloodworth the Bloodhound's office was as dark as Lucifer's soul, to use one of Gran's similes. I sat down on the cold and dusty tile floor, exchanged my Rollerballs for low-rider sneaks, and prepared to wait till the Ice Age, if necessary.

That's when I noticed the strange chap across the hall, sort of hiding in a recess in the wall in front of an unoccupied office. He was a real mouth-breather, this lurker – gargantuan, beet-faced, with semi-punk shaved head. He was wearing a lemon-colored Lacoste shirt (the collar had points, so it was one of the synthetics, rather than the pure cotton) and cranberry slacks, with the obligatory white belt. He was staring at the door to 403.

'Waiting for Mr Bloodworth?' I asked.

No reply. He took a wooden pencil out of his pants pocket and began chewing it. Just crunching it up as if it were a Baby Ruth or something. Then spitting it out on the floor.

You aren't Mr Bloodworth by any horrible chance?' I wondered out loud.

He shot me an evil look and said, 'Get the hell out of here, you little bint.' Flecks of yellow pencil coated his lips.

'Intimidation does not work on me,' I told him. 'I have every right to be here and I resent being called whatever it was you called me.'

He snorted and ate another pencil, and took our conversation no further. Nor did he leave his niche. We stayed like that for what seemed to be hours. Then the elevator doors groaned open and this big, sort of middle-aged, sort of fat – well, not so much fat as thick-chested – fellow exited.

He was dressed in a neatly pressed tan poplin suit and walked as if his feet hurt. As he drew closer, I noticed that his eyes were totally amazing. Yellow-brown and sleepy, except when they flickered, like the eyes of a hawk I saw on a class trip to the San Diego Zoo. They shifted from me to the spiked-head bozo who that moment stepped forward from his shadowy spot.

'Mr Bloodworth?' I asked.

The big man with yellow eyes turned to face me and that's when the bozo caught him in the side of the head with a fist like a travel iron.

Mr Bloodworth – for it was he – bounced into the wall, and the bozo smashed him again. As he slid to the floor, the bozo loomed over him, spitting pencil flecks, veins bulging out like worms on his arms and neck.

'Listen to me, Bloodworth,' he shouted, 'I want you to tell that slimeball of a partner of yours that Gottlieb's got more of the same for him.'

The bozo, Gottlieb, drew back his foot, apparently intent on kicking the fallen man. I rushed forward and swung my skates into that part of the bozo's anatomy where Gran suggested I hit any man who gave me a moment's trouble. Gottlieb was both surprised and pained. He doubled up, howled, and lurched forward, his hand with gnawed fingernails reaching for me.

But Mr Bloodworth was just about on his feet again. He

shouted at the bozo and that craven thug scuttled off down the hall, holding his wounded privates.

Mr Bloodworth coughed a few times and checked his teeth for possible damage. Then he pressed his left temple and winced. He tried, unsuccessfully, to brush the dust and grime from his clothes. 'Just had the damn suit cleaned,' he mumbled in a rumbling baritone.

For some reason, he smelled of chlorine.

He unlocked the door to his office and I followed him into a tiny anteroom. The mail had been deposited on the floor and Mr Bloodworth moved it around with the toe of his shoe. 'There's a good one,' he said, indicating an envelope that he obviously expected me to pick up for him.

I handed it to him and he ripped it open with his little finger.

'Who was that brute?' I asked.

'Gottlieb?' Mr Bloodworth replied in a most unconcerned manner. 'Just another satisfied customer.'

2

(Beginning: **DIE LIKE A DOG: A novel based on fact** by Leo J. Bloodworth)

This book is dedicated to my three ex-wives: Mrs Louise Lentz (née Gregory), Miss Rita Yarbo, and Mrs Irene Gallup (née O'Brien). While they may have made my life a living hell, at least they had the decency to deny me the dubious joys of fatherhood.

My sincerest thanks go also to Jerry Flaherty of the Los Angeles Post, *who was of tremendous assistance in getting this whole thing on paper.*

The Breakers
La Jolla, California

1. The Pentecostal Church of Marine Rebirth in the San Fernando Valley was a former electronics-parts warehouse that had been gutted, then partitioned into cubicles, each of which was filled with a wooden hot tub. Each tub was in turn filled with a weary businessman type, neck-deep in steamy, soothing water, being guided through a submerged Born Again experience by a healthy young woman with a solemn expression, a strong set of mitts, and unfettered bosoms. There were about twenty-five couples in the tubs, all as naked as apples. And it wasn't even noon.

The Most Reverend Buddy Fedderson and I were looking down on them from a catwalk in front of his green-velvet-draped sanctum one flight up. Reverend Buddy adjusted his wraparound terry-cloth vestment and smiled benignly at the giant egg crate of wet round humans below.

'Our philosophy is a simple one, Mr Bloodworth. Relieve the mind and body of all want and the soul will take care of itself.'

'Amen,' I added, since my mouth was hanging open anyway. 'Reverend, I wonder if you'd mind pointing out the bald head that belongs to Mr Milton DeRitter.'

Fedderson dropped a few levels of beatification closer to the earth and asked, 'Huh?'

'I'm not really here for a marine rebirth,' I confessed. 'Maybe when I have more time.'

'But what –'

'I want DeRitter. I've been on his case for nearly a month.'

Reverend Buddy's sky-blue peepers turned frosty. 'You can go fu–'

I held up my hand. 'Not in front of the holy hot tubs. Look, pal, I'm not here to cause you any grief. I just want DeRitter.'

He glared at me while his mind clicked away. Finally he said, 'I can't allow this. Mr DeRitter is –'

'Mr DeRitter is an embezzler. He isn't even Mr DeRitter.'

'You local or federal?'

'Local,' I said, not bothering to tell him local what.

'Compartment fourteen,' he said, looking past me to his office. 'Try to be as non-disruptive as you can. Now, if you'll excuse me.'

He drifted back into his air-cooled chamber and I hopped down the metal steps and wandered through the cubicles until I found a wooden door decorated with a haloed fish and the number 14. Past it, only a few steps separated me from a chest-high tub. A guy with wispy red hair and a freckled scalp was hunkering at its bottom, communicating via air hose with a hefty blonde, who seemed to be doing something below with her educated hands. Holding her head above water, she shifted her attention to me and frowned.

'Reel him in,' I whispered. 'Reverend Buddy's orders.'

She glanced up at the catwalk, then back at me. 'Gimme a few seconds. He's just about to see the light.'

A little more fondling and she submerged completely, resurfacing again a few seconds later with DeRitter. She was formidable enough to drape his chin and arms over the side of the tub without any help from him. She then carefully withdrew the air hose from his slack mouth.

His eyes were shut. He was one spent mackerel. But he did have a grin on his face.

'Wake up,' I said in his ear. 'Time to pay for your sins.'

DeRitter's pale eyes popped open. The girl, standing behind him, pressed against him, rubbing his neck.

'Easy,' she cooed. 'Relax now. You don't want to spasm or anything, honey.'

'Who the hell . . . ?' he asked me.

'Your family hired me to find you, pal. Madge. Marcus, Junior. You must remember them.'

'I don't know any –'

'Sure you do. Your name is Marcus Weill and, up until three years ago, you were the trusted senior partner of Weill and Weill, Investments, of New York, Chicago, and Paris. The Paris is a nice touch.'

The muscles in his hairy shoulders were bunching up. The wet girl gave me a nasty look, but I'd seen them before. DeRitter/Weill wasn't any slender reed. He wiped water out of his eyes and said, 'I don't know what the hell you're blabbing about.'

'Save your breath, Mr Weill. It seems to be in short supply right now.'

He moaned and, without preamble, vaulted out of the tub,

kicking the girl in the head – an accident, I assumed – and splashing me with a wave of chlorinated water. He tried to bull past me in the small cubicle. I grabbed for him, but he was too slick, so I kicked the door shut and pushed him into it, wrestling him to the ground.

He was built like a steel drum and I was glad he'd spent the last half-hour relieving his body and mind or else he might have had me for lunch.

'C'mon, Weill,' I grumbled, straddling his slippery chest with my knees pinning his biceps. 'We're both too old for this kind of crap.'

The girl slipped over the side of the tub, wetting us even more. She stood there for a moment, rubbing her head and giving us a nice long look at her. Then she flounced past us, opening the door as far as she could with Weill's head in the way. As an afterthought, she whacked the door against his nearly exposed scalp before shutting it behind her.

Weill looked foggy. He was breathing like a porpoise with a head cold.

'Your son wants the whole mess cleared up quickly and painlessly,' I said. 'You hand over whatever's left of the five hundred and fifty thousand. Then you fly back to New York and sign a few papers – including a divorce document for your wife – and you'll be free to do whatever you want, short of dipping into some other till.'

'No police?'

'How much of the loot is left?'

'I can pay it back. Fact is, I've done well out here. I manufacture vitamin packs – Vita-Val.'

'Yeah, I know. Well, if the bonding company is satisfied, there probably won't be any legal action taken. Your son doesn't want any publicity. He figures the family has been through enough the past three years.'

'The kid's a weasel and his mother is worse,' Weill said. 'Suppose I offer you twenty thousand . . .'

I shook my head sadly. 'First, I'm collecting ten percent of whatever I recover. Second, your son didn't get my last good suit all wet. And third, he'd just hire somebody else to find you, and you're not that hard to find.'

Three hours later I'd accompanied DeRitter/Weill to his bank, wired an impressive cashier's check to my client, put his errant old man on a flight east, and was standing in a barrel at Lee's on Hope Street, waiting for my suit to be cleaned and pressed.

From there my day went downhill on rollers, culminating with my being slugged just outside my office by a newt-brain named Gottlieb for whom my associate, Roy Kaspar, had done some work – evidently not to Gottlieb's liking.

Still, he would not have been able to nail me if it hadn't been for a weird little girl in the hallway who called my name at the exact moment Gottlieb made his move. Once I hit the concrete, the bastard tried to drop-kick me over my own transom. But I was a little too agile for him, so he skipped. By the time I dragged myself into the office and turned on a torch under yesterday's drip roast, I was still too woozy to notice I wasn't alone.

The kid had followed me in. I was inspecting the bruise on my chin and an inch-long slice in my upper gum when she pulled the blinds and let in the smoggy-filtered evening glare. 'Oh, Jesus,' I groaned, as a needle of light pierced my skull and lodged right behind my eyes.

'This place is fit for goats,' the kid informed me.

I squinted at her. About five feet tall, skinny as a colt, blond hair straight to her shoulders. Wearing Levi's and a T-shirt that read: NOTHING TO SAY. Like hell. She was turning up her pointy nose at my office. My cluttered desk – the mark of a successful man, my father always said; my pea-green filing cabinet with its side kicked in; and my smart, plum-colored velvet couch with lion-paw legs.

'We don't open the blinds in here,' I told her. 'The blinds are never to be opened.'

'Germs, like evil thoughts, are scattered by sunlight,' she said.

I groaned again and heard the coffee bubbling in its porcelain pot. As I poured a cup, the girl informed me, 'That puts pure bile in your system.'

'Do tell. You selling cookies or something, sister?'

She arched one pale eyebrow. 'You're the sleuth, Mr Bloodworth. Do you see any cookies?'

'No, but I've been fooled before.'

'In point of fact, my name is Serendipity Dahlquist, and I am here to secure your services, such as they are. I would not be here at all if the police – a Lieutenant Rudy Cugat – had not recommended you highly. Bloodworth the Bloodhound, he called you.'

I studied the kid over my coffee cup, wondering if Cugat had been putting her on. Or me. Or the both of us. I decided that Cugat had a downright Oriental sense of humor.

'Who do you want found?' I asked her.

She answered straight out, 'Groucho.'

'Then you've got a problem, lady. Groucho and his brothers are playing to a whole new audience these days.'

'Not that Groucho,' she shot back impatiently. 'My terrier. My sweet little terrier.'

'A dog?'

'A very special dog.'

I moved around the desk and started inching toward the door. 'Well, Miss Dahlquist, I sort of specialize in missing humans. Bail jumpers. Skip artists. The odd runaway. I can put myself into their skins, try to figure out where they're headed. Dogs, I just don't know.'

I gathered from her crestfallen expression that she believed me.

'Lieutenant Cugat was having a joke at my expense,' she said flatly.

I nodded and stood beside the open door, shifting impatiently. She started out. And then Roy Kaspar arrived, his timing as impeccable as always.

He wore the kind of sincere moustache and razor-cut hair that were all the rage at singles pickup bars that year. He was easygoing and boyish and I wouldn't have trusted him farther than the length of the cord on his blow dryer. He smiled, flashing his perfect white teeth, and looked from the girl to me. 'Christ sakes, Leo. Congratulations. You found the Lindbergh kid.'

'The Lindbergh kid was a male and he'd be older than me, Roy. But it's nice you dropped by. Your client Gottlieb left a message.'

'Was he here?' Kaspar asked casually, making sure that his open shirt collar was tucked smoothly under the lapel of his silk sport coat. 'The guy's a real Gomer. He give you any trouble?'

'None to speak of.'

'He threw himself on Mr Bloodworth in a cowardly attack,' the kid piped up, 'but Mr Bloodworth chased him away. It was awesome to see.'

I gave her a suspicious eye.

'The jerk doesn't know what the hell he wants,' Kaspar said. 'He hires me, Leo, to get the goods on his wife. Who's spectacular, by the way. So I get the job done, and when he sees it's me in the snapshots with her, he shorts out. Totally unspools. Gets downright abusive and says he won't pay. So' – he gave me a wink – 'I withheld the negatives until he came up with the green.'

I rested an inch or two of rump on my desk edge, wondering how much longer I could put up with a bum like Roy in the next office. I'd earned fifty grand or so that afternoon. Another pay-day like that and I'd be able to make the nut without him.

The girl gave out an impatient 'A-hem.'

'Oh, right,' I told her. 'I'm sorry I can't help you, young lady, so if that's all . . .'

'It certainly is not all,' she said, sticking out her little chin. 'I have traveled seventeen miles by bus and three by roller skate over curbs that have no dips to hire a detective, and I will not be shown the door until I ask for it.' She tugged a bright cloth wallet from her jeans and removed a folded $50 bill.

She had Roy's attention.

'Perhaps if you told me the problem . . .' he began.

'No way! It's the Bloodhound who is supposed to be the best. It's the Bloodhound I came to hire.'

'Cugat sent her,' I told Kaspar. 'Her dog is missing.'

'Dog?' He managed to control his giggle. 'But, Leo, I'm the firm's dog expert. Remember how I tracked down Fritz the Wonder Spaniel for NBC?'

I sighed. The guy was lower than an earthworm's chin.

'Does this fellow really specialize in animals?' the girl asked me. I shrugged. I wasn't about to encourage her to hire Kaspar. 'Some say he was raised by wolves,' I told her.

'Right,' Kaspar added. 'Me and Remus. Uncle Remus.'

'Romulus and Remus,' the girl corrected him. 'Uncle Remus was an old guy who made up patronizing fables for children.' She glared at both of us accusingly.

Either Kaspar didn't get her message or he was fearless. 'Tell you what, Miss – ah, Miss . . .'

'Miss Dahlquist,' she said. 'Serendipity Dahlquist.'

'Serendipity? That's a real Sixties name, isn't it, Leo?'

I didn't bother to answer. What the hell did I know or care about Sixties names?

'Serendipity,' he said to her, 'suppose I drive you home and you can fill me in on your missing dog. Just maybe, I might make a suggestion or two about getting it back.'

She looked him over from stem to stern. 'I'll accept your offer of a ride, assuming it in no way commits me to hire you.' She tucked her money away.

Kaspar blinked at her. 'Not at all, Serendipity. No commitment nohow. O-kay, then, soon as I pick up my mail, we'll do it.'

'Miss Dahlquist,' I said, 'I'd appreciate a moment alone with Mr Kaspar.'

She nodded, her hand on the doorknob. 'I place a great deal of faith in my instincts, Mr Bloodworth,' she said thoughtfully, 'and I am convinced that if you were to apply yourself, you would be equally as adept with animals as you are with humans.'

On that exit line she closed the door carefully behind her.

Kaspar looked sheepish. 'I'm just driving her home, Leo.'

'She's a little kid, Roy.'

'A real cute little kid, or didn't you notice?'

I pushed off of the desk and took a step toward him.

'Hey, take it easy, big fella. I'm just yanking your chain. You know I like a lot of meat on the bones. I'm going her way, is all.'

'And don't take her money.'

'What about her share of the gas?'

'Not a sou.'

'Gimme some credit,' he said, grinning his boyish grin. 'I wouldn't take the kid's bread. You know me.'

'That I do, Roy. But I keep hoping that one of these times you're going to prove me wrong.'

2. Call me a cockeyed optimist, but I figured that closed the book on Miss Serendipity Dahlquist and her missing mutt. Four nights later it flipped open again.

I was in the Irish Mist, a no-frills saloon on South Figueroa within staggering distance of my office. It boasted a clientele of big, noisy, red-faced micks with bad haircuts, mean drunks in the main, and hennaed women of indeterminate age who, when pressed, could be even meaner. The owner was a grizzled ex-stunt gaffer named Mickey O'Hanrahan who was as tough as a hard-boiled owl until he started to reminisce about his youthful days at Twentieth, working for the late director John Ford. A large photo of Ford, his mottled face wearing an eye patch and a sour-stomach scowl, occupied a place of honor on the wall behind the bar, right next to the Bushmill's.

When I'm not on a job, I begin my evenings at the Mist and try to be gone before the fights break out. On that particular night I lingered a bit too long over my fifth Harp. The Clancy Brothers were wailing about Donegal in hi-fi and I was engaged in polite but pointed conversation with a big brunette named Tamarra when a certain Mr Nolan decided to shatter a pint bottle of ale on the skull of a certain Mr Feighan, and they fell to the floor, flailing and biting each other in earnest. What with my attention divided between Nolan's attempts to gouge out Feighan's eyes and Tamarra's invigorating way of measuring the breadth of my left thigh with her ice-pick fingernails, it took me a moment or two to realize that someone was tugging on the tail of my coat.

'Mr Bloodworth, you really must pull yourself together,' said an annoyingly familiar, peevish, little-girl voice.

Tamarra took a long look at the kid and asked quite reasonably, 'Who's the squirt, Hound?'

'My name is Serendipity Dahlquist.'

'Well, don't worry, baby, you can get that fixed. Is she yours, Hound?'

'In no sense,' I replied. To the girl I added, 'This is no place for you, Miss Dahlquist.'

She surveyed the room with her critical blue eyes. Nolan and Feighan, both dripping red, were being shown the door by

O'Hanrahan. A couple of the regulars were kicking sawdust over the blood on the floor and picking up the broken glass.

'Nor is it any place for you, Mr Bloodworth,' the girl said. 'This is a place for hooligans and hookers.'

'Now wait a minute, kid . . .' Tamarra began, slipping from her stool.

The girl ignored her. 'The manager of your building, Mr Diez, told me you'd likely be there, Mr Bloodworth. I thought you'd want to know that your office has been vandalized.'

'Huh?' was the best I could do.

'Three men in suits and ties. They looked quite respectable. Once they were inside your office, I left my hiding place and told the night watchman. But he wasn't very interested. He said he didn't even have bullets in his gun. He let me phone Mr Diez at home and Mr Diez suggested I come here to tell you, rather than disturb the police, whom he felt would be more trouble than help.'

'Are the robbers still there?'

'I doubt it. Are you leaving this loathsome dive or not?'

Tamarra's eyes were tiny slits as she glared at the girl. 'He'll leave when I'm goddamned ready, kid. Why don't you run along and peddle it in some punk club?'

'Ah, Tamarra, honey, I'd better go see about the office.'

'You into kiddy porn these days, Hound?' one of the barfly humorists shouted.

Tamarra answered for me. 'Hound's nearing fifty. You know how it is – they can't get 'em young enough.'

'Just relax,' I said to no one in particular as I got to my feet carefully.

'She got a kid sister for me, Hound? She don't have to be ten years old, long as she looks like a ten-year-old.'

As the kid and I headed out, O'Hanrahan returned from depositing the battlers on the sidewalk. By then the whole room was whistling and stomping and laughing. The pub owner glowered at his customers and asked me, 'What the bejesus is goin' on?'

I shrugged. 'Tamarra called John Ford a one-eyed son of a bitch and the rest of 'em sort of went on from there.'

O'Hanrahan rushed to his bar and brought down one steel fist on it. 'All right, damn ya',' he growled at the laughing drunks, 'let's see how funny you think this is: The pub is closed for the night! Out, you bums. Let your families put up with you for a change.'

I pulled the girl through the swinging doors. There was the sound of broken glass behind us. Then shouts. I heard my name mentioned, not kindly. A couple of wobbly specimens stumbled out of the Mist and waved their fists at us.

The girl and I ran the four blocks to my office as if the both of us were kids.

3

1. The night watchman, a young adult Mexican, was standing in the rubble of Mr Bloodworth's reception area with a sheepish look on his almond-colored face. He drew his pistol.

'Señor Diez gives me this, but no ammunition,' he told Mr Bloodworth, who, after our little jog, was sweating and puffing and wheezing like a candidate for the emphysema ward. 'I am like the bull without the testicles,' the watchman added, noticing me a bit late.

'It's OK, Diego,' Mr Bloodworth told him. 'There's nothing in here worth anybody getting shot over. How's about giving me a hand straightening the place up?'

Diego puffed out his chest and shook his head. 'I must return to my duty, señor. My duty is to protect this building, not be its janitor.' With that, he left us.

Mr Bloodworth watched him go, a little smile on his lips, then weaved into his office where the contents of his filing cabinets had been emptied onto the carpet along with the contents of his desk drawers. The purple sofa had not been bothered much, however, and Mr Bloodworth flopped onto it, patting it as if it were an animal that had won a ribbon. He was still wheezing.

'You're in bad shape, even for a man your age,' I told him.

'How'd you like to get tossed out of a window, kid?'

'Barroom talk,' I replied. 'Aren't you interested in the descriptions of the men who did this?'

24

He leaned his head back against the couch, closed the lids on his yellow eyes, and sighed. 'Oh, God, I suppose so. But do you think you could do a little light housecleaning while you talk?'

'I guess,' I said. 'If you're too ancient and worn out to do it yourself.'

I bent over to start collecting the files. 'They were not much older than college boys, only better dressed. Suits and ties. One was blond, one dark-haired, and one had red hair. He was the best-looking.'

'How'd they get in?' Breathing heavily through his nose, he pushed himself off the couch, his eyes open but sleepy-looking, and waded through the debris to where a bottle of Jim Beam lay on its side under the desk. He started to drink from it.

'That could be poisoned,' I suggested.

He hesitated a second, looked from the bottle to me, and then, rather defiantly, poured a goodly amount down his gullet. He grabbed a handful of papers and tossed them every which way into one of the open file drawers. 'I'll sort 'em out later,' he mumbled, mainly to himself

'Well,' he turned to me, 'do I get to hear all about these second-story men or not?'

'Could you please put that away first?' I asked, pointing to the Jim Beam. 'The smell of whiskey makes me barf.'

He raised an eyebrow at me, then picked up the bottle and took another swallow. Sometimes men can be so childish. He drank every last drop, capped the bottle, and carefully placed the empty into a metal wastebasket. 'All put away,' he said.

'It's your mind and body that you're destroying,' I said.

'You know the one thing I like the most about you, Miss Dahlquist?' he asked. He had my attention. 'You remind me of my mother.'

Then he chuckled. Rather nastily, I thought.

*

2. It took us the better part of an hour to clean up the mess. During that time I further described the three men who broke into the office. They'd reminded me of the sort of East Coast junior advertising executives who take Gran to lunch every so often. They try to get her to appear in their commercials for dishwash or cheese dip or whatever. She always goes to lunch with them, but she never agrees to do their ads. She says that she will only promote products she herself uses. She lives with the hope that someday someone will ask her to be spokeswoman for Peal's Lady Soap or Royal Family Preserves, but I doubt they ever will.

The vandals resembled ad execs, very clean and dapper and well groomed. Definitely not your usual sneak thieves. Mr Bloodworth was not too impressed by my observations until I mentioned that the blond-haired man opened the door with a set of keys.

'Describe the keys.'

'Four or five on a ring. The blond-haired man fumbled with them until he found just the right one and he opened the door with it.'

Mr Bloodworth frowned. 'What the hell were you doing in the hallway anyhow, sis?'

'Would it be possible for you to call me Serendipity?'

'Too much effort. Let's split the difference and call you Sarah.'

It was better than 'sis'.

'I was waiting for your partner, Mr Kaspar.'

'He's not my partner, exactly.'

'He's not much of anything. He promised me I'd hear from him within three days. He's one day late.'

Mr Bloodworth's frown deepened. 'You hired him?'

'Didn't he tell you?'

'I haven't seen him in a while myself. How much did you pay him?'

'Pay him? Do I look like I was B.Y.?'

'Born yesterday?'

I smiled. 'Precisely. I gave him nothing but the promise of a reward if he should help me to recover Groucho.'

'And Roy agreed to that? To work on the come?'

I nodded. 'Gran and I put up with him for several hours while he questioned us and snooped around the apartment, looking through my things. He felt quite confident he could find Groucho. Only I haven't heard from him. I tried calling here, but I kept getting that silly phone-machine message, the one with the bad Humphrey Bogart imitation.'

'I'm a little embarrassed by that, myself,' Mr Bloodworth admitted. 'So you came here tonight –'

'This afternoon,' I corrected. 'I spent several hours in front of your locked door. I assumed one of you would arrive eventually. I had no idea anyone could keep such irregular business hours.'

'It's that kind of business.'

'Well, I'd like to talk with Mr Kaspar. If he's not sincere about finding Groucho, I will have to make other arrangements.'

'That might be a good idea, si–uh – Sarah.'

'I want to fire him myself. Where might I find him?'

He shrugged.

'Don't you know? Has the Bloodhound lost his own partner?'

'I haven't lost him. And he isn't really my partner. We share the rent is all.'

'Then where is he?'

'How the hell should I know? He has his own cases. I don't keep tabs on him, for Christ's sake. I've got my own problems, which is what you're becoming, now that I think of it.'

'Tell me where I may find Mr Kaspar and you'll be rid of me.'

He sighed again and led me from his office to the anteroom. Then he opened the door to Mr Kaspar's office, turned on the light, and grunted, 'Holy shit – uh, excuse me, kid.'

I would have told him that I'd heard the word before, but I was too amazed at what had been done to the room. It had been totally, awesomely devastated. The wall-to-wall carpet had been ripped free. Desk drawers had been emptied and smashed. A leatherette couch had been torn and gutted. Parts of a stereo radio lay scattered beside an end table, the top of which had been pried off.

Mr Bloodworth's face had turned a strange gray color. His eyes were almost open as they studied the destruction. 'They were just going through the motions out there. This is the big casino. What the Christ were they looking for?'

He picked up the empty plastic casing for a radio. 'Something fairly small.'

He did an about-face on the mess and loped back into the reception area. The desk there had scarcely been touched, possibly because it was bare of anything but a telephone and a black intercom sort of gadget. Mr Bloodworth picked up the phone and pressed a few numbers. Then he cursed and replaced the phone.

The horrible Humphrey Bogart imitation blared out of the black gadget box. 'I'm sorry but Bloodworth and Kaspar are out on a case,' it rattled on. It was Mr Kaspar doing such a lousy job of it. Gran was in a Bogart movie, *In a Lonely Place*, which I have seen any number of times on TV. She portrayed an actress, which must not have been too big a stretch for her.

'Leave your name and number at the beep,' continued Kaspar/Bogart, 'and they'll be looking for you, kid.' This was followed by the promised beep, which was in turn followed by Mr Bloodworth clicking off the machine. He pressed a set of buttons again, then waited for several unanswered rings before replacing the receiver. He looked concerned.

'No answer?'

He shook his head.

'I guess he must be out or something,' I said.

'Roy has one of these answering machines at home.'

'He must have forgotten to turn it on.'

'Maybe,' he said. 'I'd better go check it out.'

'Fine. It's on the way to my apartment.'

Mr Bloodworth gave me a curious look. 'You know where Roy lives?'

'Not exactly. He said something about it being in the same general vicinity as our apartment in Bay Heights. I mean, if I knew where he lived, I could have gone there instead of coming all the way down here.'

He didn't reply to that, merely turned off the light in his office, clicked the answering machine back on, and walked to the hall door. 'You coming?' he asked.

He looked rather stately, framed in the doorway, rather stalwart. Definitely not the sort of man who should waste his days in a bar like the Irish Mist.

3. Unlike Roy Kaspar's little black Mercedes with its wood-grain panel and tape deck and leather seats and convertible top, Mr Bloodworth's dusty gray Chevrolet was all business. It had dark tinted windows, the better to hide behind. Its back seat was covered with jackets, sweaters, strange hats, brown paper bags squashed into balls, Big Mac wrappers, greasy fried-chicken boxes, and empty beer cans. It was the car of a dedicated, working gumshoe.

It transported us to Roy Kaspar's apartment in the flatlands of Culver City, not very near where I lived at all. Mr Bloodworth headed there along Olympic Boulevard. I explained to him that we'd arrive quicker if he went down Third, then cut over just before reaching La Cienega. Instead of replying, he unlocked his glove compartment and removed a small portable radio that was tuned to the old-music station that Gran sometimes listens to.

As we continued down Olympic, I asked Mr Bloodworth how he came to choose such a unique, solitary profession, but his mind must have been on his driving, for he didn't answer. He did not, in fact, acknowledge my presence until we passed a grotty sandwich shop named Louie-Louie's, where I waved to a boy standing out front.

'What the hell are you doing?' Mr Bloodworth asked, rather suddenly.

'Waving to Jimmy Matosky, who's in my Fault and Finance class.'

'That kid goes to your school? Christ!'

'Why shouldn't he?'

'That joint's no place for a school kid. Lots of – uh – odd types hang out there.'

'You mean gay prostitutes?' I asked.

'Something like that. Yeah.'

'Well, that's Jimmy Matosky.'

Mr Bloodworth looked at me in disbelief.

'Jimmy was telling us some of the stuff he gets paid to do and the stuff that's done to him. *Très* gross, but fascinating, too, in a sort of anthropological sense, I mean.'

'Christ,' Mr Bloodworth said again, and turned his radio up louder.

4. Like a sound truck for the big-band era, we arrived at a cluster of bungalows not far from MGM Studios. On Palms Avenue. I remember the first time I ever heard of Palms, it sounded like such a nice, balmy place. *Au contraire*. It is tacky, flat and dull as tapioca pudding without raisins.

The bungalows were called the Palms Garden Apartments and they had just been redone. That is to say, somebody had slapped a pinewood finish on the old stucco to make them look smart and countrylike. I've been told that property owners do that just before skyrocketing the rent or going condo, which is what has been happening a lot in Bay Heights. 'Condo blight' is what Gran calls it.

Naturally, Mr Bloodworth ordered me to stay in the car while he went in to check Mr Kaspar's bungalow. Naturally, I disobeyed him.

There were twenty or so little wood-paneled cottages in the Palms Garden complex, staring at each other across a newly landscaped flower bed filled with dandelions and snakehead and old man of the mountains. There may have been a few mule-ears and golden yarrows poking around in there, too. The gardener must have been daisy crazy.

Several of the cottages had that vacant look. No drapes. Dark. Probably the high-rent thing. Or maybe the tenants had hay fever and couldn't take the daisies. Mr Bloodworth was at the front of number 16, hunkering down and rooting through an assortment of newspapers and other junk that lay piled against the front door. He straightened up with a grunt, turned and spotted me.

'I told you to stay in the car.'

'You can tell me whatever you wish,' I said, 'but you have no authority over me.'

He shook his head sadly, a gesture I've noticed Gran make from time to time. It must be something you do when you get old.

With only moonlight as a guide, I followed the big sleuth as he navigated a dark and muddy alley to the rear of number 16. Neither it nor its neighboring unit seemed occupied. Out front I'd heard the sounds of TV sets and people arguing. Humanity. It was very quiet now. And black as ink. I couldn't even tell if Mr Bloodworth was still in front of me.

He was, in fact, already at the rear of the cottages. There were tiny square yards back there that consisted of mud and cinder blocks. The landscaper must have run out of flowers.

Past that was a simply constructed multiple carport with a few scattered vehicles, including Mr Kaspar's little sports job.

Mr Bloodworth was pressing his face against a small glass windowpane set into the back door of unit 16, where a ghostly light drifted out like smoke. I started toward him and stumbled off a cinder block, sinking into the damp mud up to my pink socks. Mr Bloodworth moved swiftly from the back door to where I was standing. His whisper was harsh: 'Get back to the car. Now!'

'I –'

'No more of that,' he growled. 'Get back to the car or I'll spank the pants off you.'

Somewhat taken aback by the intimacy of such a rude suggestion, I turned from him and started down the alley. At the side of the cottage, I stopped and waited while he did some curious thing to Mr Kaspar's back-door lock. The door opened and he entered.

Using extreme caution, I tiptoed to the open door and peeked inside. Cold air spilled out of the room, giving me goose bumps.

Mr Bloodworth was bending over something on the floor, touching it. What he was touching used to be Mr Kaspar. Now it was just so much greenish-red flesh and bones.

4

1. Roy's cracker-box coach house had been gone over as thoroughly as his office. Near his body, the linoleum was littered with the contents of the fridge, plus ripped-open containers of dry food. The living room was mainly tossed furniture, with his few books and magazines and knickknacks scattered on the cement floor and on the tattered remains of wall-to-wall carpeting. Plants had been pulled out of their pots. A small fish tank had been tipped over, its glass broken, two guppies resting stiff on the floor with a little castle and a couple of mounds of some sandy substance. That area was still damp.

Cushions had been ripped open. The leather on two Wassaly chairs had been cut and probed. Even the Zenith TV had been smashed and gutted. It lay on rug patches, trailing its tubes and spaghetti wires.

In the bath, the medicine cabinet was open, soap cakes sliced, toilet paper pulled from its rolls. In the bedroom, the ceiling mirror that Kaspar used to brag about reflected nothing but stripped and raped bedding. The contents of bureau drawers and closets embraced shredded rugs.

I worked my way back to the kitchen, keeping my hands in my pockets like the cops are supposed to, rather than disturb evidence. Little Miss Dahlquist, the scourge of my middle age, was standing next to the stiff, scowling at Roy's cloudy, bulging eyes and distended tongue. It was not a wholesome sight.

Even less so in the glow of the open fridge. 'Having fun?' I asked her.

'I'd have thought there'd be more blood.'

There was a small brown smudge near a fading strangulation groove under the jawline. 'He wasn't shot or stabbed,' I told her, 'he was choked.'

'I can see that,' she said. 'He'd been jogging.'

'Or planning to. You feeling OK?'

'He'd finished jogging,' the kid stated firmly. 'That milk carton by his hand – he was drinking from it when the killer got him. There's dried milk on his chin and the front of his sweat suit. You don't drink milk if you're going for a run. So he'd already been. I'm feeling fine. Why?'

I knelt beside the corpse. Roy's black plastic watch was still clicking off the time in seconds. I couldn't tell if it was dried milk or what-all on his chin. Somebody had dialed the air-conditioner up full blast, but he was still starting to turn. His bladder and bowels had emptied when he gave up the ghost.

'I thought you might be getting kind of queasy,' I told her. 'The first time I saw a stiff, I had to throw up.'

'Well, for goodness' sake,' she said, 'I've seen dead people before, tons of 'em. On TV. I even saw that fellow who was shot in close-up.'

'Oswald?'

'Who? No. That fellow in Latin America somewhere. El Salvador. This general put a gun to his head and blew his brains all over the jungle. No matter what channel you watched, you got to see it about ten times.'

'Fine. Only just shut up about it. You're making *me* queasy.'

Judging by the newspapers piled up beside the front door, the body had been resting on the kitchen floor for three days.

'He's smiling,' the kid said.

'That happens when you've been dead awhile. Rictus. Some

writer called it "the ivory grin", which may be a little melo-dramatic but says it all.'

I stood up. 'We're lucky the air-conditioner's turned on high or Roy wouldn't be so easy to live with. As it is, he's getting pretty ripe. Notice that greenish color and the puffiness in the face and hands. The body tightens up during the first several hours. But after a while it gets slack again and it turns. And if you leave that door open much longer, the flies will be in here, chowing down. Not to mention the maggots and worms and carrion beetles. God knows where they come from. They like to nestle in eye sockets and ears and mouths and lay eggs. All part of the general festering and decay and rot. Television sort of skims over that part of it, kid. You rarely see flesh decomposing in prime time. I guess it's not so hot for selling frozen dinners. All that putrid and shiny green skin that peels like an overripe banana. And the sores. And the stench. And the amusing part – you'll like this, kid – the more things that happen to the body, the more the face smiles. It's Mother Nature's way of having the last laugh.'

The girl looked a little chalky. Maybe I'd overdone it. I'd almost turned my own stomach. She backed through the door; said, 'Excuse me,' and ran off behind the house. Kids should have some respect for death. I pushed the door shut but didn't lock it. Then I found a phone that worked and called the cops.

2. One of the investigating officers was named Kassarian, a dark-skinned guy with an ash-colored bag of flesh under each moist brown eye and long gray sideburns that cascaded down from a balding pate. He wore a windowpane sport coat with both pockets bulging. An unhealthy paunch partially hid his belt and pushed down his double-knit slacks so that they dusted the floor when he walked. The breast pocket of his maroon sport shirt contained four pens in a white plastic ink guard that

strained the button at his thick, loose-fleshed neck. He seemed to be fighting a losing battle with gravity.

His partner was an angular fashion plate named Sitchell, younger, conventionally handsome, and of lighter weight, both physically and metaphorically. Unlike Kassarian, whose droopy poker face glared at me balefully and patiently while I gave my statement in the rapidly overcrowding living room, Sitchell sniffed, a-hemed, shot his cuffs, adjusted his knit tie, yanked his lapels, muttered 'right-right' whenever I slowed down enough to allow it, and did everything but enter my mouth with his fingers to help me get the words out faster.

He was using some of those fingers to operate a micro-cassette recorder, which he evidently preferred to the old-fashioned notebook.

When I came to the end of my story he almost swooned. Kassarian cocked his big head and said, 'You did that very well, Mr Bloodworth. Like maybe you gave a deposition once or twice before.'

Lights were flashing through the kitchen door. A cop with a videotape backpack wandered past, followed by a delicate-looking Asian woman, who turned out to be a forensic pathologist and was shaking her head for some reason. A number of uniformed cops stood around looking at the mess and pretending they knew more than they were telling. Outside, the gentlemen and ladies of the press were gathering.

'I've been a P.I. for fifteen years,' I told him.

'Ever wear the uniform?'

I nodded. 'A while.'

Sitchell shifted his weight from one Oxford to the other. Maybe he was on diuretics. He had no curiosity whatsoever about the murder or about me, but Kassarian had enough for the both of them.

'Where was that?' he asked.

'West L.A., then Silver Lake. Fourteen years' worth.'

'That's a long run. What happened?'

'I just burned out,' I lied. Or maybe it was the truth.

'Arnie,' Sitchell whined to his partner, 'can't we put a cork in this?'

'Is he on golden time?' I wondered.

'Law school,' Kassarian explained. 'Young man on the move. Law school at night. But he still hasn't passed the patience test.' He patted Sitchell's face playfully, then came back to me. 'Lemme see if I got it all clear. Somebody tossed your and the deceased's offices downtown and you think that ties to what we got here?'

'Offhand.'

'How'd you and Kaspar get along?'

'About like you and Detective Sitchell.'

Kassarian grinned. 'And the girl, what's she to you? A relative? A ward? What?'

I scratched my head. The Asian lady glided back through the room and left by the front door, causing a lot of chatter outside. Two uniformed cops walked in, arguing about the Dodgers.

'The kid wanted somebody to help her find a missing dog,' I told Kassarian. 'She came to our office, and Roy, the – uh, deceased, offered his services.'

'I don't suppose she could have done this?'

'Strangled him and tore up the place? No, I don't suppose so, either.'

He turned to Sitchell. 'Clete, get the girl's statement from Midgen and bring them both in here.'

Sitchell went off to the bedroom, where a woman cop had been interviewing Sarah, and Kassarian asked, 'How do you figure it?'

I shrugged. 'Looks like he had something somebody wanted.'

'Was he gay?'

'I don't think so, but I don't know for sure.'

'A doper?'

'Same answer.'

'This guy was your partner, but you don't know much about him.'

'Not exactly my partner,' I said. We shared an office.'

'Then you wouldn't have any idea what his killer or killers were looking for?'

I shook my head.

'What kind of case load was he carrying?'

'He had his work and I had mine. We rarely talked about it; in fact, we rarely talked at all. We split the rent. That's about it.'

'But you got along.'

'Yeah. We got along.'

'We'll want to look at his files,' he said.

'They're downtown all over the carpet. Be my guest.'

'Your files, too.'

I smiled. 'This is where I could piss and moan about confidentiality. And search warrants. But the hell with that. If it'll help you find out who did this, the files are yours. Happy to cooperate.'

Sarah joined us, followed by Sitchell and a fox-faced woman detective named Midgen who had perspired through her jacket, no doubt because she'd spent the last half-hour with the kid.

Sitchell handed Sarah's statement to Kassarian, indicating something with one long, prospective-lawyer finger. The older dick read it and stuck his lower lip out. It didn't make him any prettier. 'Hm-m-m-m,' he hmmmed. 'Well, Mr Bloodworth, according to the young lady, you haven't been exactly candid with us.'

I glared at the kid, who looked back with wide, innocent eyes. Mentally I backtracked through my statement and couldn't find anything I'd missed. I'd even copped to entering Kaspar's bungalow illegally. I turned to the dark-skinned detective with as honestly perplexed an expression as I could muster.

'You wanna tell me about this Gottlieb fellow?' he asked.

'Sure. Gottlieb. Right. Well, he'd hired Roy to do some work for him and he wasn't happy about the results.'

'The girl says he attacked you. Tried to kick in your head.'

'He never had the chance,' the kid broke in. 'Mr Bloodworth totally vanquished that terrible man. It was something to see.'

Kassarian gave me a long look. 'This very young lady seems quite taken with you, Mr Bloodworth.'

I smiled weakly.

'Why'd Gottlieb go for you?'

'Because my name was on the door with Kaspar's.'

'So he tried to pop your skull. What d'you think he had in store for Kaspar?'

'He was a guy with a bad temper,' I said. 'Maybe he would've bounced him around a little – but strangulation . . .'

'Did Kaspar have anything Gottlieb wanted?'

'Not to my knowledge.'

'Didn't Mr Kaspar say he'd taken some pictures of Mr Gottlieb's wife?' the kid asked.

Kassarian raised an eyebrow.

'Roy may have said something about that. I wasn't paying much attention.'

'We'd better go down to your office now, Bloodworth. The four of us. Clete'll drive Miss Dahlquist.' He said to Sitchell, 'Take her out the back, away from the newsfolk.' Turning to me he added, 'We'll wait and leave through the front to cause a little diversion. Then you can drive me in your car and we can talk some more about Gottlieb.'

I nodded. Sitchell looked about as happy as I felt.

5

It was the latest I'd been up since the Emmy night when Gran took me to a party where everybody got absolutely low-down and inebriated, including Rex Ahern, the humane, thoughtful Dr Montgomery on *Look to Tomorrow*. He was supposed to drive us home, but after witnessing him in the swimming pool, drunkenly groping Winnie Purcell, who plays his daughter on the show, we discovered just how difficult it was getting a cab at that time of night way out in Malibu.

Anyway, Detective Kassarian, who had heard of William Saroyan but never read him, finally let me call Gran to tell her not to worry. I did my best to explain the situation, but she demanded to speak to the detective. Judging by the red splotches on his face when he replaced the phone, she'd told him just how silly she thought he was, detaining me.

The police did not find Mr Gottlieb's photos, but they did get his address and phone number. I told them repeatedly that he was not among those men who broke into the offices, but this did not deter Detective Kassarian from dispatching his minions to apprehend Mr Gottlieb. Well, the punk-haired ruffian deserved whatever inconvenience came his way, I suppose.

Detective Sitchell continued to complain about missing his class. He was very prissy for a policeman. Detective Kassarian informed him that the mundane examination of a victim's personal effects was fine practice for a fledgling man of law, rather like a graduate course in criminology. He suggested the young investigator write a term paper about the contents of Mr Kaspar's office.

Detective Kassarian was just as snide to Mr Bloodworth, who bent over backward to cooperate with the investigation. Perhaps the lawman would have been more pleasant had the office break-in been reported. But as Mr Bloodworth explained, nothing seemed to have been taken and vandalism does not rate a very high priority in this era of carnage and rape.

It was nearing midnight when we were allowed to go. This, after making us wait for a stenographer to take down our formal statements. When that rugged, serviceable gray Chevy pulled up in front of my apartment building, its driver seemed almost as sleepy as I was.

'All out, Sarah,' he said. I began to rather fancy that name he'd picked for me. 'It's been a long one.'

I hesitated before opening the car door.

'C'mon, kid. Outsky. If I don't get some sleep soon, they'll be planting me next to Kaspar.'

'I've a confession to make,' I blurted out.

He stared at me with yellow eyes rimmed in red. 'I don't want to hear any confession. You don't see any prayer beads hanging from my belt, do you?'

I turned and, reaching around my seat, began rummaging through the crumpled lunch bags in the rear of the car. Finally, I found the one I wanted. I opened it and took out an audio cassette and a manila envelope. I held them out to Mr Bloodworth.

He scowled at them and at me. 'What the hell is this? No. Scratch that. I don't give a damn what it is.'

'I took these from the scene of the crime,' I told him.

'You did what?'

'They were in Mr Kaspar's little car. I saw him use the tape when he was driving me home. It's an audio record of his appointments for the week. He kept it in the tape deck in his car and turned it on to find out what he was supposed to do next. The envelope was in his glove compartment.'

'You took this stuff from Roy's car?'

It must have been the lateness of the hour, for Mr Bloodworth didn't seem to be grasping anything that I was telling him.

'Yes. It was parked behind his bungalow. Locked, of course. But if your hand is small enough, you can stick it under the canvas top of a convertible and open the door very –'

'You took this stuff from his car?'

'I just said I did. I –'

'Why? For God's sake, why? Why didn't you just tell the cops about them?'

I shrugged. 'I remembered the tape when we were talking in the kitchen. You know, you were telling me about the putrid flesh and stuff and it suddenly hit me that this tape could be very important evidence, with all sorts of information about the people Mr Kaspar had just seen or was going to see. So I ran out to get it. The envelope looked interesting, so I grabbed it, too.'

'You ran out to get the tape? I thought you were sick.'

'Sick?' Whatever was he talking about? 'Lordy, I'm never sick. Never.'

'And you put this stuff in the back of my car?'

'It seemed like a good idea at the time. But I must admit I was a little worried when Detective Kassarian decided to use the Chevy.'

'You should have turned it over to him.'

I wrinkled my nose. 'I don't think he's a very good investigator. I mean, Mr Gottlieb obviously is not our killer, but Detective Kassarian was so positive. Anyway, this is something for you to follow up, not him.'

'Me?'

He just didn't seem to understand. It was definitely the late hour. 'You, of course,' I said. ' "When a man's partner is killed, he's supposed to do something about it. It doesn't matter if he liked him or not, he's supposed to do something about it," ' I quoted from one of my favorite old movies.

Mr Bloodworth sighed. 'Kid, you take this junk with you and tomorrow you phone Kassarian and tell him you have it. Me, I've got troubles enough.'

'But –'

'No buts. Just be gone now, before I pass out on your lawn.'

I got out of the Chevy, taking the tape and the envelope with me. I was sure he'd feel differently about the whole thing in the morning. 'I'll call you tomorrow. Early,' I said.

'Not if you value your life,' he replied.

A joke, I was sure. The Bloodhound would be on the job at the crack of dawn.

At the door to our building, I rattled the glass, and Leon, the black divinity student who watches things at night, pulled his nose out of a book and let me in. I watched Mr Bloodworth drive away, making a U-turn to go back down Ocean Breeze Road to the highway.

Another car farther up the block pulled out into the street, its lights off, and made a U-turn also, following the gray Chevy. It was a dark blue or green Lincoln and there were three people inside it. I would have been concerned about Mr Bloodworth, except that they'd made such an obvious move to stay on his tail with that U-turn that I was sure he had them spotted, regardless of how tired he was. After all, he was the Bloodhound and ultra-sensitive to such things.

6

1. I stopped to pick up a half-dozen buttermilk doughnuts and a six-pack of Coors and headed wearily toward my modest shack behind a little theater on Gramercy Place. If, as I suspected, the streets in that section of L.A. had been named by some homesick New Yorker, he'd have been damn disturbed to see how ratty the neighborhood had become. Maybe the names had been an anti-Manhattan gag all along.

Even though the area was run-down, it wasn't a bad place to live. Low crime. No street gangs to spray-paint your car windows for you. No hookers like on Sunset or Santa Monica Boulevard. Sort of quiet, except on weekend evenings, when the Gramercy Players celebrated their muse and parking got tight and the flourish of trumpets or whatever emanating from the stage tended to drown out my little FM portable.

Since that morning, the Players had hammered a hand-painted poster to the front of the building announcing a new production. I parked the Chevy so as not to block the sign from the view of any prospective theatergoers. I locked the car and carried my health-food dinner over to the poster. It seemed that the Players were ready to roll with *Aimwell and Archer*, a contemporary musical by Laird Blaise Bardell, based on George Farquhar's eighteenth-century comedy *The Beaux' Stratagem*. Bardell was my five-foot-three landlord. His busty but wrinkled wife, Helga, was the female lead. It promised to be one hell of a production.

As I wandered down the dark alley leading to my humble home out back, idly wondering what sort of music would be filling the air come Friday night, I sampled one of the doughnuts. A little dry, but still tasty. I longed to complement it with a sip of Coors.

I was standing before my door, doughnut in mouth and key in free hand, when two gentlemen in dark suits appeared at the side of the house, looking more improbable than ominous in the moonlight.

Their hands were empty. One of them asked, 'Mr Bloodworth?'

I stared at him. In his late twenties, red hair, freckles, dressed in a nice summer Palm Beach. He probably gave the ladies hell, presuming he liked ladies. And even if he didn't. I swallowed the doughnut.

'Why don't we go inside?' he suggested.

I replied by throwing my door key onto the roof of the Gramercy Theater. Red-top just chuckled. My front door was opened from the inside by another pleasant-looking young man, who'd been in there, waiting.

I shrugged an I'm-always-willing-to-act-reasonably shrug and took a step toward the open door. Then I swung the six-pack back and bounced it off Red-top's noggin. He gave a yip and staggered away. I rushed past him, heading for the alley. A hefty third-party beat me to it. He bent over in a scrimmage-line squat and charged, catching me at midsection with his well-tailored shoulder. That was that for my escape try and for my predigested doughnut.

I sat down hard on the antique-brick walkway and gasped for air while the boys gathered around. Red-top was rubbing his ear, but there was far too little damage there for my money. He nodded to the gridiron great, who grabbed me under the arms and hoisted me to my feet as if I didn't really weigh a hundred and eighty-four pounds stripped. As he patted me down clumsily, what appeared to be a USC school ring flashed in the moonlight.

Red-top asked me, 'Where's the Century List, Mr Bloodworth?'

I stared at him stupidly. An honest stare.

'Please,' he implored. 'We know you're difficult, but we really are getting quite tired of searching rooms. Be a good guy and tell us where it is.'

'The Century List,' I said. 'What the hell is a Century List?'

Red-top gave me an exasperated look. 'We have a project to complete, Mr Bloodworth, and you're wasting our time. I suppose you want us to believe you don't know about the Century List?'

'I think you guys want some other Bloodworth.'

'All right. Be an asshole.' He nodded, and the USC grad clasped the nape of my neck in his big hand. His fingers fiddled with some nerves back there, found what they were looking for, and squeezed. I blanked out as effectively as if he'd poleaxed me with a baseball bat.

2. There was dew on the scrub grass when I awoke. The sky was a postdawn slate gray. And my neck was as stiff as a grape presser's sock. My night visitors had emptied my doughnuts onto the walkway, where a stream of ants had beaten me to them. The cardboard wrapper had been torn from the six-pack and beer cans rested on the grass along with my wallet and the contents of my pockets. Considering their brand of thoroughness, I was not anxious to see what my house looked like. That would have to come later anyway. They'd locked the door behind them.

I pushed in the top of one of the Coorses and had a warm breakfast beer. Then I went to the theater, yanked down the rusty fire ladder, and scrambled up it in search of my keys.

*

3. At 9:30, some three hours later, the phone rang. I found it under a pile of books that had been emptied from a wall unit. I'd fallen asleep in my suit on top of a ripped mattress and was covered with cotton tufts, some of which seemed to be in my mouth.

'Hello, Mr Bloodworth, is this you?'

I waited a second before answering. 'How'd you get my home number, kid?'

'I heard you give it to Detective Kassarian. Are you all right? You sound rather distant.'

'I was asleep.'

'At nine-thirty?'

'I'm just a slugabed. Call me later. I want to talk to you.'

'Wait,' she said. 'Can't I see you now?'

'No,' I told her, and hung up.

The torn mattress was way across the room. A box spring, with only half the cover removed, was just a few feet away. So that was my next destination.

Goddamn if the kid wasn't in my dreams, too.

7

Gran was on the terrace having breakfast in the early morning sun. She always enjoys a hearty breakfast – that day it was waffles with syrup and butter and blueberries and at least two strips of bacon and several cups of coffee. She eats all that terrible junk and remains as thin as a rail and healthy as a horse. I hope I have inherited some of that from her, though I don't suppose I'll know for a few years the vagaries of my metabolism.

She was dressed for work in a tweedy suit, looking very much like the all-wise Aunt Lil Fairchild, except for a large straw sunbonnet and white gloves. I don't know why she insists on breakfasting in the sun if the sun causes brown spots to form on her face and hands, but that is her business, after all.

She called to me and so I brought my date-nut granola and pure Altadena cream out on the terrace to join her. She had been reading the morning *Los Angeles Times* and was not in good spirits. She folded the paper and placed it beside my cereal bowl. There was a photo of the Palms Garden Apartments and an insert that looked like a passport picture of Mr Kaspar, back when he was still breathing. The headline read: Private Detective Killed in Palms.

Gran dabbed at her lips and said, 'Due to some stroke of fortune, my only grandchild's name was not mentioned in connection with that sordid affair, Sehr-ee-nah.' She calls me

Sehr-ee-nah when she is displeased with me, Sehr when we are pals, and Wendy when she is being especially playful.

'Detective Kassarian kept me away from the reporters. Anyway, I don't think they're supposed to use young people's names unless they're found guilty of something.'

'I wouldn't count on the dread *Enquirer* being capable of so fine a distinction with Aunt Lil Fairchild's granddaughter.'

'I'll make sure they don't find out,' I said.

'That's a sweet girl.' She smiled at me. She has a lovely smile. 'I've the day off Thursday. Why don't we find a replacement for Groucho then?'

'Couldn't we wait a while? I mean, we're still not sure that Groucho . . .'

'If Groucho were coming back, he would have by now,' she said.

'I was thinking that Mr Bloodworth might find him.'

Gran doesn't like to frown. Wrinkles, you know. But she was frowning then. 'Sehr-ee-nah, I am serious about this. I've no doubt your Bloodworth is a fine enough chap, but his associate has been . . . has met with misfortune, and he's going to have his hands full, what with the police and the press.'

'Oh, he wants to see me. He told me so this morning on the phone.'

Her frown deepened. 'I do not think that would be wise. I really do not.'

I gobbled the granola heartily, nodding my head as if I totally agreed with her. It satisfied her immensely.

'Then we'll get a new puppy on Thursday,' she said with some finality.

'I'm supposed to play tennis with Sylvia.'

'I thought the little thing was preggers.'

'She is, but she won't be delivering for a while yet, and the doctor told her to exercise.'

Gran gestured with her hands. 'Then we'll do it the following Thursday. My dear Eric taught me never to procrastinate.'

'Gran,' I said, 'tell me again how you and my grandfather met.'

She smiled. 'You don't want to hear that old story.'

'But I do. Come on. You don't have to be at the studio for hours.'

She cocked her head to one side the way she does, and her deep blue eyes got that faraway look. 'Your grandfather and I met whilst appearing in Bob Sherwood's *There Shall Be No Night*. His first real success, my first Broadway play. The Lunts starred, of course. A wonderful vehicle for them. It was about the Russian invasion of Finland. My Eric was a proud Finn, and I a housemaid. How I admired him. Admired and loved. All during rehearsals he said barely a word to me. Then, during the performance on opening night, as he was leaving the stage and I was awaiting my entrance, he kissed me on the lips. It took me by such surprise, I was late in answering my cue and dear Lynn was glaring daggers at me.

'That was a wonderful time. A wonderful play. Then the Russians became our allies against the Germans, and the Finns sided with them, so the politics were all wrong. And Bob Sherwood, who was very patriotic, decided to close the show.

'I immediately went into *Angel Street* with Judith Evelyn and Vinnie Price, who was deliciously loathsome even in those days, and Leo Carroll, with whom I'd worked in summer stock. And dearest Eric went into a revival of Galsworthy's *Justice*. At fifty, he was pushing it a bit playing the lead, but he was glorious. It made him a star. Oh, my. What a death scene! As he lay there on stage, motionless, Palea Dunworthy delivered the line, "No one'll touch him now. He's safe with gentle Jesus."'

'Those were good days, huh, Gran?'

'Good? They were transcendent. Success upon success. And your mother was born. We were so happy.'

I looked at my reflection in my spoon. 'And he was fifty when you married him?'

'To me he was still a boy. Oh, Lord, you shouldn't do this to me, Sehr,' she said, trying to gather her thoughts. 'Not when I have to toil before the cameras.'

'Have you heard from Mom lately?'

She gave me a guarded look. 'Why?'

'I was wondering if she'd been in town.'

Gran stood. 'Too much sun for me, little girl. I'm off.'

'I'll get the dishes,' I said.

'What are your plans for the day?'

'Oh, this and that.'

She paused beside me, putting her gloved hand on my cheek. 'I wish you had more friends, dear.'

'I've all I need,' I said.

'Now that Sylvia –'

'Sylvia's just a kid,' I said. 'I can't really talk with her. She's all messed up with that dumb George, anyway.'

'I'm afraid our little arrangement has robbed you of something quite precious, Sehr. You're going straight from childhood to middle age.'

'Do you really think so?' I asked. 'Oh, Gran, do you really think so?' What a wonderful grandmother she is.

8

1. The kid entered Bay Heights Park from the west gate like I'd told her, pedaling hard. She was wearing a boy's white shirt and denims and her blond hair was tucked under a bright red and yellow crash helmet. A blind bohunk could have followed her from a mile away, but if anybody was on her, I didn't see them.

I put down the binoculars and took a sip of beer. It was nice sitting in the park under a leafy oak tree on a warm spring day, sleeves rolled up, downing a brew. The stiffness in my neck was smoothing out. The portable was playing Cab Calloway's 'Minnie the Moocher'. And there wasn't a dark suit as far as the enhanced eye could see.

Sarah circled the tennis courts and headed in my general direction. I tried to remember when I'd last been on a bike but gave that up quickly. Instead, I squeezed a thick squiggle of yellow mustard on one of several hot dogs I'd brought and did away with a third of it.

I was polishing off the tail of the dog when she pushed the bike up the hill, flushed and slightly out of breath. She lowered the bicycle to the ground very gently. 'Nobody followed me,' she said.

'Let's have the stuff, sis.'

'As I've told you before, I'd rather not be called that. I'm not your sister. We are not related.' She reached inside her shirt and removed the cassette and the envelope.

'Your request has been duly noted, ma'am,' I said, taking the objects from her. The flap of the envelope was open. I looked at her.

'Well,' she fidgeted, 'I didn't see how you could steam it open out here.'

Inside was a bright orange United Broadcasting Company studio pass. It had been in effect four days earlier, allowing entry to 'Guests of Mr Gary Grady'. The name sounded vaguely familiar. The other item was a sheet of notepaper that had Kaspar's scrawl on it. I could make out . . . $100 . . . Cent Corp . . . sign-return . . . SASE . . . Milton Rome . . . citizen . . . check Leo.'

'What do you think?' the kid asked, looking over my shoulder.

'Mumbo jumbo. I think Roy should have learned to write.'

'The SASE is a self-addressed stamped envelope. You learn those things when you enter contests.'

'That's swell,' I said, putting the stuff back into the envelope and the envelope into the pocket of my coat, which was lying beside me on the ground. I picked up my radio, which was also supposed to play tapes, if you knew what you were doing.

'You're putting it in backward,' she said.

'Why don't you have a hot dog, Sarah?' I replied, reversing the plastic cassette case.

'Is it a real hot dog or a turkey dog?'

'What's a turkey dog?'

'It's what you eat if you don't want to kill yourself with pork fat and bits of gristle and cholesterol and nitrates.'

'That'll teach me to ask,' I said. 'No. This is not a turkey dog. It's a goddamn ball-park frank, as American as apple pie.'

'What could be more American than a turkey?'

It doesn't pay to argue with kids. It's a no-win situation, like when your neurotic girlfriend asks you to teach her to shoot. I clicked the cassette into place while Sarah picked up the binocs.

'I can almost see out of these,' she said. 'We must have the same vision, nearly.' For some reason, that pleased her.

I started the tape. Kaspar's well-modulated voice began a litany of names, dates, times, and places. I took the glasses and scanned the park again while it droned on. 'Testing . . . one . . . Monday, nine A.M., tennis with Lori M. on her court . . . noon, hair at Little Jimmy's . . .' Three P.M., meet with so-and-so for such-and-such. And so on and so on.

There were only two recognizable names in the bunch, or so the kid informed me. I'd never heard of either. One was Dr Devon Helmdale, author of a diet book that mixed food and cosmetic surgery. The other was the aforementioned Gary Grady, who was about to become the host of a new talk show on UBC.

Kaspar led a very full, active life in which there were shoes to be shined, nails to be manicured, bank deposits to be made, tennis games to be played, women to be wooed. Kaspar never mentioned his ladies' last names. If he had a reason, it had died with him.

Through most of the tape, Sarah sat quietly beside me on the hill, clasping her knees to her chest. But at one point she said, 'Listen carefully. This could be important.'

'You played the tape already?' I asked.

'Shush.'

The entry was for noon of the day the forensics people decided Roy had bought it. His unsuspecting voice said, '. . . lunch with Faith D.'

I looked at the kid. 'So?'

She stared off across the park. 'My mother's name is Faith,' she said.

2. Like a good citizen I had called Kassarian that morning to report my run-in with the college boys, and he and Sitchell had wandered over to my place a few hours later to check the carnage

for themselves. They'd taken Gottlieb into custody the night before and were standing fast on the theory that either the break-ins and the murder were unrelated or Gottlieb had hired the trio.

Kassarian rather liked the unrelated theory, since that made the assault somebody else's problem. It also explained why I was up and about and not lying on the bricks as dead as Roy. I didn't bother to mention the business about the Century List. Not that he would have been all that interested; he had his man.

It was only a matter of time, Sitchell added, before they found the wire garrote Gottlieb had used on Roy.

That left me to cope with the boys in dark suits, which was why I wanted to check out Sarah's stuff. I had no idea what the suits had planned for me, so I'd met her in a nice wide-open area like Bay Heights Park.

'Well, Faith is a sort of common . . . I mean, lots of women are named –'

'Mr Bloodworth, are you going to sit there and tell me that there are hundreds of Faith D.s that Mr Kaspar could have met for lunch just hours before he was murdered?'

'Maybe not hundreds . . .'

'Anyway, my mother was probably in town then. I asked Gran about it this morning and she changed the subject. She always behaves weirdly when Mom is in L.A. and doesn't bother to call me. Mom usually asks Gran how I am and all, but she feels funny – guilty, I guess – about talking directly to me. Maybe it's because I ask her a lot of questions. I tell myself not to, but I always forget because I'm really interested in what she's doing with herself.'

'That's only natural, kid.'

'Anyway, assuming she was in town, it must have been she.'

I nodded and stood up, knees cracking, and started bagging the hot dogs and beer cans. 'I'll check it out, Sarah. If I bump into your mom, I'll get her to give you a call.'

'I was hoping I could come with you,' she said. 'I'll just lock my bike to that tree and get it later.'

'That's not possible,' I said, picking up the radio and the tape and the envelope. 'I've got a lot of work to do and –'

'And you don't want a kid underfoot.'

'Hell, that's not it, exactly,' I said, thinking that feeling guilty could be contagious around the kid. 'I was putting myself in your place. It's real boring stuff.'

'Not for me. I'd love it. And I'd be as quiet as a mouse. Gran used to call me Mousy when I was younger. I was so quiet.'

'Those days are gone forever, kid. Anyway, I'll get more done if I'm alone. Maybe some other time, huh?'

I jogged down the hill and tossed the trash into a container. Then I went to my car without looking back at her. I put the radio and the Kaspar items into the glove compartment, locked it, and then started to turn on the engine. There was a tap on the glass. She was sitting on her bike beside me, motioning for me to roll down the window. When I did, reluctantly, she handed me the binoculars, which I'd forgotten.

'See. I'm not totally useless,' she said. Then, in a rush she added, 'There's only one way you can find out if mother was here and that's by talking to Gran at the studio, and Gran is the kind of person who won't talk to you unless you are properly introduced, and I'm really the only one who could introduce you, and after I've done that I'll just sort of go off somewhere and you two can have a nice long talk, because I think Gran will be more open with you about Mother if I'm not around. If that's all right with you, I mean.'

How could I argue with logic like that? I told her I'd follow her home to put away the bike.

Unless I'd lost it all, nobody was tailing us.

*

3. Waiting for her, I had another lukewarm beer in the car and listened again to Kaspar's last tape. It yielded no more information than before, but it made me curious about his three visits to his bank in just one week. Deposits? Withdrawals more likely, considering the wining and dining the guy did.

I looked at Kaspar's notes again. Was the '$100' literal, or shorthand for $100,000? '1967 Cent Corp . . .' Corporation was the obvious guess. 'Cent' probably had something to do with the Century List the dark suits were looking for. But what's on the list? Who the hell is Milton Rome? Why was Kaspar going to check with me?

Finally the kid returned. She'd brushed her hair and tied it with a ribbon and exchanged the shirt and pants for a blue pleated dress that managed to make her look both older and younger at the same time.

'I found this,' she said, and handed me a snapshot of a woman with blond hair, sitting on a lawn, cradling a dog. The woman's face was blurred, as if she had turned her head at the moment the camera clicked. The dog, an ugly-looking mutt, was staring dead-on into the lens. 'It's Mother and Groucho,' Sarah said. 'Maybe it'll help you find them both.'

'If your mother is in town, I'd like to talk to her about Kaspar. Let's leave your dog out of it.'

She nodded as if she understood. Then she explained to me precisely where her grandmother would be at UBC and what the fastest route was to get us there. Other than that, she was, as promised, as quiet as a mouse, except for joining me in a chorus of 'Accentuate the Positive,' which KCRW-FM had the good taste to send our way.

The cop at the UBC visitors' gate waved me into a temporary parking space while Sarah telephoned the old lady for the necessary pass. The evening smog at Burbank was thick enough to skate on. The heat was at least twenty degrees higher than it had been in oceanside Bay Heights. Rows of cars sat roasting in the setting sun, their windshields sending out a glare that not even Bausch and Lomb could deflect.

In the rearview I saw the kid gesturing wildly to the phone while the fat studio cop sat back on his stool, spilling over it in fact, and chuckling at her efforts. The poor bastard probably had little enough to laugh at, dealing with television people all day. I'd have rather skinned skunks for a living.

Sarah handed him the phone and ran back to the car. 'It's OK,' she told me. 'But I'd better warn you, Gran has had some problems with a new member of the cast and she's not in the best mood.'

'Oh?'

'And I had – ah, to fib a little. I told her you were a fan of the show.'

'Show? I don't even know its name.'

'*Look to Tomorrow*, but everyone calls it *Look*. That martinet at the gate said we had to park along the back wall. I don't know why we can't just take one of those empty spots over there, so much closer to Stage Eight.'

Neither did I. One of the spaces had been stenciled recently with the name Gary Grady. I covered it with the Chevy. As we walked away toward the stages, I thought I heard the cop shouting at us, but he was too far away to be sure. In any case, I didn't want to keep an already angry old lady waiting.

4. 'Good day, Mr Bloodworth,' she said, stepping daintily over the snake pit of cables and wires on Stage 8.

The place was dark and slightly damp and crowded and noisy. A group of unkempt bums who would have been eighty-sixed at even the Irish Mist sat around sipping coffee from stained paper cups while a wired, prematurely bald little guy goose-stepped around carrying a clipboard, looking confused and bad-tempered. I figured him for the head man. Television.

'Good day, ma'am,' I said to Sarah's grandmother. If I'd been wearing a hat, it would have been in my hand. She was a handsome, intimidating woman. High, full cheekbones. Knowing blue eyes you wouldn't want to lie to. A thin mouth, but neither thin nor straight enough to be called severe. Her hair, piled atop her head, still had some golden strands mixed with the gray. She raised an eyebrow at Sarah and then gave me a smile that was designed to look patronizing.

'Sehr-ee-nah, why don't you go say hello to Linda?'

Sarah nodded and off she went, meek as mutton on the hoof.

'Linda is our youngest cast member, which you no doubt know. She and Sehr-ee-nah are quite chummy. Walk me to my dressing room, Mr Bloodworth. I'm actually glad to have this opportunity to chat.'

As we stepped into the smoggy sunlight, a short, glowering guy with a mop of black hair and a disposition like a chafed bear rushed by, almost toppling the old lady. I grabbed her elbow and settled her down. Then I started after the guy.

'No.' She stopped me. 'It's only Mr Lorenzo. He's from the New York stage, where boorishness is its own reward.'

'Looks real sour,' I said.

'Perhaps this coast isn't agreeing with him,' she said with a smile. 'He has just joined our merry *Look to Tomorrow* family. You'll be seeing a lot of him on the show starting next month.'

I followed her across a narrow street. 'Actually, I'm usually working during the day,' I said. 'Not much time for watching TV.'

'That's odd. I could have sworn Sehr told me you were an avid follower of our little continuing drama.'

We stopped at the first in a line of three Winnebagos. It

served as her dressing room. The New York actor was standing beside the one directly behind hers, talking to a workman who was carting a large crate labeled 'Air Purifier.'

Miss Van Dine gave the two men and the crate a frosty glance and, head held high, stepped regally into her Winnebago. I followed her in, much less regally, and pulled the door closed behind me. It was chilly in there.

She offered me a comfortable chair, picked up two glasses, and began to pour a couple of healthy shots of scotch, mumbling, 'That little roach. An air purifier, eh.'

'We could pour skunk oil into it,' I said.

'Is that a service of your agency?' she asked coldly.

'I was just being larky.'

She handed me my glass of hootch and took the couch opposite me. 'I'm not sure that risibility is seemly, considering the recent passing of your associate.' She downed her whisky neat. Not one to let a former great lady of the stage get the jump on me, I followed suit.

'It is because of Mr Kaspar's untimely demise and the circumstances surrounding it that I wish to discourage any future – ah, business dealings between you and my granddaughter. This nonsense about Groucho –'

'Miss Van Dine, I'm sure, as you must be, that Groucho is in that big pound in the sky by now. And I agree – do I ever – that your granddaughter and I should have no further contact.'

She frowned. 'Well, then . . .'

'It's about your daughter.'

The frown deepened into something less friendly.

'Any idea where I might locate her?'

She didn't answer right away. Then, 'Didn't Mr Kaspar tell you about our little chat?' She was perched on the edge of the couch, her back straight as a poker.

'No,' I answered. 'We only talked about the weather, the rent.

Things like that. In any case, I never saw him again after the night he took the ki– your granddaughter home. Very few did.'

She edged back on the couch as if she wanted to put more space between us. I decided to go after her. 'There's reason to believe Faith saw him the next day. Had lunch with him. That was the day he was killed. Did you know she was in town?'

A flush turned her cheeks red. 'Of course she was here. Precisely where, I have no way of knowing. As I told the late Mr Kaspar, it must have been Faith who took the blasted dog. She's the only other person besides Sehr and myself who has a key to the apartment. And Groucho didn't open the door himself.'

'Why'd she want the dog?'

'I have given up trying to figure out what Faith wants with anything. Her new friend, whom she introduced as a Mr Danny Gutierrez, showed a great deal of interest in the animal when they visited me several weeks ago.'

'How?'

She cocked one eye. 'I don't understand the question.'

'How did he show the interest?'

'He asked to see the dog. He saw it. He made some sort of oblique comment. And then they left.'

'Do you think you can remember exactly the way the conversation went?'

'If I can remember forty pages of script a day, I should be able to recall the few uncomplicated words issued by that fellow, yes. They entered the apartment, sat down. They refused drinks. They seemed uncomfortably anxious, neither saying much. Finally, Señor Gutierrez said he'd like to see that puppy he'd been hearing so much about. Faith jumped up, rather puppylike herself, and fetched him the dog. He grinned at it and said, and I quote, "Don't hold him so tight, babe. That's a pooch worth his weight in gold." Then he laughed and Faith smiled and allowed Groucho to jump from her arms and return to the privacy of his basket.'

'Where was your granddaughter while this was going on?'

'She'd just departed for the movies with her friend Sylvia. I had the feeling Faith and her cohort had been waiting outside for her to leave.'

'Serendipity and her mother seem to have a rather unusual relationship.'

'Faith's emotions, what there are of them, rest very close to the surface. She might have made a good actress, but never a good mother. My inheritance, I suppose.' She smiled self-consciously.

'Meaning that you got along with Faith like Faith gets along with Serendipity?'

'I have not loved many things in this life, Mr Bloodworth. I loved my late husband and I loved the theater, because it was something he and I were part of. Faith had to compete for my affection and came off a poor third. I wish I could have changed that, but . . . In any case, my only love now is for my granddaughter.'

'She seems like a bright little girl.'

'Very bright, and generally happy. But I wish she had more friends. She may be just a bit too self-sufficient.'

'Only children get like that,' I said.

'Were you an only child, Mr Bloodworth?'

I nodded. 'How old was Faith when your husband passed away?'

'My husband didn't simply pass away. His plane crashed while he was on a USO tour during the Korean conflict. I don't really know the precise location. Never knew what happened to him. Never even had the satisfaction of wearing widow's weeds and playing that weepy farewell scene, "Safe with gentle Jesus".

'But you asked me about Faith. She was Serendipity's age. I began sending her to private schools in winter, camps in summer. Then one fine day I received a frantic phone call from a distraught instructor at Pine Manor. Faith and another girl had packed their bags and left the school. She was sixteen. I had moved out here by then. Film work. When Faith did not arrive or telephone, I consulted a detective agency – Wilmer-Blake, you probably know them – and they found her in San Francisco. That Haight-Ashbury love-peace-and-drugs communal-living nonsense was at its peak.

'Faith refused to come home, so I flew there. I won't try to describe the condition she was in. Among other things, she was addicted to drugs. I put her into a hospital at once. She stayed there for a few days, checked herself out, and disappeared again. This time I didn't try to find her.

'Two years later she arrived on my doorstep, several months pregnant, hanging onto the arm of the extraordinary Frank Dahlquist. She no longer had a dependence on drugs. I'll give him that. But she had developed a dependence on him, which may have been just as detrimental.'

'What was wrong with him?'

She shook her head. 'He wasn't a bad-looking boy, and he certainly was not ignorant. Others found him amusing. To me, he seemed a very dark-souled fellow. Moody, indifferent. Wildly changeable. One day he'd be a thoughtful philosopher, the next a raconteur, the next a revolutionary zealot. A child of the cinema, I suppose. Or maybe just slightly mad.

'He got them into some sort of difficulty – they were not specific – and they needed a thousand dollars to travel. I agreed to give them the money if they agreed to marry and legitimize the forthcoming child. Frank agreed to it readily. To him, money was money.

'After the ceremony – if you could call that cold civil ritual such – Frank tried to pry another thousand out of me, unsuccessfully. Then they drifted on their merry way. More years passed and Faith returned with her baby girl and a puppy dog, both gifts from Frank, whose worthless hide had been shipped to Vietnam, from whence it did not return.

'I had lost my husband in one conflict. Faith had lost hers in another. Because of this, my daughter and I finally arrived at a point where we made a genuine effort to get along. She lived with me and Serendipity for a while, but she will ever be a restless girl, and there was a handsome young lawyer with very nice manners who asked her to accompany him on a tour of the Orient. Not knowing that this young man made his money by smuggling and selling narcotics, I encouraged my daughter to have her fling and promised to take good care of her little girl until it was over. Her fling has continued for eleven years. Curtain and *finis*.'

'Not exactly,' I said. 'Faith keeps popping up.'

'The proverbial bad penny. May God forgive my saying it. But she never sees me unless she's in need of something, usually something that will do her no good.'

'What did she need this time?'

The old lady picked up the scotch bottle and dropped another shot into my cup. 'Faith didn't say. Although she and that Gutierrez chap spent some time rooting around in Sehr's room. Faith has a few boxes in there. Old clothes, mementos.'

'Tell me more about Gutierrez.'

'A sooty ship she passed in the night in Mazatlan and with whom she plans to troll up the coast to a place he called Pelea de Perro – something like that – as soon as he takes care of some financial matter here.'

'What financial matter?'

She gestured extravagantly. 'Unspecified.'

'Did Gutierrez look like a businessman?'

'He did not even look like a Gutierrez. I doubt that he was pure Mexican, if Mexican at all. Almost fair, with light brown hair. Was he a businessman? Do businessmen wear their shirts open to the navel?'

'In this town? Sure. When they wear shirts at all.'

'Gutierrez wore a shirt. That much I'll give him.' She capped the bottle. 'I'll have to leave you shortly for a dialogue reading of tomorrow's pages. Or, as practiced by Mr Lorenzo, dialogue mumbling.'

I handed her my empty glass and she placed it in a little metal sink set in the bar. 'You said you told Roy Kaspar that Faith had the dog?'

She nodded. 'It was cruel of her to take Groucho, whatever her reason. Mr Kaspar was convinced he could get it back quickly.'

'Why didn't you talk to Faith about it yourself?'

'I had no idea how to reach her.'

'How was Kaspar going to?'

'I never thought to ask. Wouldn't that have been like asking a magician how he makes the tiger disappear?'

'Kaspar didn't believe in professional secrets. He'd have told you anything. For a price.'

'He was your partner,' she said.

I was tired of correcting people about that. 'I didn't like him much when he was alive. But I can honestly say I'm sorry he's not still with us.'

The stiffness hadn't left my neck entirely. Maybe Kaspar hadn't shaken those college boys' cage, but he seemed to be the only reason they were on the prowl. 'Was Serendipity there when you told Kaspar about Faith being the dognapper?'

'She was in her room watching television. I'm sure she didn't hear us. She didn't even know Faith was in town.'

Through the tinted windows of the Winnebago, I saw the kid stick her blond head out of the stage door and squint in our direction. Then she ran toward us and knocked on the glass. 'Cast call!' she shouted.

Mrs Van Dine smiled at the girl and then turned to me, dropping the smile and saying *sotto voce*, 'Please cease contact with my granddaughter after today, Mr Bloodworth. You seem like a perfectly decent fellow, but she's a strange little girl, with strange ideas. It's best not to encourage most of them.'

'I don't think I know what you mean,' I said, 'but we are of the same mind, ma'am. She's a cute, bright kid, but kids don't exactly jibe with my daily routine.'

She nodded and rose to go. I asked, 'Do you think Faith's still in town?'

'Nothing about Faith, least of all her whereabouts, would surprise me,' she said. Her sky-blue eyes didn't blink. Whatever maternal affection she'd felt for her daughter had been transferred to Serendipity long ago. It was probably a good thing for all concerned.

9

1. The wheels of Hollywood are oiled by rumor and gossip. I don't know who said that, but they were totally on the mark, and though I'm not proud to admit it, I have done my share of oiling. That is essentially the basis of my friendship with Linda de Carlo, who plays the teenage vamp, Mel, on Gran's show. She's an endless fount of low-down inside stuff, the juiciest morsel of which was that Jimmy Lorenzo had been indiscreetly sleeping with – 'slipping it to' was Linda's way of phrasing it – Laurel Lee Palmer, the floozy platinum-blond wife of Ty Palmer, the executive producer of *Look*. They'd even done the dirty deed in Lorenzo's Winnebago during a lunch break, with Ty not a hundred yards away in the commissary, happy as a clam, polishing off his Robert Conrad beefburger and an iced tea.

I was passing on this rather piquant news item to Mr Bloodworth as we trudged to the parking lot, and he told me to stop spreading calumny. I told him he sounded as if he'd spent too much time with Gran. He asked what I thought of 'that Lorenzo character', and I replied that 'slimeball' might be a fitting description. That made him smile.

At the lot a rather stodgy midnight-blue Rolls was parked in the aisle behind Mr Bloodworth's chunky Chevy with its motor running and its driver's door open. The big detective looked at the car's personalized license plates, GG3, and then glared in the direction of the guardhouse at the gate. A white-haired fellow dressed in black chinos, black windbreaker, and dark aviator glasses was in conversation with the fat guard, gesturing in our general direction and sort of frothing at the mouth. Even with his face half hidden by the glasses, he had the semi-familiar looks of someone I'd seen before. Probably in a movie or on TV.

Mr Bloodworth took off across the lot toward the angry man. For some reason I could not explain, I did not follow. The angry man and Mr Bloodworth and the guard all seemed to be talking together, though I had no idea what they were saying. Then the angry man said something to Mr Bloodworth, and Mr Bloodworth said something to him, and the angry man broke away and started walking swiftly toward the Rolls.

Mr Bloodworth followed him, shouting, 'Just tell me if Kaspar was working for you.'

The angry man ignored him. Before getting into his car, he paused, facing me. There was a dramatic dark streak in his white hair. His lean, tanned face broke into a smile. Then he got into the Rolls and slammed the door.

Mr Bloodworth was beside the blue car, growing ever more out of sorts. The Rolls's windows were even darker than the Chevy's. 'You'll talk to me, Grady, or you'll talk to the cops.'

The Rolls bolted forward and Mr Bloodworth had to take a quick backstep out of the way. It zoomed across the lot and, without pausing, shot through the gate and off the studio grounds.

Mr Bloodworth didn't exactly take his time putting the Chevy into gear. 'Let's get out of this boneyard,' he grumbled.

As we drove away from the studio and into the evening smog of the Valley, he added, 'What is it about Kaspar that makes people behave so goddamned hotheaded?'

'It's like that story by Hawthorne we had to read, about the young man who goes to a small town – on the East Coast somewhere – just after the Civil War, and whenever he mentions this relative of his, strangers beat him up or put him in jail. Finally they tar and feather him and ride him out of town on a rail. And the sad thing is, he never finds out why.'

'Sounds like a fine role model,' Mr Bloodworth said grumpily. 'Actually, if you get people mad enough, that's usually when you get the answers to your questions.'

'You mean like back there?'

'Oh, hell, that guy's obviously some sort of mental case, that Grady. I mean, he wants to park his car, but he gets so pis– so bent out of shape, he drives away instead.'

'That was Gary Grady, huh? I thought he looked sort of familiar.'

'Yeah. He's on Kaspar's tape, which is why I used his parking space in the first place. I don't know if he was Kaspar's client, or what. He wouldn't talk to me, just wanted to chew that dumb studio cop's ear off. Judging by the way the cop was kissing his Guccis, Grady must be some sort of top macher around there.'

'He's an adult comic who's starting a new talk show at night on UBC. Replacing those awful Minton Sisters and their "Weirdo Revue". Gran let me stay up one night to see their show as a kind of object lesson. It was as loathsome as anything I'd ever experienced. There were pinheads and all sorts of deformed types – general all-around jell brains, singing songs and doing comedy sketches. And the Mintons and the studio audience were laughing at them, not with them, you know. I didn't find it very amusing. Do you?'

'Sarah, I don't even own a TV set. I don't find any of it amusing. A guy sitting in front of a TV set is like a horsefly perched on the rim of a garbage pail. And I don't think Gary Grady's gonna change the contents of that pail. TV comic, huh? Doesn't that just figure.'

'Television can be very educational,' I told him.

'Sure it can, if you can't read. Or if you haven't learned to stand upright.'

He was being argumentative and ignorant and truculent. 'There are worthwhile dramas and ballet and opera and symphonies and, if you prefer, ball games and other sporting events,' I said. He opened his mouth in rebuttal, but before he could begin, I added, 'And television is how my grandmother makes her living.'

That put an end to the discussion. He muttered something I didn't quite hear, but which I took to be an apology for his momentary boorishness.

2. He remained silent all the way back to Bay City, not even bothering to turn on the radio to that Joanie station he loves so.

I accused him of being petulant but could get no rise out of him. Finally he mumbled that he was 'knocking some ideas around in his head and that he would appreciate a little quiet for the rest of the trip.' I bowed to his wishes.

As he stopped the Chevy in front of my apartment building, I asked, 'Did Gran say that Mother was in town?'

'Yeah,' he answered, staring at me with those yellow eyes.

'Well, I don't mind that she didn't try to see me,' I said. 'I got over that a long time ago.'

'That's good,' he said.

'Naturally I was hurt the first couple of times she passed through without so much as a call. But it's happened so often – and anyway, I'm more mature now, more in control of my emotions.'

He gave me his funny kind of smile and those yellow eyes softened, and I felt this weird tingling sensation in my stomach, of all places.

'I don't know if she's still here, Sarah,' he said. 'But I might as well find out.'

'Then let's go.'

He shook his head. 'This is sorta goodbye, kid. I won't be seeing you for a while.'

'Did Gran . . .'

'Your grandmother doesn't have anything to do with it. I'm gonna be pretty busy is all.'

'But I could help you find Mother.'

'I'll find her. Don't worry.' He reached across me and opened the door.

'But you're working for me,' I said.

'No. We never made that deal, Sarah.'

'Who, then? Gran?'

'Maybe I'm working for myself,' he said. 'You know, "When a man's partner is killed . . ." and all that.'

Feeling utterly miserable, I got out of the Chevy. 'When will you know something about Mother?'

He shrugged. 'Hard to say.'

'When can I call to find out?'

'I'll call you,' he said.

Were crueler words ever uttered?

3. It had been over a week, but each time I unlocked the front door I expected to have my sweet little Groucho rush up to greet me. I had hoped the memory and its accompanying silly schoolgirl sentimentality would begin to wane, but apparently I was stuck with them for a while.

That period of evening was the absolute worst time of day for me. Too late to go skating. Too early to watch TV. Gran wouldn't be home for at least an hour. I flipped through a new copy of *TV Guide* magazine, not paying much attention to the non-events of the industry, before facing the decision as to whether to go up to the solarium to see the sunset – our balcony faces south – or go to my room and turn on the early local news. I hoped I wasn't becoming one of Mr Bloodworth's flies on a garbage pail, but eventually I opted for the latter. Sunsets are no fun when you are alone and despondent. Not that TV news is all that uplifting.

Of the newscasters, I preferred the one with the round head on channel 8, who reminded me of Charlie Brown, rather than the banker-looking grump on channel 6, or the absolutely silly bunch on channel 3. As for the UBC people on channel 10, with their chimpanzee who predicts the weather, well . . . I wished that Gran would let the building hook us up to the cable system. Over at my ex-friend Sylvia's one night, we watched some really absorbing programs on an access station, including one called *The Sexual Frontier*, that was like nothing else I'd ever even imagined. But Gran says paying for cable would be like biting the hand that feeds us.

Deprived of all that exotic viewing matter, I settled for the round head, who was sitting at his beige countertop silently watching the Asian female newscaster and the black sports guy with the goatee discuss polo, a subject none of them seemed to understand at all. I felt restless, anxious, useless, unwanted. My thoughts were with Mr Bloodworth.

Finally, tiring of my schoolgirlishness, I decided to do something constructive and change the moldy linen on my bed. It was my least favorite task, even worse than toting the Hefty Bag down the hall to the trash chute every other day, and I suppose I did tend to put it off far too long.

With the roundhead jabbering in the background, I grabbed one corner of the peach-colored coverlet – which matched perfectly the pale peach wall highlights – and yanked it free of the bed. A little square object flew across the room: a green matchbook for the Bottom Rung Lounge in the Marina Inn, 'where the smart singles come to drink and dance and you-name-it.'

I assumed that someone – not Gran, certainly, who never

entered my room unbidden, who has no use for matches, and who would not be caught dead in the Bottom Rung Lounge – had lost them in the folds of my coverlet. It could have been as long as a week ago, my aversion to linen-changing being what it is.

I crossed the room to the small walk-in closet where my mother's junk was kept. Things had been tossed about in there. She could have dropped the matches. She hadn't smoked the last time I saw her, but since that time she might have embraced all sorts of filthy habits.

Eagerly I picked up the Princess phone on my red desk and dialed Mr Bloodworth's home. No answer. At his office his gruff voice, recorded, told me to leave my name and number at the beep.

'This is Serendipity Dahlquist,' I replied, not a little intimidated by being recorded, possibly for posterity. 'I have found a clue to my mother's whereabouts. I don't know if I should take any action myself, or what. Please return this call at your soonest opportunity.'

I left my telephone number and replaced the receiver, feeling as though I'd done something vaguely silly. I shrugged that off and renewed my attack on the bed.

I was standing at one corner, gathering the top sheet in my arms, when something on the TV caught my eye. Publicity photos of Gran and Jimmy Lorenzo had just appeared on the screen. Since it was not a UBC news show I was watching, I knew even before the words left the roundhead's mouth that something terrible had happened.

1. 'Hey, *compadre*,' the amusing son of a bitch who called himself Rudy Cugat shouted from a table near the window of the El Matador Cantina.

The restaurant was tall for a cantina, a two-story job with pink walls and green tablecloths and enough bullfight posters, banderillas, and other ersatz Mex crap hanging around for a real matador to go for the owner's ears and tail.

Cugat and his partner, a fat, sour-faced Swede named Ambersen, were at a prime location on the top floor beside a picture window. Through it you could look over the buildings across Bay City's Main Street to where the sun slunk out of sight into the Pacific and called it a day. That evening the sky was a reddish orange with purple clouds and jet streams trying to bring some order to the whole thing with their parallel white streaks. The sun itself was blood-red, what was left of it, slipping into a slate-black, unruffled ocean that was haloed as far as the eye could see by an ominous yellow smog.

'Beautiful, huh, Hound?' Cugat said, pointing to the mess.

'Pretty as a picture,' I told him. They'd just finished what looked like enough frijoles and refrieds to put Pancho Villa down for the count. Ambersen had a dab of tomato sauce on his top lip, and his eyes had a glassy, too-many-Dos Equis, far-away look. He'd have trouble making the weight requirement next physical-exam day, assuming the force still bothered with such things. I sat down next to him so that I didn't have to look at him or the sunset.

'O'Gar at the desk told me you'd probably be here,' I said to Cugat.

He smiled. 'Have a *cerveza*, *amigo*.' He raised his hand to summon a beer.

I reached across the table and pushed his hand down, shaking my head. 'O'Gar also mentioned that the last time you paid a tab here was when you were trying to impress a new waitress.'

'O'Gar said that, huh?' Ambersen asked with a belch.

'The Hound's just making a joke, Amby. He likes his little jokes.'

Ambersen cleared his throat and tried to clear his eyes. 'Wasn't I reading something about you in the papers, Hound? Your partner got smoked or something.'

'You'd better watch him,' I told Cugat. 'He's starting to read.'

Cugat showed me his perfect white teeth before poking a cigarette between them. 'They catch the spade who did Kaspar?' he asked around the cigarette.

'They've got a suspect. But he's not black.'

'They're all spades, *compadre*. The ones killing everybody. Spades and slants and maybe the odd Latino.' I couldn't tell if he was being sarcastic.

Neither could Ambersen. 'Damn right,' he said.

'Well, you guys are in the business, so you must know,' I said.

'What can we do for you, Hound? What brings you to Bay Cit-tee?'

'That kid with her missing dog.'

Cugat frowned for a beat, then his black eyes began rolling round like waltzing marbles. 'Oh, *amigo*, you took that beeg case, then?'

'She came highly recommended.'

'I told you about that, Amby. The little smart-mouth girl I sent to my friend Bloodworth?'

'Damn right.'

I gave Cugat my Pained Look Number 4. 'Maybe this isn't a good time. You want me to wait until you go back on duty?'

'On duty?' Ambersen grumbled. Who says we're not on duty?'

'I assumed you were just relaxing and watching the sunset.'

'We're checking out the gooks,' Ambersen replied.

'Just look at that, Hound,' Cugat said, pointing his cigarette at the string of stores, a hotel, and what appeared to be a circus tent that took up the whole block across Main. 'What a splendid scam. It's this cult, or something, run by a guy who calls himself the Swami something.'

'Sounds like you're right on top of it.'

'It's almost beautiful to watch, Hound. These goddamn yoyos line up all day to go in and give this Swami character pieces of fruit, which they buy from the Swami's fruit store down the block. He takes the fruit from 'em, along with whatever other donation they care to make, and the apple or pear winds up back in the store, where some other asshole buys it again and gives it to the Swami. Hell, the end of the day, that same goddamn apple must bring in forty, fifty bucks.'

'That's inflationary,' I said.

'That's ingenuity,' Cugat corrected me.

'Yeah. Well, Cugie, I hate to keep harping on my own personal problems, but I need a little information.'

'Of course, *amigo*. What can this humble police officer do for you?'

It was not the best place and not the best time, and he was lost in some head game that only he understood, if anybody did, but I asked him, 'You ever hear of a guy named Danny Gutierrez?'

He seemed to yellow a bit in the fading sunlight. Then he

threw off the cute act like a dog throws off ocean water, with a shimmy. He glanced at Ambersen, who was slumped back in his chair studying his empty plate with a cupid smile playing on his full lips, as if he were recalling the highlights of some distant Ole Andersen party record.

Cugat pushed away from the table. 'C'mon with me for a minute, Hound,' he ordered, leading me into an empty men's room that smelled of pine oil. A glance to make sure we had privacy and the words came low, fast, and angry. 'What's with you? You suddenly got shit for brains, dropping names like that in front of that dumb Swede. You know the trouble that can bring me?'

'I don't know what the hell you're talking about.'

'Gutierrez,' he hissed. 'The name sound familiar?'

I shrugged.

'Emiliano Gutierrez?'

'Oh?'

' "Oh" is right, you *cabron*! No *digas* fucking *tonterias*.'

'You're just saying that 'cause we're old pals.'

'I'm not joking, you goddamn gringo. You ask me about Gutierrez because I'm the only Latino who'll give you the time of day. But that pile of Swedish meatballs back there, he hears Gutierrez and right away he's thinking there's a reason my friend asks me about the goddamn big bad Mexican Mafia. Maybe I'm on the pad to them.'

'Aren't you?'

'You son of a bitch,' he said, and his face broke into a grin. 'I don't know why I love you.'

'I didn't even think about the old man because I heard that Jose Merada put him out to pasture a couple years back.'

'Pasture, right. But it is a Family always to reckon with. Merada, the proper new *jefe*, set Emiliano up in a nice sunny condo down in Oceanside. A lovely little spot kissed by the salty Pacific spray, named Oceancliff Harbor. You'd like it, Hound, especially

now you're getting to that retirement age. Anyway, Padre Emiliano is allowed to continue his minor indulgences. Nothing like
dope or whores, but enough to keep him happy.'

'Danny's what? His son? Grandson?'

Cugat smiled. 'No grandson, *amigo*. Not in that Family.
Nephew, I think. Errand boy. Bagman. Like that. Part gringo,
so there's not much they'll trust him to do.'

'Where can I find him?'

Cugat showed me most of his teeth. 'I begin to scent the
invigorating aroma of *dinero*.'

I sniffed the air. 'That's pine oil, *amigo*.'

'You cagey bastard. I don't know why I put up with you.'

He knew all right. We both did.

2. There was a period in the Sixties when Cugat and I wore the
uniform of the Los Angeles Police Department. Partners we
were, for almost five years. That ended on May 17, 1966, a night
I think about often. We were riding a blue-and-white through a
slow sweep of the Silverlake district when we heard an alarm. It
came from a mini-mall on Los Feliz where, nestled between a
cut-rate shoe store and a barber-college operation, a squat,
beige-brick branch of the Golden Pacific Bank sat with its plate-
glass window smashed in, wailing like a banshee.

Cugat braked in front of the place while I reported in.

'It's very loud, Leo,' he said.

'Then let's go shut it down.'

He squinted at the bank. Its night lights presented vague out-
lines of desks, counters. 'Don't look like nobody's home,' he said.

I took the shotgun and Cugat unsnapped his Special. He
moved for the alleyway leading to the rear of the building and I
stepped gingerly over the broken glass in the front window.

Somebody had tossed mimeographed sheets on the sidewalk
and in through the broken window, carrying some message

about Golden Pacific's link to the military-industrial complex. Brothers in war profits. That sort of crap. I tried not to let it shake my faith in American banking.

I worked along one wall to a metal box with a glowing red button light on top. It looked like a simple Weymier system, so I yanked open the box and pressed a switch. The alarm stopped abruptly.

I'd barely time to register relief when there was movement by a teller's cage. 'Police!' I shouted, pointing the shotgun. 'Come out with your hands on your head.'

They hesitated about a second, then staggered into the light. Two kids in their late teens or early twenties.

'Against the wall,' I ordered.

They scuffled forward and I studied them in the dim light. The girl was a thin and frightened dirty blonde. The boy had long black hair, a patchy beard, and intense, dark eyes focused on my shotgun. They were dressed in the standard-issue peace-nik uniform of the day – faded Levi's pants and jackets. The boy called me a capitalist lackey, which was better than some things I'd been called and also had a certain ring of truth to it. The girl was saying that they weren't robbing the place; it was the bank that was robbing America. That didn't explain the folder she'd stuck in the waistband of her pants.

'Why don't you just zip it, ma'am, until my partner gets here to read you your rights.'

'Oh, God, you can't arrest us!' she cried.

I started to pat them down. I wanted a look at the folder. The girl turned to face me. Our eyes met for a beat, then she looked past me and gave a little yelp. I felt a breeze on the back of my neck and caught a whiff of smoke. I edged away from the couple, turning, and saw a man standing in a doorway to one of the offices. His tie was pulled down and there were ash smudges on his face and shirt.

He was pointing a pistol at us.

'Drop the gun!' I shouted. 'LAPD!'

He should have been able to figure that out for himself, what with the uniform, but he didn't seem too rational. I suppose I could have taken him out with the shotgun, but the guy looked like a bank employee and I didn't want to bag any bankers. Unless I had to.

His finger tightened on the trigger.

I threw myself on the kids and tumbled them to the floor, rolling on top of them. A section of the wall exploded over our heads, showering us with plaster and fake pine paneling.

The guy with the gun stepped closer, going for a clearer shot. I rolled away from the hippies and used my right foot to send a swivel chair at him. It caught him in the groin. I followed the chair in and brought the barrel of the shotgun up against the underside of his wrist. Maybe I used more force than I had to. The guy's wrist cracked and he screamed and the gun flew back over his shoulder, bouncing on a desk and skittering off it onto the tile floor.

Behind me I could hear Cugat pounding on the rear door and shouting. I didn't turn away from the man with the smudged face, who was now yelling at me, cursing. His wrist beginning to swell up.

The kids were adding their voices to the general chaos. The girl was crying and mumbling something about their lives being ruined.

Cugat ran around to the front of the bank and came in through the window. The boy hissed to the blonde, 'Shut up, goddammit,' and she did.

Cugat glared at them and then turned his attention to the guy with the bum wrist writhing and sinking to the floor in pain. 'What the hell is all this, Leo?'

I started to tell him, but the boy picked that moment to rush the window. He leaped through it, punching out a few more inches of glass on the way. The girl hesitated before following him. She stared at me, and said, 'Please . . .'

Then she turned her back to us and walked carefully to the window and stepped through it.

Cugat said, 'Leo, don't you think –'

'Stop them!' the guy on the floor was screaming. He tried to grab my gun with his bad hand. The pain must've been too much, because he checked out.

'You just let two bank robbers leave the scene of the crime, *amigo*.'

'I didn't see you drawing down on the girl,' I said.

'You wanted me, a minority member of the force, to shoot two apparently unarmed Caucasians? Some other century, *amigo*. What happened to their gun?'

'It wasn't theirs. It was his,' I said. 'He's a real cowboy. Almost took my head off, so I had to bust his wrist.'

I pulled out his wallet. It said he was Charles Z. Dotrice, assistant manager of the branch.

'Shit,' Cugat said, 'that's trouble. Maybe we should kill him, huh?' He grinned.

'Instead, why don't you call for an ambulance.'

'What about the kids?'

'Hell, I don't know.' Police sirens headed our way. I said, 'They'll get picked up and we can I.D. 'em without much trouble.'

Cugat looked at the room. 'I better send for a fire truck, too. Lots of smoke back there.'

I dragged the unconscious Dotrice over to the window and carried him through it into the relatively fresh air.

Cugat joined me. 'Are we in the shit, or what?'

'Waist-high, I'd say.'

Two hours later, at Silverlake Emergency, Dotrice was

glaring at me from a gurney while listening to a plainclothes lieutenant tell him that the fire had been extinguished but that some money had been destroyed and the hippie suspects had not been captured.

Dotrice's reply was that he wanted my badge.

He eventually got it. I kept Cugat out of it. Dotrice hadn't been worth two badges.

3. A guy with silver-blue hair and purple eye shadow and who smelled of lilacs floated into the men's room, and Cugat, glaring at him, led me out. 'You want this Danny G., you'll probably find him at that glitz motel down the way, The Marina Inn,' he said as we walked back to his table by the window. 'Very so-fees-ti-cated club there, the Bottom Rung, where the kids toot up right on the patio, under the stars.'

'Bust 'em.'

'If they want silver-plated noses, that's their problem. The Gutierrez lizard is sharing a room in the Inn with some blond floozy.' He smiled again. 'I like to keep track of the Gutierrez Family when they are in my little corner of the world.'

Ambersen had fallen asleep. Cugat frowned and shook his head at the sight. 'You need something more, Hound? The keys to a prowl car? A riot gun for the fireplace? A kilo of Matamuris mist? What?'

'Peace of mind. Like Ambersen.'

The fat man slumped forward, supported by his stomach, wheezing through his mouth. Cugat gave his shoulder a healthy shake and Ambersen sputtered, 'Hah! 'hut?' and looked up at him with droopy eyes the color of a strawberry margarita.

'Night has fallen, *amigo*.'

Ambersen didn't believe him. He looked out of the window to be sure. Down on a shadowy Main Street, anxious supplicants were still on line waiting to see the Swami.

'Time for us to go home to our be-u-ti-ful wives,' Cugat told him.

'Damn right,' Ambersen replied.

4. Marina del Rey is an oceanside community of recent vintage (until the mid-Sixties, it was an undeveloped slough) separated from Bay City by the cheery community of Santa Monica and the scruffy town of Venice, where the Hell's Angels used to hang their helmets and chains. Usually referred to as simply 'the Marina', it consists of condos, apartment clusters, restaurants, fast-food joints, supermarts, parking lots, and boat locks, all at the disposal of young, upwardly mobile, relentlessly single adults and aging, married adults trying desperately to pass for young, single adults. It is an anxiety-ridden place that has all the warmth and charm of a college beer hall and the atmosphere of a Vegas bingo parlor.

In the early Seventies – which in Marina history is comparable to the dawn of man – a builder constructed a pair of curved apartment towers that everyone seemed to like, so another builder tried to do him one better with a trio of circular towers on the tip of one of the finger peninsulas. He got two of his towers finished before he went belly-up, leaving the third to stand like a deserted beehive of gray concrete and rust.

Of the fully constructed towers, the southern one was now a condo operation called the Casa Pacific, with a glass elevator stuck onto its exterior as if it had been an afterthought. The other tower, the Marina Inn, also had its outdoor elevator, but with the flashing marquee from the Bottom Rung, it wasn't all that obvious.

The Bottom Rung had started out as a basement night spot, but as its popularity with the salt-air and cocaine crowd increased, so did its space. That's why when I walked into what should have been the inn's lobby, I found myself on the second level of, according to a nearby poster, 'A Trio of Disco-Dynamic Playrooms Where the Inn Crowd Soars and Scores.'

The room didn't quite live up to its publicity. It was very long and dark and empty. And green. Green carpets. Green walls. Green leatherette chairs were piled atop green tables. No one was manning the silent, elaborate electronic board near the scuffed dance floor. A Chicano in a green and black busboy suit drifted by as if he were looking for a quiet spot to snooze. 'Where's the lobby of the Inn?' I asked him.

He gave me the slowest take this side of the old stoics' home and said, 'Too early. Nobody here. Come back later.'

'Where's the hotel?' I asked.

'In the elevator,' he said. 'Push three.'

There was a small sign in the outdoor elevator. It, too, told me to push three for the lobby. I figured I couldn't go wrong pushing three.

As the glass booth ascended smoothly, I stared across the road at the unfinished tower. Some bums were camped out on the third level. They had a little fire going and it looked rather cozy. I wondered how they'd gotten up there. Pushed three, probably.

The door opened to an ordinary-looking second-rate hotel lobby. It had potted plants, more green carpeting, somber furniture, dark wood finishings, and an unappealing blend of welcome and indifference.

Two pale-skinned guys with dark sunglasses and loud sport shirts were trying to pass for Robert De Niro, using their mouths, hands, shoulders, and elbows to communicate with each other while studying a Things-To-Do display against one wall. A gawky teenage boy in a double-knit suit was beating the hell out of a postcard dispenser. A flashy redhead, collecting her mail from the desk, gave me a cute little nose wrinkle as I approached, and then about-faced, leaving me in the company of a tall black clerk in a severe pinstripe three-piece, who had Cornell School of Hotel Management written all over him. He stared at me patiently.

'The house phones?' I asked.

He used a shiny felt-tip pen to indicate a bank of oxblood telephones, which I moved on to. I picked up the first in the row, scanning the desk area for the switchboard. It must have been hidden away somewhere behind the cashier's area. No help at all.

A pleasant feminine voice picked up the call. 'Mr Gutierrez's room, please,' I asked.

It took the voice barely a second to discover that there was no Mr Gutierrez registered.

'Could you check again?'

The voice suggested I talk to someone at the front desk.

The tall black guy was as happy to see me as I was to be seen by him. 'I'm trying to reach Mr Danny Gutierrez, who's supposed to be staying here.'

He took two steps to the cashier's cage and snapped his fingers at the mousy young woman there. 'Gutierrez, Daniel,' he said. The woman almost jumped out of her green blazer and, a second later, shoved a card into his hand. He glanced at it and cocked his head to one side. 'Mr Gutierrez checked out several days ago.'

'Is that "several" two, three, or more?'

His eyes frosted a bit. 'Three.' He let the word rattle on his tongue.

'I don't suppose he left a forwarding address?'

'I don't suppose,' he answered, moving toward the cashier.

'Just a minute, if you don't mind. It's important that I reach this Gutierrez guy. Is there something on that card that might –'

'Our records are confidential.'

'Sure. Most records are,' I said. 'But this is a special situation. A police matter. Maybe the police have been here already?'

He just stared at me.

'I'm actually looking for the woman who was with Gutierrez. There was a woman, right?'

'You're doing the talking, mister.'

I showed him the snapshot. 'It's not a very good picture. . .'

'Could be her,' he said. 'Especially with the dog.'

'They had this dog with them?'

He nodded. 'She's put on some weight,' he said. 'The woman, not the dog.'

'How much weight?'

'About four inches around the chest.'

I looked at the photo, then back at him. 'The snapshot's a few years old.'

'No. Her chest got fatter after she and Gutierrez moved in here. She left looking like she was stealing towels in her bra. She wasn't. We checked.'

'Well,' I said, handing him my business card and taking back the snapshot. 'My client wants to locate her, tits and all.'

He glanced at the card and shoved it back.

'Keep it. I've got more,' I said.

He bent the card in two and tossed it into a wastebasket beneath the countertop. 'Is that it?' he asked.

'I really was hoping you'd have an idea how I could reach her. Maybe a record of phone calls made from their room.'

He sighed.

'I can always send the cops over. The woman's a thief.'

'Why not send the cops, sir? I talk to cops all the time.'

'Let me put it another way.'

'Why don't you?'

I pressed a $20 bill into his palm. He deposited it gracefully into his trouser pocket, then handed the information card back to the cashier with the order 'Pull Mr Gutierrez's ticket, please.'

It took the nervous woman less than ten seconds. He handed

me a pale green carbon copy of a bill totaling $3,485 for twenty-two days' lodging, much of which seemed to have been allocated to room service during the first two weeks.

Every afternoon at five, approximately, there had been a call to a number in Oceanside, California. Reporting in to Uncle Emiliano. It suggested Danny had been in town on family business.

There were other calls – to Weed, Redding, Copa de Oro, Escondido, Ramona, El Cajon, and other small towns that cut across the state, as well as a few scattered local calls. None were to anyplace that remotely sounded like Pelea de Perro, the town Danny had mentioned to the kid's grandmother.

I recognized the UBC Studios number: Faith calling her mother. Three others to the apartment in Bay Heights. None to my late partner.

I scribbled the list onto the back of a dry-cleaning ticket, returned the hotel bill to the clerk, and told him I appreciated his help. He nodded, which was almost the same as thanking me for my twenty bucks.

5. It took another four bucks and fifteen minutes to reclaim my Chevy from a daredevil ace who'd barely mastered the 45 mph hairpin turn from the garage onto the street. Then it was another forty minutes along two traffic-clogged freeways to the office, where the day's mail was sharing the carpet with the debris from the recent break-in, which I still hadn't bothered to clean up.

The police had been through the files, which they'd replaced. But they'd forgotten the Big Mac wrappers and soft-drink cans they'd emptied in the course of their work.

The phone gizmo was blinking. Seven times. Kassarian wanted me to call. One of my ex-wives, Rita, the only one who didn't remarry, needed to know my mother's address. She didn't say why. The message was confusing because she had been at my mother's funeral. It probably meant Rita was back on lithium. A client named Gallo, not one of the wine-country Gallos, had a question about his bill. Two no-name hang-ups. And the Dahlquist kid had called twice.

The first time was to say she'd figured out where her mother was staying, which I didn't believe for a minute. The second was to tell me she was at St Martin's Hospital in Burbank, waiting for news about her grandmother's condition. It seems that somebody at the studio had tried to shove a wall on top of the old lady and her New York nemesis, James Lorenzo.

II

1. Gran was occupying center stage in her crowded hospital room. Her right eye was a yellowish-red color, which she'd unsuccessfully tried to cover with makeup. The plaster cast positioned her right arm and shoulder so that it looked like she was holding up a lorgnette, only she didn't have a lorgnette. Not yet, anyway. She was propped up in bed, in justifiable ill humor, giving Dr James D. Hauser hell, though he didn't deserve it. That kindly, elderly gentleman with blue-white hair, who had been our family physician for as long as I could remember, had only brought the bad news. He had not caused it.

'Four months?' Gran was seething. 'Four bloody months? By that time no one will remember Aunt Lil ever existed.'

'Now, Edie,' Gene Sokol, *Look to Tomorrow's* writer-director-producer, told her, 'I've instructed Faye and the new girl to plot around your absence. Aunt Lil will have a bad fall or something . . .'

'Why not a cough?' Gran said bitterly. 'A cough can grow into pneumonia and death and Aunt Lil could be put to rest without my ever setting foot back on a soundstage.'

'You know we won't let that happen,' Mr Sokol consoled her. He was balding, bearded, and very postpreppie in a casual West Coast way. 'It's going to be tougher to finesse Jimmy's sudden absence.'

'Maybe he and Aunt Lil could elope,' I suggested. Mr Sokol and Gran both glared at me. 'Just a joke,' I added lamely.

'How *is* the boy?'

Mr Sokol shrugged. 'Still out. Sedated. Broken nose. Broken leg. Maybe a concussion.'

'The poor, dear boy.'

'Don't overdo it, lamby,' said the other visitor, Lacey Dubin, Gran's longtime agent, a plump, middle-aged woman with a fondness for black pantsuits, high-proof rum (she calls it 'go-to-the-moon rum'), and the scent of lavender. 'The little twerp brought it on himself,' she continued in her scratchy baritone, 'fiddling around with Hotpants Palmer. It's too damn bad you happened to be standing there when her hubby attacked.'

Mr Sokol looked distressed. 'We don't know Ty caused the set to collapse. Sure, he was furious when he found out about the hanky-panky, but I can't believe a guy would destroy his show's major standing set just to get back at somebody for boff–'

Lacey pointed to me, and Mr Sokol scowled. 'Anyway,' he went on, 'everything is settling down now. The police seem to be satisfied that it was an accident.'

'Accident,' Lacey blurted out. 'Walls don't fall down by accident.'

'Nobody saw Ty do it, Lacey,' Mr Sokol pointed out. 'They're not even sure he was on the lot.'

'How about that grip?'

'What do grips know? Ok, so he saw somebody behind the set. That doesn't make it Ty. There were visitors passing through all day. In fact . . .' He paused at the sound of a knock on the door. Gran bade the knocker enter, using her imperial czarina voice.

It was a callow-looking policeman whose uniform was as neat as a pin. 'There's a fellow out here who wants to see you, ma'am. Name of Bloodworth.'

Gran looked at me. 'Please?' I asked.

The cop continued: 'I was told to keep visitors out, especially press. There are a lot of 'em out front.'

'He's not the press, officer,' I said.

'You may invite Mr Bloodworth in,' Gran said.

The officer tuned from the door and shouted down the hall, 'OK to send him back. The others don't get in. They might as well go home.'

Mr Bloodworth entered, carrying one of those bouquets of flowers you get from kids at street corners. Still, it was a nice gesture. I took the bouquet and placed it on a table.

He said to Gran, 'Well, Ms Van Dine, you're looking pretty damn good for somebody a wall fell on.'

Gran gave him a regal smile and introduced him to the others. Mr Sokol wanted to know if he was an insurance adjuster. Lacey asked if he was with William Morris. I said, 'Mr Bloodworth is a friend of mine.' For some reason that made all of them uncomfortable, especially Mr Bloodworth. As if I were not allowed one friend in this world.

Heading gingerly toward the door, Mr Sokol said, 'I'd better run. If there's a wrong way for those cretins to put the set back together, they'll find it.'

'Ask the kids to remember their aunt Lil. As she will remember them. In her prayers.'

'C'mon, Edie, you're only going to be out for a few months.'

'Need I remind you that's nearly a whole season?'

Mr Sokol stopped, pondered. 'True. True. Maybe we could write in the accident, do some footage on your actual recuperation. How about it, Dr Hauser?'

'Perhaps. But not for a while. Edith needs to build up her strength. At any age, the injuries she has sustained –'

'We ought to sue that goddamn Ty Palmer,' Lacey grumbled.

Mr Sokol scowled at her, but she blithely ignored him,

moving to pick up Mr Bloodworth's flowers and stick them into a water pitcher. 'That's the kind of idiotic thing those vultures outside would sew up their tongues to have happen,' Mr Sokol said. 'God, the bloody *Enquirer*! I can just see it, "Cuckolded TV Exec Tries to Kill Soap Stars!" He shivered. 'I can feel the ratings drop.'

'You mean this wasn't an accident?' Mr Bloodworth asked.

'You see?' Mr Sokol shrieked at Lacey. He turned to the big detective. 'We mean nothing of the kind, sir. Mr Palmer was probably not even on the lot when it – the accident – happened. Anything else would be pure speculation or vile gossip.'

'Sure,' Lacey snapped. 'Then who was it the gaffer spotted?'

Mr Sokol gave her a pitying look and said, 'You're incorrigible.'

'What does that make Ty Palmer?'

'I don't give a goddamn what you think, Lacey. But if you stir up the press, I'll see to it –'

'Excuse me again,' Mr Bloodworth interrupted, 'but do you mind telling me how a scandal could harm a show that deals in that sort of thing?'

Mr Sokol gave him a disgusted raise of the eyebrow. 'Did you just fly in from the moon, pal? Can't you see the difference between make-believe fornication and lust and murder and the real thing?' He sighed. 'I must be getting back. I don't have time for this. Ta, Edie. Take care of yourself.'

When the door had closed firmly behind him, Lacey let out a low laugh and said to Gran, 'Don't you love the little wart? He makes me mourn for Harry Cohen.'

'I want to go home,' Gran said with sudden finality.

'Be sensible, Edith,' Dr Hauser replied. 'You have to stay here for a few days. At least until all of the test results are in. Then, if you're feeling up to it, I'll arrange for a nurse to care for you at home.'

'A nurse?'

'Edith, you have a broken arm and collarbone, and you've fractured your right hip, which could be even more worrisome. There's damn little you'll be able to do for yourself for a while.'

'Sehr will be all the help I need.'

Dr Hauser gave me an insincere sort of smile. 'With all respect to Serendipity, you'll need someone bigger and stronger and with a better knowledge of anatomy. At least until you're ready for a wheelchair.'

'My God! Edith Van Dine. Ready for a wheelchair!'

Gran was really giving it her all. For Mr Bloodworth's benefit, I suspected.

'You'll come to my place, lamby,' Lacey told her. 'It's a big old barn, and I've a nice comfortable guest room. Clarence'll be home from Stanford and he'll sling you over his shoulder and tote you around –'

'I still think a trained nurse –'

'The trained nurse, too. I've got more room than I know what to do with, what with Ed gone and the kids running off to God knows where. Sehr will be there, too. It's nice and peaceful up in Laurel this time of year, high up above the smog and noise. And not much chance of fire or flood.'

'It sounds great for Gran,' I said, 'but I'll just hang around our apartment.'

'We needn't make any binding decisions now,' Gran said, giving me a hard look. 'Lacey, I'd appreciate it if you and James were to leave us for a few minutes.'

'Sure, lamby. C'mon, doc, let's go see what kind of trouble we can get into next door at the Beef 'n' Bourbon.'

The color drained from Dr Hauser's face. 'Actually, I should be getting back to Cedars. A few more patients to check. Edith, in spite of what you tell me, I know you have to be in pain. Are you sure you won't take a pill?'

'And wind up like Bela Lugosi?' Gran asked haughtily. But she looked very tired and hurting.

Dr Hauser shrugged. 'I'll leave these for you, in any case,' he said, placing a small plastic bottle on the table beside Gran's bed. He promised to return the next day and then ushered Lacey from the room.

Gran tried to smile at Mr Bloodworth but couldn't quite put it across. 'I'm glad you're here,' she told him. 'I've been wondering about Faith.'

'She seems to have traveled on,' he said.

'With all this wretched publicity, I would have expected her to call if she'd still been here.'

'That's more than I would have expected,' I said.

It just popped out. But Gran replied with a frown, 'Not if you were hurt or in trouble, Sehr. Your mother may be – ah, vague and a bit selfish, but she is not cruel. Or unfeeling.' She coughed. 'Child, would you get me a cola?'

'You don't like colas.'

'A glass of milk, then.'

'I'll ring for the nurse.'

'I want you to get it.'

'If you want to talk privately with Mr Bloodworth, just say so.'

Gran sighed.

Mr Bloodworth mumbled, 'Give us a couple minutes, huh, kid?'

'Not if you're going to be talking about me.'

Mr Bloodworth turned to Gran. 'Do you mind if I paddle her and throw her out in the corridor?'

It was an unnecessary thing to say, and worse, it got Gran to laugh, which must have aggravated the breaks, because she winced.

Mr Bloodworth moved closer to the bed. 'Leave us alone right now, kid, or it's no more nice guy.'

Gran nodded.

I walked to the door and swung it open.

'If you slam that door, prepare to run for your life, kid.'

But I wasn't going to slam it. I wasn't even going to shut it all the way.

2. Standing in the hall beside the door crack, I watched two policemen at the far end of the corridor on the lookout for the ghoulish photographers. I could not hear everything that was being said inside the room, but I gathered that Gran was actually hiring Mr Bloodworth to find my mother.

It sounded as though Mr Bloodworth were haggling over a fee with Gran, who was in no condition to hold up her end of the bargaining. Their voices lowered suddenly. Then I heard Mr Bloodworth bellow, 'Not a chance. Not for any amount!'

Then Gran muttered something else and figures were again mentioned.

The big man finally came to the door. I was pretending to be immensely interested in a painting of a tempest-tossed sailing vessel hanging on the corridor wall.

'C'mon in, Sarah,' he grumbled.

Gran could hardly keep her eyes open. 'Mr Bloodworth has kindly agreed to stay at our apartment until I leave this place, Sehr. I ask you from the bottom of my heart to be a good, cooperative child and make his stay as pleasant and uneventful as possible.'

'You know I will,' I said, moving beside her bed. I bent over and kissed her cheek. 'I love you more than a baker loves his cake, more than a fat man loves his steak,' I told her, quoting lines from a song we'd both sung when I was a little girl.

'And I love you, too, Sehr. More than I thought possible.'

She shut her eyes and went limp. Mr Bloodworth clicked off the light near her bed and we watched her fall asleep.

At the door I looked back at her. With her gray hair spread out over the pillow, she resembled a fairy-tale queen, even with that ridiculous black eye and the plaster arm that seemed to be shading her face from the dim fluorescent light overhead.

In the corridor Mr Bloodworth was talking to one of the cops. Whatever the topic of their conversation, it changed abruptly when I approached.

'C'mon, kid,' Mr Bloodworth said, his yellow eyes hooding over. 'Let's get this show on the road.'

12

1. There's nothing like the sharp jab of a rigid hand into your kidney area to get your attention. Especially if it's followed by the kiss of a shoe off the side of your noggin. I don't know how the guy got behind me. Other things may be going, but I've still got pretty good ears and it's not easy to sneak across a gravel roof, especially in hard-soled shoes. But he had whatever it takes.

I lost my gun when his kick flipped me over on my back, hard, on the roof's wooden-slat walkway. I lay there for a second, trying to remember how to breathe, looking up at the stars colliding with red comets and white rockets in the sky. It's some light show your brain puts on when properly rattled.

A shadow moved between me and the stars – big, dark, and spooky enough to give Samson the shakes. The face wasn't a face at all. It was bushy eyebrows and horn-rimmed glasses and a thick moustache under a formidable hooknose that reflected moonlight. The whole goddamned thing was plastic!

The figure leaned over me, a huge hunting knife in one mitt. His eyes were flat and colorless behind the glasses. So were his baggy work clothes. He grunted and said something that sounded like 'even up', and sheathed the blade.

I started to sit up and he put his foot on my chest. 'You watchin' out for the kid?' he asked.

I nodded, open-mouthed. He took his foot away.

'Tell her mother how much good you are.' The voice was

garbled, strained. 'Tell her to wise up or I'll make trouble she's never dreamed of.'

'Where is she?' I wheezed.

'You don't know?' the eyes fluttered behind the glasses. I shook my head dumbly.

That earned me a derisive snort. Then, as graceful as Godunov on a good day, he hopped over me and went away without making a sound.

I didn't know what to make of him, so I turned my thoughts to how much I hurt.

One of the things you discover about recuperating from beatings is that the pain gets more intense and the healing slows down with each passing year. So I'd decided to avoid getting banged around. I'd been pretty successful at that before the kid stepped into my life. Ever since I'd laid eyes on her I'd been getting the tar knocked out of me. And I didn't have much tar left.

Lying on my back, letting out my breath slowly, I went through a routine check of my physical status. Heartbeat seemed normal enough. Dizziness no worse than usual. The rockets and comets were gone and the stars were crisp enough for me to stop worrying about a possible concussion. That left a sore spot in my back that hurt every time I inhaled and a head that throbbed like a bad Sunday morning.

I took another painful breath and closed my eyes against the bright stars blinking over Bay Heights. Two floors beneath me, a four-poster was waiting in a guest bedroom of overcast sky blue. The bed was covered with a down comforter that had symbols of the American Revolution embroidered on it.

An hour earlier I'd dropped my battered black canvas flight bag beside that bed and given the room the fisheye, moving from one wall where a dun-colored print of something that looked like *The Gleaners* was hanging, to another that held a collection – or is it called a 'grouping' – of photographs of

Sarah. Sarah on a tricycle. Sarah as a toddler, holding a bouquet of flowers bigger than she was. Sarah on a terrace, frowning at a book and chewing on a strand of hair. Sarah and Mrs Van Dine acting larky, with the old lady pressing a long finger on top of the kid's head and the kid holding out her skirts and balancing on one leg. Sarah and her mutt staring eye to eye over the dog dish.

There were no pictures of Faith Dahlquist in the room.

I'd dropped onto a tufted chair and used an old-fashioned phone on a nearby table to call Kassarian. After a brief chat about the absence of suspicious fingerprints at either my home or my office, I asked him to put a little pressure on the guys guarding Mrs Van Dine at the hospital. He wearily informed me that I was slightly paranoid for thinking that the old lady's injuries had been anything but accidental. Then he explained that he had a heavy schedule and had absolutely no clout in Burbank. But having said all that, he agreed to make the call.

The old lady had been worried about the kid, worried enough to change her mind about me giving Sarah a wide berth. She'd even hired me to keep an eye on the girl and to try to get a line on Faith. The latter would have been a hell of a lot easier if it had not been for the former.

I still had the phone in my hand when Sarah traipsed into the guest room. 'Everything all right?'

'It's great, kid. It'll be a real treat, sleeping in a sack with a lace duster.'

'I put some pizza puffs in the microwave. They're very good for you. Made with whole-wheat flour and all fresh ingredients. No salt or sugar.'

'Sounds swell. I don't suppose you could rustle up a Coors?'

She furrowed her pale brows. 'What's the matter?' she asked. I gave her my best blank look. 'You're worried about something,' she said flatly.

'There are just some things I've gotta do before I can relax. Run along and work on that Coors, huh?'

She gave me about one-third of a smile and left the room.

I dialed a Venice number. When a woman answered, I asked, 'Estella?'

'*Si*,' she replied, guardedly.

'Leo Bloodworth. Lemme speak to that husband of yours.'

She giggled and put down the phone, leaving it aimed at what sounded like fifty kids jabbering in Spanish at a TV set that was speaking English, of a sort, Soon Rudy Cugat was saying, '*Hay-sus Christo*, Hound. Will you please get off my wet back?'

'Gutierrez drifted.'

'Ah. Bad timing, then. What more can I do?'

I read him the list of towns that young Gutierrez had phoned from his hotel.

'That *bandito* has sand in his *zapatas*. Maybe he's moving *cocaina* or *chiva* for the old man.'

'In those burgs? Where's the market?'

'I don't know, man. What's a Mexican know about northern California, except they don't like us there? I tell you what I think – drugs – and you tell me I am wrong. Fine. Leave me to the peace and tranquility of my family.'

'Tranquility? Sounds like you're restaging the attack on the Alamo.'

'Estella's *hermana* is here with her three terrors.'

'I don't suppose you've room for another kid? I got one I'd like to park for a couple of days.'

I suddenly smelled the aroma of cheese and tomato sauce. Sarah was standing in the doorway holding a plate filled with little round gobs of red-and-yellow-streaked dough and a glass of beer. Judging by the stricken expression on her face, she'd heard the last bit of my phone conversation.

'Would you take a cactus to the desert, Hound?' Cugat was asking.

Sarah placed the pizza blobs and beer carefully on the table beside my chair. Her eyes were tearing.

'A bad joke,' I tried to explain to them both.

She ran from the room. Somewhere down the hall a door slammed.

'Who's the kid, Hound? Not the little blond roller-skater? Oh, man, beware those baby Chihuahuas. They got a mean bite.'

I'd grown weary of that particular joke so I changed the subject.

'You ever hear of a town called Pelea de Perro?' I asked him.

'A town?'

'Pelea de Perro. Gutierrez might be headed there.'

He laughed at me. 'I thought all those years, riding around with me, you picked up some understanding of my native language.'

'I can hold my own.'

'Then stop thinking like a gringo. Pelea de perro isn't a town. It's a – goddamn! That explains those places you mentioned. Sure. It's the kind of horseshit thing El Jefe might be into these days.'

'Mind laying it out for this gringo?'

'*Pelea de perro* in your harsh American tongue means "dogfight".'

2. Cugat was amused but not professionally intrigued by the use of dumb animals for illegal gaming purposes. 'Big bills exchange hands,' he said, 'but the crime is . . . insignificant. Only the mutts get harmed, and so far none has filed a complaint. Of course, the goddamn bleeding hearts complain, and you know the way we listen to them.'

I knew. Fine with me, I didn't want anybody busting the games and sending Gutierrez and Faith so far back into the woodwork I'd never find them. I gave Cugat my *gracias* and let him get back to his battlefield.

In the silence of the guest room I settled into the chair, sighed, and popped one of the pizza hunks into my mouth. It tasted like cardboard smeared with catsup and cheese spread. I had another and tried to wash it all down with a mouthful of beer. Goddamn diet beer! Horse piss and dishwater.

I put down the can, pushed myself upright, and walked down the dark hall to Sarah's closed door. I knocked and got no reply.

'C'mon, kid. You got it all wrong. I'm not shipping you off anywhere.'

'Get real!' she shouted back, whatever the hell that meant.

I tried the knob. Locked.

'You're acting like a goddamned brat,' I told her.

I put my fist up to knock again. She turned on her TV set. Loud.

The hell with it. She had to open up sometime, and I wasn't about to keep standing there like a dummy begging a schoolgirl to talk to me.

I got real and went back to the guest room, where I hit the light switch and stumbled to the chair in the darkness. I found both it and the near-beer glass and swallowed some more of the dishwater. My plan was to sit there until I heard the kid open her door. I decided to shut my eyes for a minute, just to rest them.

Then suddenly I was wide awake with a lurch that started my stomach churning. The rest of the apartment was dark. The kid's TV was quiet. I blinked my eyes, as if that would do any good in the dark. Then I heard a strange sound, a low keening that made the hairs on the back of my neck straighten out.

I eased off the chair and moved cautiously into the hall.

Somebody was standing there.

It wasn't the kid unless she'd grown a foot and a half. The somebody didn't hesitate. His hand cut a shadowy arc toward my throat. I shifted my shoulder fast enough for the hard part of my head to take most of the punishment. I dropped to one knee and threw a hard punch that caught the inside of his thigh.

The guy backed away easily and keened some more. I couldn't focus on his face.

There was the grating of metal against metal and he was holding a knife. A light that somehow made it through a distant window danced on the blade. I pushed myself up and back, away from the weapon as it whisked past my face.

He stalked me, moving in. He held the knife steady, belt-high, and away from his body. He'd handled one before.

Then he stopped, chuckled, and backed away down the hall. He exited through the apartment door and closed it behind him with a soft click. I rushed into the guest room and fished my gun from my flight bag. I checked its load on my way down the hall.

Sarah's door was shut. I hoped it was still locked.

I stepped from the apartment into an equally dark main hall, straining my ears for some sound other than the TV noise from the rest of the apartments.

Footsteps in the fire stairway.

I shut the door to the apartment and hit the stairwell.

The dim red night lights at each floor level were less than illuminating or comforting. The footsteps were heading up.

As I rounded the sixth landing, the metal door to the roof clicked into place. I would have liked to jam the door shut and hop downstairs to call the cops, but there wasn't anything to jam the goddamn door. So I sat down next to it with the gun in my fist and waited for him to come to me. That was when I heard loud running footsteps on the rooftop heading away from the door. A grunt. Then nothing. The bastard had jumped.

I tried to picture the building. There was a grassy lot on one side, an alley with enough room for two cars to pass at the rear. And a building on the other side that was close to this one but a couple of stories shorter. That seemed the best bet.

And so I went out to see if he'd made it.

I did it carefully, just on the chance that the sound effects had been a ruse. Half a minute later I was on my back, watching comets explode.

3. When I staggered back downstairs, my heart skipping the odd beat and my ears ringing, the door to the kid's apartment was ajar. I went through it cautiously with my gun up and ready, for all the good that ever seems to do me.

The hall light had been turned on. And the door to the kid's bedroom was gaping at me.

It was a small room with pale pink walls and white fixtures and a white plastic TV set on silent. Clothes rested in little piles around the rumpled bed. I turned off the TV. Then I sensed rather than heard someone in the doorway.

Ducking, I spun around and shoved the gun in that direction, finger tense on the trigger. Sarah was standing there in a pink robe and slippers with Donald Duck heads on the toes. She had one cardboard pizza hunk in her hand and another in her mouth. She gobbled down the mouth pizza, gave me a patronizing shake of her head, and started giggling.

I lowered the gun and stood up, trying not to notice the way my knee popped as my weight shifted. 'Nothing funny here, kid.'

'Try looking at it from my point of view,' she said, moving past me to click on the TV.

'You been up very long?' I asked, clicking off the TV.

She looked at the dark screen and shrugged. 'Couple of minutes. I was suddenly famished.' She pointed the pizza blob at my gun. 'You going to put that away?'

'With any luck.'

I hunkered down, cracking my back, to poke under her bed. Dust balls and more rolled clothes. 'Some little housekeeper, aren't you, kid?'

'I wasn't expecting company,' she said, devouring the final pizza bit.

'What happened to the rug?' I pointed to a stain.

'When Groucho gets nervous, he can't control himself. He's very old for a dog.'

I went back into the hall and the kid followed. 'Is this the only way in or out, Sarah?'

'Unless you climb down the outside of the building, only I wouldn't advise that. There's nothing to hold on to. I've been trying to get Gran to buy a Safety-Scape. It's for earthquakes or fires. You put it around the upper part of your body and it lowers you to the ground at three feet per second.'

She didn't stop talking even though I walked away from her.

'Why are you searching the apartment?' she asked, following me.

'No concern of yours,' I lied, opening and closing closets and poking behind doors.

'Gran seems to think the earthquake thing is impractical, but I say you can never be too prepared for earthquakes. You're scaring me, you know.'

'Don't mind me, kid. I do this every night at my place before hitting the hay.'

I looked around the living room and put the gun back in its holster. 'You better get some sleep,' I told her. 'We're taking a trip tomorrow.'

'Trip? Why? Where?'

'To find your mom. Somebody gave me a message for her.'

4. Maybe she slept. I had a rough night, myself. The bed smelled of spice and felt as cozy as a Sunday afternoon in 1947. But I had grown unused to cozy beds long ago and so I twisted and turned, wondering what the kid's mother and her boyfriend had stirred up to cause some psycho to come after Sarah.

Who the hell was he? A member of the button-down brigade that tossed my office and apartment? Probably not. They weren't the kind of guys to work solo. Had he killed Roy Kaspar? A good bet.

What had Kaspar and/or Faith Dahlquist done to shake his tree? Granted, Roy set my teeth on edge just by being in the same room with me. But to get his throat in a tourniquet he must have done a bit more. Blackmail? Another good bet.

My heart was beating faster, pumping out of sync under my rib cage. Arrhythmia, to go along with a slightly elevated blood pressure. My welcome to middle age.

I flopped onto my back and began the deep-breathing exercises that a doc at UCLA Med School said would help to blow off the tension that was causing my cardiovascular system to short. They don't always work, but every once in a while they get my mind off my irregular heartbeat, and sometimes I even wind up snoozing. That night the cockeyed heart was the least of my preoccupations.

I had a dead office mate, okay, a partner I didn't much like. He was a creep, but he wasn't dumb enough to turn his back on an enemy with a garrote in his hands. So there must have been more to that. Misplaced trust? The killer could have sneaked up on him, like that spook on the roof. Jesus!

I forgot to deep-breathe.

I had a dead partner. I had a plastic-faced knife artist. I had guys in suits tossing my office and my apartment, looking for something called the Century List and talking about blackmail. I had an old lady who'd had a wall toppled on her. I also had a kid with a lost dog, and her mother was mixed up in dogfights with some lowlife from the Mex Mafia.

It was not my sort of thing at all. I mean, I am an aging ex-cop who, by using the telephone as his main weapon, has had some luck finding people who don't want to be found. Period. I don't know from dogfights and Century Lists and murdered partners. I am not Philo-fucking-Vance, for Christ's sweet sake!

I was sitting up in bed by that time. I could imagine my eyes bulging out and the veins looking like vines up my neck.

About those breathing exercises.

All right. Now that that was out of my system, I sighed and lowered myself back onto the too-soft bed and shut my eyes. The air gets sucked in through the nose and blown out through the lips. In through nez, out through lips.

Fine, then.

I decided to remove from my mind the unnecessary thoughts causing the tension. Forget the boys in the dark gray suits. Whatever set them abroad in the land, it was not the big problem. That went also for Kaspar's murder. The cops could play around with that, if they cared. It was what they get paid for.

I was being paid to take care of the kid, and she was not safe. The only way to make it safe for her was to find Faith Dahlquist and get the answers to several questions.

Fine, again.

That was the kind of work I did well. All I had to do was find Faith Van Dine Dahlquist. Queen of the Dogfights. Mistress of the Mexican Mafia. Mother of the Year.

In the morning I might even be able to con Cugat into putting the kid in some sort of protective custody. Get her off my hands until I located her mother. Of course, that might not work out too well, because . . .

The kid woke me up at nine on the button, as fresh and cheery as I was groggy and bleary-eyed. She interrupted a dream in which she and Cugat and his fat partner, Ambersen, were sitting in a Mexican restaurant looking through the window at a bank robbery across the street. The kid was waving a rolled tamale at the robbers.

'Where's that tamale?' I asked her.

'What?'

'Oh.' I cleared my throat, winced at the bright sunlight bouncing off the window, and tried to sit up in the bed.

'Sleep OK?' she asked sweetly.

'Huh? Oh, yeah. Sure. Like a turnip,' I said.

'I thought you'd want a cup of coffee,' she said.

'You thought right. Thanks.' I took it from her, smelled that fine coffee smell that rarely comes through in the taste, and took a swig.

'My God! What the hell is this stuff?'

She jumped back. 'It's – special coffee. That is, it's not coffee exactly. It's some sort of whole-grain stuff that they brew. Much better for you than coffee.'

It was too early in the morning for that sort of thing.

'It's fine,' I told her. 'Leave me alone now so I can get going in here. Lots to do today.'

She moved toward the door and I squinted at her. 'What the hell have you got on?'

'Why, whatever do you mean?' she asked haughtily.

'Well, first off, what happened to your hair?'

She touched the top of her head where a black wig was replacing her long blond locks. 'I just thought this might be more *sophisticated* for travel.'

'That probably explains the eye makeup and the shiny lipstick.'

'Gran says I could pass for eighteen, easily.'

'Nowhere this side of Saudi Arabia. Listen, kid, this isn't going to be a pleasure trip. I won't have a lot of time to play the genial host. OK?'

'Of course.'

'I mean, my full concentration will be on other things, so I may not be able to always pick up on certain sensitivities. I may step on your toes a little.'

'I wouldn't expect you to be in any way intimidated by my presence. Act any way you want. Say anything you want.'

'Fine,' I replied. 'Now go take off that stupid-looking black mop and scrub that paint off your puss. And take this goddamn soybean coffee crap away before I eat the cup.'

She picked up the coffee and started out. She paused at the door and looked at me with a raised eyebrow. 'You men are so grumpy in the morning.'

5. Cradling the phone between my neck and shoulder, I tried to comb my hair while listening to the office machine play back my messages. A thick-tongued Irish Mist regular wondered if he could see me on a financial matter. A man with a 'Say, brutha' accent informed me that unless I acted right away, my subscription to Law Enforcement Digest would expire. He promised to call back.

And then there were two messages that were provocative enough for me to want to follow up.

The first number I dialed was answered by a receptionist who put me straight through to Charles Z. Dotrice. Good old Charlie had progressed to Golden Pacific's Beverly Hills branch on Wilshire where, according to the receptionist, he was a senior vice-president. From a junior exec at a low-rent, crime-racked little outpost to a veep in the big-currency casino in Beverly Hills was a fair amount of distance to cover, even in a decade and a half.

Still, he didn't seem all that happy about his progress.

'Bloodworth?' His shrill nasal voice had lost none of its warmth. I tightened the knot of my midnight-blue knit tie while he said, 'It's about time you returned my call.'

'I sort of keep bankers' hours,' I told him.

'Very droll. Am I right that we have something to discuss?'

I frowned at the tie in the mirror, undid it, and started all over again. I hadn't anything to discuss with Dotrice back in the Sixties when he'd thrown me off the force. I didn't think I had anything to discuss with him at present. I said, 'Maybe we do, maybe we don't.'

'Still playing games, eh?'

'I can afford to,' I said. 'I picked up the tab for the last one.'

'My God, you still haven't closed the book on that?'

'What do you want, Dotrice? I've got things to do.'

'The . . .' His reedy voice hesitated. 'What shall I call it? The Kaspar Legacy?'

The goddamn tie was too long in back again. 'You're handling Kaspar's will?' I asked, surprised.

There was silence on the other end of the line. Brief silence. 'But you must –' His annoying voice broke apart in confusion. 'Look, I know that you and your partner have been . . . taking advantage of me.'

'Are you nuts?' I asked.

'Be coy then. It's only that your new partner, Kaspar, had, well, something of interest to me. Since he is no longer with us, I'm willing to talk to you about it.'

'Just spit it out, man,' I grumbled. 'What do you want?'

'You know damn well.'

'Then why am I asking questions?'

'There is the smart way, the easy way, and the Bloodworth way, eh? What game are you playing now?'

'You've gotta excuse me, Dotrice, but I'm in a rush this

morning. In a few days I'll be back in town and we can waltz around for as long as you want.'

'Wait,' he interrupted. 'I've got to see you today.' He made it sound like a command.

I hung up the receiver and looked in the mirror again. The back end of the tie was still too long, so I tucked it inside my pants.

Call number two went out to Gary Grady's office at UBC. His secretary, who struck me as an efficient but troubled woman, asked if I could be at the studio within the hour. In the background I could hear loud thumps and crashes.

'Is there trouble out there?' I asked.

'What? Oh, the workmen,' she said. 'They're completing the office. Mr Grady was quite insistent on your coming out to see him.'

'Why?'

'He said it was . . . personal.' She sounded a bit miffed to have been kept in the dark.

'It's not convenient,' I said. 'Maybe in a few days.'

There was a click and a male voice cut in. 'Bloodworth? Gary Grady here, my friend. Look, I suppose I came on a bit, uh, barbed-wire on the lot, but I've got mucho big problems . . .' There was a loud hammering and Grady's voice shouted, away from the receiver, 'Jesus Christ! Could you guys please give that a break while I'm on the phone? Yeah, use rubber hammers or dildoes or something.' He chuckled. 'Sorry,' he said, back to me again. 'Anyway, Bloodworth, I wanna talk with you. Shouldn't take long. I'd come to you, but they'll paint this place like the Kowloon Palace or something if I'm not here.'

'Your secretary said it was personal,' I said.

'Yeah. Right.'

'About Roy Kaspar?' I wondered.

'Who? Oh. No. Well, maybe. No, not really. Look. Can you come out here?'

I told him I thought I could swing it.

I made a final call and within twenty minutes Peru De Falco was at the apartment door. The kid let him in. Peru was a reasonably honest member of my profession who, though not exactly Mensa material, was big enough and mean enough to keep the kid out of trouble for an hour or two, if that was his task. At a cost of only $50. A steal. Peru's mother handled his business arrangements.

'What are the instructions again, Hound?' he asked.

'You keep Sarah, the little girl, in and everybody else out. Except me.'

He nodded his big, oddly handsome head. He was wearing a bright Hawaiian sport shirt, tan slacks, and gym shoes with straps instead of string. 'What about the mailman?'

'The mailman?'

'I once made a mistake with a mailman. You know, kinda pulled him apart. He was on'y doing his job, but I was on'y doin' my job, too.'

'I think you can forget the mailman, Peru. Unless he rings more than twice.'

Peru gave me a wink that was supposed to convince me that he understood. The kid asked him if he wanted to watch *Archie Bunker* with her. He opted for something called *The Young and the Restless*.

I left them to work it out.

6. The smartly uniformed black woman occupying the fat patrolman's stool at the UBC gate didn't quite know where Building 73 was located, but felt confident that it was somewhere in the general direction of the Hollywood Hills. She was distracted by a car full of rowdy young folks who were waving Stetsons and midmorning beer cans at her and shouting they wanted to parley with Waco Jones, whoever he was.

The woman dropped one shaky but neatly manicured hand to the service revolver on her belt. Suspecting that she was as unfamiliar with the weapon as she was with the territory, I took my leave in haste. I had a good idea where I was going anyway. A headliner like Grady wouldn't be asked to walk too far from his parking slot, so I pulled in next to the dark Rolls and followed my nose from there.

The UBC production offices were supposed to resemble little ranch bungalows in smart, contrasting shades of brown. They looked more like the prefabs I remembered from World War II. To my left was Stage 8, where a couple of Winnebagos belonging to absent members of the *Look to Tomorrow* soap opera sat vacant and baking in the morning sun, one with humidifier, one without.

Scanning the area further I spied a brown building with a white '73' stenciled on its sloping roof. As I approached it a wooden sign stuck into a square foot of parched earth in front informed me that it housed Ganymede Productions and 'The Weapy & Willy Show', Saucier/Belding Prods., Frey/Zetterman, Inc., and Julius Productions and 'The Gary Grady Show'.

The doorway to Julius Productions led to a long, unlighted hall, the most striking feature of which was a bright red runner that continued to a stairwell at the rear. There, a recent cardboard sign carried an arrow pointing up and the legend 'The Gary Grady Show'.

At the top of the stairs, the carpet changed from red to purple and led me past a room full of people, mainly young, who were talking into telephones as if their lives depended on their spiels. Workmen in brown UBC uniforms carried furniture and paint cans and brushes past them, largely ignored.

A coltish lady suddenly slammed down her receiver and shouted to no one in particular, 'All right. I've got Jerry Lewis for the twenty-fifth, but he's gonna plug his goddamn telethon.'

She crossed the room to a large blackboard where she dutifully wrote the name Jerry Lewis in a column marked for the twenty-fifth of the month. As she danced cheerily back to her desk, I stepped forward and shouted to her over the din, 'Where can I find Gary Grady?'

She looked up, frowned, and then relaxed. 'Up front. You can't miss the office. Say, are you anybody?'

I told her I hoped I was.

Grady's waiting room had maroon art-deco stuffed chairs that were filled with cardboard boxes and containers. A matching glasstop desk was filled with nothing but a date-book and a felt-tip pen. Past the desk was a door through which came the sound of a man with adenoids speaking. 'Then you say, "I guess that's why they call it the Wild West."'

'Not funny!' a voice I recognized as Grady's replied. 'I don't want to have to say it again: We're not knocking L.A. anymore. Now we *are* L.A. Is that too tough a concept for you to grasp? And will you for God's sake get me some hipper material? The kids like hip, and who else besides kids are up that late? Just the fogies, and Carson's got them.'

The charcoal walls weren't quite dry. Portraits of famed funnymen – Fields, Chaplin, Keaton, the Marx Brothers, Bob Hope, and even Johnny Carson – rested on the floor in matching chrome frames. 'Get something happening on the music scene, Weyman,' Grady went on. 'Book me into a concert or, I don't know, something flashy.'

I glanced at my watch, shrugged for my own benefit, and strolled into the maroon and gray office to find five very pale young men and women who were grouped on more of the chunky maroon chairs facing Grady. He looked very dramatic in black slacks and black silk open-necked shirt, almost too thin, his tanned face seeming darker because of the silver hair. There was something else about him: He reminded you of somebody out of your past. The guy who sat next to you in high-school chemistry. A pal in Little League. It was probably the key to his success, such as it was.

Three of the palefaces looked like triplets – two men and a woman – with sad, bespectacled eyes, freckles, and wild, wiry orange hair. They were dressed almost identically in jeans, oxford shirts, sneakers, and slope-shouldered jackets. I asked, 'Is this where they're having the Woody Allen look-alike contest?'

Somebody giggled nervously. A tall thin woman in tan slacks and an oxblood leather halter that was probably as uncomfortable as a hair shirt stood up. She was a brunette with too much eye makeup. 'Didn't you bring the blinds?' she asked indignantly.

Grady said, 'It's not the blinds guy, Pia. It's Bloodworth.'

To me he said, 'I'll be with you in a minute, pal.'

I looked pointedly at my wristwatch and strolled back into the outer office while he carried on. 'The goddamn Minton Sisters,' he said half patiently, 'didn't cut it with their parade of geeks. So don't give me geeks. They got numbers, sure, but the wrong kind of numbers. We're talking quality here as well as quantity. That's why Bradshaw brought me, us, out here – to get the kids who aren't watching anything but those goddamn music shows and maybe Letterman.'

His voice didn't give anything away – not race, creed, color, or point of natural origin. I listened to it idly as I consulted the date-book on the receptionist's glass desk. The entries began a few weeks back, probably when Grady opened his offices.

Only one name meant anything to me. Grady was supposed to have met with Roy Kaspar the day before he became my late associate. There was no indication whether he'd actually shown up.

'I don't want to downplay the 'Nam stuff, understand.' Grady's voice had a hard edge. 'Why isn't there anything on 'Nam?'

The waiting room was starting to close in on me, with its boxes and dull colors. Near the door the new carpet had already acquired a large white stain. I grinned at it.

'But 'Nam's history now, Gar,' a timorous voice offered.

'You telling me the kids don't remember Vietnam, Stu? Is that what you're saying? Jesus! That's what made me back east, you know. Gary Grady was the best comic to come out of Vietnam. The only fucking comic. So excuse me if I don't think I want to suddenly throw away my winning hand. I mean, Bob-fucking-Hope is still coming on about World War Two. Hey, gang, gimme what I need, huh? Get the hell back to your cave and whip up something better than this New York-L.A. bullshit. We on live in two fucking nights!'

I moved to the bare window beside the desk and looked down on Stage 8. That producer creep, Gene Sokol, was exiting through the stage door with the prematurely bald guy I'd seen carrying a clipboard on my visit to *Look to Tomorrow*. I wondered if he was the cuckolded husband, Ty Palmer.

Pia, the leather-vested brunette, herded the writing staff through the office. The palefaces didn't look happy, but maybe comedy writers aren't supposed to smile on the outside. Pia turned her overdone eyes on me and said, 'He's ready for you now.'

Grady was pouring a cup of steaming coffee from a chrome jug. He offered me a cup and I took it. 'This is some place,' he said. 'The sun never stops shining, even at night, and I don't have drapes.'

The coffee was instant. About what you'd expect from a guy with a glass desk.

'Then I get this color. I ask for taupe and they give me grape.' He spun around in his chrome and leather chair and pointed to three huge crates to his left, one of which had been pried open. 'I still haven't fucking unpacked and I've been here nearly four weeks already. You ought to see where they got me living.'

He slipped from his chair and bent over the open crate, carefully withdrawing a large photograph in a plastic frame. It was of a group of soldiers in olive drab, sitting in the dirt and playing cards. He rested it carefully against a wall and smiled at it. If he was in the picture, I couldn't find him.

'You wanted to see me?' I asked.

'Right. Listen, like I said about that business on the lot. Sheer hostility on my part.' He took the chair again. 'I've been under a certain pressure out here. I mean, two months ago I was just this deejay on WNX in Manhattan with a lotta local fans. Doing the comedy clubs. Now there's literally millions riding on me. It's up to me to turn the trick, you know. Everything's brand-new. New job. New opportunity. New town. New life.'

'You're from the East Coast?'

'By inclination,' he said. 'I was a Bible Belt baby. Muscatine, Iowa, you believe it? But ever since I – ever since 'Nam, I've been one hundred percent New Yawkah. My kind of people. You spend much time back East?'

'Not much.'

'Yeah, well, anyway, everything here has been totally cocked up and I guess I kinda over-reacted about the parking spot.'

'No problem. I shouldn't have parked there.'

'Smoke?' He pushed a pack of cigarettes my way and I shook my head. An inch of white bandage showed just above his right wrist.

'Hurt yourself?'

He automatically started rubbing his wrist. 'The fucking workmen. Actually, it was probably my fault. I was trying to pry open one of the crates out there and I ran a piece of wood up my arm. Nothing too serious, but it hurts like hell.

'Anyway, the reason I called you, Bloodworth, I met with your partner, Roy Kaspar, shortly before his . . . before he died.'

He paused, as if he expected me to comment on that.

'The thing is, I need some background checks on a couple of people connected with the show. The ones the network made me add to the gang I brought out with me. I want to make sure they're on my team one hundred percent. Kaspar was going to check 'em out, but the poor son of a bitch never got the chance.'

'Somebody recommend him to you?'

He shrugged. 'Pia got his name somewhere. In any case, that's why I wanted to see you. I mean, you were Kaspar's partner. I paid him a thousand-buck retainer.'

'I'm afraid you're stuck with the loss, unless you sue the estate. Kaspar and I weren't actually partners, in any sense. We shared an office, but we kept separate books.'

Grady smiled at me. 'So you're saying that you'll need another retainer?'

I finished off the instant coffee. 'If I were going to take the job.'

'Why wouldn't you?'

'You can get background investigations cheaper from a lot of places who hire good kids to do the research work or who have access to computer info. A guy like me, or Kaspar for that matter, would have to charge you the going rate for his services, which is high. How many people do you want checked?'

'Seven.'

'Well, if they're all US citizens who haven't done much traveling, it'd take maybe a week or two. I'd have to tag it at two big ones a week. Plus minor expenses, like long-distance.'

Grady grinned. 'Kaspar asked for a flat seven thou.'

'Well, Roy had a large appetite.'

'You seem like a pretty straight dude, Bloodworth. I want

you to do the job. Fuck the research kids. You get what you pay for.'

'Is there something specific you're looking for?'

'I just like to be prepared before the trouble starts. Fore-warned. I didn't get through 'Nam with my ass intact by letting other people do my thinking for me. Preventive warfare, that's the way I played it. You get to 'Nam?'

'Korea was my war,' I told him. 'Long time ago.'

He leaned back in his chair. 'Korea wasn't as messy,' he said.

I didn't bother to reply. It seemed pretty messy to me, but I couldn't see any point to that particular argument.

'You ever see me work?' he asked suddenly.

'Like I said, I don't get out on the East Coast very often.'

'I do 'Nam material. Gags. You know, like the time this Viet Cong general calls his men together on one of the finger islands. These guys are starving. Haven't seen a grain of rice in months, get it? Now this General Lakanookie, he says, "Men, I got good news and bad news. The bad news is that there is nothing left to eat on this island but bird shit. The good news is that there is not enough of it to go around."'

He paused and looked at me hopefully. I nodded, wiggled my eyebrows, and said, 'Pretty funny.'

'Oh, I see. You're one of those heavy intellectuals who don't laugh, just analyze.' He shrugged. 'That's okay. I respect that.

'To get to the point, I'm picking up a weird vibe about this whole TV gig. Like, you know, I may not be in control here. This guy who heads up the network, L. D. – fucking – Bradshaw, may have stuck me with some ringers who are working for him, not for me.'

'That's a little more than a routine background check. You sure it's necessary?'

'Lemme give you this allegory about the television business,

Bloodworth. It's about a farmer with a rooster who can't get it up.'

'The farmer or the rooster?'

'The rooster can't get it up,' he explained, as seriously as if he was giving me a synopsis of *Moby Dick*. 'The farmer complains to a buddy and the buddy gets him a rooster that is guaranteed to service every hen on the farm and then some. Sure enough, this rooster is like the Burt Reynolds of roosters. The goddamn Warren Beatty of roosters. He sees a hen and it's wham, bam, thank you, ma'am. The farmer watches him for a couple hours and then he starts worrying that the bird is gonna blow a gasket. I mean, the goddamn rooster is even going after Ole Blue, for Christ's sake.

'So sure enough, the farmer is sitting on his front porch smoking a corncob pipe and he spots some buzzards circling the sky. He rushes out there to find the rooster in the middle of the field, on his back, legs up in the air, stiff as a pike. He walks over to the rooster and bends to pick him up. The rooster opens one eye and winks at him. "Beat it," the bird tells him and rolls his eyes skyward, "when you fuck with buzzards, you gotta play their game." '

I gave him another smile. 'You sort of remind me of George Gobel,' I told him.

'Who the hell is he?'

'One of the great TV comedians of the Fifties.'

'No shit? Well, anyway, that's one of my favorites. It's not the cosmic joke, of course. That's what we're always looking for. The goddamn cosmic joke. Maybe that's what life is, do you think?'

'Why not?'

'Well, anyway, suppose I jot down the names for you.' He lowered his voice. 'I'd have Pia do it, but her name heads the list, dig?'

'It'll be a few days before I can get to this, Gary. I'm working on something else right now that's going to take me out of town for a while.'

He slumped back in his chair, a frown bothering his tanned forehead. 'Suppose we up the ante a little. To, ah, eight thou? Would that get your immediate attention?'

'Ordinarily, not only my attention but my undying affection. But I have to do this other thing first.'

I stood up to take my leave, but he rushed around the desk to head me off. 'OK, wait,' he said. 'As long as it won't be too long. Where you gonna be?'

'Why?'

'In case I need you.' He relaxed slightly. 'That sounds sorta dumb, right?'

'Suppose I give you the name of somebody who can get to work for you right now?'

'Naw. You're a straight guy. I trust you. Give me a call when you get back. OK?'

I nodded and we shook on it.

Pia was sitting at her desk scribbling what looked like a resignation letter. I asked her where she'd gotten Roy Kaspar's name. 'Roy who?' she replied.

Down the hall the telephone brigade was still at it. According to the blackboard, General Westmoreland and Charo were going to join Jerry Lewis on that show of the twenty-fifth. That sounded like quite a show. Maybe Sarah would let me watch it at her place.

13

1. My classmate Sylvia Leonidas arrived while Mr Bloodworth was out running errands. He had left behind a stalwart protector named Mr Peru De Falco, a somewhat single-minded chap who did not want to let her enter the apartment. But I convinced him that a pregnant fourteen-year-old could do us little harm.

For the record, 'Peru' is a diminutive of Perushko, a name bestowed on him by a czarist Russian grandmother. While he sat in my bedroom, his John Travolta-like face as emotionless as stone, watching the rerun of a *Love Boat* episode both Sylvia and I had already seen, we went out onto the terrace for a bit of girl talk. It was a fine opportunity to fill Sylvia in on everything that had transpired since summer vacation had begun. I must admit I wished to gloat a bit over the fact that, in spite of everything she had done to keep me from it, I was about to embark on a trip north. Only instead of being accompanied by her, her grotty parents, and icky little brother, Rolly, I was being squired by the ruggedly romantic Mr Leo Bloodworth.

When he arrived, Sylvia's reaction was, as expected, sourgrapish. Imagine her comparing him to Mr Osterwald, our beefy, red-faced, perspiring gym teacher! So what if Mr Bloodworth's face did turn slightly crimson while carrying our bags to the car? Mine surely weighed a ton, what with all the books. The poor, pathetic little mother-to-be even giggled at us as we drove away, but I could see the sickening envy that was gnawing at her entrails.

'So that's your little friend Sylvia,' Mr Bloodworth said as he shifted through the gears.

'Former friend.'

'Hang on to your pals, kid.'

'Is Mr De Falco a friend of yours?' I asked.

'In a manner of speaking.'

'I found him a bit wanting in certain areas of conversation.'

Mr Bloodworth nodded his head. 'Conversation isn't his forte.'

'He's a fine television-watching companion, though. He laughs in all the right places. And he is rather handsome when he smiles.'

'Yeah, Peru's a real heartbreaker if he sets his mind to it.'

'He seemed a bit thick around the middle,' I said.

'Well, so's your little ex-pal, Sylvia,' he said. 'She's getting quite a pot on her.'

'She's eating for two,' I said.

'Huh?' He took his eyes off the road.

'She's going to become a mommy.'

'She's *what*?'

'About six months pregnant is what.'

He narrowly missed rear-ending a Buick in front of us. 'That kid? She can't be more than fifteen.'

'Fourteen. Four months younger than I.'

'Goddamnit!' he exclaimed. 'I just don't need this.'

'It's the same age when most Ubangi females have given birth at least once. I'm sure you know that Cleopatra was queen of the Nile when she was thirteen, and Caesar was at least – well, older. Her nose was a bit too long, but a wise man one said that if it had been shorter, it might have changed the face of Europe. Then there's Juliet Capulet of *Romeo and Juliet* fame . . .'

'Kid,' he grumbled, 'we've got miles of bad road to cover and I'd appreciate it if you could just button the lip about Ubangis and *Romeo and Juliet* and Cleopatra's nose. I've got some serious stuff to mull over.'

'Mull away,' I said, looking out of the side window at the passing scenery. 'Just mull up a storm, if you want.'

The car screeched as it turned onto Olympic, and headed toward downtown LA. Mr Bloodworth consulted the rearview mirror and scowled.

'Are we going to your office first?' I asked.

He grunted in the negative, but said no more.

'Then where are we going?'

He sighed. 'Didn't your grandmother call you this morning?' He waited for me to say she had. 'Didn't she mention something about who was going to be boss on this trip?'

'She told me to obey you as if you were she.'

'Reet. Then just sit back and enjoy the ride and stop your mouth working overtime.' He turned on the radio and began searching for the awful moldy-oldie station. I began to understand that this might not be such a fun excursion after all.

We drove along for a mile or so, with Mr Bloodworth continuing to check his rearview mirror often. Eventually he asked, 'Did you tell your little knocked-up friend where we were going?'

'I don't know where we're going.'

'I mean about finding your mom.'

'I may have mentioned it. Not the finer points, of course.'

He scowled. But the dark thought that hit him must have flown almost as quickly as it landed. He shrugged. 'What are the odds that anybody would know about her? Pretty low.'

'What are you talking about?' I asked.

'That's one of the problems of spending too much time alone, kid. You start talking to yourself.'

'Well, you're not alone now, and it tends to confuse those who are with you. Not to mention the rudeness of it all.'

'Maybe you're right, kid. *Mea culpa*.'

'What?'

'*Mea culpa*. It's Latin. An old altar boy expression. Means "my fault".'

I tried to picture Mr Bloodworth as an altar boy and failed. Then I tried to picture him at age fourteen and was about as successful.

From time to time he hummed along with the music; his golden eyes moved from the road to the rearview mirror without noticeably blinking.

Finally, we turned left along Hope Street, driving past his weird office building and continuing on to Third. At the corner, beside the granite visage of the *Los Angeles Post* building, we pulled over to the western curb, where a stocky man in a rumpled seersucker suit and open-necked shirt was fanning himself with the morning sports section.

'OK, kid, get ready to meet the best goddamned reporter in fifty-two states.'

The fellow was fiftyish, fat, and perspiry, and he had a weird little moustache that looked like a gathering of mosquitoes feasting on his long upper lip. I recognized him from a beer commercial: Jerry Flaherty, the crime reporter who did all those articles about the Pasadena Mauler. It was a wonder how a man could speak such terrible English and still be considered a credible journalist.

He squinted through the smoggy white sunshine and moved toward the sound of the car's horn, walking on the balls of his tiny feet.

'Be a good girl and hop in back,' Mr Bloodworth asked.

Jerry Flaherty was peering in the window, a dopey smile twisting his row of mosquitoes. I said, 'If this gentleman would be so kind as to open the door for me, I'll be glad to nestle among the litter on the back seat.'

The stocky man raised an eyebrow at Mr Bloodworth and opened the door with an elaborate fat man's bow. I hopped out and he pushed the seat forward for me to climb over. As I cleared away Mr Bloodworth's personal debris collection to make room, Flaherty slipped into the suicide seat.

'Mind turning on the air, Leo?' he asked in a quasi-Irish brogue.

Mr Bloodworth jiggled the knobs of his air-conditioner. The stocky man twisted around to give me a smile. 'Jerry Flaherty's the by-line, doll.'

When I did not reply, he asked Mr Bloodworth, 'Who's the little Garbo?'

'Hell, Jerry, I thought everybody knew by now. Serendipity Dahlquist.'

'That her real moniker?' He rolled his eyes my way. 'That's some name, hon,' he said patronizingly. He hooked a dainty Jones's pork sausage finger into his shirtfront and pulled the material away from his damp body. 'Phew, Leo. If you don't get that cooler working soon, you're gonna have a stiff on your hands.'

'It's not that hot, Jerry. Maybe you're coming down with something.'

'I musta got hold of a bad Harp last night,' Flaherty chuckled. 'In Raguso's. Shoulda known better'n to drink Irish in a wop bar. The bottle had probably been in there for ten years. Whew. Anyway, between that and the way things are at the paper . . .'

'The *Post*?'

'Them fercockta dilettantes. Keeping up to date with the *Post* is the way they put it. Christ. You'd think that thirty years on the crime beat would count for something. I don't need 'em, ya know. Got my TV deals and my book contracts.'

Mr Bloodworth found the right button and a gust of icy air wafted through the car. Flaherty sighed. 'Like the kiss of a Killarney convent girl,' he said. 'Almost makes me forget the bloody *Post*.'

'What happened? I thought you were in solid with the Raymond family.'

'Aw, the place is full of them fercockta computer machines that bathe you in a lovely green glow while you try to write your story on a plastic typewriter that clicks at you. I refuse to create on a machine that salts your rough copy away in its innards somewhere. Till a few months ago they let me keep my own typewriter on my desk. You remember the little Underwood, Leo, the same one that saw me through the fercockta Watts riots, the student bombings, a couple hundred murder cases, for Christ's sweet sake. Anyway, the word filters down from on high that they don't want any more "antiques" on the desks.'

'Maybe they were talking about you,' I said, almost without thinking.

'Who's this kid, Leo? The Don Rickles of the grammar-school set?'

'I'm in high school.'

'She's . . . in high school,' Mr Bloodworth said. Ever the peace-maker, he tried to switch the subject. 'You were saying about your typewriter . . .'

'Right. So's I gotta use one of them green lightboxes and risk goddamn cancer of the eyeballs.'

'Can't you work at home?' Mr Bloodworth suggested as he eased the car into the traffic mainstream.

'My home? Oh, boyo, I'd stare into a thousand green machines until my eyes turned to glass before I'd put up with Moira and the grandsprouts all day.'

Mr Bloodworth shrugged. 'Where's your guy?' he asked.

'Waiting for us at Tooky Marr's. You want to tell me about this Gutierrez scumbag?'

I could sense the question had something to do with me, because Mr Bloodworth's strange eyes shifted in the rearview mirror and stared my way for a second. Then he began to tell the perspiring newsman about a man named Gutierrez who was related to an older man named Gutierrez, which made the fat man edge forward on his seat, forgetting to mop his dripping jowls.

'Ah, now that sounds more like something that might have stirred the soul of the sainted Mr Pulitzer. Never mind them rinky-dink dogfights.'

'Dogfights?' I almost shouted. 'Is this about Groucho?'

Mr Bloodworth winced, then glared at Flaherty. Out of the corner of his mouth he told me, 'I don't know, kid. Maybe. Or it might just be a coincidence.' He took us around a corner and when he steadied the car, opened the glove compartment and handed Flaherty a map of the state. He'd made red circles on it.

Flaherty glanced at it. 'Dogfights. Papa G. Don't make me work too hard for it, bucko. Is this about Roy Kaspar getting choked or not?'

'If I knew that, Jerry, I'd be talking to the cops now instead of you. It's a possible maybe.'

'Great, Leo. That's what I get from Gates,' Flaherty said, referring to the top policeman in Los Angeles. 'Possible maybes aren't worth the air they're heatin'.'

'I thought you were doing me a favor, Jerry. One you owed me,' Mr Bloodworth said with a scowl. 'If it turns into something, you've got the exclusive.'

'What could be fairer?' Flaherty put the map back into the glove compartment 'No sense my looking at it now. Tex'll tell you what he thinks. He's the dogfight expert. Me, I don't clog up the cranium with info on crimes that don't even carry a felony rap. But it seems like messy stuff for an old warhorse like Papa G. to get his fancy shoes all dirty wading through.'

I had to ask. 'What do you know about the dogs, Mr Flaherty? I mean, how do they treat them?'

'Why don't we just save it, like you said, Jerry,' Mr Bloodworth suggested.

'Allow me to educate the little lady, Leo.' He twisted around, his tiny eyes twinkling. 'These fellers take a couple dogs, American pit bulls mainly, and they put 'em in contests they call "rolls". A training fight, like the prelims at the Coliseum.'

'For somebody with an unclogged cranium, Jerry,' Mr Bloodworth said, 'you seem pretty stuffed with dogfight lore.'

'You know what a newspaperman's main weapon is, Leo? His memory. That's why his main worry is senility.'

'It's not worth worrying about, Mr Flaherty,' I said. 'You'll be the last to know if it happens.'

He gave me an open-mouth stare. 'Well, damn me if you aren't right, honey. Now where was I? The doggies. Some of 'em they rig with special choppers and shoot 'em so full of dope they could rip the hide off a rhino.'

'Please. Is this what happened to my Groucho?'

Mr Bloodworth kept his yellow eyes on the road. Flaherty asked him, 'Could this little lady be your client, Leo? You looking for her dog? Set a hound to catch a hound, you might say?'

'Something like that.'

'There could be a certain heartwarmin' side to this story. Spunky little miss and case-hardened private shamus join forces to –'

'Jerry, I told you. If there's a story, it's yours.'

'Sure, boyo. Don't get your back up.' He asked me, 'What kind of a pooch was it?'

'He was . . . is a proud little terrier. The breed is known as "the white cavalier", because it was taught for generations to defend its master but to never, never provoke a fight.'

'Well, let's hope its defenses are up to snuff or else it's the big boneyard in the sky. Some of them bowwows can take the head off a razorback.'

'Jeeze, Jerry,' Mr Bloodworth said with a measure of impatience, 'put a sock in it, huh?'

'As you wish, sire,' Flaherty said, resting his head against the seat. 'That's what I heard though. Could take the head off a razorback.'

2. Tooky Marr's was a barroom, which came as no great surprise. A desperate, dismal place in the shadow of the San Diego Freeway whose owner-barkeep was a wizened and arthritic black man who'd had something to do with boxing or wrestling, if you believed the posters and photos that decorated the long, dirty, pea-green room.

The few customers at 11:30 in the morning eyed us suspiciously as Flaherty grabbed Tooky Marr in a hammerlock and the old man humorlessly allowed himself to be led around the bar to meet me. His dark eyes were covered with a film as gray as his apron. His right ear had closed in upon itself, like a flower crimped before blooming. There were thick and thin streaks of scar tissue under his eyes and over the bridge of his nose. When he spoke, his words were slurred. Still, there was an olde-worlde dignity about him.

'It is a pleasure to welcome you, miss, to Tooky Marr's Wonder Bar.'

Mr Bloodworth was staring at us with some apprehension. I shook Tooky Marr's gnarled hand.

'Any friend of Mr Flaherty's is welcome here,' he went on. 'Mr Flaherty talks about Tooky Marr's in his column. Once, twice, I don't know how many times. People start to come in.

Young, old, white, black, brown, yellow, and any variation thereof. They all read Mr Flaherty's column.'

Flaherty didn't hear any of that nonsense. He was at the far end of the room talking to a man in a cowboy hat who was sitting by himself in a booth. I said to Tooky Marr, 'They read his column because they're amazed at how much punishment the English language can take and still prevail.'

'Do tell?' the old man replied, thinking about it. 'You know, I never looked at it in just that way.'

Flaherty must have been listening after all. 'Give the kid a Coke with some cherry juice, Tooky. Maybe it'll sweeten her disposition.'

'Is it hot enough for you, Mr Flaherty?' I asked.

14

The way Sarah rode Jerry Flaherty that morning in Tooky Marr's, it's a wonder he didn't deck her. Maybe not a wonder, exactly. I'd seen him deck women before, but never little girls.

Still, most little girls weren't like our Sarah.

While Tooky hobbled behind his bar to rescue a Harp from its cold, watery grave for Flaherty, she raked her eyes over every square inch of the big barroom. 'What a dear little place,' she said. 'I suppose you spend many fruitful hours here.'

'One for you, too, Mr Bloodswert?' Tooky asked.

'Oh, I suppose so.'

Flaherty squeezed into a booth beside the weird-looking black rhinestone cowboy. The man was wearing a Tom Mix ten-gallon topper, only unlike Tom's, his was a bright yellow with a peacock-feather band. His shirt was a dark-blue silk with yellow piping. The rest of him was mercifully hidden by the chipped imitation-oak table, but the tip of one shiny bright red boot winked as it moved in time to some music only his ears could hear.

Flaherty leaned across the table and said something to him and the cowboy turned toward me. His eyes were hidden by large, very dark sunglasses that were approximately the same color as his skin. He looked like a six-and-a-half-foot ant on his way to a Martian rodeo.

The kid wasn't interested in him, probably because he'd

allowed Flaherty to sit with him. She was observing two winos on the nod at the far end of the bar, sipping through straws stuck into a small wooden keg. 'What are they drinking?' she asked Tooky.

'Oh, missy, that's just the leftovers. See, I pour all the booze customers leave in glasses into the keg and I lets the boys take a few swigs each for a quarter.'

She turned to stare at me, as if this proved some point she was trying to make. 'We'll be on the road soon,' I said, giving her a weak smile.

Flaherty waved me to the table. The kid started to join us, but I suggested she play a new electronic game that Tooky had been coerced into installing by some friendly amusement-company salesmen in sharkskin suits. It had space monsters on it. The kid carried my quarters to it as eagerly as if she'd been sentenced to spend the rest of the week watching tires being patched.

Flaherty slipped from the booth. 'I'll leave you and Tex to chat.'

I took the seat opposite the cowboy ant. His smile was as sincere as a pimp's passion. 'Mr Flaherty tells me you're interested in the ignoble sport,' he said in what sounded to my ears like a genuine Brit accent. 'The vile in pursuit of the violence.'

'Dogfights?'

'Dogfights.' He lifted a briefcase atop the table. It was a deep cordovan with bright brass corners. A pretty thing. I wondered who'd picked it out for him. He clicked it open as Tooky arrived with my Harp and a Lone Star for the ant. When Tooky had begun his long march back to the bar, the ant called Tex said, 'How well do you know the dogfight territory?'

'I'm a stranger, myself.'

He sighed and his manicured fingers plucked from his

briefcase a digest-size magazine titled *Roll Call: The Monthly Best of Breed*.

'I am the publisher's West Coast representative,' he said. 'Our advert rates are quite reasonable, considering our circulation. I think a quarter-page would be just what you need.'

'How much?'

'A mere fifty dollars.'

I peeled two twenties and a tenner from my wallet and rested the bills on the magazine's cover, partially hiding a bad pen-and-ink sketch of a very angry dog with furrowed brows and bared teeth. Tex lifted them, gently tested their composition, and deposited them into the briefcase, which he then shut.

'Nothing fancy,' I said. 'How's about "Compliments of a Friend"?'

He showed me some teeth. 'Well, now, mah man,' he said, 'suppose'n we take it from the jump.' I nodded, wondering which accent was the fake. Probably both.

'So. You got about a hundred thousand 'yats who subscribe to *Roll Call* or *Pit Dog Report* or some other book that tells 'em where the action is in their area. That's all over the US, but you figure for every guy who subscribes, they's four or five others who leech his copy, dig? Say a half-million citizens who like to see Rover get his guts ripped out.'

I sipped at the Harp. 'How many in California?'

'A high percent. Enough for five to ten rolls going just about every night somewhere in the state. And maybe five major matches every week. Once a month you got a weekend convention. Dudes take their old ladies, their kids. Party time. Like an old-fashioned family picnic with shredded dogs.'

'Everything is listed in there?' I pointed to the magazine.

'We don't bother with the rolls, man. Those are really small-time. Owners are just testing their mutts to see if they're game or if they'll cur out. That is, if they'll put up a good fight or turn tail. A roll lasts for maybe twenty minutes. The dogs get cut up a little. Nothing heavy-duty. Nothing for crowds.

'A fight, now, lasts until one of the dogs goes belly up. Usually about an hour, but I heard of one that went on for five hours and the winner of that one didn't look no better than the loser.'

I picked up the book, flipped through it.

'We list the big events. Many of the fights. All the conventions. Like, you got conventions this weekend' – he took the book from me and looked at it – 'at Riverside, Wasco, and Weed.' He handed it back.

'How the hell do you get by with this? You're listing illegal fights. Don't you get any heat?'

'Involvement in a dogfight, even the staging of a dogfight, is not a serious crime, *amigo*,' he said, slipping into a Latin cadence. I tried not to notice it. 'It is, of course, a federal crime to use interstate transportation or the mails to promote dogfighting. But' – he wagged a long black finger at me – '*Roll Call* isn't promoting dogfighting. It prints only facts and paid advertising. And each issue carries an editorial deploring the brutality of the sport.'

'Better watch out or you might pick up a Nobel Prize.'

'We are also nonprofit, by the way. Whatever we net is used to lobby against the – ah, restrictive laws that deprive ethnic minorities of the sports that are so much a part of their cultural heritage.'

'Dogfights? Which culture is that?'

'Anglo-Saxon, I believe,' he said with a smile. 'But I was thinking more of the sport of cockfighting. All part of the same oppression.'

He nibbled at his Lone Star. Across the room the kid's machine was exploding in beeps and bongs and twitters. Flaherty was standing beside the pay phone staring at Sarah with a bemused expression.

'What's your angle?' I asked Tex.

'Angle?' he asked me back, feigning innocence. 'I'm in publishing. Many fine magazines. I sell advertising.'

I glared at him. A multi-accented Martian ant cowboy ad salesman.

The kid's machine stopped its space music and she walked over to the table. 'I'm out of quarters,' she said.

The cowboy ant smiled at her.

'Your hat glows in the dark,' she told him. 'I've never seen anything quite like it'

'I had it made in Italy.'

'That just shows what the Italians will do for money.'

I handed her a couple of bucks and suggested that she get Tooky to break them into coins. Tex, the cowboy ant, watched her go. 'Precocious child,' he declared.

'And then some. What can you tell me about Emiliano Gutierrez?'

'Let me put it this way,' Tex said, going British again. 'Dogfighting is becoming a major business throughout these colonies. But especially right here in the Golden State, where the weather allows conventions the year round and where the Latin worship of the macho mystique is as strong as the redwood. In a large convention with three hundred or so participants, an amazing amount of currency changes hands. You'll find blue-chip gambling, narcotics – I understand that if one ingests the proper medication, the rending of a dog's flesh can become a transcendent religious experience – prostitution, and the sale of weapons, from handguns to howitzers.

'Now, with all this high finance taking place, and with only minimal opposition from law enforcement, and that mainly at the behest of the cruelty-to-animals people, also known as cranks, is it surprising that some branch of organized crime should want a hair of the dog?'

'Gutierrez.'

'Precisely.'

'I'd heard that El Padre was doing it strictly as a hobby.'

'A most lucrative hobby.'

'How much, do you think?'

'A ball-park figure? Three million annual net, just in this state.'

I goggled at him. 'Jesus, and they're letting the old man fool around with it?'

'So far, Jose Merada has been happy to get the old man out of his hair, but he can't ignore the bottom line too much longer. Then he'll give the old bull something less pricey to bang his head against.'

'I'd think the cops would be impressed by the bottom line, too.'

'Maybe. Once they bother to think about it. The Humane Society is trying to educate them and maybe they can. But it's not easy to teach an old cop new tricks. And, it can be dangerous. Last year a Humane Society investigator got himself torn to pieces by some very game animal up past Sacramento. Semi-accidentally,' he added, slipping into his southern-black mood. 'Some junked-up pit bull got locked into the guy's motel room with 'im. Nobody'll ever know how it happened, 'cause the brain-fried Fido ain't talkin' and neither is the ghost of the Humane.'

'Nice,' I said, feeling a little queasy.

'Oh, there're gonna be more examples, you can bet. Man into dog chow. Guys welchin' on fight bets. That sort of thing. Old Dominion isn't gonna let any big loser off the hook.'

'What's Old Dominion?'

'That's the company name Gutierrez is using. Old Dominion Management. Nice sound, huh? If your bout is protected by Old Dominion, you got bouncers to handle your little flare-ups, all bets are insured, your concessions are well stocked, and interference – from the Humanes, ASPCA, or whatever – will be minimized.'

He flashed his teeth, then consulted a rainbow-colored plastic watch on his wrist. 'Time I be off,' he said. 'An ad salesman can't let the grass grow under his ass.'

I explained that I was trying to locate Danny Gutierrez and handed him the map with the list of phone numbers that Gutierrez had called from his Marina hotel. Tex glanced at them. 'Well, these'll give you an idea where Little G. is heading. Probably belong to the local organizers. Car salesmen. Supermarket owners. Members of the Rotary. You dial a number, you get a switchboard. Then what? You ask for the guy with the dogfights?' He chuckled. 'These numbers won't do you much good specifically, 'less you got the password. But they can put you in the right location. I mean, Little G.'s gonna be dropping by to collect Old Dominion's share of the pot, you can guarantee.'

'So I use the area code to figure out the location, then check the magazine to find out the date of the fight in that area.'

'There you go. He'll probably be at the big bout near Weed tomorrow,' Tex said, with no noticeable accent at all. 'Top of the state. Then he'll work his way home to papa.'

He stood up, exposing pink pants tucked into his cherry-red boots. 'There are two promising hounds mated at Weed, both one fight shy of being true champions. Should be a solid bout, if you have the stomach for it. I personally don't, but to each his own.'

He put two fingers to his hat brim, just like Randolph Scott used to, and picked up his cordovan briefcase. On his way out he gave another Scott salute to Flaherty, who was on the phone.

I was flipping through the book when the kid joined me. 'Who was that tasteful character?'

'An advertising salesman,' I replied, standing up. I slipped the magazine into my coat pocket, along with the map and phone numbers.

Flaherty cradled the pay phone and met us at the bar, where Tooky had positioned a fresh Harp for him. He said, 'A Beverly Hills face-lifter just got dusted in his office. I should probably get over there. I don't suppose it would be on your way?'

'We're catching a flight up north and we're running late,' I said. 'What happened to that guy who used to drive you around? Benjy? Benny?'

'Benjy. Oh, he went to crap and the rats got him or something, boyo. Undependable.'

'I've never understood how somebody could live and work in this town for thirty years and never learn to drive.'

'A minor failing,' he said. 'Hell, maybe I won't bother. You seen one Beverly Hills murder, you've seen them all. Let the TV vultures pick over the bones. I'll stay here and have another of Tooky's fine beers. Tex come through for you?'

I nodded. 'You're a pal, Jerry.'

His smile twisted his moustache. 'Anything for a friend. Or a good story, boyo. Where are you headed, exactly?'

'Up the state. Fly into Sacramento, then rent a car.'

'You know the lay of the land up there?'

I nodded. 'About seven years ago I went up after that alderman. Claymore. Harlan Claymore, remember? I had to chase him all the way to Vancouver before I grabbed him.'

'Happier days,' Flaherty said. 'Younger days. Well, *vaya con Dios* to you, Leo.' It was my day for dialects. He dangled his bottle of beer. 'One for the road?'

He looked lonely. I felt bad about using him and running, so I hesitated. Sarah, who'd been watching us, shifted from one foot to the other and said, 'I have two quarters left over. Why don't both of you gentlemen have sips from the dreg cask. On me.'

I gave Flaherty a sheepish look. 'See you soon, buddy,' I said.

Flaherty emitted what sounded like an Irish chuckle. 'That's a real feisty little lady there, Leo. You got your work cut out for you and that's the Lord's truth.'

There was not much that I, or anyone, Sarah included, could add to that. We went.

15

1. 'Are you sure you need your book, little girl?' the stewardess with the pouter-pigeon breasts asked me in sickly-sweet condescension. We'd arrived at LAX just in time to board an immediate flight to Sacramento. It was simply a matter of purchasing our tickets and walking onto the plane. For some reason Mr Bloodworth checked his luggage, but I carried mine on board, where the stewardesses proceeded to stick it in some cranny or nook. They were not anxious to dig it out again.

'We'll be in the air for nearly forty-five minutes,' I reasoned. 'I'd like to pass the time reading.'

'Try one of our magazines.'

'I suppose I could make do with a copy of *Omni*,' I said.

'Oh, I'm afraid we don't carry that one. How about *Newsweek*?'

'I'd rather have my book.'

The stewardess looked imploringly at Mr Bloodworth, who had been silently studying his awful dogfight magazine, lifting his strange-colored eyes only infrequently to contemplate the stewardesses as they flounced by. 'Sir, I'm trying to explain to your daughter the difficulty of –'

'I'm not his daughter,' I said.

Mr Bloodworth smiled and said, 'Not my daughter,' and returned to his magazine.

Frustrated, the chest-heavy stewardess backed away with a

fixed smile on her overly made-up face. 'I'll try to find your bag, dear,' she told me.

'I guess the customer may still be right, huh?' I asked Mr Bloodworth, who mumbled something. He opened his map and started making notations on it with his pen.

'I understand the stewardesses on this line are particularly promiscuous,' I said.

'What makes you think so?' he asked.

'Bill Rudolpho, a boy in my class, dated two of them.'

'A fourteen-year-old kid went out with some of these dames?' He shook his big head in wonder. 'Probably drives a Ferrari, Either that or he has an overactive imagination.'

'If anything on him is overactive, it's his prostate. He showed us videotapes of them, the three of them, on his waterbed.'

Mr Bloodworth's face twisted into a grimace. 'Before this is over, kid, you're gonna have me in some cardiac ward.'

I will never understand his attitude toward sex. The man seems to be absolutely afraid to talk about it even. I was on the verge of confronting him on that point when the pouter-pigeon stewardess waved at me from the front of the plane. She had my suitcase.

Five minutes later I was back in my seat, perusing my very own book. 'Could we visit Croaker College?' I asked Mr Bloodworth.

'Where?'

'Croaker College. In Sacramento. According to this book, it's the only school in the world where frogs are taught to jump. For the Calaveras County contest.'

He scowled. 'I think we'll have to pass that by, Sarah. What the hell book is that?'

'*An Eccentric Guide to the United States*. I bought it when I thought I'd be motoring with the Leonidas family. As long as we're going to be so near, I don't see why we couldn't take just a few minutes –'

'We're gonna be real busy, kid. Maybe you and your grand-mother can visit the frogs when she gets better.'

'She hardly gets any vacation. And when she does, we usually go to New York to see plays.' I flipped through the book. 'Do you think we might be passing through Castroville? It's the arti-choke capital of the world, it says here.'

'You ever try to sleep on a plane?' he asked.

'No,' I replied huffily. 'But I understand how it is with senior citizens and if you want to nap, please feel free.'

'Maybe I'll do just that, kid,' he said, leaning back against the cushions and shutting his eyes. His chiseled profile was outlined sharply by the circle of blue sky visible through the window beside his head.

With his eyes closed, he smiled.

'Pleasant thoughts?' I asked.

'Those stewardesses your school chum had on his waterbed, you don't see any of 'em on this flight by any chance?'

I was reminded of the words of Gran's and my favorite writer, the incomparable Dorothy Parker: 'She could not laugh at his whimsicalities, she was so tensely counting his indul-gences . . .' That would not happen to me. Someday I would introduce Mr Bloodworth to the works of Mrs Parker. But not until he was ready for them.

2. I was not impressed by Sacramento Metropolitan Airport, a styleless, frantic place, decorated in a most unimaginative color scheme. Abandoning hope of ever finding a redcap, Mr Blood-worth bore the weight of our luggage manfully all the way to the car-rental booths.

For some reason, he selected CalCar. I'm sure that the bru-nette with the white pleated miniskirt behind the counter had nothing to do with his decision.

He patiently filled out a long, complicated rental agreement and handed it to the girl. While her busy eyes leaped over the document, she asked, 'You'll be paying for this with what kind of card, Mr Bloodworth?'

'No card. Cash.'

She blinked at him. 'Oh, I'm afraid we don't handle cash here. Robberies and all.'

'Let me get this straight, honey. You won't take US currency?'

'I'm afraid not,' she said, batting her eyes at him unmercifully. 'But we accept all credit cards.'

'I don't use 'em,' he growled. 'They're the reason the economy is so messed up. How about a check, then?'

Before she could point to the sign behind the desk that answered that question, I took out my wallet and handed her my Gold PacCard.

Mr Bloodworth squinted at me. 'Where did you get a credit card, kid?'

'I've always had one,' I said. 'When I was born, my father opened one of those basic ten-dollar savings accounts for me, and ever since, Golden Pacific Bank has sent me a credit card every year.'

'Jesus,' he said, shaking his head. 'A responsible workingman they turn down simply because he's self-employed, but they automatically send one to a kid? Banks!'

Miss Short Skirt handed me the charge slip to sign, then led us out of the building to a mini-parking lot filled with gnarled and clenched-looking tiny cars.

'These are the Death Cars,' I said in horror.

'What's that?' asked Miss Short Skirt.

'These cars conflagrate on contact. I've read about them in *Mother Jones*.'

'They do what?' the no-brain girl asked.

'They seem a little – ah, small,' Mr Bloodworth noted.

'Well,' the harpy said in a huff, 'if you're willing to pay for your own gas, I can let you have a medium-size Chevy. I think we have one left.'

When we arrived at the automobile, a two-tone gray and tan that we would have to live with, Miss Skirt handed me the keys before washing her hands of us. I tried not to smile at the big man's woeful look.

'Maybe you'd better drive, huh?' I handed him the keys.

He unlocked the trunk, tossed in the luggage.

'Wait,' I said, and rooted around in my suitcase, withdrawing a few items. 'You can close it now,' I told him.

He did, muttering under his breath. Then he slipped behind the wheel. I chose the back seat. 'As long as I rented this car, I think I'd like to be chauffeured, if you don't mind.'

'Not if you're quiet about it,' he said, adjusting the rearview mirror and studying the general activity around us. He backed from the little lot and eased the car into the traffic that was departing the airport with us. He started humming a tune that I think was 'Won't You Come Home, Bill Bailey?'

'Is anything wrong?' I asked.

'Wrong? What makes you think anything's wrong?'

'You hum when you get nervous.'

'I never hum when I'm nervous, and anyway I wasn't humming. You better get your ears fixed, kid.'

His eyes darted from the road to the rearview mirror. Behind us was an assortment of cars, none of them in any way distinguishable that I could see. I settled back against the vinyl and flipped through an itinerary book I'd prepared while still naively trusting the Leonidas family to come through. 'I don't suppose we'd have time to visit the state capitol?'

'Not really.'

'Or Sutter's Fort?'

'We're not even going through Sacramento, Sarah. We pick up Highway Five at this corner and then we're heading north.

You won't be missing much. They tore down most of the great old houses to build a mall and a bunch of highrises.'

'I'd heard the city was kind of nice.'

He shrugged. 'It's not bad. I was trying to cheer you up about missing it, but you're a big girl, you ought to be able to take a certain amount of disappointment.'

I couldn't tell if he was having sport with me, but I was not averse to the 'big girl' designation. We both lapsed into silence as he guided the rental onto Highway 5, heading for towns with names like Zamora and Colusa. California had such exotic-sounding locales.

As we bounced along, the fertile countryside kept changing colors as alfalfa fields gave way to broccoli and almonds, as far as the eye could see.

Mr Bloodworth began humming again as we passed Dunningham. We were now being followed by only a few cars.

Ours speeded up.

'I guess you've spent a good deal of your life on the hunt,' I said, 'accompanied by only your metal steed, traveling vast landscapes on a seemingly everlasting crusade.'

'I don't know as I'd put it exactly that way, kid. But I do spend a lot of time on the road.'

'Alone?'

'Mostly. I sort of like it.'

'But then, when you return to your homeland, there's only more solitude.'

'I could always buy a hamster.' His yellow eyes flicked in the rearview. One car was keeping pace several lengths behind, a silver Ford with tinted windows and a personalized license that read SOTBROS, whatever that meant.

As I studied it, a dashing, cream-colored classic Jaguar convertible whizzed past the Ford and then our car, going full-out.

The driver glared at us and, as he zoomed away, raised a gloved hand with the middle finger showing.

'What's bugging him?' Mr Bloodworth asked, squinting at the departing car.

I tried to change the subject. 'Why aren't you married?' I asked him.

'Huh?'

'I was wondering why you weren't married,' I said. 'An attractive, compassionate, semi-sensitive man like you should have a soul mate.'

'Jesus, kid, could we talk about something else?'

A behemoth of a diesel truck roared down upon us. When he drew alongside, he blasted his horn and almost blew our car off the road. Then he roared away. Mr Bloodworth, his knuckles white on the wheel, stared after him. 'What's going on with these people?'

I pretended I didn't have the foggiest idea. 'If you were to marry –'

'Sarah, I have married. Not once, but three times. The first time was youthful folly. The second time was middle-aged curiosity. And the third – well, the third was, I guess you could say, senile stupidity that took ten years off my life and taught me a very important lesson.'

'Which is?'

'Never to discuss my private life with any woman, regardless of age, religion, or sexual preference.'

'Sexual preference? You mean she was a dike?'

'Please, kid, do us both a favor and change the station. Or maybe I will.' He turned on the car radio and began twisting the dial.

Somehow he found another moldy old record show. A man with a nasal condition was singing about losing his Sugar in Salt Lake City. I waited patiently for another car to pass us by.

It was some low-slung foreign number. Its driver's little capped head barely showed above the windshield. His reaction was amazing. He honked his horn and pointed a gloved finger at me. Mr Bloodworth stared at him and frowned. Then he glanced back at me.

'What're you up to, kid?'

'Nothing.'

Without any warming, he twisted the steering wheel to the right and screeched off the highway at a little town called Arbuckle. He stopped the car at the side of the road and we had a brief discussion, the topic of which is neither important nor relevant to these chronicles.

The discussion over, Mr Bloodworth drove back onto the highway. Immediately I saw the true purpose for his having left it. The silver Ford with the tinted windows was parked on the soft shoulder, waiting for us.

16

1. I didn't mind the guy in the Jag who shot us the finger, nor the semi that nearly ran us off the road, nor the lightfoot in the Alfa who nearly blew his country cap, but it was the laughing cops in the state police wagon that did me in. 'What the hell are you doing back there, kid?'

'Nothing.'

'Don't give me that "nothing".'

I pulled off the highway at the Arbuckle exit, then braked at the side of the road and waited for the shell dust to settle. 'C'mon, kid, give.'

'Could this town have been named for Fatty Arbuckle?' she asked innocently.

'He wasn't the kind of guy they named towns after. Give me what you're hiding behind your back.' I reached over the seat, no longer an easy chore what with the goddamn headrests.

'I read a book that said Fatty Arbuckle was probably innocent of his supposed sexual offense.'

'There is innocent and there is innocent. You're making me real mad, kid.'

She sat there, smiling as if she were getting ready to pick daisies. It was time for a new approach. 'Uh, you gotta excuse me. Sometimes I forget how young you are and I get mad because you behave like a real little girl. Which, of course, you are.'

'I don't . . .' She couldn't finish the sentence. She handed me a book-like object titled *Road Signs*, designed, it said, to make car travel more fun. It consisted of twenty heavy cardboard signs held together by two metal rings at the top. The signs offered suggestions to other drivers, such as 'Suck Eggs, Creep', 'You're a Cutie', 'Let's Neck', 'Get Lost, Nerd', 'Eyes on the Road, Pervert', 'Get Off My Tail', and so on.

'I was bored,' she said.

I shrugged, put *Road Signs* in the glove compartment, and said, 'No harm done.'

'I'm not a little girl,' she said, about a fraction of an inch from bawling.

'Of course you're not,' I said. 'Now let's get going.'

'You forgot your seat belt.'

'I don't use a seat belt, kid. Danger is my business.'

We picked up the highway at the next street. The boys in the gray Galaxy were waiting for us by the side of the road, wondering where we'd gone. I flipped open the glove compartment and took out the road signs. I flashed them a 'Suck Eggs'.

It didn't stop them from falling in behind us. I couldn't figure out their game. The car was not a rental, not with personalized plates that read SOTBROS. If not a rental, then it was waiting for us at Sacramento Municipal. Who knew we'd get off the plane there? Just Flaherty. Maybe there was a car waiting for us in San Francisco, too. Or Santa Rosa, or Red Bluff, or any of the places we might have plane-hopped. That could make the guys state cops, only silver-gray Galaxies are not their style.

More likely we'd been followed to LAX, where somebody used the old cabdriver gag at the airline desk. 'Miss, could you tell me where the guy and the kid went? They left a bag in my cab.'

Then a phone call goes out to somebody to pick us up at Sacramento.

Fine, that meant the guys were either hoods or off-duty local cops, often the same thing, or even weary old private eyes like me. Hell, they could've been anybody and they were arrogant enough to keep an open shadow, the purpose of which is usually to make the shadowed party as nervous as a nun at a rapists' picnic.

'You're humming again,' Sarah said. I was starting to worry about her and whether I could handle those guys in the Galaxy. I turned the radio louder and was rewarded with Big Joe Williams and Basic giving out with 'April in Paris' one more time.

Beyond the fast-food joints and gas stations and the occasional billboard lurked vast, flat farmland, broken by lakes and gorges and creeks and campsites, and in the far distance was the treetop outline of Mendocino National Forest. The whole goddamn state seemed to have been designed for vegetarians and junk-food junkies and recreational-vehicle owners. Since I fit comfortably into one of those categories, I pulled into a DemiBurger franchise, a few miles north of Corning.

'Do we really have to?' the kid asked, looking glumly at the giant neon-outlined figure of Smiling Sammy Soybean.

'We've been at it for nearly three hours. Don't you want a burger or something?'

'But the DemiBurger is half Class Z beef and half soybean. There's nothing real about it. It might as well be made out of fat and sawdust.'

'Then get some fries or something. Or use the rest room while I chow down.'

The Galaxy had parked near the highway at the turnoff, waiting. So far they were just trying to rattle us. I wondered if they had a phone that could change their instructions at any moment. But people don't usually put phones in Ford Galaxies.

'I guess I am a bit peckish,' the girl said, hopping from the car. 'Mmmmm-ahhhhhhh.' She stretched and kicked her legs. 'It's good to move around. You must be all cramped up.'

'I'm used to it, kid,' I said, trying to get my left knee to work.

We hobbled into the joint, where the kid had some kind of chicken deal while I downed two of the fake burgers and a couple of Coorses that our waitress smuggled in from the cooler out back. Our table was near the big front window where I could watch the Galaxy and make sure its passengers stayed in place. Before I polished off the last of my soyburger, I waved it around a little and licked my chops. Just in case the boys in the car had forgotten to pack their lunch.

It occurred to me that they might have forgotten other things. I hustled the kid back to the car and took off as if I had something definite in mind.

I poured it on the few remaining miles to Red Bluff, the Tehama County seat, a pleasant little town on the Sacramento River. I turned off the highway and, at a slightly reduced speed, began navigating through the simple grid layout of the burg.

It was a nice, relaxed, early-summer afternoon in residential Red Bluff, with the palms and cottonwoods protecting the well-kempt lawns from the shimmering sun. The kid said, 'What are you up to now, Mr Bloodworth? Or would you rather keep it a secret?'

'Just giving you a Chinaman's tour of Red Bluff, Sarah,' I said.

'They're still behind us,' she replied.

'So they are.' I adjusted the radio to bring in the last fading signal of Hoagy Carmichael singing 'Ole Buttermilk Sky'.

We spent nearly an hour twisting and turning through the town. The kid saw a couple of museums from the front, St Peter's Episcopal, the City Center, some libraries. The Galaxy kept pace.

When we arrived back at the highway, instead of returning to 5, we headed west on 36, toward Trinity Forest. There were fewer roadside attractions, fewer diners and service stations. I wondered if the boys in the Galaxy got the point yet.

It took nearly an hour and a half to arrive at Peanut, the

goober capital of California. I'd never been to the goober capital before, nor did I know my way around Trinity Forest, but there was a promisingly deserted-looking, unidentified road that cut north through the tall timber.

'This is certainly scenic,' the girl said.

'Yeah. Lovely. Great old trees.'

'Are you purposely giving them the opportunity to attack us?'

'I sorta hope it won't come to that,' I said. 'We're pretty defenseless.'

'You have a gun.'

'Not to speak of. It's in back, in my bag, in three pieces. The airlines frown on passengers who carry guns.'

'Then what is your plan?'

'It comes under the heading of "Waiting Game" in the detective manual. Chapter Seven. Lulling the enemy into false optimism.'

'I think we're the ones being lulled.'

'They might have read the book, too. There's always that chance.'

She looked back as the gray car slunk along behind us, the sun bouncing off it at irregular intervals as the treetops would allow, making it appear to leap forward every few seconds.

'Kid, do you mind if we talk a little about your mom? It might help if I could get some sort of fix on her,' I said.

'I don't have much of a fix on her myself. The short time I lived with her, both with my dad and Gran, I was a very small child and I have no conscious memory of those days. Only vague flashes. Boxes piled high with clothes. New empty rooms. Always moving. I remember the faces of men. Most of them I'd rather forget.'

I'd been avoiding the nits and grits of the situation because I continued to assume that Sarah was an almost typical fourteen-year-old, impressionable and excitable enough to fly into a fit at the thought of her mother shacking up with the kind of weasel who'd turn a buck by maiming and killing dumb animals for the pleasure of sick and/or jaded assholes. But Sarah was in no way typical – at least I hoped she wasn't. And she definitely did not seem to be subject to fits.

'You've seen her with guys,' I said, in my best diplomatic manner. 'Is she – uh, in control of the situation, or –'

'From what I have been able to observe,' she cut in, 'on the odd occasion when Mother has invited me to lunch or dinner with her even odder escorts, I'd say she was the clinging-vine type, who hangs all over the guy, dotes on him. Even when they step on her, like that awful slimo singer. It's probably because she lost her father so early.'

'Uh, yeah,' I said, my mouth dry.

The Galaxy looked as if its driver had come to a hard decision. It was moving up fast. I floored the Chevy and we roared through the little town of Hayfork.

'You think she took your dog?'

'If this Gutierrez wanted Groucho, she would have taken him. Never mind that it was the dearest thing I possessed. Never mind that it was my last link to my father. Never mind that it would be used in a manner both cruel and in –'

She didn't finish and I didn't have the time for any kind words. The Galaxy was trying to snake around our left. Its heavily tinted passenger window was lowering by inches and I thought I saw the barrel of a gun poking through the opening.

I put my foot to, and very nearly through, the floorboard and the Chevy bucked forward, rattling like a notions wagon. Neither car was built for back-road dragging, but ours was newer. We bounced onto Route 3, which was slightly more populated. I'd hoped that the pursuit would have ended by then, but I was getting the feeling that it was not a day when things worked out.

'Duck down, kid!' I shouted, and for once she listened to me.
'Who are they?'

'It doesn't really matter too much at this point.'

I shot past some old bird in one of those baby Caddies and
almost sent him into a gully. He wiggled all over the road, but
the Galaxy made it past him, too, gaining again.

It was a car length behind me. I saw the flutter of a pink silk
shirt and a hand with a gun sticking out of the window. Then
the Galaxy made a few jerky motions and began to die. The son
of a bitch coughed and sputtered and then it just gave up the
goddamn ghost.

That was when they started shooting. Two guys staggered
out of the car. Dark-skinned, but not black. They took professional stances, bent at the knees, and snapped off a few rounds,
aiming low.

The Chevy bucked beneath us and threatened to spin out.
'What's happening?' the girl shouted.

'They hit a tire,' I said, wiggling the wheel and applying the
brakes very gingerly.

The car was dancing a rumba, but I didn't think it wise to
stop too soon. 'This is awful,' the kid noted.

'It's not as bad as if we'd been the ones who ran out of gas.'

'Is that what happened to their car?'

'If you want to tail somebody, you ought to be damn sure
your gas tank is bigger than theirs.'

'Phew – I smell burning rubber.'

'That happens when you ride a flat, kid. Relax. We'll put a
few more miles between us and those *pistoleros* and I'll stop and
throw on the spare. We'll make it into Weed by five or six with
plenty of time to get a line on the fight tonight.'

Only we didn't have a spare. And we didn't hit a service station
until we'd passed Whiskeytown, some fifteen kidney-pounding
miles along Route 299. By then the rim of the busted wheel

looked like an octagon. It took an ageless mechanic with ice-water eyes and skin like jerky and his partially Mongoloid young assistant the better part of two hours to batter it into its original shape and slap on a new Goodyear. While they hammered and cursed, I sat on the Coke machine sipping Dr Zestos, nibbling fritter chips and studying the cars as they whipped by.

The kid shot me accusing glances every bite and swig I took of the poisonous substances. It was a lovely way to spend an afternoon.

The bill for the tire and the labor came to $73.25. The guy with the tanned hide couldn't change any bills, wouldn't take my traveler's check, but he was more than happy with the kid's goddamn credit card.

2. Just after seven, with the sun ducking out of sight for the day, we arrived at the Algonquin Motel on A10, which *Roll Call* had accurately described as being in the shadow of Mount Shasta. The Algonquin consisted of a dull, flamingo-colored brick one-story U, in the center of which was a vacant swimming pool. The old neon sign had given up the ghost of the 'quin' section of the name, leaving a dim 'Algon' and 'No Vacancies' to keep the odd traveler entertained.

A very understated parking area had been set aside in front of a scrub-grass garden. I pulled into a slot next to the only other vehicle, a dusty pea-green pickup.

Before I could get out of the car, the door under a sign that read 'Manager' opened and a khaki-clad youngish fellow with a crew cut shuffled out to meet us. He positioned himself so that I couldn't move the car door without hitting him, and pointed to the sign. 'Just like it says, Jack. No vacancies.'

I looked at the empty lot. 'Everybody at the fight?'

'What fight would that be?'

'The dogs.'

He squinted. 'I wouldn't know about that,' he said. 'A coupla miles up this road you'll run into Selecosta's Lodge. You and your little girl might find a room there, if you're lucky. Cars been coming by here all day.'

The office door opened again and a guy in a green T-shirt, cutoffs and logging boots walked through it. He was wearing a web belt and a holster that was unbuttoned, displaying a gun handle, which he rubbed with his right hand. His head jerked back and forth like a rooster's when it struts.

'What's wrong with your friend?' Sarah asked. 'Brain fever?'

'Cabin fever's more like it. You folks move it, huh?'

'What's up?' the man with the pistol shouted.

'Nothing,' the man in khaki shouted back. 'More tourists.'

'You shouldn't advertise if you don't want business,' Sarah scolded him. She showed him the Algonquin ad in *Roll Call*. He took the magazine, studied the page for a bit, looked at the cover, and tossed it back to her. 'That's an old ad, miss,' he said. 'My buddy and me just took this place over six weeks ago.'

'Trouble?' the man with the gun wanted to know.

'Naw. Lighten up, for Christ's sake.'

'Any idea where the fight's being held tonight?' I asked the man in khaki.

'Naw. You can find that out at Selecosta's. You better get outa here, now.'

I jiggled the shift into reverse and circled back onto the highway. The gun-toter joined his buddy and they both stared at our car until we were well away.

'Do you know what that was all about?' Sarah asked.

I shook my head. 'People are funny, as Art Linkletter made a fortune proving.'

'They were policemen.'

'Oh?'

'And that was a convict motel.'

'A what?'

'A convict motel. California's prisons can't hold all the criminals, so the state bought a bunch of motels where they put the convicts who have only a short time to serve.'

'You been holding out on me, kid? You got an opium pipe bath there?'

'It's true. There are convict motels. I saw it on TV.'

'Oh, sure. Right. You believe everything you see on the tube? *The Incredible Hulk*? All the cops-and-robbers crap?'

'One of the governor's men was on *The Sy Lewis Show* explaining all about it and why we needed to raise sales taxes to build more prisons?'

'More prisons and less TV stations. I'd vote for that.'

'Don't be purposely obtuse,' she snapped. 'There are convict motels and Sy Lewis asked his guest where these motels were and the man said all over the state. Then Sy asked him where they were specifically, and the governor's man said, "Oh, you wouldn't want to upset a lot of nice neighbors, would you?" But people do have a right to know.'

I chuckled. 'Convict motels, eh? You're really something, kid.' I fiddled with the radio and managed to drag in a not-too-distant station playing what sounded like the old Bob Crosby Bobcats' version of 'Ain't She Sweet'.

Ten miles nearer to Weed, Selecosta's Lodge awaited us by the side of the road – a homey nest of log cabins in the midst of renovation. A brand-new cheery neon sign displayed an outline of Mount Shasta in the sunset glow of evening with the light changing colors as it approached the mountaintop.

'It looks like a volcanic eruption,' the kid sneered, negative as always.

A shell drive cut through the buildings to a large lot at the rear where a tiny log cabin was labeled 'Office'. Inside was a comfortable pine-paneled room with scattered oak furniture and an oak reservation desk, behind which a young girl was seated, dividing her attention between a copy of *Cosmopolitan* and a small black-and-white TV where an announcer was browbeating a contestant with the question 'What was the name of Tonto's horse?'

'Scout,' I said.

The girl looked our way and jumped. 'Oh,' she said, 'I didn't hear the bell over the door.'

'Loud TV,' I said.

'I guess that must be it.' She was a tall, pale teenager with long wavy hair that she hadn't bothered to comb in a while. She smiled at Sarah, exposing a set of barbed-wire braces on her teeth, and said, 'Hi, I'm Larue Selecosta. You're checking in?'

I asked if we could have adjoining rooms and she consulted the keyboard. 'I can let you have eight and nine,' she said. 'That's in Cabin E.'

'Pretty busy, huh?' Sarah asked.

'Sure are. Ever since we opened up the new place, business's been real good. And with the convention, this weekend is gonna be wall-to-wall visitors.'

I filled out the little white registration card while Sarah asked, 'How long have you been open?'

'Here, about four months. In the old place, the Algonquin, for as long as I can remember. Maybe twelve years.'

I handed Larue the card, which she ignored. 'Are you sixteen yet?' she asked Sarah.

'Almost,' my fourteen-year-old traveling companion answered.

'Me, too,' Larue confided. 'I can't wait.'

I put my finger on the registration card and moved it back and forth on the desk to catch her attention.

Sarah asked, too casually, 'Why'd you leave the Algonquin?'

'Oh,' the girl replied airily, 'just got a real good offer for it.'

Sarah moved closer. 'From the state?'

Larue got a stricken look on her face and said, 'You know?'

'That it's a convict motel? It sure looked like it to me,' Sarah said.

'You're not supposed to know,' Larue said in a hushed voice. 'That's supposed to be a secret. Folks around here would be madder than wet cats if they found out we let 'em put criminals in the Algonquin.'

Sarah gave me a look of triumph.

'I'd better go get my ma,' Larue said.

I reached over the desk and grabbed her shoulder before she rushed off. 'Hold on a minute, honey,' I said. 'Sarah here didn't mean anything. No use worrying your mom about something that won't be discussed again.'

'But –'

'Why don't you just give us our keys and we'll unpack and you can get back to your reading and watching, or whatever.'

'She'll swear I told you. I told somebody once and she grounded me for a month. No movies. No dates. No fights, either, even though Ironmouth was entered. Ironmouth is ours. Pride of our kennel. After tonight he'll be a grand champion, for sure.'

'Where is the kennel?' I asked.

'Out back, past the cabins.' She turned to Sarah. 'You going to the convention tomorrow?'

Sarah hesitated. I said that we were.

'I hope I can, too,' Larue said eagerly. 'I heard Papa saying something about Hogjaws and Silver Sam being entered. I've seen both of them fight and you couldn't ask for gamer dogs.'

'You sound like you go to lots of fights,' I said.

'Since I was little-bitty,' Lame said. 'Only lately they been leaving me behind to watch the desk here. Pa and Ma and Roberto go and they leave me behind. Pa says the fights are getting a bit rough these days for girls. Lots of guys with guns and stuff.' She looked from Sarah to me. 'Oh, I didn't mean you shouldn't. That's just Pa. He's a mite, uh . . .'

'Conservative,' Sarah finished for her.

'I was gonna say cautious. Anyway,' she said to Sarah, 'if you wanna look at the kennel sometime, I'd be glad to show you. Unless you've seen a professional fighting-dog kennel before.'

'No. I'd love to see it, Larue. Thanks.'

Larue smiled and took our registration card. 'That'll be two hundred,' she said to me. 'In advance.'

My mouth dropped open. 'Don't you have something without the view?' I asked.

'Huh?' Larue replied, frowning.

'He's just making a joke,' Sarah told her. 'He means the price is high.'

'It's for the weekend,' Larue said to me. 'With the convention we do that. A weekend rate, Mr . . .' studying the card, '. . . Mr Bloodworth.'

I endorsed four fifty-buck traveler's checks, which passed Larue's scrutiny. She was sticking them in a drawer under the countertop when the front doorbell tinkled. Larue jerked erect, anxious. Three people walked in – a middle-aged couple with more money than style, judging by their clothes, and a tall, dramatic-looking woman in her late thirties wearing a man's oxford shirt, beige slacks, and her head wrapped in a white turban, the likes of which I had not seen since Maria Montez went west. She was smiling at the short man in the money-green sport jacket and responding to something he had just said. 'Mr Sandhurst, I definitely do not need any samples, thank you.'

'My husband tells every pretty girl the same thing,' said Mrs Sandhurst, a dowdy number in a lime-green jumpsuit.

'Well, my daughter, Larue, will check you right in, folks. Then Roberto will have the van ready to take you to . . .' – she paused, turning to me, one eyebrow cocked – 'to the, ah, contest.'

'You go, Henry,' Mrs Sandhurst said. 'All I wanna do right now is slip into a hot tub and get into my evening meditation.'

Since I had the benefit of Mrs Selecosta's attention anyway, I pushed it. 'I wonder if I could hitch along with Roberto in the van.'

'This is Mr Bloodworth, Mom,' Larue said. 'He and his daughter –'

'Niece,' I corrected. Sarah's eyes narrowed, but she said nothing.

'He and his niece just checked into Cabin E.'

I rattled the keys at Mrs Selecosta in a gesture of friendship.

'You haven't stayed with us before, Mr Bloodworth. I'd have remembered.'

'Likewise, ma'am,' I said, 'especially at these prices.'

She gave me a half-smile. 'Will your niece be going with you tonight?'

'No. Maybe tomorrow, during the day.' I kept my eyes away from Sarah and on Mrs Selecosta.

'If Ironmouth hasn't fought by the time you get there, bet on him,' she said. 'You might just get your money back for the rooms.'

She turned and strode past the counter and through the doorway leading to the rear of the building. Sandhurst watched her go. 'Quite a woman,' he said, almost involuntarily.

'She's enough to make you believe in James M. Cain,' I agreed.

3. The kid sulked the whole while I dumped the luggage out of the rental and into our cabin. She resented my leaving her behind. By the time Roberto honked for me, she was positioned in front of her TV set, staring at a trio of poodle-headed

country singers as if she wanted to scalp them. I didn't bother to tell her goodbye.

Roberto was a cousin of Mrs Selecosta, whose maiden name I discovered was Dulciana Portello, and whose family had a vineyard somewhere in the Napa Valley. Roberto was happy to be away from the valley. He preferred driving people around to picking grapes, the latter being a job for young boys and elderly men and women, but no way for a man of twenty to squander his prime years. Roberto felt it in his bones that his cousin's husband would be devoting more and more time to the dogs and less and less to the motel, which was fine with him. He expected to take over the business before too long, if he worked hard and applied himself. He was short, with a thin body and a ferret-like face that he made more so by cultivating a very lank handlebar moustache.

The Selecostas had stocked the van with booze and beer, and Sandhurst poured himself a very dark highball while I popped the top on a Miller's. 'You from around here, Mr Bloodworth?' he asked.

'The L.A. area,' I said, following him to our seats while Roberto barreled down the highway.

'I'm from San Francisco, myself. Born there, raised there. Made my first fifty million there.'

'Oh? What business are you in?'

'I like to say I'm in sperm,' he said, giving me a jack-o'-lantern grin.

'Sperm?' I asked.

'I had a little company, Mr Bloodworth –'

'Make that Leo,' I said.

'Fine. Leo it is. And I'm Henry. Anyway, Leo, I had this little company that manufactured a doodad that, in layman's terms, keeps the color on a TV set locked in. Simple damn device one of my boys came up with back in the early Sixties just about the time all the networks went to color. Hell, man, I went from a pissant with a tiny electronics plant in Oakland to king of the goddamn valley in less than sixteen months. Nine years ago I said the hell with it all and sold out and retired.'

He took a long pull on the hooch. Roberto flipped on a tape that sounded like two guitars being smashed together in a sleet storm.

'But retirement wasn't for me, Leo. Not by a long shot. That's when I started looking into the sperm market. Bull semen. Cloudy gold, I call it.'

'You sell bull semen?' I repeated, trying to get it straight in my mind at least.

Henry Sandhurst winked a bloodshot eye at me. 'I just started out with bulls. But I'm not a guy who thinks small. I took a look at the big picture, as it were. What's good for the cow is good for the country. Get me?'

'Not exactly.'

'Well,' he said, pouring his drink into one, 'well, you've got your horses, sheep, and, as we shall see in a few minutes, dogs. That's what got me going on this dogfight business. I can really get my rocks off watching a good bout. The better the dog, the better the fight. Everybody's looking for the super-animal.'

I nodded. 'Except for those who are looking for the super-human.'

'Aha.' His red-veined eyes brightened. 'You've hit the nail right on the nubbin, Leo. Superhuman. And how do we get a superhuman, pray tell? Two years ago I created my finest achievement, CGI. Controlled Genetics, Incorporated.'

Roberto swung the van off the highway and down a macadam road postmarked 'Shasta National Forest'. There was a pickup by the side of the road, with two good ole boys in khaki who were enjoying a few beers and checking on the traffic. One of them shone a light at us and waved at Roberto. Roberto waved back and ground the gears getting away, proving what a man he was.

Henry Sandhurst was saying, 'Pasadena, Seattle, Princeton. Evanston, Illinois. Baton Rouge, Louisiana. I've got banks in every one of them cities and a whole bunch in various stages of preproduction all across the country. Human goddamn sperm banks. Filled with giz from movie stars and Nobel scientists and football players. It's amazing how easy it is to get guys to make a deposit when the inducement is right.'

'Artificial insemination, huh?'

He frowned. 'That's a very Fifties term, Leo. Very negative. *Artificial* is a no-no word. *Controlled genetics* sounds so much nicer, don't it? Hey, you know, I like to tell people I'm into a whole new kind of designer genes.'

'That's very droll, Henry,' I said, watching Roberto enter a more secluded section of the forest. We'd begun to pass parked cars and buses and trucks. Benzes and baby Caddies and VWs and Pintos and Jeeps. A very democratic gathering.

Henry was a bit peeved by my lack of enthusiasm over his exciting new money-maker. With an edge to his voice, he asked, 'And what do you do to pay the bills, brother?'

'I'm a surgeon. Specialize in vasectomies. We're expanding into animals. Get that Beverly Hills doghouse business,' I added with a wink.

He bought it, which was fine with me. I had other matters on my mind. Roberto had braked in front of a small auditorium surrounded by a copse of tall trees. About a hundred yards farther on, a baseball diamond looked sad and lonely in the moonlight.

Roberto killed his lamps. He popped open the front door. 'I'll be right here when you're ready to split,' he said. 'We got about fifteen more guests inside, so maybe I'll be running a bunch of them back. But I'll be here for you, too.' He pointed at the cooler. 'Might as well take a drink with you. They get an arm 'n' a leg for 'em inside.'

'I've come to spend money, boy,' Henry Sandhurst told him. 'Not to save it.'

Roberto seemed happy that I left the van with a beer in each hand. I had to stick one in my pants pocket to get at my wallet at the door, where a big-jawed baldy in undershirt and black Levi's waited for me to lay $20 on his callused palm. He stuck the bill into a black metal box.

'Is Gutierrez here?' I asked him.

'Goo– what?'

'Danny Gutierrez,' I said, staring at a nose full of blackheads.

'Sounds like a spic. Spic'd have to be a damn fool to come here. The boys get their blood up, you know.'

'Is there somebody here from Old Dominion Management?'

'That'd be Eddie Charteris, Slick,' he said, his eyes shifting to an arriving crowd of yahoos. 'He's inside. Sharp-looking feller with a leetle moustache. If I see him, I'll tell him you're looking for him, Mr . . .'

'Slick'll do,' I told him.

The building was a gym with a basketball court, grandstands, and a track around the upper area where fight fans lined up for a bird's-eye glom of the matches. As high as the ceiling was, the place was cloudy with cigarette smoke and smelled of it, cheap booze, sweat, and something stronger and nastier. There were about six hundred people, all of them white. Men mostly, but more women than I'd expected. Out-of-touch chauvinist me.

I pulled the pin on a Miller's and threaded my way through the crowd to its center where a boxlike pit had been constructed out of plywood. Each of its sides was about five yards long and a shade less than a yard high. A rug covered the hardwood basketball floor, but I couldn't tell if it was to protect the dogs from the floor or the floor from the dogs.

The crowd was as noisy as central lockup on a full-moon night. And about as ugly. Faces were flushed, wet with sweat and bloodlust. Hands held drinks or money or cigarettes. Some of them smoked dope. Some were popping pills with their beer. Some appeared to be English professors in tweeds. Others were farmers in bib overalls, women in slacks or evening gowns. A butcher had come straight from the market, still wearing a blood-smeared apron. Some, you couldn't tell where they'd come from or where they thought they were going.

They were calling for the fourth and final fight of the night. The Selecostas' pride, Ironmouth, which, according to 'Just Pete', a deep-voiced, skeletal expert on my left, was a throat dog that had ripped the underneck off its opponent in the previous match. In the second match, a reddish bull named Snapper had curred out. But as my new friend gleefully informed me, the owner had bowed to the desires of the crowd and blown the 'yaller dog''s brains out in front of them all. 'Almos' better'n a fight,' he told me. 'Sometimes they just set the dog loose. But that could fuck things up if he mated with some other dog. You got to get rid of them cowardly animals right away, keep the breed strong.'

When Henry Sandhurst passed by, I introduced him to Just Pete and they took to each other like long-lost brothers in blood lust. I excused myself and, as I continued to stroll among the sports lovers, a wiry little guy in a white shirt and black slacks hopped into the pit, snapping the crowd to instant attention. He was the referee. He was followed by the breeders and seconds and the animals, a white bull named Majesto and a brindle answering to Deathboy.

By the time I'd circled the pit, not seeing anyone who even remotely resembled a handsome moustached fellow named Charteris, each breeder was straddling his dog, in opposite corners of the pit, holding him tight by the nape of the neck and grabbing a handful of skin along the back. The referee, a man with more guts than sense, stood between them in the center of the pit, shouting some mumbo jumbo about Louisiana Rules.

Sandhurst made a thousand-dollar bet on Deathboy. 'It's a very even match,' he told me. 'Both are game dogs who've won four matches apiece. The winner will be a grand champion. He'll retire and maybe do some work for me.'

'What's that in the ref's hand?' I asked. It looked like a knife carved out of wood.

'It's a breaking stick,' Sandhurst told me, as if everyone should know. 'It's – well, a sort of knife carved out of wood.'

'What's it for?'

'To pry a dog's mouth open.' He chuckled. 'I've seen 'em break like kindling. Those animals weigh less than fifty pounds, but they could gut a German shepherd weighing three times that much. The shepherd has no jaw strength. Now, if we could breed an animal with the size of a shepherd and the –'

His dream of a German superdog ended when the referee shouted, 'Pit 'em!'

For one brief second there was silence in the auditorium. And stillness. Then the referee leaped to one side and the dogs charged, crashing into each other in the center of the pit, going up on their hind legs.

The crowd began to scream, plead, yell, calling their dogs by name. Cursing. Cheering. The dogs were as silent as death, their tails working like out-of-whack metronomes. Sandhurst was muttering, 'Goddamn, goddamn,' over and over again, as if he were angry.

'What's the matter?' I asked.

'That goddamn Majesto is a rider.'

'A what?'

'A rider, you idiot. You see that? He takes hold in the top of

Deathboy's shoulder and he'll stay there until tomorrow. As long as it takes to wear the poor dumb bastard down. Look at 'im. Deathboy still thinks he's got a chance.'

Evidently Deathboy's breeder thought so, too. He'd moved to within inches of the struggling dogs, whispering to his mutt. Majesto's breeder, with a smile on his face, stayed a few feet away, urging the dog to hang in there. 'You're top dog, Majesto. You're on top, old boy. Just hang in there. You can outlast 'em all.'

The crowd continued to scream. Deathboy tried his best to twist his head around, snapping at Majesto's neck, but he couldn't get the proper leverage. After what seemed like hours, but was actually minutes, Deathboy got lucky. Majesto's hind leg slipped on the carpet and the dogs broke apart. Their breeders grabbed them and pulled them to their corners, keeping their heads turned away from the ring.

Blood was flowing down Deathboy's fur, and Majesto's white pelt was spotted with red, too, though it may have belonged to the other dog. Deathboy's breeder, a fat, eager-looking man of middle years, cradled his mutt and crooned to him. Then he proceeded to suck mucus from his animal's nose. All right, they're man's best friend, but man should draw the line somewhere.

'You ever see two bitches go at it, Leo?' Sandhurst asked.

'Not that I recall.'

'They're even gamer than the males. Bloodthirsty little bitches.'

I opened my second beer and was about to hit it when I spotted Charteris. He was standing at the far end of the crowd, with a moustache and a matinee-idol profile, as advertised. Beside him was a woman with platinum hair who was either a hooker or liked that look.

He came toward me through the crowd, which seemed to

part in front of him. The woman stayed where she was. He asked, 'You looking for me?'

'Right,' I said. 'I'm –'

'I know who you are,' he cut in. 'Follow me.'

He turned and led me back through the crowd. A big guy in Levi's and a purple shirt, built like a sidecar, moved in between us. As if by accident, his V-shaped back separated me from Charteris. I tried to move past him on the right and he wheeled around. He had a small head for so large a body. He also had a handful of rolled quarters.

I barely saw his fist and then I didn't see anything else. I felt myself flying backward in a hail of shiny quarters. There were faces staring down at me – male and female. Judging by their anxious, maybe even sadistic, expressions they might have been watching the dogs. Except for two. One was a very handsome red-haired woman who seemed worried. I didn't think I knew her. The other was Charteris, who said through clenched teeth, 'You got a bad name-dropping habit, pal.'

And that was that.

4. When I woke up, there was no crowd, no noise. Just a pale white ceiling shimmering in fluorescent afterglow. I felt light-headed, as dreamy as a prom kid on Quaaludes.

Somewhere in the room, men were talking. I was too relaxed to move my head to look at them. 'I can only go so far with you on this,' one of them said.

'You'll go as far as I tell you,' the other replied. 'Don't start pretending you're a virgin.'

'I still have nightmares about that. No matter what the cause, a man should never take another man's life.'

'Since when did you get Born Again, Corvan? Cut the crap. The idea is to do this asshole before he does us. It'll be just like those Save-the-Dog sneaks. Grunt'll stick around to help you with the mutt after you feed it the green dragons.'

'I can't do this.'

'Sure you can, baby. I've seen you in operation. You're a guy doesn't mind a little blood on his apron.'

Their voices made me smile. I wondered what they could possibly be talking about.

17

1. I've never liked watching television away from home. In a city the size of New York, one would think it would be terrific. But a few years ago when Gran and I were in Manhattan – ostensibly for her to promote *Look to Tomorrow*, but actually for her to see old friends and visit old places – we stayed at a charmingly seedy hotel named the St George, overlooking Central Park. I absolutely loathed the television at the St George because it was so snowy and vague. And the local shows were populated by perfectly dreadful, aggressive types who all but foamed at the mouth trying to be witty and chic. I was forced, instead, to spend vast hours at the window, looking down at the park, which, I must say, was not without its diversions.

At least Selecosta's Lodge had newer sets than the St George (better plumbing, too, now that I think of it), and there was a cable hookup that brought San Francisco stations in as clear as crystal. Gran has constantly fought me on the cable thing at home. She says it is against the American system of free enterprise. First they destroyed the neighborhood grocery store with the bloody supermarkets. Now they're doing away with free television. Actually I suspect that if Gene Sokol were to sell *Look to Tomorrow* to cable, Gran's attitude might shift somewhat. Regardless, that evening, left to my own devices by the chauvinistic Mr Bloodworth, I settled in for an assortment of strange amusements, most of them sexually oriented.

I was sitting in shocked contemplation of Howard Phelps's *Love Bazaar* – in which one Howard Phelps, a sad little man with a sallow, blue-whiskered face and a portable TV camera, confronted men and women along San Francisco's Market Street and talked them into accompanying him into a nearby apartment-house hallway where he offered them money for their clothing until, not infrequently, they wound up standing there starkers – when there was a knock at my door. I clicked off the set and peeked through the eyehole in the door. It sounds like a simple thing, but they invariably put those holes much too high for the average young person, who really needs them, to use without straining and hopping.

I removed the chain from its slot and opened the door.

'Hi,' Larue Selecosta said. 'I thought that since your uncle went to the fights, you might want some company.'

'I was just watching TV.'

'Oh?' she said. 'Howard Phelps?'

'Yes,' I admitted warily.

'I used to watch him all the time,' she said, rolling her big brown eyes, 'but it's the same thing over and over. Mom says it's all fake anyway, that those people he interviews are porno actors or exhibitionists and not just people. Bor-ring. Later they show some very, very gross movies, where they do the deed and everything. But I guess you get all of that in L.A.'

'No,' I told her. 'Penetration is not allowed on TV in L.A. It's self-censorship.'

'Pene-what?'

'Doing it.'

'Oh? Cripe, I thought that'd be all you'd get down there. Anyway, there's time before the movie to see our kennel, if you want.'

'I'd like that. It's more fun than old Howard Phelps, I bet.'

'For sure.'

I rummaged around for the cabin key, shoved it in my jeans pocket, put on my teal-blue jacket, and followed her out. I stared at the dark room next to mine. 'How much longer will the dog fights last?' I asked her.

She shrugged. 'Hour, maybe. Hard to say, because you never know how long the animals will keep going, how game they'll be. Daddy's come in at two, three in the morning some nights.'

Most of the cabins we passed were dark. Evidently everybody was at the fights. But us, of course. I hoped that Mr Bloodworth was enjoying himself.

The kennel was a goodly distance from the cabins, more for reasons of odor, though there was only a slightly doggy smell, than for noise, since the dogs were uncommonly quiet. Their high chain-link cages were laid out in the form of a resting cross, four of them, one empty now, with what looked in the dim light of a sentry bulb like green canvas covering three sides of the cage so that the poor animals couldn't see each other. Their cages were big, clean, and sterile-looking. They reminded me of pictures I'd seen of prison cells.

Larue introduced me to the dogs, which she called 'animals'. 'There's Li'l Bit,' she said, indicating the smaller of the three, a brindle-colored beast stretched out with its chin on its paws. 'He's in keep now, in training, which is why we've been giving him a special pro-mix food. It makes him a little wired, but Daddy says that's OK. He'll be fighting next weekend up near Yreka.'

'How many fights do they have around here?'

'Oh, there's rolls all the time. Practice matches. And conventions at least once a month. And fights in between. When we first got into it, maybe six or seven years ago – I was real little then – it was an occasion. But it's been growing and growing, till now I believe Daddy puts in more time with the animals than he does with us or the customers.'

'Does he make a lot of money with it?'

'If he wins, which he probably will tonight. I heard him tell my mother that Ironmouth had already paid for all this and the other three animals. There's a lot of money in stud fees. Li'l Bit is almost too small, but he's got a lot of power. And he is game. Do you have animals where you live?'

'One. A bullterrier. British, though. Not like these.'

'These all come from the British,' Larue said. 'But they been bred bigger and tougher, with stronger jaws. See that rope hanging from the top of Li'l Bit's cage?'

I nodded.

'Well, he hangs from that by his jaws. Strengthens the bite and builds up the neck muscles. He weighs in at a little under forty pounds, which is light, but he could make hamburger out of a big ole shepherd.'

We moved to another cage, where a white bull lay on its side, its head away from us and the light. I asked, 'Do they ever use British bulls in fights?'

'Not around here,' she said. 'That wouldn't be very sportsman-like. They might use 'em for rolls, just to give a champion a work-out.'

'Oh.'

'That there's Mrs Ironmouth. She's carrying right now, so before long we'll be needing a few more cages, unless Daddy sells 'em. Bitches put on a real good fight, too. They can stand more pain.'

I winced. 'Don't you just hate to think about your – animals getting hurt and maybe killed?'

She tossed her head airily. 'Not if they behaved honorably. I'd absolutely want to run inside and hide if an animal of ours curred out and refused to fight. But that's not likely. Look at Spam over there,' she said, pointing at the third cage where a red bull sat on its haunches, staring at us. A clean white bandage was wrapped around his right rear leg.

'Spam? That's a weird name.'

She grinned. 'Daddy says it's because he's all solid-packed meat. Spam went up against a leg dog last month. That's a rough one because the artery in the hind leg is easy to get at. Especially if an opponent is naturally so inclined.'

'That's what a "leg dog" means?'

'Right. It's nothing you can teach 'em. Some are neck dogs or face dogs. It's the thing they feel best about going after. Anyway, this leg dog bit a hole in Spam's back leg and the blood wouldn't stop. So he's a poor ole loser of a dog. Some breeders would've killed him, but Daddy doesn't blame him because he had the bad luck to come up against a leg dog.'

'That's most kind of your daddy,' I said, trying to keep the sarcasm to a minimum. Not that it wouldn't have been lost on Larue. She was too busy being Lady Dogfight.

As we passed an odd-looking treadmill contraption that was mud-spattered and rusted, I asked her about it. 'Oh, that's something Daddy bought when he was just getting into dog breeding.'

'Doesn't look like you use it much.'

'Well,' she said, frowning, 'that says it all. You see, this feller came by and sold it to pa. One day Jim Beaufort, who's from Louisiana, visited us and saw Ironmouth running on the treadmill and he began to laugh and he told Pa, "Why, Joe, I thought you were raising a fighter here and not a goddamn greyhound." Pa had to laugh, too, once he realized the silliness of it all. But he's never stopped looking for that black dude who sold him all the junk.'

'Black dude?'

'Yes. A big black guy who dresses like a cowboy, but very fancy-like.'

'He doesn't sound like he'd be too hard to find.'

'Around these parts, he is,' Larue said.

I led her back to the cages and hunkered down near the infirmed Spam with his sad dog's eyes. 'You said earlier that your father didn't let you go to the fights very often because they'd gotten too rough. Rough how?'

'Oh, a bad element, I guess. You know that whenever there's any kind of money to be made, sort of – well, outside of the law, so to speak, there's people who want to cut themselves in on it.'

'You mean like the Mafia?'

'Like that, yes.'

'Italian hoods with guns and all of that?' I asked in wonder.

'Not exactly. But gangsters, certainly. And there was something that happened last year . . . Anyway, I don't go to the fights. But I'll be going to the big day tomorrow. You should get your uncle to take you.'

I said I'd ask him. 'About these gangsters . . .'

She kicked the dirt with her sneaker and turned away. 'I'd as soon not talk about that,' she said.

'Something happened, huh? Maybe they hurt somebody?'

She looked around and, satisfied that we were alone, told me in a hushed voice, 'There was this feller from the SPCA. A policeman, sort of, only he was in plain clothes and he didn't tell anybody who he was. He got himself killed. They said a dog tore him apart. But Pa said a dog wouldn't do that under normal conditions. He thought it was real suspicious.'

'What'd the police say?'

'Oh, they didn't appreciate some guy coming in here trying to do their business for them to begin with. I don't suppose they cared what killed him. Fact is, nobody much cared, not when it turned out the feller was here to put an end to the fights. But Pa decided it was time for me to stop going so much.'

'That's awful,' I said.

'Right enough,' she replied. 'I love the fights.'

'I mean about the dead man.'

'Oh, that, too.'

'Who do they think did it?' I asked.

'The dog was named Barney. Dr Corvan – he's the vet around here – he put Barney to sleep. Barney had never attacked anything before except other dogs. And kittens, of course.'

'I mean who do they think was behind it all?'

'Oh, there's this feller, Mr Charteris. He's the representative of the bad element. Only comes to town for the conventions.'

'You sure his name wouldn't be Gutierrez?' I asked.

'Is that Chicano?' she asked.

'Spanish, at least,' I said.

She smiled. 'Well, I hardly think Pa or the rest would be doing business with a Chicano. We don't have the tolerance toward Chicanos you have in the southern part of the state.'

'It's a wonder you let them drive along your freeways.'

'If there was a way to stop 'em, I suspect we would.'

At that I stood up, dusted off my Levi's, and told Larue goodnight. I'd had my fill of her and her dreadful ignorance. God knows, life is short enough; we shouldn't have to waste too much of it on bigoted fifteen-year-olds.

2. It was nearly 1:30 when someone knocked on my cabin door. I'd fallen asleep watching *Love Me Fast Before I'm Thirty*, a dreadfully gamy little movie in which fellatio played a large part. When the knocking woke me, a whole new cast of characters were going through the same basic motions on the TV screen. I clicked it off and opened the door to an anxious Larue and a perplexed little guy with the mustached face of a weasel. It was her second cousin, Roberto. I didn't much like the look of him, so I took a step outside the cabin rather than invite them in.

'What's up?' I asked Larue.

'Roberto came back a while ago from the fight,' she said. The weasel nodded his head.

I glanced over at Mr Bloodworth's still-dark room. 'Your uncle wasn't with him,' Larue said quickly.

'What happened?' I asked, trying to keep the panic out of my voice.

'I am not so sure, exactly,' Roberto said. 'I think he insulted a lady and a man hit him. A very large man.'

'He would have had to be very large,' I said. 'Where is Mr – my uncle?'

'That I couldn't say precisely.'

'Tell her the rest,' Larue prodded him.

'The lady was with Mr Charteris. He got this large man to carry your uncle away from the fights.'

'Carry him where?'

Roberto hesitated. There was a sudden burst of laughter, glasses clinking, from the direction of the office. Roberto shied from it. 'I should not have said anything.'

He looked at Larue accusingly.

'Roberto recognized the car that the Charteris feller was driving, a nice white Mercedes, parked in front of Dr Corvan's hospital. I bet that's where they took him.'

I was silent, trying desperately to think of what I should do next. 'Could you drive me there, Roberto?' I asked.

He gave me a down-the-nose look. 'No way, little babe. This boy don't mess with Charteris for any reason.'

There was more laughter, then Mrs Selecosta's voice shouting for Roberto. He looked relieved to hear it. 'Got to get some ice or booze or something. Big victory night for them.' He backed away, then ran toward the office.

'I'm really sorry about your uncle,' Larue said, as if he were dead already. 'What're you going to do now?'

'Where's that hospital?' I asked.

'It's a veterinary clinic, just off the highway on A10. You can't miss it, but it's too far to walk. And anyway, it's not a good place to be just now.'

'But my uncle's there,' I reasoned.

'Maybe they're just, you know, fixing him up so he can get back here.'

I stared at my cabin. 'I'm going to call the police,' I said.

'Won't do much good,' she said. 'There're only three of 'em and they're over at the victory party at the office right now, drunk as skunks. They were at the fight when Charteris took your uncle. They were there when they took that SPCA man, too.'

'What about the highway patrol?'

She shrugged. 'You ever try to get a policeman to listen to anything a kid says? Anyway, maybe your uncle and Charteris are friends or something. You could look like a real silly if you went busting in on 'em with the highway patrol.'

Dammit! I thought. Dammit, dammit, dammit.

Larue must have thought I was fusing out or something. She began to back away. 'I figured you should be told, anyway,' she said, 'about your uncle.'

'Thanks, Larue. I appreciate it.' I wasn't thinking about her at all. She gave me a little wave and ran off to join the party.

I went into the cabin, unlocked the connecting door, and entered Mr Bloodworth's room. It didn't take me long to find the car keys. They were on the bed. I'd have found them immediately if he hadn't put his suitcase on top of them.

3. Fortunately there was a little booklet in the glove compartment that told me all sorts of important things, like where you put the key to turn on the engine, and how by pressing a button near the floor you can elevate the seat to a height at which you can at least see over the dashboard.

Oh, God, it seemed so hopeless. Only the thought of poor Mr Bloodworth in danger gave me heart to continue.

I turned the key in a clockwise direction. There was a convulsive motion, then nothing. I consulted the manual. I pressed my foot down on the gas pedal, held it, then released it. I turned the key again. This time the car jumped and something caught. The engine rumbled, then hummed loudly. I pulled the knob marked 'Light' and it came off in my hand. It was the cigarette lighter. Driving was no breeze, that's for sure.

I found the 'Lights' knob and used it. Headlamps blazed out illuminating the front of Mr Bloodworth's empty cabin. I looked down at the automatic gear device. I was in 'P'. I took a deep breath and threw the car into 'R'. To my chagrin, it shot back. I jammed my foot on the brake, stopping the car within inches of a nice quiet two-toned brown car parked behind me.

Perspiring freely, I eased the lever into 'D', which the manual informed me would put me in a forward motion. Keeping my foot on the brake just in case, I crept forward, turning the wheel until I was aimed at the front drive. Then I took my foot off the brake.

The car moved forward slowly. The hum of the engine was sort of comforting. I gave it some gas and drove out of Selecosta's Lodge and away from its dippy, erupting-volcano neon sign.

On the highway my fear lost out to the exhilaration of actually controlling an automobile. It was speed, freedom, independence, and power, all on four wheels. Driving was infinitely better than skating. I was so caught up in it that I almost forgot the purpose of my journey and slightly overshot the A10 turnoff.

I shoved my foot on the brake and the car spun crazily to the left, right into the path of an oncoming truck of such size and proportion that I still shudder to think of it. It was like a steel

Moby Dick bearing down on a poor little minnow of a Chevy. I killed the engine, of course. All I could do was sit there and brace myself for the crash.

The semi waited until the very last moment; then, with a great gust of wind that rocked the car and the terrifying blast of a clarion from hell, it easily drove around me. I thought I heard laughter as its red taillights disappeared into the distance, leaving me drained and ashen and totally fed up with this driving business.

There was no other traffic, so I took my time getting back to the alternate road. Before I could make the turn, the white Mercedes Roberto had mentioned approached the intersection and paused briefly. I couldn't see the driver, but I got a good look at his passenger, a woman with metallic blond hair who squinted as my headlights illuminated her side of the car.

The Mercedes' driver didn't wait for me to turn. He wheeled onto the highway and roared away toward Selecosta's Lodge and points south.

The urge to follow the car was strong, but not strong enough to make me forget Mr Bloodworth's peril, so I nosed the Chevrolet onto A10 and drove along it slowly, looking for Dr Corvan's clinic.

There was not a great deal of commerce that near the turnoff – a darkened gas station; a bait place where you could buy hunting and fishing permits; a discount shoe store named Heel 'N' Toe; and a white, seemingly windowless concrete square with block lettering that read: Dr John L. Corvan, Animal Hospital. Two cars were parked in front.

I drove past the cars about a hundred yards to where the trees and underbrush had yet to be mowed down in the name of progress. Heel 'N' Toe, indeed.

I parked the car just off the highway, which sounds easy enough but was in fact an ordeal, especially when the shell-and-gravel shoulder gave way and the car nearly slid down into a deep drainage gully. We were on such a slant that I couldn't open the door on my side. Instead, I slid over, let the passenger door swing open, and dropped nearly four feet to the bottom of the gully. There was the chance that the car would come tumbling down on top of me, but I preferred not to hold on to such negative thoughts.

I approached the 'hospital' through the woods. There was a door at the back of the concrete square and several windows, the purpose of which, I assumed, was to give Dr Corvan a clear view of his patchy yard area where many species of animal were housed in rows of cages. One of them was howling at the moon. The others were mildly restive.

The chain fence surrounding the yard seemed abnormally high, but it was not unlike a schoolyard fence that I had mastered time and again. If your feet can fit inside the links, it's just a matter of not losing your head when you reach the top. In this case there was a row of barbed wire, and I was forced to drape my blue jacket over it.

I tried not to make much noise, but the dogs began to stir as my feet hit the ground. A few barked. I looked at the building. Dim lights glowed through the rear windows. As I moved closer, a naked bulb flashed on and the back door opened.

I ducked behind a nearby tree and waited.

A fellow bigger than even Lou Ferrigno stepped into the yard. He was dressed in a purple polo shirt and tight pants. He was one of those peaheads, like the villain who gives Popeye so much trouble. His face was red and raw-looking, as if it had been worked on by a meat tenderizer. He called back into the building, 'Hey, Corvan, these mutts can tell something's in the air. C'mon out and pick the lucky dog.'

A thin, balding man in a white smock left the building, reluctantly. He was a black man with a prominent nose and little gold-rimmed glasses that rested on it. 'I really don't want to do –'

'Come off it, doc. Cut the crap, huh? Let's just get the job done. Find us a killer dog.' The big man paused by one of the cages. 'Gawdamn. What's this bugger?'

'Hmmm . . . let me see . . . oh, a timber wolf. Bill Slater caught him up near the Oregon border. Don't know why he didn't just kill him.'

The big man grinned. 'Maybe he's gonna put him up against Ironmouth.'

'Quite impossible,' Dr Corvan answered. 'You can't train him. We're waiting for his leg to heal from the trap. Then Slater is going to set him free.'

'This Slater sounds like a fucking idiot.' The big man picked up a branch and poked at the timber wolf, which charged against the cage.

Dr Corvan was almost as agitated. 'Please don't, Grunt. He's difficult enough to handle. And we don't want to upset the other animals unduly.'

'They's upset enough,' the brute said, poking the branch at the wolf once more.

Actually, that branch seemed like a good idea. There was a nice one, as thick as a baseball bat, near my foot. I bent down and drew it toward me.

'Whoo-eee, he's a tough-enough sucker,' the big man said, backing away from the cage. 'Well, which one of these doggies's got a treat in store?'

The vet pointed to a cage near the bottom of the first row. The big man hunkered down on his haunches and stared into it with some skepticism. 'Seems kinda quiet.'

'He shouldn't be any trouble,' Dr Corvan said.

'Then you get him out,' the appropriately named Mr Grunt replied.

Dr Corvan shrugged, and bent over and unhooked the latch. Mr Grunt danced back a few steps. The black vet reached into the cage and began to coax the dog out.

'C'mon, old boy. C'mon, Fireball, old boy.'

Mr Grunt snorted. 'Some Fireball.'

Finally a gray bullterrier stepped charily from the cage. Dr Corvan grabbed him by the scruff and back and said to Mr Grunt, 'You'd better get the poor fellow.'

'Please, doc, don't get so goddamn sentimental. It's him or us, remember.'

The yard light went out after he entered the building. The moon was evidently bright enough for whatever they had in mind.

When Mr Grunt returned, he was carrying Mr Bloodworth over his shoulder as if he were a feather pillow. He had a small sack in his free hand. 'Well?' he asked.

Groaning, Dr Corvan lifted Fireball awkwardly and started carrying him in my direction. I slunk back and pressed against the rough bark of the tree.

Mr Grunt dropped Mr Bloodworth on the ground roughly, not five feet away from the vet and the dog. I was amazed to see that Mr Bloodworth's yellow eyes were open. He was awake, but there was an awful slack look to his mouth. I wondered what these fiends had done to him.

He stared at Fireball. 'Nize doggy,' he slurred.

'You think so, huh?' Mr Grunt said with a snicker. He opened the sack and took out – I find it hard to recall this experience – took out pieces of animal, pelt still bloodied, hunks of meat. He started toward Mr Bloodworth with them.

Fireball picked up the scent or something, because he went rigid.

Dr Corvan said, 'Hold on, Grunt. First things first.' He removed a hypodermic needle from his smock pocket.

'That's gonna send the mutt into outer space?'

'It's a powerful amphetamine,' Dr Corvan said. 'I don't like doing this on the clinic grounds.'

'Now, doc, like Charteris told us, it's a real simple – ah, what was the word?'

'Scenario.'

'Right. Scenario. This guy is snooping around your cages, he accidentally sets Fireball there free, and the poor dog goes into a frenzy and takes him apart.'

'Nize doggy,' Mr Bloodworth repeated.

Dr Corvan squirted a few drops of the liquid amphetamine into the air. 'It should take about thirty seconds to become effective. By then you'd better have that – ah, material on him and away from you.'

Mr Grunt reached down into the bag. 'This really gonna work?'

'It did before, God help me,' Dr Corvan said. 'Be sure you place it near his throat.'

Mr Grunt reached his arm out to Mr Bloodworth, holding the bloody pelt. I shouted 'No!' and stepped out from behind the tree with my branch-bat poised.

Dr Corvan was straddling Fireball, holding his neck with one hand and about to apply the hypodermic with the other. He twisted his head toward me just as I swung the branch at his face, shattering his glasses, and for all I knew, his nose and cheeks. He screamed and fell back as the dog raced from his arms toward Mr Grunt and Mr Bloodworth.

Mr Grunt had enough presence of mind to toss the pelt away, but the dog hit him all the same, knocking him onto his back.

I rushed to Mr Bloodworth, who was sitting up and looking at the tableau in the moonlight as if he were enjoying it. 'C'mon,' I said, trying to pull him to his feet.

Mr Grunt and the dog were rolling over in the leaves and

earth. Dr Corvan's dark hand covered his face and blood was beginning to trickle down over it. 'It's now or never,' I told Mr Bloodworth.

He tried to stand, but his legs wouldn't support his body. He tumbled again to the ground. There was a horrible snap behind me and Fireball emitted his first sound, a death yelp. Mr Grunt had broken the animal's back! He tossed the dog aside and turned his head slowly until he caught me in his piglet eyes. There was blood on his face and arms, and gashes and cuts. But he didn't seem to be at all affected by them.

'What the hell are you, I wonder?' he asked without emotion, moving slowly to his feet.

Mr Bloodworth was entirely useless, poor man. 'Sarah?' he called, helplessly trying to right himself.

I backed away toward the hospital as Mr Grunt advanced. He took his time. He knew he could outrun me, I suppose. As he passed Mr Bloodworth, that gallant man grabbed for his legs and got kicked in the head for his trouble.

There was only one thing to do. I pretended to stumble and fell back, grabbing a handful of dirt and leaves. Mr Grunt moved closer, grinning now, with blood dripping off his chin. When he was close enough, I jumped up and threw the dirt into his face. He snarled, wiping his eyes. By the time he cleared them enough to see, I was on my way.

He naturally thought I was headed for the clinic, where I might escape. But that would have left him out there with poor Mr Bloodworth. I ran for the cages instead.

Still wiping his eyes, the big man charged the back door. When he got there, he looked around, puzzled, staring at me across the yard. He began walking toward me, slowly. He was grinning.

I let him get near enough. Then I opened the timber wolf's cage.

Mr Grunt was pretty surprised, but he didn't have much time to think about it. The wolf went for him, snarling and growling. Dr Corvan had done a fine job on the animal's leg. It worked as good as new. Mr Grunt screamed and raced for the door to the hospital, but the wolf fell upon him before he could make it.

I turned away and ran back to Mr Bloodworth. Dr Corvan was on the ground beside him, his hand still to his eyes, moaning about the Angel of Wrath. Mr Bloodworth, who seemed to be rallying, told him that I was indeed a wrathful angel, and that he should never forget it.

Using a tree for support he managed to stand upright. 'How do we get out of here, kid?'

'Through that door.' I pointed to where the wolf was doing terrible things to Mr Grunt.

'Maybe we ought to let them finish,' he said. 'You better get me something I can use if that animal comes for us next.'

But we didn't have to worry. The timber wolf let loose a bloodcurdling howl and pranced away from Mr Grunt's lifeless body. Its silver-gray head stared at us. Then it turned away. It raced gracefully across the yard, leaped to the top of the cages, and vaulted over the fence. It disappeared into the forest.

Mr Bloodworth staggered forward. He looked from Mr Grunt to Dr Corvan, who was sitting on the ground rocking back and forth and spouting religious gibberish. 'Well, kid,' he said, 'you sure play hard ball.'

4. Somehow we got the car door open and I slipped behind the wheel. Mr Bloodworth waited on the side of the road till I worked the Chevy onto the asphalt. Then he slipped in beside me. He was still dazed. He said, 'I wonder what kind of fairy dust they sprinkled on me?'

'How'd it make you feel?'

'I – I'm not sure. I was out of it. Then I woke up with a kind of rush. Very strong. Then my stomach started flip-flopping and I just mellowed down to a point where I didn't feel like moving.'

'Heroin, maybe,' I told him.

He stared at me. 'Don't start that, kid. Heroin? Jesus! You sure?'

'That's how this boy, Larry Niles, told me it'd feel if I did heroin with him. I didn't, of course.' I applied more gas and we zipped along the highway toward Selecosta's.

'Heroin! Christ, suppose they'd given me an overdose or something?'

'Larry Niles told me it's practically impossible to overdose on heroin alone. Deaths are caused by multiple drug use. Heroin plus something. Usually alcohol.'

Mr Bloodworth winced. 'I had a beer at the dogfight,' he said. 'Who the hell is this Niles character, a pusher?'

'No. He's captain of the Bay High rugby team.'

He put his head in his hands. 'Why do you tell me these things?' he said.

'What things?' I couldn't imagine why anything about Larry Niles would affect him so.

'It's just that – it's goddamn depressing, is what. You depress me, kid.'

'You're not yourself,' I said. 'Later on you'll realize that I just saved your life.'

'That you did. And I won't forget it.' He yawned, nestled his head against the cushion. 'Maybe I'll just take a short nap.'

'You do that.'

A raccoon picked that moment to dash onto the highway and freeze in my headlights. I hit the brake and swerved around the critter. Mr Bloodworth's eyes popped open. 'Hold on here! You're driving? Since when do you drive?'

'Since about an hour and a half ago.'

He sighed and leaned back against the cushion again. 'You want to take over?' I asked.

'Too late for that,' he said.

18

1. Whatever it was they'd pumped into me at that barnyard funny farm, it was slow dying. The kid had to help me out of the car and up to the door of my cabin. I was as wobbly as a waltzing giraffe. Sarah led me inside the cabin and turned on the light.

'Chain the door,' I told her. 'These people are raving goddamn loons about their favorite pastime. And there is no law in Creed.'

'What?' she sensibly asked.

'Don't ask me to explain anything I say under the influence of drugs.' I slumped on the bed and she jammed an ugly redwood straight-back under the doorknob. I rolled over and got my wallet out. It looked more or less intact. My good friend Charteris had said he knew who I was, but did he really know what I was doing there? Was that why he tried to have me killed? Was it because I mentioned the name Gutierrez?

'Roll over and lean back and I'll pull those ugly shoes off for you,' the kid said, looking almost too pleased with herself. She'd done a good night's work, by any standards.

'I'll get 'em,' I said, trying and failing. She yanked 'em off without hesitation. If they'd been tied any tighter, she'd have taken my heels off, too.

'Now get some sleep. You look awful.'

'Thanks. I've been sucker-punched, doped to the gills, and kicked in the chops. If I looked good, I'd be worried.'

'You'll feel better in the morning, when we're back on the trail.'

'What trail?' I asked. 'Whose trail?'

She smiled smugly. 'That Mafia killer, Charteris, and my mother.'

I narrowed my eyes at her, wondering if she was a witch.

'She was with him tonight,' the kid said, reading my thoughts. 'I saw her. She's had cosmetic alteration to her face, but it was her, all right. In a white Mercedes. Heading south in a hurry, away from that awful clinic. I don't think they wanted to be around when your "body" was discovered.'

'You could have followed 'em,' I said.

'It was a question of priority.'

I gave her a smile. 'I'm glad it worked out that way. For what it's worth, she wasn't around when Charteris gave the order to plant me. She probably didn't know anything about it.'

'I hope she hasn't fallen that low. That Gutierrez fellow sounded bad enough. Now she's traded him in on one even worse.'

I shook my head. 'Same guy. Different name. He's lying to these old redneck boys about who he is and who the Old Dominion company is. He's lying to them about everything. That's why he was so bent out of shape about my mentioning his real name. He probably thought I was one of the competition, or some other enemy. For all I know, he might be scamming his uncle and worried about that. He's got a real guilty conscience.'

'Do you think I should call the state police and send them out to that animal clinic?' she asked.

I looked over at the phone. It had a dial, but that didn't mean it couldn't be monitored from the office. We couldn't risk an anonymous call. 'I don't think so, kid. Not if we want to get out of here in the next month or so.'

'But that Corvan is a cold-blooded killer,' she said.

The state cops would get there and find a man who'd been mauled by a wolf, and Corvan, who'd been partially or completely blinded by vandals. There would be no evidence of anything that could be pinned on Corvan. It was not worth our getting involved in the mess.

'He's not the same old Corvan,' I said. 'We'd better settle for that. Now get out of here and let an old man sleep off his dope.'

She wasn't convinced about Corvan, and I was glad she wasn't, but she walked from the room and through the connecting door. She didn't shut it. I heard her slipping the chain lock on her door and fixing another chair in place. With great difficulty I pushed myself onto my feet and got the covers down on the bed. Then I proved what a guy I was by pulling off my pants without falling headfirst onto the throw rug. Huffing even more than usual, I worked into the cool sheets and pulled a coarse wool coverlet over my body and up to my neck. Then I went to sleep.

Sometime in the night, I opened my eyes to find Sarah standing in the doorway between my room and hers. She was wearing a skimpy T-shirt and pink panties. She reached into my room and flicked off the ceiling light, which I'd left burning. She paused, framed in the doorway with the light from her room behind her. She seemed larger, fuller in body. Provocative. I shivered. I was afraid of what I was thinking. I reacted in typical adult fashion. I squeezed my eyes shut and pulled the covers over my head.

When I awoke it was nearly ten in the morning and Sarah had already packed. She was standing by my bed calling my name. I opened my eyes cautiously. She was wearing denims and a pink T-shirt and she looked even younger than usual, thank God. I breathed a sigh of relief and told her to get out of my room. My head felt sore. My mouth was dry. I hoped that the dope, whatever it was, had taken a hike out of my system.

2. Seven messages had been left on my office machine. A very piqued lady slurringly inquired as to why I had not shown up at the Irish Mist on Thursday night to get drunk with her. Office City, the firm responsible for my letterhead – a magnifying glass, within which is my name and business address, all nicely embossed – wondered if I'd be needing a new supply. Not for the next decade, probably, unless the roaches discovered the unopened boxes. A Mrs K. R. tearfully complained that her 'dear friend' was missing again. The last time it had taken me over a week to find her 'friend' clinking pineapples with another elderly lady at the poolside of the Mauna Kea Beach Hotel on the Big Island, and another thirty-six hours to talk him into returning with whatever was left of the $40,000 Mrs R. had invested in his Sleep Machine.

Sarah's grandmother had phoned, the recording of her trained voice assuring me that she had nothing serious on her mind. Only the curiosity of an old lady in a hospital bed with too much time on her hands. She was followed by some unidentified party shouting something rude into the machine. And finally, both Gary Grady and Charles Z. Dotrice had left their home numbers with requests that I use them immediately.

I explained to the operator that I wished to place a few L.A. calls and charge them to my office. She told me that this could be done automatically and gave me an endless pattern of numbers to dial. I replied that hanging on to that many numbers was more than I could handle and would she please put the first call through herself or get the hell out of the business and leave space at the big switchboard for someone who could.

Edith Van Dine's voice sounded considerably sunnier than the last time I'd seen her. Part of that may have been because I'd put Sarah on the horn before we had our chat. For a moment I was afraid the kid would mention the fracas the night before, but I should have known better. She gave the old lady the usual nonsense about how much fun she was having, adding, 'And Mr Bloodworth is teaching me how to be a detective.'

I gave her a crooked smile as she handed the phone back to me. Mrs Van Dine wanted to know where we were, so I gave her a rough idea, adding that we were heading south. I explained that I didn't know exactly when we'd be returning and she said that was all right, since she'd be in the same place whenever we got there.

She was feeling better; hardly any pain. Just a bit useless. But her producer, Gene Sokol, was having the broken wing written into the script so that she could go back on the show whenever her doc said it was okay, possibly in six weeks.

The calls to Grady and Dotrice were not so cordial. The Eighties' answer to Bob Hope was already at work. He was convinced someone on his staff was undermining his efforts and he wanted the traitor found immediately. I told him I was at the northern end of the state, in the shadow of Mount Shasta, as it were, and it might take me a while to work my way to L.A. I gave him the number of Eddie Gorman, an investigator who is thorough, almost as presentable as yours truly, plus he'd put in time in Vietnam, which I somehow guessed Grady would find comforting.

He still wasn't happy, but at least he'd lowered his voice a few octaves by the end of our conversation.

Dotrice, whom I'd caught midprune in his garden, could not understand how a professional businessman could take off across the country without so much as a secretary to field his calls. He hated talking to answering machines. I inquired if that hatred included his shouting vile things into it and he admitted that he had.

He wanted to see me within the hour. When I finished chuckling at that, I suggested we might meet in Copa de Oro in about three hours. Maybe at a restaurant with a nice garden.

The man was totally without humor. When could we meet in Los Angeles? I asked him how the middle of the week sounded. He replied that the matter was extremely serious. I suggested he give me a hint, and that set him off again. He shouted that I knew damn well what he was talking about, and this time he hung up on me.

The Selecosta family – Dragon Lady Mother; rumpled, pot-bellied Dad; and wan, plain Daughter – watched us from their little office cabin in the pines while I eased the car out of the parking lot. They seemed to be waiting for something. The car to explode. The earth to open up under the front wheels.

More likely they were waiting for the SPCA people to show up with a golden key to set their doggies free and lock *them* in a cage. They'd traveled cross-country to find happiness in northern California and some son of a bitch with a little niece was trying to take it all away.

They were wrong. Sure, they'd stood by and let some bozo cart me off to feed me to the spaniels. But the hell with 'em. Time would settle their hash. The boys who eventually call the shots on outlaw activities would soon elbow in, push a small-timer like Gutierrez aside, and start pulling the strings. They'd order idiots like Selecosta to slow down or speed up their dogs, and Selecosta and his noble sportsmen pals would make a brave show of taking a stand, and one morning they'd awaken to discover that during the night their kennels had been transformed into canine slaughterhouses.

Sarah waved at the little Selecosta girl, but the girl didn't wave back. 'I guess we're the enemy, huh?' Sarah asked me.

'I sure as hell hope so,' I replied.

★

3. Copa de Oro looked like our next destination. Gutierrez had called there from his Marina Inn and it was listed in *Roll Call* as the site of a large weekend match. It was also in the direction that the white Mercedes had been headed, according to the kid. Copa de Oro one hundred and sixty miles south of Mount Shasta, in the heart of the gold-rush country.

The kid nixed breakfast and I didn't like staying around the area so we took off for three hours of uninterrupted highway travel. Sarah amused herself by reading to me from her weird paperback library. 'Listen to this,' she said enthusiastically. 'There's a place right near San Simeon called Dr Tinkerpaw's Castle and it's made entirely of bottles, crates, and old junk. It's a full eight-level building. Look, here's a picture.'

'It'd help if you took that book out of my face when I'm driving,' I said, as even-tempered as possible.

'Could we visit Dr Tinkerpaw's?'

'Maybe, kid. If time is on our side.'

'It says it was built by an old fellow named Art Beal. He's in his eighties and his neighbors think of him as a hippie. Hmmm, I wonder when this book was printed. Anyway, this Beal says he never married because he's a member of the Detergent Club. Do you know what that is?'

'Haven't any idea.'

'It's a club with members who work fast and never leave a ring. Is that supposed to be a joke?'

'To an eighty-year-old codger, most of life is. Or none of it is. Sounds like Beal is a happy sort!'

'I wonder if one could visit the building without having to meet him?' she asked.

It made me feel better that she was back to sounding and acting and, well, looking like a kid again. 'Hungry yet?'

She nodded.

We took the 32 turnoff, going west toward Chico, and almost

immediately approached the gravel parking lot of a barnlike restaurant.

I nestled my car into one of the few empty spaces near the walkway. 'You want to eat here?' she said with disgust.

I looked up at the yellow and red building. The sign said: 'Maude and Jerry's Bad Food Palace'. 'It's a little strange,' I told her, 'but it looks like it's doing a good business.'

'What about that?' she asked, pointing to a sign in the window that read: 'The Worst Cooking in the Great Northwest'.

'It's a gimmick, kid. That way, when they serve pretty good food, it tastes like it's great. It's all promotion and advertising.'

'It's dumb,' she said, slipping out of the car.

'We don't have to eat here,' I said, following her to the door.

'Might as well.'

It was a very large room with a long counter and maybe twenty-five tables, all but one of which were occupied. We made it a full house. An elderly waitress with close-cropped gray hair and a relatively clean gray uniform brought us our menus and informed us, 'The only thing lousier than the food is the service,' and walked away.

'I like this place,' the kid said with a smile.

When she got the opportunity, she ordered a tuna sandwich on whole wheat and let the waitress persuade her to sample the barley soup. I asked for a roast beef sandwich. The waitress said she'd try to find a few slices that weren't too old.

'What are you going to do about Gutierrez and my mom?' Sarah asked when we were alone.

I took my time answering. My immediate desire was to stomp Gutierrez into the sod, but there were several things I wanted to discuss with the woman first. What had been her business with Roy Kaspar? Why had she and her murderous boyfriend taken the kid's dog? How could she have turned her back on her own little girl with no curiosity about how she was doing? Maybe I'd stomp her when I was finished with Gutierrez.

'I'm not sure what to do about them,' I said. 'I want to ask your mom about your dog.'

'I don't think she has Groucho,' Sarah said.

'No?'

She shook her head, sending a few blond strands over her ears. 'If he'd been in the car with them, I'd have known. Without that dear little animal even sticking up his head or barking or anything, I would have known.'

The waitress brought our food. It was good and filling. And cheap. It even passed the kid's nutritional scrutiny. The cashier smiled as she put the money into an ancient cash register. She pointed to a sign over the door: 'Come Back Anytime Your Stomach Can Handle It'.

The kid ran to the car and hopped onto the back seat. 'Nap time,' she said.

'Make it a quick one. We'll be in Copa de Oro in less than an hour.'

As it turned out, neither of us was telling the truth. The kid didn't sleep. Instead, she played that road sign game with our fellow motorists. Some honked. Others shook their fists at me. The hell with them. It was good to see a kid act like a kid.

A few miles past Chico, the divided highway was replaced by a narrow blacktop that added to driving fatigue and pressure.

One of the new little Pontiacs tried to pass me, held in for a few seconds, then dropped back, barely avoiding a head-on with a Fleetwood roaring down the other lane.

There was a brief hole in the oncoming traffic and the Pontiac made its move again. I slowed down to give it some help, but instead of passing, it began crowding me off the highway.

There was open country to the right, almond fields forever, glinting brown and green in the midday sun. The Pontiac's rear fender kissed the side of our Chevy and the steering wheel shimmied in my hand. 'Hang on, kid,' I shouted as the right front tire bounced off the tarmac and bit into the gravel alongside the road.

The Chevy dived off the blacktop at an oblique right angle, putting its game – but not quite game enough – shocks to the test. A tire blew and the car did an about-face, kicking up a fogbank of dust. The engine shook and coughed and died. I felt something wet on my forehead. Blood. I'd cut my head on the visor and I hadn't even noticed.

The kid had been thrown to the floor. She crawled back onto her seat, groggily.

'You OK?' I asked.

She shook her head, trying to clear it. Her monkey face was scrunched up into a confused frown.

'Anything hurt?' I was a little more insistant.

'No, I don't think so.'

'Jesus, kid, what kind of sign did you flash those yahoos? They were so mad, they tried to cash our checks.'

'Sign?' She didn't seem to know what I was asking. 'Oh, sign. I didn't flash them any. I wasn't fooling with that anymore.'

'Honey, as crazy as most people are today, they rarely run you off the road for no reason.'

'I swear. I'd stopped playing with the signs.'

'I'm not calling you a liar or anything, Sarah, but –'

My door was thrown open. A brown, mustachioed face was grinning at me through the settling dust. He was wearing a thin white short-sleeved dress shirt and dark trousers. The gun in his mitt was leveled at my chest. 'Hands on the wheel, *cabron*,' he said. His eyes were crossed.

The Pontiac had pulled off the road about fifty feet away. Another, similarly dressed Mexican headed our way from it. They both looked in pretty good physical shape, except for the one's eyes. His buddy opened the rear door and said to the kid, 'C'mon, young lady, out of the car, *date prisa.*'

'Now just hold on, boys,' I said. 'Let's sort this whole thing out.'

'Hands back on the wheel, *hijo!*'

'All right. Just tell me what you want.'

Cross-eyes turned to his pal. 'He wants to know.' He grinned. 'Tell him then.'

'The little *muchacha* comes with us.'

'Why?'

'Like you doan know, *cabron,*' the other guy snarled. He leaned through the door and grabbed for Sarah's foot. She gave it to him. In the throat.

He staggered back, away from the car, clutching at his neck and coughing and cursing. Cross-eyes looked from me to him, the gun wavering in his fist. I relaxed my grip on the steering wheel.

'You all right, brother?' Cross-eyes asked in Spanish.

'Watch Bloodworth,' was the reply, also in Spanish. 'I'll take care of the little girl. She will not surprise me again.'

'Should I hit him with the revolver and aid you with the little girl?'

I decided to go for his gun. If the car had been more roomy, I'd have made it. The goddamn seat squeaked as I began to shift my weight. Cross-eyes, half-panicked, grabbed his gun with both hands and pushed it into my temple.

I could feel my nerves jumping like worms on a griddle. I eased back against the seat and forced my eyes forward, away from the gun and the Mexican. Traffic shot past less than a hundred feet away. You'd think one of the bastards would glance over, see a man holding a gun, and send back a cop.

Maybe a highway patrol car would pass. Maybe my blood pressure would go back to normal.

'Come on, little witch,' the man behind me urged Sarah. His voice was rough and he cleared his throat every other word.

She didn't move. He sighed.

Cross-eyes slipped into Spanish again. 'I don't like standing here in the bright sunlight with a gun in my hand. The police will come.'

'Don't worry,' came the reply. 'Bloodworth will be the one in trouble, not us.' In English he said to Sarah, 'Come with us immediately or my brother will begin to shoot the ears off Bloodworth.'

Not a sound from the girl. I started to turn my head to see what she looked like, but Cross-eyes' gun muzzle held a fascination I couldn't break.

Finally Sarah said, 'Kidnapping is a federal offense of the most heinous type. The FBI will hunt you down like rats and put you behind bars forever.'

She seemed to be getting through to Cross-eyes, but his brother only laughed. 'Tell that to Bloodworth, who took you from your home and – what is it? – cohabited with you.'

'That's outrageous!' she shouted. 'He is a fine, decent man. A gentleman of the sort you would never understand in a million –'

'Hey, *esse*, it sounds like a woman in love, eh?' Cross-eyes said.

'The courts may not see it your way, little girl,' his brother said. 'They may feel we got more right to be driving you around than him.'

'You guys shot at us yesterday,' I put in, adding the lie, 'I saved the bullet they pulled out of our tire. I bet it fits this gun.'

'So we shot a tire,' came the reply behind me. 'We shoot what we aim at. Come on, girl. We are behind schedule by almost a day. It is not our way.'

Cross-eyes added to me, 'It is acceptable to damage a short-eyes, *cabron*. Even the police agree on this.' He tightened his finger on the trigger.

'Wait!' the kid shouted. 'Don't hurt him. I'll go with you loathsome creeps.'

She slipped out of the car.

'Get your luggage,' Straight-eyes ordered, and Sarah did as she was told.

The three of them backed away, toward the Pontiac. Sarah gave me a concerned look.

'Sorry, kid,' I said. 'Try not to worry. They're not going to hurt you.'

'Should I cut up his tires?' Cross-eyes asked.

'Waste no more time on him, brother. He is going nowhere.' To me, he said, 'You are too smart an *hombre* to worry the police, Bloodworth. I bet you ain't got any kind of legal paper allowing you to travel with this underage girl. Even if you do, remember, *cabron*, you on the wrong side of the fence. We on the right.'

'You're working for the girl's mother?' I asked.

He rubbed his throat and didn't bother to answer. He pushed Sarah into the Pontiac and waited for Cross-eyes to join him. They were gone in seconds. My mental afterimage was of Sarah sitting beside Cross-eyes on the back seat, staring at me plaintively and helplessly through the rear window.

19

1. 'You know exactly whom we are, little lady?' the man with the straight black, old-fashioned Beatle hair and the crossed eyes asked.

'I know who you are,' I replied. 'Dark and evil insects who should, by rights, wither and die in natural sunlight.'

'No, no,' he said, unaffected by my insult, 'we are the Sotos.'

The tall, surly driver muttered something in Spanish, which the talkative one ignored. 'My brother is Bartolo and I am Juan, named for our revered great-great-great-grandfather, the famous Juan Soto.'

'We are sixth-generation *Californios*,' Bartolo added.

'What do you *Californios* want with me?'

'We take you to your mother,' Juan answered.

'Or maybe you take us,' Bartolo joined in.

'Why?'

'Because we are paid to do this,' Juan said, as if the answer were obvious.

'Paid by my mother?'

'The honor of our profession forbids us to be specific on that point,' Juan said.

'But this weird honor of yours allows you to kidnap a – a helpless woman at gunpoint?'

'You have it topsy-turvy,' Juan said. 'It is like the gringo view of our beloved ancestor. You have probably been taught that Juan Soto was a lawbreaker, a pillager, a despoiler of women.'

'I haven't been taught anything about him,' I said. 'I've never heard of him.'

Juan's jaw dropped. 'Goddammit!' he shouted. 'You see, brother, they don't teach these kids nothing anymore in the schools.'

'Be quiet,' Bartolo said, eyes on the road.

'How can I be quiet when I hear of this total ignorance of our great-great –'

'Dammit, Juanito,' his brother snarled. 'We don't even know if we are his relations.'

'Did not our father –'

'Tequila talk,' Bartolo snapped.

'Why do you speak of our sainted father in this manner?'

'Shut up, Juanito. Give your jaw a rest.'

'Shut up? You shut up, you – you Tonto.'

They began shouting at each other. Juan leaned forward and his gun almost slipped from where he'd tucked it in his belt. It was just hanging there.

I grabbed for it.

I'd barely touched the metal when his big hand closed on my wrist. 'Na, na, *chica*,' he said. 'Naughty girl.'

'What?' Bartolo asked.

'Nothing,' Juan answered. He looked at me with his sadly crossed eyes.

'You should have those fixed,' I told him. 'Your eyes.'

He scowled. 'Fixed? Hell with that! They are the eyes of the great Juan Soto from whom we are descendants. His eyes, too, were crossed. But they did nothing to deter his noble tasks. He was a defender of the poor, in the days of the great gold rush. He and his band of *caballeros* rode the land of Santa Clara

County, stealing from the wealthy tyrants and sharing the spoils with the poor and destitute.'

He went on like that for most of the trip. At irregular intervals he would stop to argue with Bartolo. They were a strange pair, more annoying than dangerous. I managed to get some sleep.

The sun was starting to set as we drove past a sign reading: Vacaville.

'Just where are we headed?' I asked.

'To San Jose,' Juan answered. 'To find your mother.'

'But I thought . . .'

'What?'

If Mr Bloodworth was wrong about mother and the vile Gutierrez having Copa de Oro for their destination, then there would be little chance that he would have any idea where I might be. No chance that he could aid me in escaping the wearisome Sotos. The immediate future looked bleak.

'Wassamatter, *chica*? You think we headed somewhere else?'

Bartolo let out a whoop. 'I bet Bloodworth,' he said between chuckles, 'I bet he gets the same reception we did in Copa de Oro.' They both began to chortle riotously, shouting at each other in Spanish. I tried to get some glimmer of what they were saying, but the only thing that sounded familiar was the name of the late film star Steve McQueen.

'In point of fact,' I said loudly, 'Mr Bloodworth and I were on our way to San Jose when you ran us off the road.'

'Sure,' Bartolo said, the word virtually dripping sarcasm. 'That's why you were traveling in the other direction.'

'We were planning on circling back. We were trying to – escape a – dangerous – ah, killer. An awful man.'

Bartolo shook his head, as if in pity. But Juan seemed intrigued by my improvised story. 'What did this awful man look like?'

'Juanito, do not encourage her to lie more.'

'Of course I'm lying,' I said. 'I make up stories all the time about men over six feet tall who carry guns and who, in this case, tried to kill Mr Bloodworth last night. Tried to sic a crazed dog on him. He said he'd kill anybody he caught with me.'

The color drained from Juan's face. 'Bartolo, it could be the same –'

'Shut up! If you must wag your tongue, do it in our native language.'

So they gabbled Spanish at each other for the next sixty miles. In junior high I'd studied French and ranked very high, but even that language, rattled so fast, would have stumped me.

Finally Bartolo asked me, 'When was it that the *hombre* tried to kill Bloodworth?'

'Last night, like I said.'

'What time?'

I told him I wasn't sure. 'Midnight, maybe.'

Juan said, in English, 'Ah, so it could not have been him, unless he did not phone us from El Lay.'

Bartolo snarled, 'Do not talk like a fool.'

'But we don't even know what the bastard looks like.'

'We know what his money looks like. We know he wants to reunite the girl and her mother. Enough!' Bartolo glared at the highway. 'You are behaving like a child, Juan. Listening to the lies of a child.'

I told Juan, 'You really shouldn't put much stock in the judgment of someone who thinks an almost fifteen-year-old girl is a child.'

Juan gave me a grin that was almost pleasant to see. 'You know something, *chica*? You goin' to be one dangerous woman when you grow up.'

'If she is allowed to grow up,' Bartolo said.

★

2. 'Is this not "the garden valley of heart's delight"?' Juan asked rhetorically as we drove through an unending stretch of amazingly fertile farmland. In the fields the workers were harvesting what looked like three-foot-long carrots.

'It'd be wonderful,' I agreed, 'if it weren't for the nitrous-oxide emissions that pollute the air we breathe.'

'Huh? What is that?'

'Ignore her, for your sanity,' Bartolo said.

'What is this? Nitrous what?'

'The exhaust of a car, brother. Do not listen to her. She will drive you crazy. All women drive you crazy.'

That, of course, started them off again. Twenty minutes later, with the Spanish still flying, the Pontiac passed the San Jose Civic Center, drifting slowly in the traffic on Guadalupe Parkway, if one could believe the signs.

The Sotos seemed to have some destination in mind.

Eventually, Bartolo parked in front of the Rama Inn Motel. Originally it had been a Ramada Inn. The new owners had apparently tried to conserve as much of the neon sign as the law allowed. The result was a gross double entendre, but no worse than I expected.

Bartolo glared at me. 'We are going in there together, miss. And you are not going to cause us any trouble, because if you do, we track down that fat old Bloodworth guy and break his legs permanently.'

I looked at Juan. 'You'd really do that?'

He shrugged. 'Be nice, *chica*. Then there will be no need to make that decision.'

OK. So I was nice.

20

Sheriff Eric Ludmeuller of Copa de Oro was only twenty years old – the youngest sheriff in the whole United States, if you believed him, and I had no reason not to. He fancied, quite correctly, that he bore a remarkable resemblance to the late Steve McQueen in his salad days when he appeared on TV as a Wild West bounty hunter. To add to this similarity, Ludmeuller wore a jaunty little Stetson pushed forward on his small head. He walked with his butt in the air.

And he carried a sawed-off shotgun, just like McQueen did in that old series, though it would probably do him as much damage as the poor soul it was aimed at. He gave me a flinty Steve McQueen glower and slammed the cell door shut.

I felt bad about having to spend the night in the Copa de Oro hoosegow, worse that I'd lost track not only of the kid but the red-haired Ceeley McDermott. Her small Buick had been the third car to pass my way after Cross-eyes and his brother took off with the kid – the first to stop.

'Trouble?' she asked, looking over at the useless Chevy. I nodded. 'Want me to send back a mechanic from Copa de Oro?'

'I'd rather get a lift there. The car's a rental. Let them worry about it.'

She was handsome rather than beautiful, with the kind of cheekbones that females prize more highly than the love of a good man; a straight, thin nose; full mouth; and rich, free-flowing red hair. All right, so she *was* beautiful. I had that feeling of having seen her before, but I didn't know where. A dream maybe.

She gave me a long, vaguely disapproving look, as if trying to decide if I'd turn out to be a rapist or an insurance salesman or some other bad choice of traveling companion.

'My name is Leo Bloodworth,' I offered, trying for the most sincere smile at my command. 'I've got a real need to reach Copa de Oro as soon as possible.'

She unlocked the doors and tossed a pigskin briefcase onto the luggage resting on the rear seat. I opened the door and put my suitcase on top of the pile in the back, then slipped in beside her.

'What happened to your car?' she asked, lighting a cigarette.
'Blowout.'

She made the proper sounds of consolation and exhaled a gust of tar and nicotine and smoke.

'I know this is going to sound dumb,' I said, 'but I get the feeling I've seen you . . .' I stopped. There are some things you can't bring yourself to say, even if they're true.

She gave me a sidelong, tongue-in-cheek, raised-eyebrow look and concentrated on her driving. 'Your forehead is bleeding,' she said, and yanked a tissue from a box perched on her dash, waving it at me until I took it. She didn't say anything more after that.

Forty minutes later we were in Copa de Oro, a still-rural town that is supposed to be sitting on top of a major gold deposit. Whatever money was to be made there had come from nature's wonders on top of the ground, however, not from below it. The agribusiness was thriving in that part of the state, and ever since the Copa de Oro Dam had been constructed in the late Sixties, the recreation dollars had been piling up, too. But it hadn't changed the town all that much.

'Where shall I drop you?' Ceeley asked as we drove past

rows of Victorian houses along a thoroughfare called Paley Street.

'I guess you're in a hurry to be on your way?'

She lit her sixth cigarette from the butt of her fifth and said, 'To tell you the fucking truth, Leo, I don't even know where I'm going. So I'm in no particular hurry to get there.'

The cigarette in her lips was meant to make her look tough and independent, but the fact that it and her bottom lip were trembling undercut the effect. 'What're you leaving behind?' I asked. 'Boyfriend, husband, or what?'

'Husband. Eight years' worth.' She fogged up the car with more smoke. 'I tried leaving him fifteen or twenty times, but I always let the bastard talk me into going back. This time I decided to do a job of it. I emptied the savings – mine, not his – and gave notice at the bank where I've been clerking and piled whatever I could into the car and I've been driving ever since.'

'From where?'

She made a vague hand gesture before flicking her cigarette ash into the tray. 'It's not important.' Since she was heading south, I assumed she was coming from the north. Crescent City? Eureka? Weed? Someplace where they were running a help-wanted ad for a beautiful red-haired bank clerk.

'What happens if he finds you?'

'How can he when even I don't know where I'm going?'

'There are people you can hire who'll find anybody.'

She smiled. 'Jay's too cheap, among other things. And the other things make "cheap" look good. Not that he'd have anything to do with that sort of person.'

'What sort of person?'

'A hired – snoop. A private detective, or whatever. One of those awful, greasy little men who take money to leech off people in trouble. Even Jay wouldn't stoop that low. What was that?'

'Just mumbling to myself.' I stared out of the window.

'Anyway,' she went on, 'my time is your time.' She showed me her strong, lovely profile.

'If it's not too much trouble, I'd like a lift to Feather River Boulevard. It's coming up.'

'What's there?'

'A motel. The Casa de Oro Motel.'

'A motel, huh?'

'That wasn't a suggestion,' I said without humor. 'Just drop me off and you can be on your way.'

'Is something bothering you?'

'No,' I lied.

'Something I said?'

'Nothing at all. There's the turnoff,' I told her.

She cornered on two wheels and squeezed into a traffic slot on the boulevard. 'I hope this is the right direction,' she said.

I told her I thought so. She heavy-footed the gas. 'Suppose you tell me your story, Leo.'

'Nothing to tell.' Cars passed us by. Workers going home. I was a worker, far from home, going . . . where?

'Married? Kids? That sort of thing.'

'Haven't been married for a while.'

'Kids?'

Just one, I thought. Not mine, but definitely my problem. Hell, Sarah could probably take better care of herself than I could.

'Earth to Leo, come in, please.'

'Huh? Oh . . . no kids.'

'Just a gruff old bachelor, eh? Well, there's the motel.'

'Great. Pull in behind that Dodge.'

She did. 'This isn't such a great place, Leo,' she said, turning up her nose at the series of run-down wooden bungalows past the neon entryway.

'It'll do,' I said, reaching for my suitcase.

She put a hesitant hand on my arm. 'Listen, you wouldn't want to drive on with me for a while?' she asked.

I studied her face a little longer than I had planned. She seemed worried, high-strung, and on edge about something. I didn't know what I could do to help. I had other matters like a kidnapped kid on my mind. The smartest thing I could do was to grab my luggage and wave goodbye.

'I should only be a minute or so in here,' I told her. 'I have to get some information from the owner. If you feel like waiting . . .'

'I'll be here,' she said. She tried out a smile and it worked. So what if she was a bigot about private detectives? We all had our little failings.

There was a rosy-cheeked old dame named Mrs Crosswell behind the counter in the office. She gave me an anxious smile. The place looked pretty vacant, which bothered me. With a big fight on tap, it should have been as busy as Selecosta's. I mentioned the dog matches and she nodded and excused herself, I assumed to check the latest information.

When she returned, she had her back up. She didn't know a darn thing about any dogfight in the happy little town of Copa de Oro. I questioned her about her ad in *Roll Call*, which listed her motel as a source of fight information. She allowed as how the advert must have been placed by the motel's former owner.

No, she had not seen two Latins traveling with a Caucasian teenage girl, and if she had, she would certainly not have let them stay in her motel. I started for the door and she remembered that she had seen the Latins. But that had been yesterday and there had been no girl with them.

Had she given them a room?

She was working on an answer when boot heels hit the front entryway and the door to the office flew open. Sheriff Eric

Ludmeuller duck walked, Steve McQueen-style, into the room and into my life, his rather small hand resting on his holstered Mare's Leg.

'Palms on the counter, mister,' he said in a vaguely southern twangy voice.

'Huh?'

He pulled the sawed-off shotgun from its holster and waved it under my nose. It smelled of neatsfoot oil. 'Press the flesh to the Formica. Now.'

The way he was holding his gun made it very easy to twist it away from him and blow away his upper torso. I thought that would be a rather extreme reaction to his order, so instead I obeyed it. He patted me down, finding some amusement in my telephone beeper and little else.

He explained that one month ago, the day he became the youngest sheriff in the whole USA, he had declared war on those who would destroy man's best friend for sporting pur-poses. He personally closed down the games. He ran the previous owners of the motel out of town, along with other involved parties. He saw to it that Copa de Oro citizens who owned pit dogs were persuaded into taking up some new, less obscene hobby. He had vowed to treat any 'would-be gamester' who set foot in his town to an evening in his newly sanitized jail.

At my request, he let me fish my wallet from my coat with my fingertips. I showed him my state license. He studied it, holding it high so that he could keep one eye on me. 'This sup-posed to impress me?'

'Not at all, sheriff, but it should prove I'm no – ah, "would-be gamester".'

'Then why'd you ask Aunt Mildred about the fights?'

'There are two men I'm trying to find. I had reason to believe they'd be at the fights.'

'Why're you looking for them?' He didn't lower the gun.

'A divorce matter, sheriff. Nothing to do with dogs or gambling.'

'Divorce, huh? These guys got names?'

'Names? Yes, well, they're brothers. And they're Latin. And . . .' I stopped, because I realized that if the two Latins had visited the motel yesterday, as Aunt Mildred had told me, Sheriff Ludmeuller probably knew more about them than I did.

'Cat got yer tongue?' he asked with a boyish grin. 'You wouldn't happen to know what line those boys are in, huh?'

I shook my head.

'They're private detectives. Just like you, Bloodworth. Had their licenses. They weren't really interested in dogfights neither. They were looking for a missing woman who was supposed to be at the fights. Only they ain't no fights and ain't likely to be any. So I didn't believe 'em. Turned out they was, indeed, PI's from down in Sacramento. Brothers, like you say. Name of Soto. I set 'em loose this morning. Now it's your turn in their cell.'

'C'mon, sheriff. You got no reason to lock me up.'

'Got no reason to shoot you, neither, but I could. And I might.' He moved in closer and whispered, 'Frankly, the cell's got better beds then my aunt's got. And the price is better, too.'

As we exited the Casa de Oro, I was wearing handcuffs, which is what Sheriff Ludmeuller's book said a prisoner should be wearing. His dun-colored Mustang with its now-dark bubble light on top was the only car near the motel office. Ceeley McDermott's Buick was noticeably missing and with it my suitcase, my clothes, my gun, and my notes. Not to mention my sense of humor.

'Where's your wheels, mister?'

'Just off the highway near Chico. A rental job. I had to ditch it.'

'Trouble, huh?'

'Yeah.'

'Well, you got more now.'

I sighed. 'Sonny, you're gonna have to make up your mind,' I told him.

He tensed. 'About what?'

'Just who the hell are you gonna be when you grow up, Steve McQueen or Jack Webb?'

He curled his lip and poked his gun into the small of my back, pushing me into his Mustang. We were almost at the lockup when he turned to me, scrunched up his face, and asked, 'Just who the hell is this Webb guy, anyway?'

21

1. It was car-cophony enough to make even the deaf scream out in pain. Auto horns blaring. Brakes squeaking. Shock absorbers jouncing. It was even worse than that Cage concert the freshman class had been forced to endure at the Bay High auditorium.

The ridiculous-looking low-riders with their big whitewall tires and tail fins poking in the air were lined end-to-end in front of the motel. Evidently this was the big cruise street in San Jose. If you were Chicano and owned a car, it was where you hooted and honked the night away. Lucky us.

Bartolo scowled at the cars and downshifted, waiting for a break in traffic so that we could leave the parking lot. Juan was his usual ebullient self, absorbing every one of the souped-up cars with his anxious crossed eyes and his full mouth set in a perpetual wide grin. 'Like when we were young, eh, Bartolo?' he chuckled.

Bartolo glanced at his wristwatch and fired off something in rapid Spanish. The tone was harsh, but it didn't bother Juan, who said to me, 'My brother chooses to forget that he once owned a low-rider that would put any of these to shame.'

Bartolo growled, 'Shut up, fool. Where would we have got money to buy one of these pieces of tin? We were too naive to be thieves, too stupid, too –'

'Too Catholic,' Juan completed for him, crossing himself. Bartolo looked at him and almost smiled. 'But we did have that old Buick, eh?' he said.

'The one Miguel painted red like flames,' Juan added, his dark eyes dancing.

'He even painted the hood ornament red, that Miguel,' Bartolo said, gloom again descending. There was a sudden opening in the line of honking extroverts and he piloted the car right through it. The other drivers shouted and waved good-naturedly. Juan waved back, shouting something incomprehensible.

Bartolo's bad humor was getting me down. The man would not cheer up. It was as if his brother had soaked up all of the family's high spirits.

'I agree with the *chica*,' Juan said to Bartolo. 'We should eat at the Giant Artichoke place.'

'It is nowhere near our destination, goddammit.'

'But we're here in San Jose, and the *chica*'s book says this Giant Artichoke is a wonder. They serve nothing but artichokes. Even out of season. And it is decorated all in green. The doors are like the leaves of the artichoke.'

'Have you lost all of your senses? We are on business here. We are not out to sample the food at local restaurants.'

'We have to eat someplace,' I added.

'Exactly,' Juan agreed. 'Don't tell me, Bartolo, you do not like artichokes, when I have seen you eat . . .'

'All right!' Bartolo shouted.

He muttered to himself as he twisted through a series of narrow streets until we arrived at Stephens Creek Boulevard. Ten minutes later we were seated at an artichoke-colored table, on artichoke-colored chairs, enjoying tossed artichoke salad and marinated artichoke hearts on toast.

The french-fried cheese and chokes seemed to lift Bartolo's spirits somewhat, but even then he kept checking his watch.

'What's the matter, Bartolo?' I asked. 'Do you have a late date or something?'

'No, *chica*,' Juan said, checking out the artichoke cake at the next table, 'there is to be a telephone call to our rooms later and there is much to do before then. We are going to need your help.'

'Please be specific,' I said.

Bartolo's face dropped all expression, except perhaps a touch of weariness. 'We need you to identify your mother for us. At the fights tonight.'

'Why?'

'It is not necessary that you know.'

'It is, if you expect me to cooperate. For all I know, you two might want to hurt my mother.'

'We will not even talk to her, I promise,' Bartolo said.

'I need a reason. Only animals obey without reason.'

Bartolo slammed his fork down on the table and leaned toward me, speaking through clenched teeth. 'How is this reason? If you do not do as I say, we will break your fingers and toes.'

I turned to Juan. He looked from me to his brother. 'Don't talk that way, Bartolo,' he said. 'She will help us. She knows we will not hurt her. Or her mother. Or anybody we don't have to. She will help us, I guarantee.'

'Oh, you guarantee. That certainly relieves my mind.'

'What's with you, Bartolo?' I asked. 'Did you bite into a bad artichoke or something? You're turning this into a most unpleasant experience.'

'I got news for you, child. This is supposed to be unpleasant. We are not here for a good time. We are earning a living, in spite of the way my brother sometimes acts.'

'If it were not for the way your brother acts, I would not dream of going to the fights with you tonight.'

We glared at each other for a few seconds, then Bartolo signaled for the check. Considering the way things were going, I did not try to talk him into visiting the Mystery House, which was not very far down the road. According to my book, the widow of the heir to the Winchester Rifle fortune somehow got it into her head that as long as she continued to add rooms onto her house, she would never die. She kept the carpenters busy for thirty-eight years, when her theory was proven faulty, not that she cared much at that point. Even though I desperately wanted to visit this testament to odd-ball behavior, I did not think Bartolo would go along with my suggestion at that time. But there was always tomorrow.

2. According to Mr Wilson Tassler's 'The Great State', in the 1890s there was a steam railroad that connected downtown San Jose to Claypool Park, a three-hundred-fifty-acre area filled with natural mineral springs. Mr Tassler, of course, had no reason to think that some eighty years later the park would be used by a bunch of crummy sleazoids who made money by setting poor animals at each other's throat, literally.

We made our way there along Route I30, traveling a semi-ominous shady country road to where a group of fellows flagged down the car and poked their dust-covered noses inside. One of them, a spooky young person with a dent in the middle of his forehead, as if he'd been hit with an ax in childhood, blinked sleepy eyes at the Sotos and said, 'You greasers got the wherewithal to buy your get-through tickets?'

Both Bartolo and Juan glared at him for a second. Then Bartolo said, 'I think we can manage the price.'

The dented head nodded. 'Well, your money's as good as anybody else's.' He turned to his pals and added, 'Once you clean the chili sauce off it.' They laughed at his original backwoods wit.

As we drove slowly by them, a squat, bug-eyed cretin goggled at me and said, 'That little spic looks as white as you or me,' and the dented head replied, 'White as you, maybe.' And they all laughed again. The Sotos were very silent. 'Hey,' I told them, 'you can't expect those guys to be international diplomats. Look at the business they're in, crowd-checking dogfights.'

'It's OK, *chica*,' Juan said, truly depressed for the first time since I'd met him. He stared down the road to where several other local boys were trying to keep the gamblers' cars in some sort of parking order.

According to my books, in the palmy days of Claypool Park, there had been a large spa, complete with boathouse, hotel, restaurants, and even a casino, and people had traveled hundreds of miles to spend time there. Only ruins – old brick-and-cement foundation, a portion of a wall, scattered hunks of concrete in the moonlight – remained. The spot was used for picnics now, and for dogfights. I wondered if the old bleached wood building had once housed the casino. It was circled by brightly lit windows. Smoke and noise escaped through the broken panes. The place seemed crowded, hostile, and frightening.

Bartolo parked at the far end of a mass of cars, keeping sight of the front entry where two men in Levi's stood collecting money. 'They may give us trouble,' he said, almost to himself. He opened the glove compartment and pulled out an awful tan rain hat that had stains all over it. He tossed it to me.

'What am I supposed to do with this?'

'Stick it on your head. Hide your hair under it.'

'I will not wear this smelly thing.'

'Be sensible, *chica*,' Juan said. 'If we go walking in there with a blond young lady, those people are sure to make some comment. That is the way life is. But if you are just some kid in a dirty hat, well . . .'

'We must all pay the price of prejudice,' I said, and just as one would dive into a cold ocean, I shoved my hair up and pulled the filthy hat down over my ears. Juan had to turn away before he burst with laughter, and even Bartolo smiled.

But they were not laughing at all when we arrived at the entrance and the man sitting there, with a blond crew cut,

Levi's, and an undershirt on which a snarling dog seemed to emphasize his prominent breasts, said, 'Thirty bucks, boys.'

Bartolo, his wallet in hand, indicated a sign that read: Admission $5.

'Oh, thass for locals. You folks don't look like locals. Ten apiece.'

'Even for the kid?'

The man with breasts looked at me and said, 'Hell, yeah. This ain't no movie theater.'

Bartolo handed him the money. Juan took me by the arm and pushed me inside the big room. It was like Roy's Burgers at noon – crowded, smelly, loud, people pushing people around, shouting. An awful place. I saw no one even near my age, except for a sad-faced girl in a green and pink silk dress whose mascara had dripped down her face like some weird punk makeup. She was with a bigger woman with jet-black hair whose arm rested on the shoulder of a little man with diamonds on his glasses.

'Do you see your mother?' Bartolo asked me.

I scanned the room. Ugly faces. Horrible faces. Brutal. Greedy. And worse. I started to feel faint and realized I had been holding my breath.

The bulk of the crowd was gathered around a pitlike area, where two men were holding their dogs – bullterriers – and cooing to them.

'Well?' Bartolo asked.

'No,' I said, unable to take my eyes off of the dogs.

'Let us move around.'

They dragged me through the crowd, but I continued to stare at the men with their dogs. I didn't want to see what was about to happen, but I didn't have the willpower to look away.

Juan put his hands on both sides of my face and physically turned my head until I was looking into his crossed eyes. 'Watch the crowd and not what happens with the dogs. You do not want to see that.'

But for some horrible reason, I did. As soon as he released me, I looked back.

The two men faced each other, holding their dogs securely. Then, on a signal, they let the dogs loose. Immediately there was an attack. The two dogs met in the center of the pit and began to rip at each other's neck and face!

The room began to shimmer and close in on me. I felt myself swaying. Nausea. The works. With a strangled shout – Juan told me about it afterward; I didn't hear it myself – I bolted for the door and out, past the man with breasts, to the parking area.

The man with breasts shouted something about getting my hand stamped, but I didn't care about that. I rushed through the cars, stumbling, scraping my knee on jagged racks. Then I stopped, taking great gulps of air. All I could see was the face of one sweet dog being ripped open by the other. There were other images, too. Violent images, including that of Mr Bloodworth being kicked that first day we met. And I saw my mother, poor silly woman, being beaten by whom? Was it something I saw before, or had I imagined it or projected it from something she or Gran had told me?

The Sotos found me. Juan hunkered down beside me and stared at me helplessly. I must have looked like Bette Midler at the end of *The Rose*, or something. Bartolo pushed him aside and bent down. He slapped me hard, knocking the crazy images from my head. I began breathing semi-regularly again.

I had never fallen apart like that before. It was a good lesson. I would never let it happen again.

'You OK?' Bartolo asked.

I nodded.

'When the fight is over, we will go back inside,' he said.

'No,' Juan said. 'We will wait here.'

Bartolo looked at his brother as if to argue, but he restrained himself.

'If her mother is inside, she will leave sometime,' Juan reasoned. 'We will watch the door. The *chica* is not going back into that place.'

Bartolo looked at his watch. 'Our call comes through at midnight. We don't even know if they are inside.'

I looked at the cars. 'They're using a white Mercedes,' I said. 'I don't see it. Maybe they're not here. Maybe they're somewhere else, like Copa de Oro.'

We were sitting in the Sotos' car when the white Mercedes arrived. It parked to our right, five or six rows behind us. A sort of handsome dark guy hopped out and moved through the parked cars to the front door, where he nodded to the man with breasts.

'That's Charteris, or Gutierrez, or whatever his name is. The guy Mother's traveling with.'

'There's no one else in the car,' Bartolo said.

'I guess he left her behind.'

'This guy doesn't look Chicano,' Juan said. 'He is supposed to be Chicano.'

'That is probably why he is useful in this situation,' Bartolo said. He turned to me. 'You are certain this is the same car? There are more Mercedeses in this state than oranges.'

'It was missing a hubcap, just like this one.'

Juan said, 'We will follow him to wherever he stays and then we tell our client and . . .' He looked at me.

'And what?' I asked.

He shrugged. 'Whatever it is the client wants.'

'Who is the client?'

'Someone who –'

Bartolo cut him off with another Spanish tirade and Juan shut his mouth and did not say another word.

Bartolo consulted his watch for perhaps the hundredth time that night. 'We are going to miss the call.'

'Maybe not,' I said. And before they could stop me, I opened the back door and ran toward the Mercedes.

The driver's door was unlocked. I opened it and hopped inside. Bartolo and Juan rushed after me. I'm not sure why – sheer perversity, probably – but I slammed the door in their faces and locked it. I grinned at them. Then I started poking through the glove compartment and ashtray, trying to find something that might indicate where the malevolent Mr Gutierrez and my mom might be staying.

Juan began to pound on the window. I looked up. He was pointing toward the front of the building. Gutierrez was leaving, carrying a briefcase. He was in a hurry.

The Sotos slid away from the Mercedes. It was too late for me to open the door without Gutierrez spotting me. I hopped over the seat and tried to hide in a ball in the rear floor well. Then I remembered the locked door. I snaked my hand up past the front seat and pushed up the lock just as there was a sound of someone rattling keys. I hugged the floor of the car.

Gutierrez got into the car and tossed his briefcase onto the seat next to him. He started the car. He smelled of some horrible musk perfume. Barfville. He hummed and half sang a Mexican song that had the words *Laredo* and *muy bien* in it. The Mercedes moved quietly and eerily over the country road.

I raised my head and saw to my horror that there was something resting on the floor of the car not a foot from my nose. It was big and furry and it looked alive. Then we passed under a highway light and I relaxed. It was a wig, a silver wig like the one my mother had worn the night before.

My nerves were entirely too overworked. I remained flat on the floor, trying not to breathe too loudly, staring at the silver wig, until the Mercedes left the highway and traveled a minute or so. Gutierrez stopped it and turned off the ignition.

He got out of the car and I heard footsteps going away. Then a knock at a door and the door opening. When it clicked shut, I poked my head up cautiously. I was at one of the Sleepytime Motels. The familiar neon sign of the couple in nightshirts, pulling up the covers, blinked down on me and the rest of the cars parked beside the little green-and-white cottages.

I crawled over the leather seat and let myself out of the car. The Sotos were parked by the curb. Bartolo had his finger to his lips. He got out and moved past me to the cottage marked 'Lovebirds 3'. He waved me to join him.

We stood just outside the door and listened. Gutierrez was laughing and saying something about 'only eighteen thousand'. A woman's voice told him to be satisfied with whatever it was.

Bartolo looked at me and mouthed the words, 'Your mother?'

I nodded. He took my arm and we moved away from there and back to the car.

Suddenly, I jerked my arm away. I had a great desire to rush to my mother, to find out what was happening.

Bartolo must have sensed what was on my mind. 'It would be unwise,' he said. 'That Gutierrez *hombre* is no good. He could hurt you.'

'She wouldn't let him,' I said.

'She's under his spell,' Bartolo said. 'Women do terrible things. Men, too, when the situation is reversed.'

I wish I could have trusted her more, but she had never given me any reason to. It was rather awful to realize that I felt safer with two very odd brutes than I would with my own mother.

'We'd best go back to the motel and wait for our call,' Bartolo said.

'I could stay and keep an eye on this place,' Juan suggested, not realizing that he'd made a joke of sorts.

Bartolo considered it, then shook his head. 'They will be here until morning. We will return early. It would cost us another thirty or forty dollars for you to get a room here, brother. Our expenses are already too high and we have not even received a portion of our fee.'

He started the engine and eased away from the Sleepytime Motel, waiting until he was clear to turn on his headlamps. Juan seemed bothered by something. Finally he asked me, 'You and your mother, you don't know each other so well, huh?'

'Maybe too well,' I said.

'I mean, she's back in that room with that – fellow – and –'

'What are you doing now?' Bartolo asked him.

'It is just that, you know, mothers . . .' He looked at me. 'You don't get along, huh?'

I didn't know how to answer that. I guess I loved her, all right, but I didn't know how else I was supposed to feel. I didn't want her hurt, emotionally or physically, by Gutierrez. But I'd long since stopped worrying about how her lovers treated her. That was her business. It had nothing to do with me.

'Before you tell your client where my mother is, you should get your money, don't you think? I mean, once he knows that, why would he bother paying you?'

'A good question,' Juan said.

Bartolo looked as if he were sucking sour balls. 'He will pay.'

'Why?'

Bartolo's reply was to floor the gas pedal and race for our motel.

3. The phone rang exactly at midnight. Bartolo, who was resting on his bed in undershirt and suit pants, jumped up and snatched the receiver. 'Yes,' he said into it. 'We have them located. But before we discuss that we would like some money for our services. As a sign of good faith. We have been at work for several days and . . . yes . . .'

Bartolo looked at me. Juan was staring at his brother anxiously, leaning half in, half out of his twin bed. I was on a little port-a-bed, as curious as Juan.

'Yes . . . in Los Angeles . . . yes. But that will cost more . . .'

Bartolo waved to his brother to hand him a pencil and paper. Juan threw open the drawer to a bedside table and dug out motel stationery and a pen.

Bartolo began writing names and addresses. 'That is fine, but the money . . .' He nodded impatiently. 'My brother and I are selling a service, You must pay for the service.' He shook his head. 'No, no. We know nothing about you, except that . . . yes, I realize we have the girl, but we do not know . . . Ah, that makes a difference. No, of course not. Tomorrow then, for certain, the money will be sent to our office. I warn you, we will keep the girl until we are sure of the money.' He sighed. '*Si*. They are reposing in the Sleepytime Motel on East San Fernando, in the Lovebirds 3 cottage . . .. He is a tall *hombre*. *Distinguedo*. Moustache. He is using the gringo name of . . .' He snapped his fingers at me.

Ordinarily I do not reply to snapped fingers, but I was hoping to learn more. 'Charteris,' I said.

'Charteris,' he repeated into the receiver. 'He drives a white Mercedes with the license plate reading DMNION. He collected money from the fights. Since there is another fight tomorrow night, it is safe to assume he will be in place for a while. We could go back tomorrow and . . . Oh? But I think . . . Yes, you are the boss, but . . . Yes, of course.'

He replaced the receiver and said to his brother, 'He is wiring the money tonight. We will wait until morning and phone Consuela to make sure it has arrived. Then we will carry out his request.'

'Which is?' Juan asked.

'That we forget about the man and woman. They are no

longer our concern. We must return this one to Los Angeles to a . . .' – he looked at his scribbles – '. . . a Mrs Van Dine.'

'My grandmother,' I told him. 'Suppose you don't get your money?'

'Then we still have you,' Bartolo said. 'We will get the money.'

'How? Suppose this client doesn't care what happens to me?'

Bartolo looked at me strangely. Then he uttered a rather harsh word, the translation of which I was happy not to know. He whirled on his brother. 'She's right. We don't know if we have been told truth or lies. I am afraid I have not acted wisely this time, brother.'

Juan hopped off his bed and sat down next to Bartolo, putting his arm around his shoulders. 'Let's not worry about it tonight, Bartolo. If the money does not arrive, then we worry. Then we figure out something else to do.'

Bartolo nodded. 'We know where this Gutierrez and the woman are. Maybe we can get our payment from that end somehow.' Juan moved back to his bed.

While I was brushing my teeth, they, very modestly, went to bed in their undershorts. Bartolo was apparently satisfied that they would not be beaten out of their money, but he still was not able to fall asleep very quickly. Juan began snoring almost as soon as I put out the lights. But Bartolo twisted and turned for at least an hour.

I slipped from the port-a-bed and, very carefully, lifted the phone from the table beside Bartolo's head and carried it as far away as I could. I covered it and my head with my blanket and punched a seemingly endless succession of numbers into it. There were a few beeps and twerps and then the number began to ring. On the third ring, there was a click, then Mr Bloodworth's voice. Even recorded, it did much to comfort me.

22

1. The Ellington Orchestra was playing in the Hollywood Bowl and the night was crisp and cool and starbright as we looked down dreamily at the musicians swinging on the half-shell stage. We were at the top of a grassy knoll that was soft and dry under our spread blanket. The girl with me was my high-school sweetheart, Marion Olsen, a sweet-faced blonde with an upturned nose that had never quite recovered from a severe sunburn the summer of '48.

We'd been sipping orange blossoms from a Thermos and were pleasantly woozy and the sounds coming from Otto Hardwick's sax and Barney Bigard's clarinet and Cootie Williams's trumpet seemed to be surrounding us, tying us in ribbons, pushing us into each other's arms . . ..

Oh, God, don't let me be dreaming, I prayed. But there was that hand on my shoulder, shaking me. And a voice coming from another world entirely.

'You look like ten pounds of man-ooer in a five-pound bag, Bloodworth,' Sheriff Ludmeuller said.

I sighed and squinted up at him from the bare ticking of the cell cot. 'Don't spare my feelings, sheriff. Tell me what you really think.'

He snorted. 'What I really think is that you're a dumb ole boy who thinks he's a smart ole boy. But that's your kettle of carp. Far's I'm concerned, we got no business. You check out.

Your license checks out. Get your rumpled butt out of my jail and out of my town and everything'll be A-OK.'

I swung off the cot and sat upright, my head still buzzing from The Duke's music and the memory of Marion and her sweet freckled nose.

'There's a rusty Schick around here you can use,' Ludmeuller said magnanimously as he headed away from the cells.

I seemed to be the only lucky soul in the lockup. The drunk who'd been occupying the suite next door must have left an early wake-up call. Ludmeuller gestured to me from the door leading to his office. He held out a razor with a brownish blade and a can of spray foam. He kept his eyes away from them and me, as if he were embarrassed by all of us.

2. As I stepped from City Hall, a sudden dry breeze blew away the half-dozen little bloody toilet-paper pieces I'd stuck to the nicks on my chin and jaw. My back hurt. My heart was fibrillating. But my mood picked right up when I spotted Ceeley McDermott's car parked down the street.

She was behind the wheel, sipping from Styrofoam. With her free hand she reached into a paper sack beside her and handed me a similar cup filled with reasonably hot coffee-flavored water. Finally, she broke the silence with 'I bet you thought I'd run out on you.'

'It crossed my mind.'

'When that baby-faced lawman charged into the motel, I figured I might as well find a place for the night other than the one you got.'

'Smart,' I said, meaning it. I looked over my shoulder at my suitcase on the back seat.

'There wasn't a hell of a lot on TV, and I couldn't find a good book,' she said, 'so I went through your stuff.'

'That was smart, too.'

'Your socks have lost their elastic. Never wash them in hot water.'

'I'll pass the word along to Fong's Hand Laundry.'

'You have a gun,' she said.

I sipped my near-coffee. 'Helps to soothe my paranoia. Speaking of which, could you get this car moving before the Cincinnati Kid draws down on me again?'

She shrugged, flipped down the glove-compartment door, and placed her cup on it. Then she kicked over the engine and eased away from the curb. 'The permit for the gun says you're a private detective.'

'Permits never lie.'

'I didn't think so,' she said.

She picked up her cigarette pack, but I stopped her before she could shake one free. 'Save that for an hour or so, huh? Give both our lungs a break. I had a bad night.'

She arched one eyebrow, shook out a cigarette, and said, 'Chuck you, Farley.' Then she lit up. She blew smoke in my face and added, 'I'm right on the cusp of going back to that little boy sheriff and spinning him a yarn that'd put you under the jail.'

'What's your beef?' I wondered.

'How much is the bastard paying you?'

'What bastard?'

'My husband. The low-life son of a bitch.'

I smiled at her. 'Snuff out the smoke and I'll tell you all about it.' She took one last, long drag and jammed the barely used coffin nail into the crowded tray. 'Happy now?'

'Lady, I haven't been happy since the spring of 1963. But I'm sorta pleased to report that I'm not working for your old man. I wouldn't know him if he bit me on the leg.'

'He might,' she said. She lifted her coffee cup and used it.

'Remember, you picked me up,' I said.

'Then *what*?' she asked.

'What what?'

'What are you doing here?'

I supposed she deserved some sort of story. 'There's this little kid,' I began. I told her about Sarah and her dog and her family. I told her about Gutierrez and the dogfights and the Soto brothers. I didn't bother getting into my late partner or the knife wielder who'd attacked me at the kid's building, or the guys in charcoal gray who left me lying on my front stoop.

When I'd finished she said, 'OK. You're the private eye. What do we do now?'

'If you're game, we drive to Sacramento.'

'What about your car?'

'Ludmeuller notified the rental place. Let them worry about it.'

She casually dropped her empty coffee cup on the floor, at my feet. 'Why're we going to Sacramento?'

'That's where the Sotos are from. They're private eyes, too. I imagine they've been hired to get a fix on me and the kid.'

'Set a thief . . .' She flashed me an insincere smile. 'I was only fifteen when I lost my virginity to one of your – breed.'

'What am I supposed to be, a spokesman for the industry? It takes all kinds. Just like people who work in banks.' When she didn't say anything, I added, 'That must've happened at least fifteen years ago. You might want to stop poking at it.'

'It's not that easy.'

'I guess not,' I said. 'Did the guy rape you?'

'No, dammit. He just never called again.'

She fired up another cigarette and we were both silent for a while. Then she asked, 'Who knew you were flying to the Sacramento airport?'

'Huh? Oh, I thought about that. Somebody must've followed the kid and me to the airport in L.A. and conned the information out of the girl at the reservations counter. They tipped the Sotos to be waiting.'

'And the Sotos followed you from then on?'

'We ditched 'em,' I said. 'I assume they second-guessed our next location.'

'Then they must've known about the dogfights.'

She was pretty damn good. 'I guess they did,' I said.

'What does that tell you?'

I could think of only two people who knew I was traveling to the fights – Jerry Flaherty, and my old partner, Cugat. 'Nothing. Tells me nothing,' I said.

'OK,' she went on. 'They drove to Copa de Oro, where they were going to wait for you at the fights. Only there weren't any and the boy sheriff locked them up,'

I nodded. 'Then they doubled back, expecting us to be heading to Copa de Oro. They picked us up somewhere along the highway, swung in behind us, and snatched the girl.'

'Why'd they do that?'

I shook my head. 'Desperation?'

At Yalta City the good highway gave out. We bumped along for a few minutes before she asked, 'Why didn't they take her before?'

'I guess the order only came through after we got away from them.'

She nodded and began frowning again. She was really into it. I was tempted to tell her even more of the tale to see what she'd come up with. 'Did you get their address from Ludmeuller?'

'He wasn't terribly cooperative,' I said. 'But I can find it easy enough.'

'How?'

'The phone book,' I said smugly. 'The guys are private detectives. They're in business. They list their phone number.'

'But they may not list an address,' she said. 'I'd imagine there are those in your profession who would discourage people from knowing where they might be found.'

'Most of us have an office of some kind,' I said huffily.

'Or a rock to crawl under,' she replied.

3. Less than two hours later, we were parked between Route 5 and the Sacramento River in what was laughingly called the Old Business District of the city. When Sacramento was turned into a series of freeways going everywhere, Steckler Street, like many of its neighboring thoroughfares, had been left to fend for itself, cut off from the mainstream of activity. Planners had hoped to turn the area into a sort of Old Town, complete with boutiques and restaurants, but as of that moment it was still waiting for a wrecking crew. And Steckler was another degenerating boulevard littered with car lots and motels and office structures like the Cabrillo Building.

It was an ancient, squat flat-top with elaborate granite exterior that included tons of filigree, matted with a green mold thanks to the damp wind off the river. Most of the building was devoted to the selling of moderately old automobiles. But if you were so motivated, you could find an entrance at the rear that opened onto two flights of dusty wooden stairs leading to a landing with twin pebble-grain doors. According to a painter's unsteady hand, one door led to Jesus Domino, Photographer, the other to Soto Investigations.

The latter was locked tighter than Gene Autry's pants. Beyond its pebble-grain, no light showed. Domino, however, was wide open for business, such as it was. A thin Hispanic woman sat at a desk behind a dark wood counter and in front of a thick black curtain, scowling through Coke-bottle lenses at an account ledger as if it were telling her unpleasant secrets. From behind the curtain a male voice was making cajoling sounds in Spanish.

The woman looked up from her paperwork. She offered a mechanical smile and rose from her chair. She walked briskly to the counter. Her askew eyes had a Jerry Lewis 'Nutty Professor' look behind the thick lenses. 'Passport photos?' she inquired.

'We're trying to find your neighbors,' I told her.

Her head swiveled jerkily until she was looking at the common wall that separated her from the Sotos' den. She replaced the smile with a frown. '*Que?*'

I showed her my I.D. 'Business,' I said. 'I think we can do a little business. *Dinero.*'

She studied my identification carefully. The Spanish stopped behind the curtain. 'The Sotos *hermanos*, they gone somewhere,' the woman said finally. 'Been away for a couple of days. I don't know when they come back. Sometimes they gone for weeks.'

A tall, gray-haired Latin in black polo shirt and slacks emerged from behind the curtain. Before it fell back into place, I got a glimpse of a very young girl resting on a purple divan, covered by some sort of robe. The man stared at us and then at the myopic woman. 'What's the problem now?' he asked the room in general.

'No problem,' I said.

He gave me a look that said there was always a problem. 'He want the Sotos,' the woman in glasses said.

The gray-haired Latin made an 'o' with his mouth.

'It's important,' I added. 'Could mean a few bucks for them. Or somebody.'

The man seemed interested.

'Like I tell you,' the woman snapped, 'they gone. I give them a message for you when they get back. OK? Maybe a week. Two weeks.'

'Who takes care of their office while they're away?' Ceeley asked.

The woman acted mildly surprised, as if Ceeley had been given no permission to speak. But she answered, 'Nobody.

Not that we know of. I guess the office just takes care of itself. My husband and me have all we can do to take care of this place.'

I nodded. 'Thanks for your time,' I said, and shooed Ceeley out. I got down on my hands and knees in front of the Sotos' door and looked through the thin space between the door bottom and the Cabrillo Building's threadbare carpeting. Nothing but dust and pale sunlight.

I brushed off my trousers and elbows and walked with Ceeley back down to the car.

'Well?' she asked.

I pointed to a dreary-looking fast-food joint across the street. She grimaced. 'Christ, you're not going to take me into a place named Chickee-Likee?'

'Coffee's a safe order,' I said.

But judging by her face as she sipped hers, I may have overstated the case. I gave her a grin from across the lunchroom, where I waited for the Sotos' office phone to ring. It sounded three times and Mrs Domino picked it up. I put the receiver back on its hook and joined Ceeley in the battered booth she had selected. Its black Naugahyde had been tortured by knives, razors, and cigarette butts. All sorts of rude suggestions had been carved on the Formica table, but it was positioned for a fine view through a streaked display window of the rear entrance to the Cabrillo Building.

'You sure you don't want a Chickee-Likee?' I asked while we both watched the building.

'I'd rather go down on Charlie Manson,' she shot back.

'They must have loved repartee like that in the bank.'

She paled and gave me an oddly sheepish look. 'I was never comfortable enough at the bank to . . . I never used much of any kind of language there, good or bad.'

'Lucky me.'

'I'm sorry if it offends you,' she said.

'Hell, no. No offense taken,' I said. I glanced around the greasy lunchroom. We were the only customers. A tired black man in a gray apron sat on a chair behind a pink-topped counter, inspecting his clotted grill with bloodshot eyes and humming to himself. 'A guy in my sleazy line of work doesn't get offended at anything that happens. As a matter of pure fact, I like women who curse a lot. Gets the old blood pumping.'

She let out a sigh. 'Have you any plans for real food sometime tonight?'

'That's up to Mrs Domino. She's related to the Sotos. Sister, probably. Genetic eye problem. She's taking care of their office. She's the stumbling block. With her out of the way, I can talk her husband into giving me the Sotos' itinerary. I might even find out who hired 'em.'

The difficult part was waiting for the woman to leave the office. Ceeley groaned when a delivery boy brought the Dominos' lunch. By 1:30, a mailman had visited the office, one little girl had left the building, and two had gone in. We'd had a half-dozen cups of Chickee-Likee's finest mocha-java and Ceeley was ready to jump ship.

She stood up and said, 'The hell with doing it your way.' She picked up a dime from the change scattered on the tabletop, then marched to the phone. She riffled through the directory while both I and the counterman watched her with vague interest. She turned to the counterman. 'Is there a post office near here?' she asked him.

He blinked and croaked, 'The Old Town branch is two blocks over.'

'Fine,' she said, and popped the dime into the box and dialed a number.

'Hello,' she said in a semi-shrill voice, 'to whom am I speaking? Good. Mrs Domino, this is Mrs Phillips at the post office, Old

Town branch. We have a registered package for you from . . .' – she paused as if consulting a registered package – 'from somebody named Soto . . . Well, we can deliver it, of course, but probably not before tomorrow and it has "Rush" stamped all over it. Possibly you could drop by and pick it up . . . Let me see now. It just says Soto, but . . . well, I'm not sure.'

Ceeley gave me a shrug, then said, 'Maybe it could have been sent to Soto care of you. Yes. I'm sure that's it . . . Oh, Mrs Domino, I'm sorry but you'll have to sign for it yourself. Maybe we'd better just send it out tomor . . . Fine. That'll be fine, Mrs Domino. But we do close at five P.M..'

She slipped the receiver back onto the hook and dusted her hands walking back to the table.

Within minutes the myopic woman rushed from the building and headed toward Old Town.

'I'll take it from here,' I told Ceeley, and moved toward the door.

'The hell you will,' she said, following.

'Have you got a camera?' I asked her.

She nodded. 'In my luggage. But I need film.'

'Not for this. Get it.'

It took her a minute or two. In another minute we were opening the door to Jesus Domino, Photographer's, very quietly and moving around the counter. Ceeley yanked back the curtain while I aimed the camera and clicked.

Domino was at his camera. Two little girls were on the divan doing things that even big girls shouldn't do. I handed my camera to Ceeley and said, 'Take this down and get the film to the lab in a hurry.' She nodded and went off with the camera. Domino frowned at me and bit his lip, and the little girls looked at him, puzzled and afraid.

'Put some clothes on,' I said to them. To Domino I suggested, 'Let's go next door.'

'Eh?'

'To the Sotos'. You're gonna tell me how to find them.'

'But I can't –'

'Either that or I show the cops the picture I just took.'

'The cops don't care,' Domino said. 'You don't scare me.'

'OK. Scratch the cops. Suppose we go to the papers? Or TV? You're gonna be a very famous photographer, Jesus.'

'Shit,' he said. He went to the desk and opened a drawer. 'Those *pendejos*, the Sotos, nothing but trouble. *Imbecils*. My wife has all the brains in that family.'

'That must be why she married you,' I said.

'You mentioned a few bucks when you were here before.'

'Back then I hadn't caught your action with the little girls. How old are they?'

'Old enough.'

'Sure. What . . . fifteen?'

'Hey, man, I'm a photographer. I take pictures. Nothing really bad. No heavy stuff. Just pretty pictures. A little flesh here and there. A little touchy-kissy. Nothing that gringo David Hamilton don't do. They sell him in bookstores and me they sell in porno joints. You tell me the difference.'

'I'm still curious. How old?'

'Um . . . fourteen.'

Goddammit, Sarah's age.

The girls, dressed now, came out from behind the curtain. Apprehensive and chalk-faced, they circled us to get to the door as if they expected me or Jesus to do them some vague harm.

'You don't got to go,' he pleaded with them.

'Sure they do,' I told him. 'And if they come back, they'll get their butts tossed into a jail cell.'

The girls hurried out, slamming the door behind them. Domino shook his head. 'Shit, man. Them Chihuahuas know more at fourteen than you gonna learn your whole life. They gonna be back here, only now they think they can bring the heat down on me, they gonna charge me a goddamn arm and leg. You great for my business, man.'

'Fact is, Jesus, I'd like you out of business.'

'Then what happens to those kids, huh? They start to peddle it on the avenue. They a commodity, man, and they know it. They sell it any way they can.' He scribbled the name of a motel on a piece of paper and handed it to me. 'Here, take it and get the hell out of my face.'

I looked at it. 'Is this some kind of joke? The Rama Inn?'

'That's what they tell Constanza. No joke. They were there last night and today, probably. They waiting to see if somebody sends them money. She just went to the post office to see if it has arrived. Anyway, they gonna phone here soon to check in. If they moved, they'll tell us where.'

'When's the call coming through?'

'I don't know. When the crazy bastards feel like it.'

'Do they keep records in their office?'

He laughed. 'Records? Who you think you dealing with? Price-Waterhouse? Records! These guys can barely write. *Pendejos*. Juan, he got his ass knocked around in Vietnam. Bartolo, got no excuse. I don't care why you want 'em, what you want to do with 'em. They give me a royal pain in the ass, anyway. Them with their *Californio* bullshit. Men of honor. Just who the hell are they to tell me how to live my life? And their sister, she's the worst.'

'Who are they working for?'

He laughed. 'They don't even know, the assholes. They got paid some money in cash. Fast. Wired to 'em. Then they were supposed to get more. Maybe it'll happen, if the assholes are lucky enough.'

'What are they being paid to do?'

He shrugged. 'Who knows? Maybe Constanza, but if you expect her to tell you anything, you got less smarts than Juan.'

I started for the door. 'If you warn them, I'll have to come back here,' I said.

'Why the hell would I warn them? Then I got to explain to Constanza why I sent you to them. I be better off if I just pack up and hit the road, anyway. I been thinking of that. Going back south, where I was born. Getting into the easy money down there. This is shit. I should move back south. These goddamn Sotos are too much for a man to take.'

I shut the door on him. Ceeley was in the hall, leaning against a wall with the camera in her hand. 'You picked up some grease,' I told her, pointing to her hands.

She looked down at her smudged fingers. 'It's that kind of place,' she said.

We barely made it to the car before Constanza turned the corner, chugging swiftly to her husband's office. She had a disappointed look on her pinched, myopic face. It was likely to be there a while.

23

'I ought to take a stick to her,' Bartolo snapped at his brother as he shoved me roughly into the rear of the car.

Juan kept busy by loading the luggage into the trunk, but not too busy to make little clucking noises, like a nursing quail. He slammed down the trunk lid and he and Bartolo got into the car, Bartolo driving, of course.

'Bad little miss,' Juan said to me, a silly stern look on his cock-eyed face. I certainly felt no guilt. If Bartolo hadn't gotten so incensed by the long-distance call charged on the bill and if he hadn't made such a scene accusing the motel manager of trying to pad the bill, and if the manager hadn't called the number collect, and if the operator hadn't been so sloppy as to let Bartolo hear Mr Bloodworth's answering machine, there wouldn't have been any problem. I had been betrayed by a series of circumstances beyond my control.

We had spent most of the morning in the motel room waiting for their sister to call from Sacramento with the news that their mysterious client had wired money to their office. Why they hadn't asked him to send it directly to the motel, I'll never understand, but when I mentioned it to Bartolo, it just made him more furious.

At eleven, he left us to check on things at Sleepytime and to bring back food. It was nearly two when the brothers decided the money was not going to arrive. It was quarter to three when we drove past the Sleepytime Motel.

Bartolo had come up with a simply awful plan of action. We would keep track of Mother and low-life Gutierrez in hopes that their unknown client would be entering the hunt himself. Bartolo was sure that, having refused to pay them, he would now continue the job himself. If, on the other hand, no weird-looking stranger should join the procession of people following Mother and the gross Mr G., Bartolo would be forced to introduce himself to them and ask their help in figuring out precisely who the cheating client might be. The poor deluded Sotos!

Fortunately, it appeared as though neither of those avenues would be explored. As we parked near the entrance to the motel, Bartolo screamed, 'The goddamn Mercedes is gone!'

Juan looked at him helplessly. 'Maybe they just went out for an early dinner.'

Bartolo jerked open the car door, slamming it behind him. Juan's mouth was open, but he didn't have a chance to say whatever was on his rather simple mind. He turned to me. 'I guess he wants us to wait.'

'He may need help,' I said.

'He would have asked.'

'If he'd wanted you to wait, he would have said so.'

'Ha! Don't think you can trick me into leaving you in the car alone,' he said.

'I was thinking no such thing. We can both help Bartolo.'

Juan shook his head and smiled. 'You're a hot pepper is what you are, miss.' He got out of the car and held the door for me. 'You promise nothing funny?' he asked, too late really if I'd had that in mind.

'I promise,' I answered in truth, walking quickly with him toward Lovebirds Unit No. 3.

The door must have been open, because Bartolo had already

gone into the room. As we approached, he stepped back out into the motel yard. His face was an unhealthy shade of yellow. He jumped when he saw us. 'It was unlocked,' he said in a strange, strangled voice.

Juan, curious, moved toward the room. As did I. What we could see of it looked a mess. Near the door was a piece of bed linen with a dark brownish-red stain on it.

Bartolo grabbed my arm and turned me around, almost dragging me away.

Juan stood in the doorway. He started to step in but changed his mind. '*Madre de Dios!*' he uttered in a heartfelt manner.

'What is it?' I asked.

Bartolo didn't answer. He hissed to Juan, 'Shut the door.' Juan obeyed, then stepped back to us.

'Was there, ah, anything else in the bathroom?' he asked.

Bartolo shook his head 'Take the girl back to the car. I'll join you.'

'Where are you going?'

'To talk with the motel manager.'

'Is that wise, brother?'

'We have no choice. How else do we find out where they have flown?' Bartolo said.

Juan looked warily back to the closed door to No. 3. 'Do we really want to know?'

Bartolo glared at him. 'Have we been paid?'

Juan shook his head.

'Then we want to know.'

He strode quickly to the manager's office and Juan led me back to the car.

'What was in there?' I asked.

'A real mess,' he said.

'What kind of mess?'

'Nothing for you to worry about.'

'There was blood on that sheet,' I persisted.

'You crazy. Blood? Sheet? You don't know what you're talking about.'

'Was – was somebody hurt in there?'

He shook his head. 'I'm pretty sure, no. Nobody was. No human being.' He was obviously keeping the truth from me, but I couldn't pry it out of him. I didn't try too hard, because I knew that sooner or later, in conversation with his brother, he'd tell me enough for me to figure out what horrible thing had occurred in that motel room.

Bartolo joined us in about fifteen minutes. He seemed wiped out by the day thus far. He turned on the ignition before replying to his brother's first question. Only when we were on the road did he say, 'It cost me five dollars to find out the bastard Charteris – Gutierrez – made a call to the Sea and Sand Motel in Oceanside. And another three dollars to call the motel myself to make certain he'd reserved a room there tonight.'

'Oceanside! *Caca!* That's almost to *Mehico!*'

'So, brother, you want to go home and forget it?'

Juan whined, 'Such a long way. Hundreds of miles. So much gas. And we have to pay the rental place for each mile.'

'It is a matter of pride to be paid for one's work, brother,' Bartolo said. 'We will not be charged for this car or for anything else out of our own pocket. We will make that son-of-a-bitch client pay.'

'It may be wiser to let it be, Barto,' Juan said, scrunching up his face. 'Back there. All that blood . . .'

Bartolo cut him off in Spanish with one of the longest nonstop sentences known to man, jerking his head in my direction from time to time. Poor, stupid Juan would turn and stare at me with a woeful countenance, making that quail clucking noise.

'Was someone hurt back there?' I asked, once Bartolo had quieted down.

'No,' he shot back. 'You keep silent.'

'I have a right to know.'

Bartolo harrumphed and said, 'That Gutierrez and maybe your *madre*, they messed up that room real bad. But they must've been quiet about it, because the manager of the motel remains in ignorance of the condition of the room. Naturally, I did not educate him. He will discover it soon enough.

'The two of them were there when I checked just after noon. They must have . . . done what was done and then they drove away. The manager thought he saw them leave at five or so. He is expecting them to return and use the room for one more day. The bill is paid through tomorrow.'

'There was blood in the room,' I said.

Bartolo did not reply. But Juan, looking totally miserable, told me what they had found.

Though I did my best not to, I could not help crying. I begged them to drive back. To let me see for myself. They ignored my request, which was, of course, the smart thing to do. I pulled myself together. No more tears. Juan, watching me, started shaking his head sadly again.

No more tears, I commanded myself.

24

1. Ceeley's Buick ate up the highway while I chewed the inside of my mouth and wondered how the kid was making out. If that slimebag Domino was on the emmis about the Sotos' sense of morality and honor, maybe Sarah was in clover. I probably should have been worrying about the Sotos.

'What's bothering you?' Ceeley asked.

'Who's bothered?'

'You are. You hum when you've got something on your mind.'

'That's ridiculous. I hum when I'm happy.'

She shot me a skeptical look. 'Right. You spend a night in the slams. You stick your big nose in a kiddy-porn operation. The little girl you're supposed to be taking care of is in the company of a pair of – well, fairly skiffy characters. And we're headed toward an address that's probably as phony as my hair color. And you're happy.'

I turned on the radio. All it pulled in was A.M. punk rock. Country rock. Pop rock. News. News rock. Christ! I turned it off. The woman was smirking at me. On her, even a smirk looked good. 'For somebody who's a phony redhead, you've got a redhead's skin.'

'Is that a compliment?'

'Yeah, I suppose. What I mean is, it's a nice pale skin with little freckles. No warts or anything. Or liver spots.' I checked the backs of my hands.

'Wow, Leo, I've heard silver tongues before, but you . . . Keep it up and I'll follow you anywhere.'

Swell. I needed smart talk as much as I needed another heart fibrillation. 'OK. Forget I said anything. I was out of line.'

She frowned and looked at me as if I were one of the more pathetic sights all week. 'Out of line?' She had a nice healthy, explosive laugh. 'My God, Leo, what have you been doing the past thirty years? I wasn't criticizing your little pass. I was just having fun with your lame follow-up. How long has it been since you gave a woman a compliment?'

I shrugged. 'About six years ago. I thanked my last wife for her promptness in signing the divorce papers.'

'How many times have you been married?'

'Too many.'

'Practice is supposed to make perfect.' She lit another of her endless cigarettes. 'Anyway, I *am* a redhead. But not quite this shade. More like a candied apple or . . . your face right now. A little too vivid.'

I threw up my hands. 'Christ, lady, I guess I do get embarrassed. As if you didn't know, you look real good. And if we were bumping into each other in a bar, I'd certainly buy you a beer.'

Using two fingers, she moved the wheel several inches and neatly skirted the rear of a truck that was clotting our lane. 'With that approach, Leo, do you get much?'

'What kinda question is that?'

'An icebreaker, maybe. Don't you ever think about sex?'

I gave her a long look. 'Lady, saying you're impulsive is like saying Ali was a kinda good fighter.'

'You didn't answer me.'

'Well yeah, sure I think about it. When the time is right.'

'That, I take it, is not a compliment.'

'I meant when there's more time. Or a different time. Right now, I've got work to do.'

'Ah, the old work ethic. Work first. Fuck later.'

I yawned and turned away from her and rested my head against the seat, shutting my eyes.

'What's the matter now?' she asked.

'Women who use the word "fuck" usually spend more time talking about it than doing it.'

'Well, well, well,' she said, exhaling smoke in my direction, 'you sound like somebody's father, Leo.'

'I'm old enough to be yours.'

'But you aren't. And that's what makes all the difference, when you're talking fucking.'

'You're doing the talking,' I said. I turned toward her and opened my eyes. 'But if it'll save time in the long run, why don't we just pull into the nearest motel and get it over with and then maybe you can drive me to San Jose before your glands start twitching again.'

She gave me a deadly smile. 'Isn't it nice we're getting to know each other so well,' she said. Then she made the car jump forward until we were damn near flying to San Jose.

2. 'Well?' she asked as I sauntered back to the Buick from the Rama Inn.

I got into the car and said, 'Head back down Guadalupe Parkway. We're looking for a Sleepytime Motel.'

'We could just tuck ourselves in here,' she said around a cigarette.

'Let's let the smart talk go until there's less stress in the air, huh?'

She nodded and took off. 'The photographer creep give you bad directions?'

I shook my head. 'They left here a few hours ago.'

'Why'd they switch motels?'

'They didn't. Gutierrez is at the Sleepytime. Or he was.'

'How'd you find that out?'

'An investigator has his ways,' I said.

'Oh?' She was staring at me.

'The kid left a message on my recording machine back in L.A.'

'You mean we went through all that crap in Sacramento for nothing? You could have just called your office?'

The radio rock music suddenly didn't seem so bad.

We made it to the Sleepytime in jig time. There seemed to be some sort of commotion at the unit the kid had said was Gutierrez's. A handyman and two maids stood at the door while a small, sour-faced guy with a brush moustache and all of his scalp showing tried to shoo them away.

'This is dreadful,' he was saying to no one in particular as we hurried his way.

The room was caked with dried blood. All over the carpet. The bed linen. Splattered on one wall.

'Jesus,' I said, without meaning to.

The baldy with the brush turned to us. 'Oh, my word!' he exclaimed. 'I'm sorry. We've had a spot of trouble.'

'I'll say,' Ceeley added.

'We have a number of very clean, beautiful rooms, however,' he informed us, stepping away from the carnage site and shutting the door on it. 'If you'll just follow me to the office . . .'

'What the hell happened in there?' I said, not moving.

His eyes glazed a bit. 'Nothing to worry about.'

'Nothing? There was blood all over that room, Mac.'

'Blood. Yes,' he said very primly. 'And they looked like such a high-class couple, too. Savages. Degenerates. On dope, probably. But you mustn't be concerned.' He paused, as if to think something out, then said, 'Let me show you something, so you won't worry as much.' He turned back to the room, then paused with his hand on the knob. 'It's not my intention to shock the lady. Perhaps she –'

'What the hell is it?' I asked, too loudly. I was on the edge of panic and I probably scared him. He opened the door and I almost climbed over him into the room.

There was a dog on the carpet. It looked a lot like the picture of Sarah's mutt, Groucho. It wasn't in very good shape.

Somebody had cut its head off.

25

1. I tried to feign total naiveté as I walked back to the brothers who were waiting by the car. We were at an Exxon station near Seal Beach and the moon was glistening on the purple-blue ocean – a lovely sight if one has the opportunity to savor it. I didn't. Nor did I get the chance to see any seals, assuming they were up at nearly 10:00 P.M.

Bartolo shouted for Juan to drag me into the car, if necessary. Juan opened the door and politely allowed me to take my time getting in. 'What was that stuff with the gas-pump guy?' he asked.

I opened my eyes wide as if I didn't understand the question. 'Was that money you handed him?' he asked.

'No, I just gave him back the key to the rest room.'

Bartolo started the engine. He said to Juan, 'You took her money from her, like I told you?'

Juan moved his head from side to side as if he were physically ducking the question. 'She didn't have all that much, brother. Twenty dollar.'

'But you took it.'

'Not exactly.'

Bartolo spun the wheel to the right and pulled over to the side of the road. He shouted at poor Juan in Spanish for what seemed like an hour. Juan turned purple as a plum. Finally Bartolo just put his head against the steering wheel and began counting in Spanish. '*Uno . . . dos . . . tres . . .*'

Juan looked at him in consternation.

'Are we going to sit here all night?' I asked. 'I'm famished.'

'Hungry, yes,' Juan agreed.

Bartolo raised his head from the wheel and looked heaven-ward. Then, without another word, he steered the car back onto the street and drove away, taking whatever turns necessary to put us back on Route 5.

'Aren't you fellows hungry, too?' I asked. 'We haven't eaten for hours.'

Juan put his finger to his lips, indicating that I should be silent.

I saw no reason to be silent. I had every right to voice my opinion. I was sleepy and out of sorts and I was very depressed over the sad fate of my poor dear Groucho, for I was convinced it was he who had been treated so badly back at the motel. So I was in no mood to be cordial to the two fools who had probably kept Mr Bloodworth from saving my dog's life.

True, they could not have known what their delaying tactics would yield. Still, ignorance is no excuse, which was especially unfortunate in the case of the Sotos.

2. What with our stopping for barely edible fast-food chicken – absolutely rife with monosodium glutamate, sodium nitrate, and God knows what other poisons – we arrived late at the Sea and Sand Motel on the southern outskirts of Oceanside. In the bright moonlight I could see in the distance, along the coast, a replica of a light tower atop the Cape Cod House, the sort of place where decent people dine, people who are not on the run in the company of crazy Mexicans.

Bartolo drove slowly into the ugly motel with its tiny orange bungalows and red roofs, studying the parked cars. No white Mercedes. He should have known better. We circled the parking area and returned to the office.

'Why don't we get a room here and wait for them?' I asked.

Bartolo looked at the tacky bungalows and wrinkled his nose.

Juan said, 'We have to sleep somewhere.'

Bartolo nodded and got out of the car.

Juan turned to me. '*Chica*, can we please have peace tonight? Bartolo is ready to turn the corner. I know him. He can become wild, not know what he is doing.'

'I see no reason to cater to or sanction his fits. I am not here by choice.'

Juan sighed and got out of the car, too. He stood beside the door waiting for his brother to register for us. Why, I wondered, did young people not have to register? To be young and female is to know prejudice.

Bartolo hustled us into one of the hideous little orange bungalows – which had pale pink walls, wouldn't you know, and red and pink lisle bedspreads – and we were in the midst of unpacking when Bartolo slapped his head and said, 'Goddammit! They will not be coming here. This is the last place they will come.'

Juan asked, 'What are you saying, Barto?'

I, of course, knew exactly what he was saying and explained it. 'Gutierrez made this reservation before the – the horrible thing at the Sleepytime. He knows that the motel had a record of the call. So he won't come here, where he might be traced and –'

'And what?' Juan asked. 'He killed an animal in his room. This is a very sick thing, but it is hardly a serious police matter.'

'Do you forget how he makes his living, my dumb baby brother? Gambling is not legal. Dogfighting is not legal. He does not look for trouble, not even small trouble. He will not come here.'

Juan shook his head. 'If he doesn't want trouble, why does he do that in his room?'

I said, 'Maybe he didn't do it. Maybe somebody else did. Maybe your client even.'

Bartolo and Juan looked at each other. Then Bartolo sat down on one of the twin beds and picked up the phone. He punched an 8, then 1, and then ten more digits.

Juan asked, 'Constanza?' Bartolo nodded.

Juan turned to me and said, 'He's phoning our sister. She'll know what to do.'

'Why? Is she the brains of the family?'

It was not easy to insult Juan. He nodded and said, '*Si*. Very smart, Constanza.'

Bartolo's conversation was in Spanish. It didn't make him any happier. When he hung up, he turned to me. 'A man who sounds like Bloodworth was looking for us,' he said angrily. Then he turned to Juan and added, with a rare smile. 'He gave Jesus a difficult time.'

Juan grinned back.

'Jesus has threatened to leave Constanza. He says he can no longer work with all the distractions due to our business.'

'You think he will really leave this time?' Juan asked hopefully.

Bartolo shook his head. 'Where would the bastard find a home as comfortable or a woman like Constanza?'

'He is a pig.'

'Yes, but she loves him.'

'Your sister loves a pig?' I asked. 'And she's the smart one?'

Bartolo ignored me and said, 'Jesus sent Bloodworth to our motel in San Jose.'

'He didn't tell him about this place?'

Bartolo answered with a sigh of exasperation. 'How could he? Even we did not know where we would be staying.'

Juan nodded, relieved.

'Of course,' Bartolo went on, glaring at me, 'we do not know what this little – little girl said to Bloodworth's telephone machine.'

'She didn't know we were coming here then.'

'Maybe she left some kind of message for him back at that gas station. He could be here any . . .' He shook his head. 'I am getting as foolish as you, Juano. Bloodworth and his woman left Jesus in the afternoon. They would have to drive to San Jose, and then, even if they found Gutierrez's motel there, I imagine the mess might hold him up quite a while. He could still be there, trying to figure it all out.'

'What was that about Mr Bloodworth's woman?' I asked.

'He's with some redhead, Constanza says.' Bartolo added to Juan, 'The woman reminded her of Rise.'

Juan, that buffoon, raised his eyes to heaven, shook his hand as if it had been burned and made animal moans. 'That Bloodworth won't have much else on his mind if she looks like Rise.'

'When you boys are through with your filthy pipe dreams, you might want to concentrate on finding Gutierrez's trail. I don't plan on spending the rest of my life with worthless wretches like yourselves.'

'Don't worry about our finding Mr Gutierrez,' Bartolo said. 'I know how to find him.' He got off the bed and headed for the door. Juan started to follow. Bartolo spit some Spanish that froze him to the carpet. His reply was short. Bartolo answered that, pointing to me and then to the closet.

'Oh, no,' I said defiantly. 'You're not putting me in there.'

'You'll get in there and like it, you little witch.'

'Brother, that is no way to talk to an *inocenta*.'

Bartolo's reaction to this was surprising. He took a deep breath and apologized to me. They were some pair, the Soto brothers.

★

3. Juan's taste in TV was predictably awful, running to half-hour sitcoms featuring girls with their breasts bouncing around and displaying as much intelligence as your average aphid. It seemed to make him both horny and superior, an unbeatable combination.

He'd rolled the set from the wall and placed it between the two beds so that we could stretch out and watch with pillows propping our heads. It was very comfortable, but Gran had once warned me that watching TV in bed could eventually alter a person's character for the worse.

During commercials I discovered from Juan that there was a connection between Gutierrez and a local resident by that same name who was a very highly regarded member of the Mexican criminal element. He lived in a full-security complex named Oceancliff Harbor, near the new Oceanside Marina. Gran and I had visited that very place. One of her cronies was in retirement there, an elderly gay gentleman named Miles Baumgarten, who wore a green velvet smoking jacket with his initials on the pocket and who affected a British accent and pretended that life was one big Noël Coward play. He would positively turn to stone if he knew that one of his neighbors was a Mexican Mafia man.

'Suppose Gutierrez has already done whatever he came here to do and has moved on?' I asked Juan.

He shrugged. 'Then, tomorrow, Barto calls this important man's home and uses the name of one of our cousins – a distant member of the family, actually – and tries to get a new location for Gutierrez.'

'Why doesn't he just do that first?'

'*Chica*, you do not understand how difficult it would be for Bartolo to have to use this cousin's name. The man is worse than garbage, though he is of our blood.'

'Then let's assume that Bartolo finds Gutierrez. What then?'

'He will speak to Gutierrez and find out who our cheating client may be.'

'And he thinks Gutierrez will tell him? Just like that?'

The poor deluded cross-eyed boob gave me a patronizing look. 'I know it is hard for you to understand, *chica*, but it is to Gutierrez's advantage. When there are two, ah, opposing parties, if one is working for one party and then offers to change allegiance, the other party should be quite, ah, happy.'

'This Gutierrez is a heartless killer. I told you what he tried to do to Mr Bloodworth.'

'Bloodworth was opposing him. We want to aid him,' Juan said, as if he were talking to a five-year-old.

'Mister Bloodworth was following him. Just like you and Bartolo are following him.'

Juan frowned. 'Barto can take care of himself.' But he was no longer all that confident.

It was doing me no good making Juan nervous and apprehensive, so I ended our conversation. We watched the screen in silence for a while. UBC promoted Gary Grady's new show every half-hour, telling us how funny and wonderful and youthful it would be. They continued to stress youthful, though I could see nothing youthful about the fellow. He must have been at least thirty-five.

Juan had a bit of trouble concentrating on the screen. Bartolo was taking longer than he expected and he kept consulting his watch anxiously and sipping from a succession of warm beers he had purchased at the gross fast-food parlor where we'd eaten.

'Don't worry,' I tried to comfort him. 'Your brother can take care of himself, like you told me.'

'He is not as tough as he seems. He has a big heart.'

'Yours is not exactly pea-size,' I said. 'Don't worry. Try to sleep.'

He nodded. 'Maybe you're right. My brain is weary.'

I let that pass without comment. He pushed himself off the bed and went to the closet. He found extra pillows and blankets in there and tossed them onto the floor. 'You get ready for bed, too, *chica*. I'm sorry, but Bartolo said you must sleep in the closet, locked in. You should not have phoned Bloodworth last night.'

I looked at the blankets on the closet floor. There seemed to be just about enough room for me to sleep with my legs straight out. 'Must you lock the door?'

'*Si*.' He was definitely not happy about it.

I didn't have the energy or the heart to give him much of an argument. Like a very tired young lady, I dragged myself to the bathroom, performed what Gran calls my 'evening ablutions', and then headed reluctantly to the closet. Though I did not resist the confinement, I did manage to leave him with one of my special pitiful looks, guaranteed to induce industrial-size guilt in much stonier souls than his.

When I had stretched out on one blanket and he had covered me with another and made sure the pillows were comfortable, he gave me a sad goodnight and shut the door. I felt a momentary tightness in my chest in the dark, close quarters, relieved in no way by the dreadful click of the lock. Through the door, Juan said, 'Sorry, *chica*. I mean it.'

I knew he did. I closed my eyes and thought about Mr Bloodworth and his new red-haired lady friend. I hoped he wasn't going into his famous dim bars, cavorting with the demimonde, when he should have been looking for me. No. If he'd gone to the Sotos' office, he was on the trail. The Bloodhound was on the trail, no matter who the redhead was. My thoughts skipped to Gran, and poor, forever-gone Groucho.

And then, I suppose, I fell asleep.

★

4. There was a thud that shook the floor and woke me. That was followed by a grunt and gurgling noises. With my eyes wide open, I could see objects in the dark closet – a few empty hangers overhead, the brass doorknob, a sign covered by a plastic square, screwed into the door.

There was another thud, very near. Then a little yelp noise, more human than not. Then something crashed into the closet door. The knob began to turn. I recoiled from it.

I heard the lock click open as the knob continued to move. Then the door swung outward on a sight as horrible as any I ever hope to see. In the light of an overturned lamp on the floor, Juan was on his knees by the closet, dressed in his underwear, the awful little jockey shorts that look like slingshots. There was blood gushing from his throat, pouring out in torrents. His sad crossed eyes looked at me pleadingly and then became uncrossed and went up into his skull.

I tried to scream, but no sound would come. I moved forward to help the poor man, still not quite registering the full horror. Before I could take a step, the door was slammed in my face by someone else in the room. The lock clicked shut again. I shouted, 'Bartolo? Please. Let me out.' But I realized as I was saying it that Bartolo wasn't there to hear me.

A muffled voice said through the door, 'Stay where you are, girl. Safe and sure, flower girl. There's nothing but death out here.'

There was something chillingly familiar about the singsong and the name 'flower girl', but I couldn't come to grips with it. The image of Juan covered in his own blood expanded in my mind, crowding everything else out. I backed away from the door as far as I could and began to shake. Even with all the blankets wrapped around me.

The voice began to croon, 'Show me a rose, I'll show you a stag at bay.'

My teeth were chattering. I could not stop shaking, not even after the singing stopped. I don't know how long I was in that closet. It was nearly dawn when Mr Bloodworth rescued me. By then I must have looked as if I'd turned the corner.

26

1. The false-alarm terror of the motel room in San Jose had been the perfect warmup for what we found at the Sea and Sand in Oceanside. This time the blood was human and still warm. The poor son of a bitch in his skivvies near the closet had been cut long and deep and he'd bled fast.

I wasn't surprised to find him. I'd already discovered his brother in the car parked in front of their orange and red bungalow. His body had been draped along the front seat, decranked by a garrote, just like Roy Kaspar. During the night anybody seeing him would have assumed he was just another drunk who hadn't quite made it back to his motel room.

The bald-headed manager of the Sleepytime in San Jose had told us that two Mexicans and a young girl had been headed to Oceanside in search of Charteris. He figured they'd probably be too late. He had already phoned the Sea and Sand's manager, a Mr Carpiellier, to warn him about the sort of pervert that Charteris was. It was his hope that he might eventually get Charteris to pay for the damage to his room.

I doubted that he'd swing that one. He didn't even know the guy's real name, and Gutierrez had several more-pressing commitments and would not be staying at the Sea and Sand, where half the world was expecting him. But I thought the Sotos might, considering their linear approach to life.

We got there at 2:00 A.M. Ceeley, who'd been sleeping, or

trying to, rubbed her eyes and coughed. Her makeup had long gone and there was the pattern of the vinyl upholstery on her cheek. On her it looked great.

Her reaction to the first Soto brother was to light a gasper with a very shaky hand. Mine weren't much steadier as I took the pieces of my .38 from the suitcase, fumbled them together, and slipped in some shells.

Inside the motel room, Ceeley didn't stop to study the second, bloodier Soto. She said, 'I don't see the girl.'

I made a quick scan. Blood. Bed linen dragged across the carpet. More blood. A lamp resting on its side. A tipped-over end table. A TV set canted at an odd angle near the bed. I stepped over the body and the blood and went into the bathroom, poking the air with my gun. Nothing in there but towels, used and fresh; twin imitation-leather shaving kits, one unzipped; and the kid's little pink travel kit. Back in the bedroom, Ceeley had shut the front door and was leaning against it. She looked paler than usual, which was damn near chalklike.

'I'd better go outside,' she said.

I nodded, moving toward the closet. The door handle was sticky with drying blood. I used the tail of the bed linen to turn the knob. The lock popped out and the door swung open. No blood in there. Just Sarah, shoved into a corner, shivering and grinning at me like one of those pathetic strays you see in doorways along Hollywood Boulevard.

I backed away, found the kid's suitcase, and scooped up her jeans and T-shirt and underwear and tossed them into it. Then I lifted her out of the closet. She was as rigid as a marlinspike. One thin arm went around my neck as if it were a life preserver and a little hand grabbed my coat lapel and tried to pleat it. I wrapped the blanket around her, then grabbed her luggage.

Ceeley was waiting near the car door. She took the luggage. The kid and I almost fell into the back seat on top of the suitcases that were piled on the floor. Ceeley slammed the kid's stuff into the trunk and got behind the wheel. I raised my head and looked back. In the predawn shadows, nothing else seemed to be stirring at the Sea and Sand.

Extricating myself from the girl, I told Ceeley, 'I'm sorry, but I've got to go back.'

'What the hell for?'

'I have to check something. Park down the street away from here. If it gets crowded, I don't want you two involved.'

I turned my attention toward Sarah. The shivering was coming in intermittent spurts now and the rigidity of her jaw was loosening. I pried her fingers from my lapel and tried to get her to lie down on the seat. She wouldn't bend her body.

'Flower girl,' she said, for no apparent reason.

'C'mon, Sarah. It's OK now. Everything's fine.' I wondered how much she'd seen, what she could tell me when she rejoined the party. Then I was hit by a thought that made me shiver. 'Maybe we'd better get her to a hospital.'

Ceeley looked over her shoulder. 'Are her lips blue?'

'Nope. Sort of pale, though.'

'Is she hurt? Neck or back? Any bleeding?'

'Uh, I don't think so. No bleeding that I can see.'

'Trouble breathing?'

'Nope.'

'Let me get back there, you oaf.'

I stepped backward out of the car and she raced around and took my place. She ran her hands over the kid's face and arms and got her to sort of lean back on the seat until she was lying down. 'Give me your coat,' Ceeley said.

She took it and rolled it into a ball and put it under the kid's feet. Then she covered her with the blanket. She turned to me. 'I don't think there's anything wrong physically. But we should get her to a hospital, to be sure.'

'No,' the kid said suddenly. 'No. I'll be all right. No hospital. Nothing happened to me.'

'All right,' Ceeley said to her in a soft voice. 'Just lie down. Just relax, honey.'

'Don't call me that,' the kid said. 'My name is Serendipity.'

Ceeley shot me an indignant look and I grinned back at her. The kid was OK. 'I'll only be a few minutes,' I told them.

I moved quickly back to the Soto's car. I let myself into the back seat, being careful to use my shirt cuff. Then I leaned over the seat and began pawing through the dead man's clothes. I didn't waste too much time with that. His wallet was gone and one of his pants pockets was turned inside out.

I was about to get the hell out of there when an object on the carpet caught my eye – a thin, rectangular slab of granite, two inches long. I slipped it into my shirt pocket and went back to the girls.

We got away from there without bumping into any nosy citizens.

2. The kid was herself again, which meant she was hungry. We wound up at a wood and glass drive-in joint overlooking the Pacific called the Grab It and Growl. There we shared an early-bird breakfast with a bunch of guys in polyester suits with their sample cases safe between their ankles. Aside from Sarah's reaction to Ceeley, and especially to Ceeley's cigarettes, the meal went normally enough. We were all too weary to trade insults.

While putting away two bowls of Kadota figs in cream and a box of some kind of crispy flakes, Sarah told us of her adventures with the hard-luck Sotos. The kid was tougher than I was. She hesitated only slightly before describing the horror of the night she'd just spent.

'Maybe I really hadn't heard his voice before,' she said, ending her tale. 'Maybe I was just imagining it.'

'You're sure it was a male voice?' I asked.

'It was deep,' she said. Then she opened her eyes wide. 'It wasn't Faith, I'm sure of that.'

'Gutierrez,' Ceeley suggested.

'No. There wasn't even the hint of an accent, and it was deeper than his voice. And . . . spookier.'

I took a sip of the worst coffee this side of the Chickee-Likee and flipped the 'flower girl' business over in my mind, along with the song about flowers. A rose. Show me a rose. Sarah remembered only that part of it. If it meant anything, it wasn't going to come to me that morning. It had been nearly forty-eight hours since I'd slept and my mind and body knew that for a hard fact. Ceeley had grabbed a few hours' rest on the road, but she wasn't exactly penny-bright either. And the kid was limp lettuce.

We'd had our fill of motels, so we checked into connecting rooms at the Manor House in Oceanside, a solid old hotel that had weathered earthquake, rainstorm, and computerization. The desk clerk wore a boiled collar and a carnation in his lapel. The bellhop was old enough to call me 'sonny'. And the bed had a mattress covered by crisp, clean sheets and a light wool blanket.

Aching in every joint, I flopped over on my stomach and dug my fists under the pillow. I wanted to check out the Mafia Man at Oceancliff Harbor, but he could wait. Sarah didn't know his name, but I did. Cugat had told me all about the guy, Gutierrez's uncle Emiliano, the man they called El Jefe.

I yawned. He probably didn't get up before afternoon, anyway. Fine with me. With the drapes closed, I couldn't tell what time it was. Not important. The bed was soft. I felt myself going. I didn't hear the connecting door open or any movement in the room. But I sort of came alive when I felt a tall, strapping woman suddenly in the bed with me, pressing against me. I turned slightly and was enough of a detective to find her lips in the darkness.

When we came up for air, I asked, 'The kid asleep?'

'Really? That's what's on your mind right now?'

I stopped thinking about the kid for a while.

3. I woke feeling rested and pleased with myself. My watch said that it was in the 4:00 P.M. vicinity. Ceeley must have gone back to her room with Sarah. I stretched, bounded from the bed like a young man of – oh, say forty-two – and cha-cha-ed across the floor to the bathroom.

Shaved and showered and feeling just fine, I put on my rumpled duds, walked jauntily to the connecting door, and gave it a discreet knock. The kid invited me in.

She was sitting on the edge of one of the twin beds, the one that had been slept in, fully dressed in jeans and T-shirt and giving me a scornful look.

'Where's Ceeley?' I asked.

'Where do you think she is, Mr Detective? She's gone. Left hours ago. She told me to be sure to let you sleep, that an old duffer like you needed his sleep.'

'She didn't say that. Where'd she go?'

'She didn't confide in me.'

'C'mon, kid. This is serious.'

Sarah hopped off the bed and went to a polished maple writing table. She picked up an envelope and handed it to me. Hotel stationery. With my name on it in Spencerian hand. The letter had a nice economy to it.

'Dear Leo,' it read. 'I'm sure you're enough of a pro to know that we do what we must to get the job done. Some things we enjoy, like this morning. Some we don't, like now. You know the game. You told me a bunch of half-truths. I told you one or two. Call me next time you're in the City by the Bay and we can swap stories and lies and secret tricks of the gumshoe trade. I'm listed under my real name, Gwen Nolte. Love.'

I slipped the letter into my coat pocket. The kid was watching me very carefully. 'Well?' she demanded.

'Her real name is Gwen Nolte. She's a private detective from San Francisco. I've heard of her. Supposed to be real good at serving papers. Works for a group of lawyers and a few other money clients.'

'I knew she was a phony the first time I laid eyes on her,' the kid said.

'So did I,' I told her. 'The night I got tagged at the dogfight by Gutierrez's pals, she was in the crowd. Only she never mentioned it. She told me she was a teller in a bank, but she didn't talk like a bank teller. And the way she smoked, I don't think she could have stood being without a cigarette that long. Finally, she was too damn good at the Sea and Sand. Regular citizens don't walk in on a homicide scene and calmly shut the door behind them.' I smiled.

'What?' the kid asked.

'When I was dragging you from the closet, she must've been outside in the car, going through Soto's pockets.'

The kid eyed me skeptically. 'Why didn't you tell her you were on to her?'

'I was waiting to find out what her game was.'

'And what was her game?'

I stared at her. 'If you're a good kid, maybe I'll tell you.'

'You don't know.'

'Oh, I know, all right,' I said. 'The Bloodhound always knows.'

'Sure,' she said sarcastically, crossing the room to snap her suitcase shut. My effectiveness with the opposite sex seemed to be on the fritz that day.

27

1. The red-haired trollop sneaked out of Mr Bloodworth's room at about 11:00 A.M., shutting the door quietly behind her and tiptoeing across the carpet. She spent a few minutes in the bathroom, then returned wearing a cotton dress that was too bright and too young for her. She put her cosmetics case and other tools of her trade into a soft tan canvas bag and was zipping it shut when I asked, 'Going somewhere?'

She jumped and grabbed the spot where a normal person has a heart. Then she regained her composure and put on an insincere smile. 'I thought you were asleep.'

'You didn't commit any harm on him, did you?' I asked, nodding my head in the direction of Mr Bloodworth's room.

This time her smile was more genuine. 'No. He's healthy as a hog.' She continued putting her gear together for a quick departure.

'Does he know you're running out?'

'Aren't you sleepy? You had a rough morning.'

'I'm not in the least sleepy and I asked you a question.'

'No. He doesn't know. I'm going to write him a note – of explanation.'

'Were you two intimate?'

She cocked an eyebrow. 'You might put it that way.'

'Then you're lovers?'

She bit the inside of her mouth and frowned. 'Given the right set of circumstances, we could be. But you seldom get the right set of circumstances.'

'Then you care for him? A great deal?'

'Probably not as much as you do.'

So she had some degree of sensitivity. I watched her sit down at the writing desk and scratch out a message for Mr Bloodworth. She moved her lips while she wrote – I've always considered that the sign of a near-illiterate. Eventually she folded the note and stuck it into an envelope. She sealed the envelope, as if I would stoop to read someone else's letter.

'When was the last time you spoke with your mother?' she asked suddenly.

Talk about confusion! What did that have to do with anything? 'I don't know. A year ago, maybe.'

'You didn't see her last week, when she and Gutierrez were in L.A.?'

I shook my head.

'Have you got a bankbook?'

'What?'

'A bankbook. A savings book. With Golden Pacific.'

'I – I used to.' It was the reason I had a Gold PacCard.

'What happened to it?'

It was a very odd question and it provoked a very odd sensation in me. 'I'm not sure, really. I haven't seen it in a while.'

She nodded, then picked up her luggage and headed for the door. 'Let him sleep,' she told me. 'He's going to need as much rest as possible if he's planning what I think he is.'

'What might that be?'

'Oh, no. If he hasn't figured out his next move, I don't want to put any ideas in his head. So long, Serendipity. Try not to grow up too fast. Being an adult is the shits.'

'Uh. Before you go – is he – I mean, is he a good lover?'

'That depends on if you're talking tenderness or warmth or just, you know, the basic goods.'

'I don't know what I mean. That's why I asked. I've never – that is to say . . .'

'Well, my suggestion would be – and I admit to a certain amount of experience in these matters – that you don't rush right in and find out for yourself. Take three or four years to observe all the mistakes your pals make. The pregnancies and the herpes and the God-knows-what-all. Then you find yourself some tall, tanned, bleach-brained nineteen-year-old – that's the prime time for males, by the way, nineteen – and a gynecologist with a sense of humor and have yourself one hell of an eighteenth summer.'

It was patronizing, but I had to give her points for originality. 'You still didn't answer my question about Mr Bloodworth.'

'Well, from my point of view, men are either stirrups or stallions. You step on the stirrups to mount the stallions. Leo may spend more time at a slow trot than a full gallop, but you wouldn't want to risk stepping on him. Not without good cause. Make sure he gets the letter, huh, lady. And take care of yourself.'

With that she was gone. The red-haired strumpet was gone.

2. It was a number of hours before Mr Bloodworth strode into the room with a big, beaming smile on his face. His yellow hawk eyes traveled about and registered the fact that I was there alone. His chin dropped to the carpet.

'Where's Ceeley?'

'Left about three hours ago. She told me not to wake you, that you needed your sleep.'

'Left? Left to go where?'

'She didn't confide in me,' I said, a bit peeved that he chose not to inquire about my state of mind after the nightmare I had been through.

'C'mon, kid, this is serious.'

'I can see that.' I picked up the letter and handed it to him. He tore it open and devoured it with his eyes. He didn't read it aloud, but that was all right. I'd already steamed it open in the bath. It seemed that the woman known as Ceeley was in fact a San Francisco private eye named Gwendolyn Nolte. I wished she had told me that before leaving. I had all sorts of questions about that fascinating line of work. I was considering a similar career for myself.

Mr Bloodworth, as dejected as ever a man was, sank into a chair and stared morosely at the carpet. He gave me a brief summary of the letter and I reacted as if it were news to me. 'So she put one over on the Bloodhound, eh?' I asked.

'It might look that way to a kid,' he bristled. 'Actually I've been playing along with her, till I could figure out her game.'

'What is her game?'

'You let me worry about that,' he answered gruffly.

'Well,' I said, evoking a cheeriness I did not feel, 'I'm all packed. Where do we go now?'

'Where, indeed,' he mumbled, adding a heartfelt, 'Dammit. Damn all dames to hell.'

'Ceel– eh, Gwendolyn thought your next move might require a great deal of effort and energy.'

'Huh? Oh. She probably thought I'd go to see old man Gutierrez. Used to be the head of the Mex Mafia. But there doesn't seem to be much point now in rattling his cage. I think we'll head back to LA. so's I can dump you with your grandmother and get on about my other business.'

I couldn't believe it. 'But nothing's solved. Nothing's explained. The Sotos have been killed. There's a murderer out there, ready to strike again.'

He shrugged. 'I feel old and tired, kid. Not up to shagging after killers. The cops'll get the guy sooner or later.'

'Later, huh. After he's found my mother, maybe.'

'OK, let's look at that,' he said, leaning back in the chair and staring at a corner of the ceiling. 'Let's say Roy Kaspar and your mother and Gutierrez got somebody mad at 'em in L.A. This "somebody" used a garrote on Roy. He used the same weapon on one of the Sotos and took the other one out with a blade. The guy who chased me in your building had a knife.'

'Groucho's head was . . .' I couldn't finish the sentence.

'Right. That's very interesting. I read something about . . . yeah, the Viet Cong mutilated domestic animals to terrorize villages. Now that's real interesting . . .'

He seemed to be drifting away. 'Are you all right, Mr Bloodworth?'

'Huh? Oh, sure. Right. The knife. Yeah. That's interesting, too.' He reached into his pocket and pulled out a strange-looking gray-black stone. He ran his thumb over it. 'OK,' he said, and from the look of him the Bloodhound was back on the scent. 'We've got a killer. My guess is he hired the Sotos to lead him to – well, let's say, Gutierrez. The Sotos were killed because they stumbled onto his identity.'

'It must have been Bartolo. Poor Juan couldn't have even stumbled onto his own feet.'

'This guy hired 'em, I'm sure. They thought we knew where your mother and Gutierrez were and they followed us. But why did the Sotos put the snatch on you?'

'They didn't know what Mother looked like. They needed me to identify her. They told me that.'

'Well, I guess I'd better go talk to El Jefe,' he said. 'I'll be back for you soon.'

'We'll go see him together!'

'Uh – uh, he's not a nice man. I'd be worried about you and I wouldn't get as much out of him.'

So we went to see El Jefe.

When we checked out of the hotel, Mr Bloodworth discovered that the redhead had paid the bill and had even arranged a rental car for us. This seemed to infuriate him, but I silently and begrudgingly applauded Miss Nolte for a sense of style I had not thought she possessed.

3. Oceancliff Harbor was a series of very expensive condos – according to Gran, a year ago they'd started at a half-million, and I shuddered to think of what they were selling for now – that were designed to look seaworthy but modern. Lots of smoked glass staring out at the Pacific, and terraces and balconies and sun decks from which to court the cancerous sun.

While we paused before an iron gate, waiting for a reply from the Gutierrez buzzer, some handyman must have turned the switch causing a totally fake waterfall and stream to start rippling throughout the complex.

'Cute,' Mr Bloodworth said about the water. Then he turned to me and said, 'This is my last and final word, kid. Get back in the car.'

A metallic voice that sounded too refined to belong to a Mexican Mafia man asked, 'Yes? Your business, please?'

'My name is Leo Bloodworth. I'd like to talk to Mr Gutierrez about his nephew, Danny.'

There was a pause, then a woman's voice asked, 'Who is that with you?'

'Ah, Miss Serendipity Dahlquist,' the big detective replied, a bit hesitatingly.

More silence. Then the woman said, 'Face the camera, please.'

Mr Bloodworth turned toward a TV camera that was perched on top of the stone fence. I hadn't noticed it before – but then, Mr Bloodworth was taller and nearer the machine and he was a trained observer. I faced the camera also.

The woman's voice continued, 'Young lady, are you the sister of Danny's woman?'

'No,' I replied.

'You have the same name, the same family name.'

'She's my mother.'

'I will send Pepe. You wait.'

Pepe turned out to be a bantam rooster of a man in a purple velvet suit. He approached along a path beside the fake babbling brook, nimbly hopped over a footbridge, and greeted us with a wide smile under his black moustache.

'*Saludos*,' he said, withdrawing a large revolver from a gray suede holster under his jacket. 'Excuse, but we have a procedure.' With his free hand, he found a key in his coat pocket and opened a metal door built into the wall near the gate hinges. He pressed a switch behind the door and the iron gate swung open slowly.

'This is certainly more of an ordeal than going to visit Miles Baumgarten,' I muttered.

'Who?' Mr Bloodworth asked.

'A friend of Gran's who lives around here.'

Pepe requested that we take one step forward. We obeyed and he grinned, reached into the little wall recess, and threw a few more switches. Then he locked the metal door.

Mr Bloodworth and I had to stand aside to let the iron gate swing shut.

Pepe put his gun back into his holster and took a position just ahead of us. As we followed him up the path to the house, Mr Bloodworth asked, 'Did you scan us back there?'

Pepe nodded happily. He was very good-natured. 'Neat, huh?' he said. 'It's made by the same company that does the airports.'

'What happens when somebody tries to bring a weapon in?'

'That depends.'

'On what?'

'On who they are.'

'What about relatives like Danny?'

'I think he would not be allowed to bring one in.'

'Has to leave his knife outside, huh?'

Pepe grinned wider. 'Knife? Now that would be a rare sort of weapon for Danny. You are familiar with Juan Belmonte's observation that the closer one works to the bull, the tighter the grip of fear on the entrails. It is my belief that Danny, who is my own cousin, would work the bull from a distance of not less than four hundred yards. He is not a man for close work of any kind. No knives for that one. Guns are another matter.'

The Gutierrez condo was three times the size of the old Mr Baumgarten's, a tri-story bunkerlike building of gray concrete trimmed in white wood. It had been built about a hundred yards from a promontory that looked down, very far down, on a ragged coastline and the foamy surf of the Pacific. A rough wood stairwell went down the cliff to a small private beach where a girl or a tiny woman rested on a towel enjoying the late evening sun.

The gray building was surrounded by the babbling brook, accessible only by a wooden footbridge. That must have made the former Mafia chieftain feel even more secure. Though if someone had really wanted to harm him, I don't suppose they'd have hesitated to wade through some dippy fake brook.

Pepe brought us into the house through a spacious kitchen where two maids and a butler, all black, prepared finger sandwiches and drinks. Another butler entered the room through a swinging door, bringing with him the loud chatter of lady talk.

'Having a party?' Mr Bloodworth asked.

'The usual,' Pepe replied.

We went through the swinging door into a long, white hall with a pale peach carpet. Contemporary paintings had been hung precisely at adult eye level, with little gallery lights shining down on them. It looked as coldly efficient as the County Art Museum.

Pepe moved us quickly past an open entryway to a large room where, facing a splendid picture-window view of the blue sky and the Pacific, twenty-four or more elderly people sat at tables playing cards and chirping like magpies. Nearly all of them were women of the coal-black-dyed-hair variety. There was, however, a scattering of plump gray-haired men, looking as if they would have preferred being anywhere else in the world.

One of them had the biggest head I'd ever seen, with a lion's mane of white hair in shocking contrast to his burnt-orange jowly face. Mr Bloodworth stopped to look at the old guy and Pepe said, 'This way, please.'

We continued on up a flight of stairs – simulated-stone slabs that seemed to be floating on the wall. Tacky, actually. Mr Bloodworth asked Pepe, 'What's going on downstairs?'

'Canasta,' Pepe said. 'The game of choice at Casa Gutierrez.'

'Is that a card game?' I asked.

'Before your time, kid.'

'Just about everything was,' I grumbled.

Pepe said, 'To quote the great Cervantes, "The bow cannot always stand bent, nor can human frailty subsist without some lawful recreation."'

'What are you talking about?' I asked.

Pepe shrugged. 'Card-playing. Or, rather, the art of enjoyment. Youngsters read it, grown men understand it, and old people applaud it,' he went on in his silly, confusing manner.

We continued up past the second floor to the top, then along another hall straight out of the County Museum, only with a plum carpet. The paintings were all nude women. Mr Bloodworth eyed them furtively.

Pepe rapped quietly on a closed set of double doors and they were opened by a handsome Latin woman whom I judged to be middle-aged. In her forties if she was a day. She was in some sort of office. Unlike the rest of the horribly modern house, the furnishings here were Early American – a rolltop desk, good high-back chairs with worn armrests, a small cot positioned beneath a skylight and covered with a patchwork quilt. A long dark wood table held an assortment of fabric swatches, sketches, pincushions.

One side of the room was glass, facing the ocean and leading to a balcony. The other side was a wall papered with drawings, photos of women in stylish dresses, fashion junk of all kinds.

The Latina introduced herself as Carlotta Gutierrez. She dismissed Pepe and indicated that we should be seated. She studied me with a playful smile. 'So you are Faith Dahlquist's daughter, eh?'

I nodded.

'There is more than a small resemblance.'

'I don't see it, myself,' I said.

The woman's dark eyebrows went up. 'Do I detect a touch of trouble in the family?'

Mr Bloodworth said, 'Ms Gutierrez, ma'am, I wonder if I could have a few minutes with El Jefe?'

'With my father? Why?'

Mr Bloodworth made a helpless gesture with his hands. 'Uh, your father . . . well, let's see. Danny would be your – uh . . .'

'My brother Tio's son. Tio brought dishonor to the family by marrying an outsider, a very stupid Nordic girl, of all things. I bring dishonor by not marrying anyone.' She continued to look at me. 'At least, I have not married in the conventional sense. You have much nicer hair than your mother, girl.' She reached out and touched it.

Oh, Lordy. Mr Bloodworth looked ever more uncomfortable. 'Ah . . . Miz Gutierrez –'

'Carlotta.'

'Carlotta. I'd like to talk to your father about Danny.'

'Why?'

'I'm trying to locate him. At least, I want to find Faith Dahlquist. I assume they're together.'

'A logical assumption. But what you ask is impossible. My father talks with no one.'

'Isn't that him playing canasta downstairs?'

'Yes. I meant he talks to no outsiders. Pride, you know.'

'What's pride got to do with it?'

'My father suffers from premature senility. He has a repertoire of perhaps five rather droll stories that become rather tiresome after the fourth or fifth reprise. As a result, he talks to no one, except the canasta players, who are no keener of wit than he.'

Carlotta Gutierrez turned to me. 'So you want to find your mother?'

'Yes,' I said carefully. 'I'm worried about her.'

'You should be. Danny is about as dependable as a raincoat of seersucker.'

'It's possible that both she and Danny may be in danger,' Mr Bloodworth said.

'What danger?' Carlotta asked.

He hesitated. 'Possibly something connected with Old Dominion.'

'The dogfights? I cannot believe that anyone . . . It is true that our family's influence weakens in the northern areas of the state. That is why we use the not-always-reliable Danny. Thanks to his mixed blood, he can pass for Caucasian, making him an "acceptable" collector. But I hardly think any of our business associates would dare harm him.'

'If your father is not in full control of his –'

'My father has been the way he is for a number of years,' she said, her eyes flickering. 'When he was – replaced, our family was granted several small but viable enterprises, including Old Dominion. It was understood that I would be in charge, and no one complained. I think I have more than proved myself. So I refuse to believe that any harm might come to Danny from that quarter. Unless I initiate it, which I have not.'

'For a family free from danger, you keep pretty tight security.'

Carlotta shrugged. 'There is no sense being foolish.'

'Then you might want to rework your gate procedure. Once Pepe was satisfied I wasn't carrying a gun, he turned his back on me. If I'd wanted a weapon, I could have taken his.'

'Pepe is a surprising fellow,' Carlotta said airily. 'It might not have been that simple.' She turned back to me. 'Now I have a question: What kind of woman is your mother? Might she be likely to push Danny to leave the Family?'

'He's quitting the dogfight racket?' Mr Bloodworth asked.

Carlotta wrinkled her nose at the word 'racket', then answered with a nod. 'I will have to hire someone else, a gringo, to do the job, but at least I may be able to trust the gringo, a luxury I did not have with Danny.' She walked past me and picked up a swatch of orange material. She held it near my face. 'This is a good color for you, darling.'

'When did Danny give you notice?' Mr Bloodworth asked.

'During his visit last night. He was twenty-four hours late with his delivery and it was . . . a few dollars short. I railed at him, as was expected. He then informed me that he no longer needed to be "the Gutierrez Family's delivery boy". I explained that he was a member of the Family, and he laughed.'

'What are his plans?'

'I was hoping this little beauty might be able to tell me.'

I shook my head.

'No? Pity.'

'Was my mother here last night, too?'

'No. I did inquire after her, to be polite. Danny answered me so brusquely I suspected that the romance might be short-lived. Then, when he told me of his decision – their decision, actually – that he become more independent, I realized that I may have underestimated her influence. Heterosexual politics is not something I fully comprehend.'

'You know where we might find them?' I asked.

'He mentioned an appointment in L.A.'

'Did he seem nervous? Frightened?'

'A little less arrogant than usual. That might be construed as fear.'

Mr Bloodworth edged toward the door. 'Thanks for your time, Ms Gutierrez. We'd better be on our way.'

She headed him off at the door. 'It was a pleasure. Perhaps the young one might wish to stay, allow me to fit her for a nice dress. I could send her back in our limousine later.'

'I think I'll leave now with Mr Bloodworth,' I said.

'Not the wisest choice,' she said, opening the door.

Pepe was standing there, waiting to lead us out, his smile still in place. At the gate he said, '*Adios*. I shall remember not to turn my back your way again.'

Mr Bloodworth gave him a lazy smile. 'You should always watch your back,' he said.

The iron gate swung shut between them. Through it, Pepe said, 'Be concerned for your own back, *señor*. There are men waiting for you near your car. Three men. Very rude gringos.'

'Hey, Bloodworth! It's about time!'

The man calling to us had bright red hair. He and two others, neatly dressed in gray suits, were standing beside a bottle-green Lincoln towncar that blocked the walkway in front of the complex. The last time I'd seen them, they'd been breaking into Mr Bloodworth's office.

The redhead said, 'C'mon, Bloodworth, you're going to make us catch that going-home traffic.'

The detective turned back to the gate.

'Sorry, *señor*,' Pepe said. He was no longer smiling.

'At least take the kid inside.'

Pepe shook his head. 'My orders are clear. This has nothing to do with the Gutierrez Family.'

'I wouldn't go back in there, anyway,' I said. 'That Carlotta is creepy.'

'At least you could phone the cops,' Mr Bloodworth complained to Pepe. 'I don't even have a gun.'

The Latin looked at us sadly. '*Vaya con Dios, amigos*,' he said.

The three men came toward us. 'Don't worry about your rental car, Bloodworth,' the redhead said. 'You and the baby doll can leave the driving to us.'

28

1. I didn't have a hell of a lot of alternatives. So we got into their car. The same USC grad who'd dumped me in front of my apartment sat across from me in back. Red-top and the kid were in front. We waited while the third guy transferred our luggage to the trunk of the Lincoln. He was a thin, medium-size fellow who looked eighteen and not quite weaned. He slipped in under the steering wheel and turned to Red-top. Red-top gave him a nod and the guy got us going.

Route 5 was starting to pile up with cars as we headed north to L.A. There was still plenty of sun, but the smog filtered the brilliance out of it.

Red-top said, 'My name is Holz, Bloodworth. That's Butler on your right and Dimitry behind the wheel.' I looked at Butler, who gave me a quick smile. The side of his face was blotchy and there seemed to be a pesky yellow mouse developing under his right eye. I wondered if Pepe had done the damage. If so, I owed him one.

Holz continued: 'A little bird told us where to find you. She was worried you couldn't handle the Gutierrez people.'

'They were real hospitable,' I said. 'Just regular folks.'

'You can never tell with the Chicanos,' Holz said. 'They'd as soon cut you as tip their hats.'

'So you drove down to help us out,' I said flatly. 'Thanks.'

'We could have handled it with a phone call, actually,' Holz said. Butler turned his head lazily to look at him and it caused Holz to shift gears. 'Anyway,' he went on, 'we drove down so we could have a chat on the way back.'

'About what?'

'The kid's bankbook. What else?'

'That's what that two-faced Ceeley asked me,' Sarah said, hopping around in her seat. 'I don't know what happened to my bankbook.'

Holz blinked at her, then addressed me. 'Did you train her, or was it Kaspar and her old lady?'

Butler gave a little snort and looked out of the window. We were passing a large concrete dinosaur that some dedicated soul had constructed beside the highway for no apparent reason.

'I don't know what the hell you guys have got on your mind,' I said, 'but I do know you're facing the stringy end of a kidnap rap.'

Holz shook his head, feigning wonder. 'You're beautiful, Bloodworth. You and that scumbag Kaspar try to extort money from the bank and you say we're in trouble.'

'Extort what money from what bank?'

Butler's deep voice answered with no small sarcasm. 'I think it was a nice round fifty thousand, from the only bank in California worth your confidence, the Golden Pacific Bank. With over three hundred branches.'

'Jesus Christ! You guys work for that banana-head Dotrice. And that means that Ceel– Gwen . . .'

Holz tensed. 'The Nolte woman is not an employee of the bank,' he said stiffly. 'She does occasional odd jobs for us.'

'Well, doesn't this just . . . Excuse me, guys. I thought you were run-of-the-mill skullbusters. I sure didn't know you were bank skullbusters. Where'd Dotrice find you, in the Collection Division?'

'We're in Security,' Holz said.

'Insecurity is right,' the kid said.

Holz ignored her. 'Let's settle this bankbook thing, shall we?' he asked me.

'She doesn't have it. She told you.'

Holz exhaled through his nose and nodded to Butler, who, in less than a second had me pushed face-forward against the car's rear door. The guy was an ox. He had me pinned, one-handed. With the other, he played with the door handle.

'You're an annoying bastard, Bloodworth,' Holz said. 'You have about a minute to start talking before we dump you out on the freeway.'

The window was cold and clammy against my face. The afternoon traffic zipped past. If I survived the fall, there was no way I'd avoid being hit once or twice by cars going an average of fifty-five miles an hour. 'I don't know anything about any goddamn bankbook!' I shouted.

'You let him go!' The kid was shouting, too, and sinking her fingers into Holz's red hair.

Suddenly Butler's hold relaxed and he slid away from me. 'We're being assholes,' he said to Holz, who was grabbing the kid with one hand and trying to extract her fingers from his hair with another.

Addressing me, Butler continued, 'A few days before he ... died, your partner, Roy Kaspar, and Faith Dahlquist set up a meeting with Mr Dotrice at the bank. He thought it was about a loan. They showed him a bankbook indicating that a savings account for one Serendipity Dahlquist had been opened in the year 1968.'

'The year I was born.'

'The originator of the account – the addressee of record – was a Frank Dahlquist. His widow, Faith Dahlquist, wanted to know what happened to the account. Fritz' – he indicated Holz – 'went to check it out. There was no record of it in our computer.'

I rubbed the back of my neck. We were doing eighty past the San Clemente off ramp. I wondered if the property values around there had been lowered because of the Nixon association. 'How far back do your records go?' I asked.

Holz said, 'If the account had stayed open, it would have been in the computer. Even if the service charges had been slowly eating it up.'

'Then it was closed out. Probably by Dahlquist.'

Holz shook his head. 'No. That was checked. There was no record of the account. None. Period.'

'But Sarah's been getting credit cards from the bank.'

Holz scowled and said to Butler, 'We never thought of that.' To me, he continued, 'The cards are issued by another part of the bank entirely. Dahlquist wanted to keep control of the savings account, but he must have put the kid's name on the card account. Probably didn't want to be liable for her diaper charges.'

'I still don't get it,' I said. 'What's the big deal? A fourteen-year-old savings account, worth about a hundred bucks, slipped through the floorboards.'

Holz opened his mouth, then closed it.

'Kaspar and the Dahlquist woman tried to hit up Dotrice for fifty grand,' Butler said. 'So there is something more to it. Take our word for it.'

'What?'

'It doesn't matter,' Holz said.

'Suffice to say,' Butler told us, 'Dotrice was upset enough to send us out to retrieve that bankbook and the Century List by any means necessary.'

'What's the Century List?' I asked.

'That's none of your goddamn business,' Holz said, glaring at Butler.

Butler shrugged it off. He leaned back and stared out of the window again.

I said to Holz, 'You and Dotrice must get along real well. Between you, you don't have the brains of a fig bar. If I really was part of the extortion scheme, which you seem to believe, I'd already know all about the Century List. Even if I'm not involved in the scam, I could possess information you need to know. So, what's the harm in talking about it?'

Butler said, 'It's a typewritten list of names and account numbers from the year 1966.'

'But Sarah's bankbook was from 1968,' I said.

'We were not informed of the connection,' Butler replied.

'Why is the list important?' I asked.

'We don't know,' Butler said.

'Why is it called the Century List?'

He shrugged. 'Don't know that either.'

'Did Dotrice tell you to kill Kaspar to get the stuff?'

'C'mon, Bloodworth,' Holz said disgustedly. 'Kill a guy for a bankbook and a sheet of paper just because our boss asked us to? Do we look like that kind of idiots?'

Butler and I exchanged glances and we both laughed.

Holz didn't think it was so funny. 'We weren't really gonna throw you out of the car,' he said. 'But that may have been a mistake.'

'Mr Kaspar didn't have that list,' Sarah said, suddenly.

She had their attention. I shook my head, but she didn't see it. 'He'd made notes about the list. Scribbles, really, that Mr Bloodworth and I found in my room. He wouldn't have bothered to make those notes if he'd had the complete list itself. Mom must have it. Or that Gutierrez person.'

Holz looked at me and smiled. 'See? That's all we want. Just a little cooperation. We were thinking the Dahlquist woman might have the list.'

'Do you know where she is?' I asked.

'We will,' Holz said.

'The same way you found us, right?' I asked. 'Through the Gutierrez Family.'

Holz blinked at me.

'That one just registered,' I said. 'I've been wondering how, in the last couple of decades, Golden Pacific became one of the largest banks in California, and Dotrice went from lowly branch manager to one of its chief executives. During that same period the Mexican Mafia has been expanding, too. El Jefe had all that cash from Tijuana gold and coke and girls and the transportation of illegals and whatever else makes up their portfolio. Those millions might have looked very tempting to a struggling little bank. I imagine the Family and Dotrice could be real close.'

Butler scowled. 'The Gutierrez Family has an account with the bank. As for that other crap about drugs and whores, money has no history. If all the currency that had been earned illegally were to be pulled out of circulation, we'd be back trading corn for beefsteak.'

'Money has a history, all right,' the kid said. 'Everything has a history. What you're saying is that money has no conscience.'

Holz shook his head at Butler. 'I think we've all had a little too much to say. Let's just wait for Mr Dotrice to do the rest of the talking.'

'Who is this Dotrice person, anyway?' Sarah wanted to know.

'Just a guy who got Bloodworth kicked off the police force a while back,' Holz said nastily.

'I got myself kicked off,' I said. 'But Dotrice helped.'

The kid looked at me, her brow wrinkled. I smiled at her. She said to the occupants of the car in general, 'You call yourselves bank executives, but you're nothing but common thugs. Bullies and thugs.'

She continued on like that for a while. Nobody seemed to care. I let my cluttered mind drift elsewhere. Tiny mysteries had been solved. Gwen Nolte had been hired by Dotrice to locate

Faith Dahquist, with information on her whereabouts being provided by the Gutierrez clan.

I wondered if the Gutierrezes knew why Dotrice was looking for her, or if they cared. In any case, when Gwen couldn't get a fix on the couple, she stumbled across me and figured I might lead her to them. In Oceanside, she gave up that idea and either went off on her own or was taken off the case by Dotrice. Probably the latter, since Faith Dahlquist was now back in the Los Angeles area and Nolte's specialty was the north. Her note to me more or less indicated that she was going home.

So much for that. I moved on to more pressing matters. The reconstruction of events. Why did Faith take Roy Kaspar to see Dotrice? Well, she didn't have the chutzpah to squeeze the banker by herself. Danny knew there was a tie between the bank and his family, so he opted to stay in the background. And Kaspar had already elbowed into their scam, so they used him. Question: If Holz was straight about Dotrice not having had Kaspar killed, could Danny have done it? Or Faith? Unlikely, but not impossible.

The logical assumption was that the guy who dumped me on the roof of Sarah's building had done the jobs on Kaspar and the Sotos and even the kid's dog, Groucho. Groucho . . . that was something else to think about.

My head started to throb and I experienced that chilling sensation I get in my stomach when the rhythm of my heartbeat goes askew. My doc says I shouldn't be able to feel it, but I do.

I opened my eyes. The sun was dipping down in a violet-gray sky. We were bumper-to-bumper on the San Diego Freeway. Holz and Butler had their heads back and eyes closed. The kid was kneeling, staring at me intently over the front seat. I winked at her and closed my eyes again.

Knives, garrotes, beheaded dogs, banks, Mexican Mafia

families, spots on the carpet, dates. God help me, I was beginning to make some sense of it all.

2. Two hours later we were about fifteen feet under Wilshire Boulevard, in the first basement of the main branch of the Golden Pacific Bank, walking toward an elevator that opened either on command from the penthouse or when unlocked by a special key. Holz tried to buzz Dotrice, and when that didn't work, he used his key. It wouldn't work either.

Puzzled, he ran his finger over the slot and pressed. The elevator door opened. 'We better get that fixed,' he said to Butler.

We entered the elevator. Holz pressed the PH button and we ascended at a slightly less than thrilling speed. The door opened on a carefully antiqued, dark wood office whose walls were lined with books. It was the kind of room that radiated trust and confidence. Holz said, 'Dimitry, maybe you'd better go tell Mr Dotrice we're –'

He didn't finish because Dotrice was already there, at his desk. The desk faced the elevator, but the leather chair had been turned away from us. He seemed to be looking out of a large picture window at the dark purple sky and the tops of various overpriced shops across Wilshire Boulevard.

'Mr Dotrice?' Holz called.

No answer.

Holz and Dimitry walked toward him, circling the desk. I spotted Dotrice's hand, clutching the arm of his chair, and I drew the kid to me. Dimitry touched Dotrice's shoulder and the chair spun around.

Dotrice didn't look like his old self, but it wasn't his fault. He'd been given the garrote, just like the others.

Holz said, 'Holy shit,' and his legs gave out. He sat down on the rug.

The kid struggled in my arms. I pulled her back to the

elevator. 'We're going now,' I said to Butler, who didn't seem to believe what his eyes were telling him. 'You guys have a pretty full plate without worrying about us and kidnap charges.'

Holz tried to stand. 'But . . .'

'Phone the cops right away,' I said. 'You can alibi each other. Say one word about us and you can kiss your careers, and maybe even your freedom, goodbye.'

'But . . .' Holz repeated.

I didn't spend any more time with them. I yanked the kid into the elevator and sent us down.

29

Lordy, would it never stop? Wherever we went, murder most brutal followed. Or preceded. Or something.

Before the elevator doors closed on Mr Dotrice's office, I had a long look at the dead man in his chair – glassy-eyed, whey-faced, his tongue lolling out of the left side of his mouth. A dark purple line circled his bruised throat. Mrs Franklin, our physical-endurance instructor, once explained that when enough adrenaline is released in the body, by fear or whatever, strength may be intensified tenfold. Which I guess is why a spindly scare-crow like the late Mr Dotrice could have been able to dig his fingers into the armrest of his chair and rip away a patch of studded leather.

Mr Bloodworth was, I'm afraid, terribly shaken by the murder of his old adversary. In making our getaway, he kept fumbling with the lock on the green Lincoln and I had to use one of my hairpins to open the door and hot-wire the car. I'd never done anything like that before, and I was amused to dis-cover the method employed by a young tough on the soap *Wait Till Tomorrow* to be absolutely workable.

Gran was happy to hear from me. She sounded in wonder-ful spirits. Mr Bloodworth had cautioned me to say nothing to her of the murders – to spare her the worry and anxiety – but I did inquire about the bankbook that seemed so important to everyone. She thought there had been one in that box of mementos in my closet, though she hadn't looked into it in years.

She was dismayed that we'd been unable to locate mother. Again I offered no details. And when she neglected to mention Groucho, I decided to let that whole episode pass, too.

She had moved in with her raucous agent, Lacey Dubin, and wanted me to come stay with them. I told her that I preferred to stay at home for a while. She asked to speak with Mr Bloodworth and I pushed the truth a bit by saying that he was unavailable. He was available in body, but he was also distracted to the point of being entranced. Behind those hard yellow eyes, his mind was churning over heavy thoughts and he simply wasn't . . . well, available.

Finally, not long after Gran had rung off, he leaned back in the chair, blinked, and turned to me. 'You tell your grandmother I'd be dropping you off?'

'Ah, no. Not exactly. I thought I'd stay here for a few days.'

'Well, you thought wrong,' he said.

'I don't want to go over there, and Gran said it was all right. Lacey's son, Clarence, is home from college. I don't want to have to deal with him.'

'What do you mean "deal" with him?'

'He wore a mood ring when he was in high school.'

'I don't know what you're talking about,' Mr Bloodworth said, standing up. 'Come on, get your stuff!'

'No. No. That's not all. He and his cousin, Phil Armbruster, once cornered me in the swimming pool and did things to me.'

'C'mon, Sarah . . .'

'They did! Clarence touched me here.'

He shook his head. 'He must not have gotten much out of that.'

'What an absolutely awful and rude thing to say! Just because

I'm not like that Nolte cow who pulled the wool over your eyes . . .'

'You're mixing your barnyard images, kid.'

I ran to my room and locked the door. He knocked on it a couple of times. 'C'mon, Sarah. I don't have time for this.'

Finally he shouted 'Dammit!' and walked away. I pressed my ear to the door. He was on the telephone. I opened the door and tiptoed into the living room, where I could hear better.

'. . . I'm not sure, Cugie. Just see what you can find out . . . I know it's getting late, but computers don't sleep, do they? It's nothing definite but yeah, maybe it'll give me a few answers . . . No kidding? Dotrice, huh? Well, what the hell are you so goddamn mad about, *amigo*? Since when was Dotrice one of your favorite people? . . . That's what I thought. OK, if you find out anything, call me here.'

He gave that policeman, Cugat, the telephone number of the apartment. Then he rang off and turned. And saw me. 'Let's go, kid. To grandma's house.'

'You'll miss your phone call,' I said.

'I know Cugat. He won't get anything done until tomorrow.' He frowned. 'Dotrice's murder really lit a fire under him, though. And it wasn't even in his jurisdiction.'

'Did he know Mr Dotrice a long time ago, too?'

'Yeah. He and I were partners when . . . Yeah, he did.' Mr Bloodworth drifted off again, the way he does, and just as abruptly came back. 'OK, chop-chop. Time to go.'

I didn't move. I said, 'I wish I'd remembered to ask that Holz creep something when he was in a talkative mood.'

Mr Bloodworth took a deep breath and looked at me expectantly. 'Well? What'd you want to ask him?'

'If the bank had hired the Sotos, too.'

He thought a second. 'Not much chance,' he said.

'Why not? They hired that Nolte.'

'You told me that the Sotos didn't know who hired them. Dotrice wouldn't have been mysterious. Besides, as much as I hate to say it, Nolte only stuck around to see if you knew where your mother and Gutierrez were. The Sotos were aware of the fact that you didn't know any more about their whereabouts than they did. No, somebody else hired them. The same guy who killed them.'

I had to agree. I said, 'Then it makes sense, doesn't it? Dotrice hired a detective because Mother and Gutierrez had tried to get money from him. The killer probably hired the Sotos for the same reason.'

'That's a good logical assumption,' he said.

It also reminded me of something. I ran back into my room. I was rooting around in the memory box when he came in and sat on the bed.

'What're you looking for now, kid?'

'The bankbook. Gran said she remembered seeing it in here.'

'Your mom already went through that box,' he said. 'That's probably where she found it. She wouldn't have put it back.'

He was right. No bankbook at all. Just a lot of junk I'd seen a million times, like my baby book with the fat cherub – nothing like myself – in the middle of a stage, wearing diapers and bowing to an unseen audience. As I went to place it back in the box, a piece of paper poked out.

It was a list of names written in an unfamiliar hand. Probably my father's. The names included Bernadette, Grace, Joan, Jane, Janis, Freedom, Liberty, Serendipity, Sunrise. I'm glad they settled on Serendipity, which has a certain giddy uniqueness without being totally absurd.

I turned the paper over. It was a mimeographed letter. 'What've you got, kid?'

He read it over my shoulder.

Dear [Blank]:

I am most pleased to inform you that you have been awarded the sum of $10,000 for your efforts in keeping America the great nation that it is. Please be assured: This is a serious, bona fide offer from the Century Corporation. Each year our executives, acting under the direct bequest of the corporation's founder, Malcolm R. Seevers, select twenty-five United States citizens who have in ways, obvious or subtle, demonstrated their love of home and country. Each is presented a tax-free sum of $10,000 in appreciation of his or her good citizenship.

Ordinarily this letter would include a cashier's check in your name. However, we have reason to believe that this address is not your most current. Therefore, hoping that our letter will be forwarded to you, we ask that you provide us with your present address. Send it in the enclosed self-addressed stamped envelope. We will then send you, with absolutely no obligation on your part, a check for $10,000.

Cordially,
Milton Rome, for the Century Corporation.

Mr Bloodworth was grinning at the letter.

'What is it?' I asked.

'A con to find out somebody's address.' He abruptly stopped smiling. 'C'mon, kid, I've got to get you to your grandmother, now.'

He folded the letter and stuck it into his pocket.

'Is it important?' I asked.

'To somebody. C'mon, Sarah. Time's wasting.'

'I don't want to go there. Please. I just want to spend the night in my own bed for a change.'

He checked his watch. 'That's not a good idea.'

'I'll be OK. I can lock the door and everything.'

'Double-bolt it. Stay in this room with that door locked, too. And if anything even a little bit strange happens – any odd noise, strange odor – call the cops and tell 'em somebody's trying to rape you. Then hang up and call the fire department and tell 'em the building's on fire. That'll get you fast action. I'll be back in an hour or so, with luck. I'll call first so you'll know it's me coming in.'

Neither he nor I really expected any trouble at the apartment. But after he left, I was struck by a very strong feeling of apprehension. The door was double-bolted. I'd slipped the chain into its slot. I even shoved a chair under the doorknob. Then I went into my bedroom, locked that door, and turned on the TV, with the sound down really low so that I could hear anything like a creaky floorboard or a rattling or a tapping.

There was nothing much on the tube except reruns of programs that had been dreadful when new.

The Gary Grady Show was debuting a little later, with guests that included a popular group, The Slag. Ordinarily, I was not interested in modem music, but I'd grown quite fond of The Slag's opera, *The Tree Cried Out*, which I felt signaled the introduction of sanity into pop composition.

I had barely settled in when the phone rang.

'Hello, Serendipity. How are you, honey?'

'Uh – hi, Mom.'

'What's all that noise?'

'Just the TV,' I said, dragging the phone to the set to turn down the volume.

'You sound fine.'

'So do you,' I lied. She sounded frail and nervous. It was noisy where she was, too. Guitars twanging in the background.

'Darling, I . . .' She moved her head away from the phone and whispered something. There was a muffled reply. Then she was back. 'Darling, I want you to come here. I want to see you.'

'When? Where?'

'Now. I'm up the coast in Hermosa. It's less than an hour by cab. Have you any money? Of course you do. You're a self-sufficient little thing. Not at all like your mom. Hurry, I need you.'

'Wait,' I almost shouted, afraid she'd hang up. 'Where are you, exactly? In a bar or something?'

'Oh,' she giggled. 'Sometimes I have no sense at all. I'm at this music place. Rock City. You must know about it. Don't all you kids know about it?'

'I've heard of it. The cabdriver will know,' I said.

'Hurry, please, dear. It's so important.'

'Mom, do you have a bankbook of mine?'

'What?' Her voice went up a few octaves. 'I don't . . . bankbook . . . ?'

There was more mumbling from Gutierrez, or whoever was with her. Then Mother said, 'Is that policeman, Bloodworth, with you?'

'He's not a policeman. How do you know about him?'

'We can discuss that later, honey. Is he there?'

'No. He'll be here soon.'

'Then you're alone?'

The question disturbed me, but I answered it truthfully.

'Good,' she said. 'Don't tell your grandmother or . . . anybody where I am. Not Bloodworth. Nobody. Please.'

'There's a man who's trying to –'

'Darling,' she cut me off, 'I really can't talk any longer. I want you here. With me. As soon as possible. Your mother wants you and needs you, baby.'

I'd dreamed of hearing those words. But the dream had ended long ago. 'I suppose that Gutierrez fellow will be there,' I said.

'Oh, God!' she cried suddenly. 'Don't make me do –' And we were disconnected.

So, I phoned for a cab. Then I dialed Mr Bloodworth's answering machine to let him know where I was going and why. We should obey our parents. But only to a point.

30

At nine o'clock I was sitting on a creaky old swing on the dark porch of a little gray and white house on Fransen Street in Bay City, a block off the beach. The air smelled of honeysuckle and faintly fishy ocean. The wild ivy that covered the front lawn all the way to a white picket fence rustled ominously in the still night.

Inside the house, a TV set blared and kids laughed and coughed and their mother shouted at them. Every few minutes she'd appear at the door to ask if I wanted something – iced tea, a beer – and I would shake my head and tell her, 'No, thanks.'

I'd spent a busy few hours exchanging the lifted Lincoln for my car and getting the kid fed and tucked away in her apartment. She'd pulled some stunt to coerce her grandmother into letting her stay by herself. I didn't think she'd have any trouble, but I told her what to do should it arise. Then I drove to Bay City and Fransen Street, where I waited for the man of the house to come home.

At 9:30, Rudy Cugat left his unmarked Ford whistling 'You Belong to My Heart'. His pastel suit was a phosphorus lime-green in the moonlight. He unhooked the latch on the white picket fence and stepped gingerly on flagstones through the ivy, then up the porch steps to his front door. His hand was on the knob when I said, 'Working late, *amigo*?'

He turned, crouched, and his hand shot quickly to his chest, then stopped. He squinted in my direction. 'Hound? What the hell are you doing out here in the dark?'

'Enjoying the night air, like folks used to before television.'

He lifted his shoulders as if to shake the tension out of them and joined me at the swing. He used his handkerchief to dust off a section of the wood first. The swing creaked but it held us. Quality workmanship.

'What's up?' he asked.

'Anything new on Dotrice?'

'Strangled by person or persons unknown.'

'I picked up that much on the car radio.'

He shrugged. His long fingers reached inside his coat and withdrew a folded computer printout. 'I was gonna drop this by tomorrow.'

I angled the sheets toward the lighted front window and looked them over. 'Fast work, Cugie.'

'It's just the war records. There was no criminal history on either of the guys. Is it what you want?'

'Sort of,' I said.

'You gonna tell me about it?'

I put the sheets in my pocket. 'Why not?'

He scowled at me. 'What's with you, *amigo*?'

The ivy rustled. 'You've got ants in your plants,' I told him.

'Rats,' he said, curling his lips. 'They come from Beverly Hills.'

I gave him a polite smile.

'No joke, goddammit. Beverly Hills is fulla rats. Big as Dobermans, some of 'em. And mean.'

'You think they get gout, eating all that rich garbage?'

He grinned. Maybe I was the same old Hound after all was what he was thinking.

I asked, 'Why'd you get so bent out of shape about Dotrice?'

'Bent out of shape? Me? Just surprised.'

'And disappointed, huh?'

He scowled and reached inside his jacket again. This time I watched him carefully. He took out a cigarette pack and lit one. 'Say what you're going for, Hound.'

'A few days ago, Dotrice told me my partner had been shaking him down. I assumed he was talking about Kaspar. But when he mentioned Kaspar by name, he referred to him as my *new* partner. What he was telling me was that both of my partners had been putting the bite on him. No wonder he had doubts about me.'

Cugat didn't say anything. He seemed to be listening to the laughter of his kids inside the house.

I asked, 'Were you working with Kaspar and the Dahlquist woman?'

'Huh?' He looked genuinely confused.

'The bankbook and the scam letter,' I prompted.

'Man, you're talking like some freebase fish.'

'If you weren't with them, you must have had your own hook in Dotrice.'

He started to reply, but his wife appeared at the door. In Spanish, she asked if he was coming in to dinner. He said he'd already eaten.

He might as well have slapped her face. She stood there a few seconds, as if in pain, waiting for him to amplify his statement. When that didn't happen, she went mopily back to her job of shouting at their kids.

Cugat said, 'Estella's sister fills her head with bullshit and she starts thinking I screw some new woman every night before I come home. I don't have that many screws left in me.'

I had no interest in his love life. I said, 'Tell me about Dotrice.'

He played with the pleats on his pants. 'We had a business arrangement.'

'Long-term?'

'Fairly long-term, yes.'

'Since about May 17, 1966?' I asked.

'Yeah. Since that night,' Cugat said, with so little affectation I barely recognized his voice.

'What was your lever?'

'The money that was supposed to have been burned in the fire.'

'As I recall, it was a sack containing a hundred thou. Total loss.'

'Yeah,' he said. 'But I don't think that more than twenty-five thousand got burned. Dotrice had been working late when the kids busted in. They used this amateur Molotov cocktail. A real smudge pot. Dotrice, being something of an opportunist, set fire to the money himself. Then he left his office and took his shots at you and the kids. I don't think he was trying to actually connect, but you never know with bankers.'

'What tipped you?'

'One of the firemen. Guy named Hemphill. He went in and sprayed the room. It was mostly smoke. The bag and the money burned pretty good, but Hemphill told me it sure didn't look like any hundred grand in twenties and fifties, which is how Dotrice described it.

'So I visited him the next day at his home. You should have seen him, Hound. Had his wrist in a cast sticking out of the god-damnedest black silk robe. The guy even had little velvet slippers with some kind of crest on 'em. So very fancy. Anyway, I told him I'd had the ashes bagged and tagged and that they looked a little skimpy and that I would probably have to run them past the lab to find out just how much really got torched.'

'He buy that?' I asked.

'He was – dubious. But I assured him that the lab could probably reproduce every bill.'

'Is that true?'

'Who the hell knows? To a very nervous man, it sounded

possible.' Cugat lit another cigarette. 'So we had our chat and he opened a small account in my name at the bank. He would put money into it and I would draw it out. I split it with Hemphill for nine years, until poor old Hemp sucked in too much smoke in one of those hospital arson things.'

I glared at him. 'You could have got Dotrice to lift his boot from my neck. I could have kept my badge.'

'If Dotrice had done that sudden a switch, it would have looked hinky to the captain. We might all have been in the soup.'

'I took the full whacks and kept you clean and you didn't feel you owed me anything?'

'Owed you? Jesus, Hound, I was already splitting the loot with Hemphill.'

'Not money, you son-of-a-bitch! My job. The only goddamn thing I cared about.'

'Look, Hound. You broke the bastard's wrist. And you let the kids go. That had nothing to do with me.'

I nodded. 'You're right about that part.'

'I never could figure out why you just let 'em walk that way. It wasn't like you. I mean, you were no pushover.'

'I've never been able to figure it myself. The girl said something about them getting married. My marriage to Louise was springing leaks. I don't know. Maybe it was just that they were dumb kids and they would have gone down as bank robbers.'

'But that's precisely what they were, *amigo*.'

I shrugged.

'Hell. So you set the pigeons free. It was a long time ago, *amigo*. No sense going through it all again. It has nothing to do with us anymore.'

That's how much he knew.

A chill swept through me. I tried to shake it off, but couldn't. Cugat leaned toward me, frowning. 'Hey, you OK? You don't look so good.'

'I'll be all right,' I said. 'Let's get back to Dotrice. I assume that if he'd steal money from his bank, he'd also steal from his depositors.'

'The man was as crooked as a ram's horn,' Cugat said. He was still studying my face. 'You need a shot of booze or something?'

'Naw. I need a telephone.'

Cugie's wife tried to quiet the kids while I dialed. Neither of us had much success. The phone rang thirteen times before I gave up. Then I tried my number on the odd chance that Sarah had left some word.

Cugie watched, unimpressed, as I beep-beeped my gizmo past a message from a divorce lawyer and another from a theater owner whose night manager was double-ticketing. Sarah's serious little voice came through, finally. 'Sorry,' she said, 'but I have to go out. Mother called and wants me. I'm going to . . .'

I put down the receiver and turned to Cugat. 'It sounded like she said she was going to Rock City.'

'There is such a place, Hound, which you might know about if you ever read the papers or watched TV. It's like Disneyland, only with nothing but music. Or the crap that passes for music. New Wave. Fusion. Dirty dancing. The kids flock to the place. So do the dope peddlers and the pimps and the porno scum.'

'Where is it?' I asked.

'Slow down, *amigo*. You look like you're coming down with some bad bug.'

'Where?' I repeated through my teeth. 'The girl's in trouble.'

'The Chihuahua?' He put a hand on my shoulder. 'That serious, huh?'

I glanced at his wife and kids and nodded. I didn't know what to say.

'I'd best come with you,' he said.

Estella Cugat had other ideas.

Cugie shot back at her, 'The hell with that. I owe this man.' He pushed me to the door.

Estella asked, 'Will you come home tonight?'

'Don't I always?' Cugat replied.

'I never know for sure,' his wife said softly behind us.

It didn't slow him down any. He suggested we use his car, with the attachable red bubble and siren. That was fine. He'd always been better than me behind the wheel. He shot us down Main, past its darkened boutiques and noisy singles bars, to the freeway.

'Hound, maybe you can fill me in, now, eh?' Cugat said as we bounded down a ramp onto the freeway, heading east at a brisk seventy-plus through the light night traffic.

'What do you want to know?' I asked him back.

'Start with the blond girl's connection to Dotrice.'

'Her mother was blackmailing him.'

'And you thought I was working with her? Hell, man, I don't even know her mother.'

He was quiet for a second, then he went on: 'There is the theory in Homicide that the same person who did Dotrice took care of your Roy Kaspar. Naturally, they will not release that to the papers.'

'I'd already figured that out,' I said. 'What about Helmdale, the plastic surgeon?'

Cugat frowned as he drifted into the far left lane. 'What we have is on that sheet I just gave you. He was found dead in his office on Camden in Beverly Hills. Place had been looted. Wife said he moved here from New York because he thought it was safer. Some junkie busted in and struggled with him and killed him.'

'Choked him,' I said. 'No junkie. It's the same guy.' Jerry Flaherty had been moaning about a plastic surgeon's murder the day Sarah and I left him to catch our plane. I had no reason to think the death was connected in any way, but it hadn't cost anything to check it out. And it had paid off.

Everything seemed to be connected. I smiled. I was starting to think like a man suffering from paranoia. I was starting to think like the killer.

'Hound, you OK?' Cugat was chewing the inside of his mouth.

'Sure,' I told him.

'Three goddamn murders!'

'You can add two dead PI's down in Oceanside to the list, too,' I said.

His eyes shifted to me. 'What the hell are you mixed up in?'

'I'm still trying to put it together.'

'Well, we got a nice long ride in front of us.'

'Not too long, I hope.'

He kept his eyes on the road for a few miles while he continued to chew the inside of his mouth and make his moustache wiggle. Finally, he asked, 'This little girl, you think she's with the killer now?'

I didn't want to think about it. He said, 'Maybe I'd better call through to Hermosa and have them send some people out to Rock City.'

We were maybe thirty minutes away. The Hermosa cops could get there quicker. But they might rush in and screw everything up. Maybe Sarah was with her mother and Gutierrez and not with . . . 'We don't have any hard evidence, Cugie. We would wind up looking like donkeys.'

'Then let's forget those Hermosa assholes.' He smiled at me. 'Hell, it is only one man, eh, Hound?'

'Might be three people,' I said.

He shrugged. 'Beeg fucking deal. We can take 'em, no?'

'I sure as hell hope so, *amigo*.'

'You need a pistol?'

I nodded. He reached under his seat and came up with a little .38. I checked to make sure it was loaded.

'If you have to use it,' he said, 'get rid of it *pronto*. No registration.'

'A throwdown?'

'It only becomes a throwdown after you have thrown it down,' he said stiffly. 'Until that time, it is a weapon of self-protection.'

'I appreciate your help.'

He patted his chest and brailled out another cigarette. The speedometer jumped up ten notches. He took a deep draw and sent the smoke out of a break in his window. 'When the son-of-a-*putanna* did for Dotrice, he took four hundred a month out of my pocket. I want first shot at him.'

'It'll be first come, first served,' I said.

He laughed. 'Goddamn, Hound, you and me in the car. I feel like a kid again. It's like old times, no?'

'Almost, *amigo*,' I told him.

31

Naturally, the cabby – a black man named Mohab Sebaz Ge, according to his taxi license – balked at taking a young person all the way from Monica Heights to Hermosa. I had to show him three $20 bills before he would put his battered red and white machine into drive.

Then he insisted on talking nearly the whole trip, prattling on about various gurus, maharishis, and perfect masters he had known and served and chanted with in an effort to find not only peace of mind but the ultimate contemplative state. Finally at El Segundo, an area that resembles industrial waste at its worst, he lapsed into a chant that sounded like a dying pack mule. That lasted until we arrived at the gate to Rock City.

Neither he nor I was ready for it.

'Jesus, Mary, and Joseph,' he said, reverting to his primal religion. We were staring at an expanse of land the size of two football fields and housed colorful tents and platforms and banners and klieg lights and occulting white lights flickering on Day-Glo billboards. A monster electronic billboard spelled out tonight's special treats. Huge white statues loomed up – Elvis Presley, a rather unattractive woman in a long dress, a black man with a guitar, the soulful John Lennon – nearly twenty-five feet high.

Thousands of people milled about them, drinking, smoking, and in general acting weird. The giant parking lot was crammed with every manner of automobile from hot rods to Rolls-Royces.

Barbed-wire fences had been constructed to surround the area like the concentration camps in those ancient movies about World War II. Instead of Nazi soldiers, clowns and punkers and greasers and space creatures and God-knows-what-all roamed the outer edges of the area trying to control the crowd of mainly unruly teenagers who pushed into turnstiled entryways, shoving their tickets into the hands of other oddly costumed types. Loudspeakers from at least six different sources blasted the eardrums with a cacophony of sounds passing for music.

Mohab Shebaz Ge halted his cab at the entrance to the jammed parking lot and looked back at me questioningly.

I searched the crowd. My mother was nowhere to be seen. For the first time I began to wonder if this was another of her scatterbrained plans that had misfired. Or, worse yet, had it been a ploy to get me out of the apartment, so that she and Gutierrez could . . . do what?

The meter read $38.20, so I gave Mohab the two twenties. 'You may keep the change,' I said.

'A dollar eighty cents for a forty-mile ride,' he whined. 'And I gotta deadhead back.'

'Offer it up to your perfect master,' I told him, slamming the door behind me.

Before driving off, he shouted a very rude word at me – very rude, coming from a fellow who had achieved total peace of mind.

I concentrated on the teeming crowd of dreadful people and wondered what to do next. If Mother were there, where would she be in this bedlam? The possibilities were infinite.

A tall boy wearing a black leather vest over his tanned chest and a leather Lone Ranger mask stood beside one turnstile, collecting admissions. 'Ticket?'

'I don't have one.'

'Fourteen bucks, babycakes.'

I could not believe it. Fourteen dollars? For what? I had only one $20 bill left and I was not about to throw good money after bad.

A line was forming behind me. 'Pay or no play, blondie,' the masked fellow chided.

Furious, I prepared to make way for the fools ready to squander their money, when a tall man appeared and called out, 'Wait!'

He, too, was wearing a costume of sorts. His jacket, pants, and silly-looking peaked Foreign Legion cap were cut from the ugly greenish-yellow-tan camouflage material sold in army surplus stores and ridiculously overpriced boutiques like Camp Beverly Hills (a place I avoid like the plague). He had on one of those absurd plastic glasses-and-big-nose disguises with black eyebrows and moustache. He was smoking a cigar that made him look like that Cuban fellow, Castro.

He whispered something to the leather boy and handed him a folded bill of some denomination. The leather boy waved me through the turnstile, raised his eyebrows, and said, 'Enjoy yourself, sweetpants.'

The man in camouflage croaked, 'C'mon. Your mother's waiting.' His voice sounded as if he were trying to disguise it.

'Is your name Gutierrez?' I asked.

The camouflaged man began to laugh so hard he almost dropped his cigar. It was a high-pitched, slightly hysterical sound. Definitely not a healthy laugh.

32

1. 'What'd the kid's mother have on Dotrice, exactly?' Cugat asked me, too casually. We'd left the freeway and were speeding through the teeming streets of Compton toward Hermosa Beach.

'Remember a couple of years back when the state controller started nosing into the way some banks were playing fast with their inactive accounts?'

'I don't pay much attention to banking news, Hound.'

'Me neither, as a rule. But I'd done some work tracking down owners of unclaimed property, and the story caught my eye. Seems there are a hell of a lot of savings accounts that people forget about. The law says that once an account stays inactive for seven years, a bank can start deducting service charges. But first it has to make a good-faith effort to notify the owner. Eventually, the money in the account is supposed to wind up going to the state. So the controller got pretty well frosted when he discovered that one of the biggest banks on the West Coast was service-charging the accounts into the ground. There was the case of a nine-year-old boy who learned that forty-seven fifty had been deducted from the fifty-dollar account that had been opened for him when he was born.'

'Forty-seven fifty ain't exactly grand larceny.'

'The ball-park figure that the controller was tossing around was twenty million in less-than-legal deductions.'

'And Dotrice was pulling down that kind of loot?'

'He had his own thing,' I said. 'From what I can figure, he dummied up something called the Century Corporation.' I pulled the mimeoed letter from my pocket and flashed it at him. 'It says that the lucky recipient is the winner of ten grand for some imaginary act of good citizenship. He mailed the letters out to the names and addresses on his bank's dormant accounts. If he got an answer back at his P.O. box, he didn't touch the account. But if the letter came back Address Unknown, he closed out the account and siphoned off the money.'

Cugat was amused. 'And the little girl's mom found out about it?'

'Yeah.'

'Then she and Gutierrez socked it to Dotrice?'

'With Roy Kaspar's help.'

Cugat nodded. 'Yes. They probably used Kaspar to brace Dotrice. Gutierrez would have wanted to keep a low profile around the bank, since his family owns a hunk of it.'

'How'd you know that?' I asked.

'Hell, I know lots of stuff. I'm sort of in the information business.'

'Dotrice wouldn't have told you, unless . . .' I gawked at him. 'Unless you're the one put him and the Gutierrez Family together for the deal.'

'Hey,' he said angrily. 'Let's cut out this extraneous bullshit and concentrate on the situation at hand, eh?'

'I just like to know who's covering me, *amigo*,' I said.

He looked genuinely hurt. 'You never worried about that before.'

'That was a different lifetime.'

'Then let us focus on this one, and on a man who has killed several people. He is our main concern.'

'The kid is my main concern.'

'Then remember that, and stop digging up the roots of our friendship.'

He swerved. About five hundred people were streaming out of a movie house where a *Star Wars* triple feature was ending the goddamn fable once and for all. 'Maybe I should hit the siren,' he said.

He handed me the red bubble and, automatically, I plunked it on top of the car while Cugat made noise.

The crowd gave us a wide berth.

'This little girl must be something special, eh?'

'She is that, all right,' I said. 'Did I tell you she saved my life?'

He shook his head as I pulled in the bubble and put it away. My heart started fibrillating so I leaned back against the seat and started breathing in and out, slowly. Cugat gave me a nervous glance. We didn't talk much after that.

As we approached Rock City – the home of the most useless collection of music, musicians, people, and portable architecture I ever hope to see in my lifetime – the garish electronic marquee was spelling out: TONIGHT . . . THE . . . GARY . . . GRADY . . . SHOW . . . DEBUTS . . . LIVE . . . FROM . . . THE . . . JIM . . . MORRISON . . . PAVILION !!!

Cugat looked up at the sign. 'This Grady is one of the guys I ran through the computer for you.'

I nodded and asked if he'd ever seen the comic.

'Sure. In ads and on TV,' he said as he flashed his badge at some jerk dressed in a diaper who was guarding the parking gate.

'Then you know what he looks like.'

'I just said so.'

'Fine. Because he's the bastard were after.'

2. Grady was making it easy for us, or so I thought. He was set to appear on stage at the Morrison Pavilion in ten minutes. A

pirate, whose cheap cologne would have made walking the plank a relief, pointed the way and Cugat and I set out through a sea of teenage California flotsam. They floated, drifted, giggled. Some merely stared. Some leaned against statues or slipped quietly to the ground, where roving bands of thugs hired by the Rock City elders collected and carted them off to the main gate and tossed them to the perils of the outside world.

Cugat seemed even more distressed by the wasted youth than I, probably because of his birth-control-free family. Parents, do you know where your little nippers are? Pray they're not at Rock City.

We passed a small, partitioned stand where fabricated juice was being dispensed at a buck a squirt. Cugat pointed out an ambitious youngster who was adding a brown-bagged liquid to the juice for two more dollars. 'The land of free enterprise, eh, Hound?'

At what appeared to be a community lavatory kiosk, a young couple was in the last throes of coital bliss, standing up. 'Christ, Rudy, doesn't anybody patrol this place?'

'You want us to start arresting kids for screwing, *amigo*? We don't even have cell space for the killers.'

We closed in on the stage at the Morrison Pavilion, a raised cement platform surrounded by wooden slat seats arranged amphitheater-style, all now filled. Two video cameras and one hand-held were manned by technicians, and a large assortment of crew members were gathered on stage listening to their earphones for instructions.

I didn't see Grady.

I took the left side of the open-air stage. Cugie the right.

An announcer strolled to the middle of the stage while a pair of overweight, long-haired, poorly dressed boys set up what looked like large building blocks, but which were some sort of sound-amplification system. The announcer was pale and just this side of prissy, with a razor-sharp pompadour that could have been shot from a grease gun. His glasses were the size of rearview mirrors. He was dressed for success in a mint-green velvet jumpsuit. But even though he looked like something you'd hang out of your window on St Paddy's Day, his voice was as deep and rich and comforting as Walter Cronkite's.

'Welcome, guys and gals, to *The Gary Grady Show*. Gar will be out in a minute, and when he shows, we want to hear a nice, happy, enthusiastic round of applause. I'll be standing right next to that camera with a sign in my hand – show 'em the sign, Mickey. . . Right, that's the sign. It says "Applause". When you see that, you clap like, well, like you just found out you don't have the clap.'

A few chuckles.

'That reminds me of a story about this real pretty girl. Only sixteen, but she had this strange rash on her . . .'

He droned on. I looked across the pavilion to Cugie, who looked back and shrugged. We edged in closer to the stage area. Cugie said something to a guy wearing earphones.

'. . . and the doctor tells her, "Would you mind, miss, if I showed this to my associate?" . . .'

Cugat was pointing to me, waving for me to join him. I cut through the stands, passing in front of the announcer, who looked down and ad-libbed, 'Was it something I said, officer?'

I scanned the stage as I walked. Still no goddamn Grady. The announcer got off a punch line aimed somewhere below the belt. The spectators responded with shrieks of laughter. It was that kind of crowd.

'What's up?' I asked Cugat.

The crewman next to him gave me his headset. 'It's for you,' he said.

I slipped on the phones and a voice said in my ear, 'Bloodworth, you old bounty hunter. So you finally made it, huh?'

'Grady?'

'Who else, supersleuth! Hey, tell the spic to hold it right there.'

Cugat was edging away from the stand. I grabbed his shoulder and he stopped, looking at me questioningly. Covering the mouthpiece, I asked the crewman where the hell Grady was.

'In the Tower of Power, dead ahead.' He indicated an ugly tower that rose up far above the pavilions and tents and squat buildings like a medieval turret. 'This whole place is wired to it,' the crewman went on. 'He's up in the top. There's a lounge up there for the veeps.'

Grady's voice said, 'You look like a tiny white ant down there, Bloodworth. Like a bug on the jungle floor.'

'I want to talk to you, Grady. About that job you mentioned.'

'Let's take a meeting on it, huh?'

'I'll come on up.'

'Your pal, he's gonna be working for me, too?'

'Sure. Two for the price of one.'

Grady chuckled mechanically. Then he got to the point. 'Time to stop fucking around, pally. She's with me.'

Out of the corner of my eye, I saw that the crew members had turned to face the tower, too. They must have been plugged into our conversation.

'Say something to your big buddy, Serendipity.'

Sarah's voice was loud and clear. 'Mr Bloodworth, there're just the two of us up here. Mr Grady asked the others to leave –'

'Are you O.K., kid?'

'I'm –'

'She's right as rain, Bloodworth. She wants to see her mother, but she's being very patient. I like that. It's not good to push people, you know.'

'Nobody's pushing anybody,' I said.

Was the announcer still playing to his audience? I couldn't tell. The crowd was a blurred mass of grinning faces.

'Everything was golden,' Grady continued. 'All the crap of the past was out of my system. I was on a winning streak and – blam! They started pushing. Everybody. You work like a son of a bitch to make something of yourself and there are always the bastards who try to grind you down to their size. The goddamn Tops in 'Nam who'd look right through you like you were a n— or something. The studio fuckheads who throw their goddamn little Sunday brunches and forget to invite you. Sure they forget.'

'Calm down,' I said. 'None of those people is anywhere near this place.'

'They're everywhere, Bloodworth. That's what I'm trying to tell you. They were put on this earth to fuck things up. To complicate things. All you can do is try to simplify matters, to get rid of the complications. Like doctors get rid of cancer. You cut it out.'

'Just take it easy.'

'Oh, sure. I get the one chance I've been waiting for all my life and what happens? Some goddamn grubbers come along and try to grab it away from me.'

'Maybe it can be worked out.'

'Hell, it was one-step-over-the-line time about three hours ago.' Which meant, I suppose, that he'd killed Faith Dahlquist.

'Send the kid down, Grady.'

'She likes it here, near me.'

'You're a very nice man, Mr Grady. But I really should go now. Those people are waiting for you on stage, anyway.'

'Did you hear that, Bloodworth? She thinks I'm a nice man. Should I let it go at that or should I tell her that –'

'Grady! Your fans are waiting. Look at them. There must be a thousand or so. And the viewers at home –'

'Which one of us is psycho, Bloodworth? There isn't gonna be any show. At least not the one they're expecting. That reminds me of the story about the monkey with the glass eye . . .'

'Why don't I come up there? Our conversation would be a little more private.'

'Come on up. But come alone. We'll tell some jokes and smoke some smokes.'

'Send the girl down first.'

'We'll wait for you up here,' he said, clicking off.

'What's going on?' a floor manager asked me as I took off the headset.

I ignored him and turned to Cugat. 'You'd better make a phone call. But get 'em to come in quietly. He's ready to pop. And you could start moving these people out.'

'How the hell do I do that?'

'Tell 'em there's free drugs in the parking lot. I don't know.'

'You're not going up there?'

'I thought I would.'

'That's real bush-league, Hound.'

'He's got the kid.'

'That's too bad for her. It won't help her any if you die with her.'

I turned from him and started through the crowd. Cugat trotted along behind me. 'He wants me up there alone,' I said.

'Don't worry. I'm not going with you. But think it over. Don't rush up there like a cowboy with a cactus up his chaps. He'll do you the minute he sees you.'

'Maybe not,' I said. 'He passed on me once. Maybe he still thinks he owes me.'

'Huh?'

'You handle things down here, *amigo*. I'll take care of them in the tower.'

We were at Rock City's dead center when everything fell

apart. First the lights blinked and went out. Then, in the darkness, the loudspeakers were turned up full gain, blasting eardrums with some screechy music crap. The kids, screaming in either fear, ecstasy, or stoned agony, began running. Panic took over Rock City in a matter of seconds.

Cugat shouted, 'Find yourself a hole, Hound, before the crowd –'

That's as far as he got before a mass of wild-haired cretins swept him off his feet and sent him crashing into a concrete statue. I started back to help him, but the crowd made its own eddies and waves. I was shoved away.

The idea was not to panic and not to fall. That required a few well-placed punches that made me feel better than they should have. I couldn't even see Cugat, didn't know what his condition was.

There were more screams now and more fear. The music got even louder. White lights began to flicker and the whole frantic panorama seemed to be moving in fits, like one of those old Chaplin movies.

Over the din and increasing madness came the calm, mellow voice of Gary Grady from every speaker. 'Hey, boys and girls, isn't rock 'n' roll fun?' He paused, then went on: 'Stay tuned for the end of the whole fucking world in just five minutes. Or maybe four minutes. But, hey, who's counting?'

33

1. I suppose I should have been surprised when Gary Grady removed his full-face mask, but I was rather past surprises. He led me into a tall building that he referred to as the Tower of Power. Its first four levels were mainly wires and fuses and cables and whatever else mechanical or electronic that was needed to keep everything functioning. It would take a mind more steeped in physics than mine to describe the operation adequately. My memory is of oddly cool, calm, pale-lighted metal halls where serious men and women observed dials and listened attentively to electronic bleeps.

Gary Grady and I entered an elevator. He pushed a combination of buttons on the door panel and we were whooshed directly to the top of the tower, where the door opened on a round room that looked like a futuristic lighthouse. Chrome and black and tinted glass all around. A thick black carpet covered the floor. The walls were black with dashes of polished chrome. The furniture consisted mostly of white leather chairs and plush black velvet sofas – some perverted interior decorator's idea of casual elegance. On the couches, draped like debauched pixies, was an assortment of slimy fellows in Day-Glo short pants and short-sleeved shirts, sucking on cigarettes and chatting about sexual matters I'd prefer not to have to repeat.

Bare-faced, Grady looked like your everyday military nut case – camouflage pants tucked into parachute boots; knife strapped to his upper thigh; cartridge belt, holster, et al. He introduced me by name to the lizards and I discovered to my dismay that they were the group, Slag, that I had been pining to see. In person, with their brightly colored Little Lord Fauntleroy clothes, they seemed nothing more than limey perverts.

With them were two oily types in elaborate silk shirts and expensive designer jeans – their American agents – and a frenetic fellow with yellow spiked hair, wearing black, who was the manager of Rock City.

Gary Grady offered me a chair and I sat down to listen to their absurd talk. The American agents were trying desperately to affect Cockney accents, which even the Slag boys found amusing. They started mocking them in what I thought was an obvious manner. But the agents either missed it or chose to ignore it.

Drinks were poured and consumed. Marijuana was smoked, but there was no stronger drug use that I could see. Through it all, Gary Grady neither smoke nor drank. He continued to stare at me, smiling, making me totally uncomfortable.

After an hour or so of that, he turned to the others and said, 'You gentlemen wouldn't mind leaving me alone with my – little girl for a few minutes, would you?'

The man with the spiked hair said, 'Be my guest, Gar. Just remember there's a show in a half-hour.'

'How could I forget?'

The Slag boys looked at me and then, cackling obscenely, filed past us and into the elevator. As Mozart proved so long ago, talented musicians need not necessarily be gentlemen.

Alone with Gary Grady, I asked, 'When's mother going to be here?'

'Soon,' he said, locking the elevator door. 'We don't want anybody surprising us, right? C'mere to the window. Check out this view.'

I moved beside him and looked out of the floor-to-ceiling window at the crowd below as it milled and thronged. 'How can mother get up here if the elevator's locked?' I asked him.

He turned his head to stare at me. 'Does anyone know where you are?'

'Mother,' I said.

'Besides her.'

His dark eyes were nearly mesmerizing. My mind told me I was in some sort of danger, but I didn't feel it in my heart. I didn't honestly believe that this man would do me any harm. 'No. I told no one,' I answered.

'Hey, come on, now,' he said with a wink. 'Lies will hold you down in size.' He led me around the room, still looking out of the window. 'Didn't you mention it to your friend Bloodworth?'

I had to be truthful. 'I – I left a message for him.'

'Good,' he said. He seemed genuinely pleased. 'I want to talk to him. I have a great deal of respect for him.'

'So do I.'

'Of course you do,' Gary Grady said. 'You must think of him as a sort of – father figure.'

What an odd notion. 'Not really,' I replied. 'Not at all.'

He paused when we were in front of a flat black electronics board, similar to the one in the director's booth on Gran's show. It was positioned flush against that section of window so that it would be possible for someone to sit at it and watch the main stage area clear across the park while using the sliding tabs and monitors and mikes.

Gary Grady indicated that we should both sit down at the board.

He flipped a switch and one of the monitors began to glow, a sixteen-inch TV screen on which two men were threading their way through the crowd. Mr Bloodworth and that Latin policeman named Cugat. When they moved out of camera range, Gary Grady pushed another button and they appeared on the screen again, captured from a different angle.

'Isn't this something, honey?'

No answer seemed necessary. Mr Bloodworth and the policeman arrived at the main stage. I could barely make them out by staring out of the window, but on the TV screen they were quite prominent. Gary Grady smiled and removed his knife from its scabbard.

'He didn't come alone, did he?' he asked himself. 'Well, it's blown, anyway. It had to be this way, in the end. There are too many of them, moving around through the jungle, closing in. You can't keep track of them all, and it's the one you don't see who –'

'Are you all right?' I asked.

He turned to me and smiled. 'Sort of a setback. I thought for a while I would make it, but, hell, I won't just lie down for them. You wouldn't want me to do that, would you?'

'I'm not sure what you're talking about. But I do wish you would put that away,' I said, indicating the knife.

He looked at the weapon in his hand, nodded, and put it on top of the black console in front of him.

'Are you and my mother friends?' I asked.

'A long time ago,' he said. 'But you know how old friends, when they pop up in your life, tend to bring disorder and confusion.'

'No, I don't,' I told him.

He gave me another of his strange smiles and turned to the monitor, where Mr Bloodworth and the policeman were standing beside the stage and a dreadful person was telling jokes. Gary Grady pressed a key button that cut off the comedian mid-story. He said into the microphone, 'This is Grady; see that big dude in the brown suit to your right?'

'Grady?' came the voice through the speakers. 'Where the

devil are you, man? You're supposed to be here to introduce Slag.'

'A hitch, buddy. Get the big guy for me, huh?'

'But the time . . .'

Grady picked up the knife and said coldly, 'Get the guy, now, goddammit. His friend's standing right next to you.'

He must have been talking to one of the floor directors, because this pudgy fellow with earphones tapped Detective Cugat on the shoulder and told him something and Detective Cugat began waving to Mr Bloodworth, who then trudged through the crowd.

'Give him your headset,' Gary Grady ordered the pudgy fellow. The Bloodhound puzzled out how the set worked and put it on.

'Bloodworth, you old bounty hunter,' Gary Grady said with a grin. 'So, finally you return my phone calls.'

'Grady?' Mr Bloodworth asked, twisting around and looking through the crowd. He covered the mouthpiece and said something to the pudgy crewman, who pointed in our direction.

'That's right, Bloodworth. Up here. You know what? You look like a little bug on the jungle floor, trying to find some pant leg to crawl up.'

'About that job you wanted me to do,' Mr Bloodworth said. 'I've got all the time I need now.'

'All-reeti,' Gary Grady shouted. 'Let's take a meeting on it.'

'Come on down, Gary, and we'll discuss the whole thing.'

'Just you, me, and your pal, huh?'

'Sure.'

Grady's laugh was eerie enough to make most of the other crewmen turn our way. 'Don't fuck with me, Bloodworth,' he said, no longer smiling. 'I know exactly who that guy is.'

He turned to me. 'Talk to your big friend, honey. Tell him you'd like him to visit us.'

He pressed a tab on the board in front of me and I said, 'Mr Bloodworth, I'm up here in the tower with Mr Grady, but I don't think it's necessary for you to come. We're waiting for my mother.'

'She wants her mother, Bloodworth. But she has been patient. That's good, because some people should not be pushed.'

'Absolutely,' Mr Bloodworth said. 'I don't believe in pushing anybody.'

'Hell,' Gary Grady muttered, seeming to sink inside of his army garb, 'it don't make a whole lot of difference. It was one-step-over-the-line time a while back.'

Mr Bloodworth suggested that Grady send me down, and I started to get up from the chair, but Grady grabbed my arm and pulled me back. He shook his head. 'Stay a while, princess. The view will be spectacular.'

He turned his attention back to Mr Bloodworth and began telling him a joke, of all things. In the middle of it, he picked up the knife and began tapping it against the window. He seemed quite crazy, almost foaming at the mouth. But I was more sorry for him than afraid of him. He wasn't interested in harming me. I could see now that it was Mr Bloodworth he was after.

He told him to come up alone. Then he gave him the elevator combination needed to send it to the top of the tower. I tried to shout to Mr Bloodworth not to come, but my mike was dead.

I watched as the noble detective and his friend Cugat started toward us. Gary Grady was fuming. 'Alone, I said, you son of a bitch,' he hissed at Mr Bloodworth's image on the screen. 'I'd better teach you and the greaser a lesson.'

And with that, he ran his hand across the bank of switches and turned the whole park into terrifying darkness.

There was an awesome silence at first. Then he twisted a few knobs and the Slag's recording of 'Mince Meat' blared out across the open area so loudly that it reverberated off the tower.

There was a pounding coming from the elevator shaft. Someone seemed to be stuck in there – a man with either a high-pitched voice or one affected by panic. Grady said, 'Shit, I'd better get that going again.'

He found a switch that shot a pinpoint of light on the control board. Then, with a grin, he began punching buttons and twisting dials until the elevator began to whir.

'Will you look at this, flower girl?' Gary Grady asked, indicating the panic and turmoil and insanity of the crowd below as it reacted to the darkness and now the flickering of powerful klieg lights.

But it wasn't the people being bashed and trampled below that caused my goose bumps to rise. It was the knowledge that my instincts had been wrong, whatever their reason. The man beside me was the same man who had called me 'flower girl' back in that motel in Oceanside, after he had cut the throat of the good-hearted Juan Soto.

He was staring down at the crowd below with a grin on his face. He put the knife back on the counter to use both his hands on the electronics board. I slipped from my stool. He was still concentrating on the crowd. I moved around behind him to within a few feet of the knife.

He was chuckling to himself. He started talking to the crowd about the end of the world. Lord, what a loony!

Only a few inches more and my hand would be on the knife. If only he didn't turn away from the window. My fingers touched the hilt. And he turned, his crazed face grinning wildly. He grabbed the knife from my fingers. I backed away as he slipped off his stool. Behind him the night exploded in white light every few seconds. The music battered the smoked glass of the tower.

I grabbed a cushion from one of the ugly couches and threw it at him. He caught it on the point of his knife and gutted it in his effort to toss it aside. 'A man comes into the world naked and alone and he should leave it the same way,' he said. 'He will be known by his actions and deeds and not by his intentions. And his people should not be made to suffer or pay for his mistakes.'

I couldn't make hide nor hair out of what he was saying. Not that my mind was free and clear to do so, even if I'd wanted to. There was nowhere to run, really. He had locked the only door, the one leading to the elevator shaft.

I backed away as far as the round wall would let me. When he got within kicking distance, I tried to defend myself that way. But he was too good for that. He pushed in against me, grabbed my wrists in one hand, and yanked me from the wall. He pushed the blade against my throat and said, 'You have survivor's blood in your veins, kid, but there comes a time when even that's not enough.'

He dropped my arms. I started to pull back, away from the knife. 'Don't even think about it. Just – relax a second. Put your hands behind your back, like a good girl.'

When I didn't respond, he pressed the blade harder against my neck. I could feel a little wetness there. The monster had cut me.

He grabbed my wrists again with his hand, holding me in front of him like a shield, the blade still against my throat. He pushed me to the elevator door, which he unlocked. Then we moved back to the console, where he turned the dimmer, throwing the room into total darkness.

We could both hear the elevator coming up.

2. The elevator moved closer. My neck stung and was getting damper, with blood or perspiration, I couldn't tell. Blood, I assumed, since I was growing increasingly light-headed.

The elevator stopped. Gary Grady released my wrists, but

held me in place with the pressure from his knife. He used his free hand to take a pistol from his belt and point it at the elevator.

The doors took an eternity to open. When they did, the car was as dark as the room. But in the reflection of the white bursts of light from outside, we could see it was quite empty. Gary Grady shouted, 'Bloodworth, you son of a bitch! Where are you?'

'Maybe,' I said weakly, 'maybe . . . he's found another way up.'

'Impossible,' he snapped. But he wasn't sure. He turned to the glass window and there was a clatter and thud inside the elevator. With my last bit of strength, I twisted away from Gary Grady's knife and threw myself on the console, pushing the dial controlling the room lights. Then I fell to the floor.

Gary Grady stood over me, a knife in one hand and a gun in the other. He looked like something hot from hell. He started to bring the knife down and I turned my head. Through his legs I saw Mr Bloodworth, who had dropped through the top of the elevator, where he'd been hiding. He picked up his gun from the floor where it had fallen during his jump. I doubted that he could pick it up, aim, and fire it fast enough to do me any good.

But I was wrong to sell the Bloodhound short.

Just before I fainted, he shot four times, the bullets entering Gary Grady's chest, neck, and head.

Mr Bloodworth said later he had been merely trying to wound him.

34

1. Getting up there wasn't the problem, once I got past the idiot manager of the place, a fuzz-brain with a droopy crew cut who was not bearing up well under the pressure. He kept running around the base of the tower, shouting for somebody to bring him some drugs, any kind of drugs.

That left me with an affable bearlike fellow named Sandy, the building manager. He had just spent the roughest ten minutes of his life and was turning philosophical about it.

He sent the elevator down to the basement, and I, on the first floor, stepped through an open door onto its metal canopy top. The resourceful Sandy had given me a pair of work gloves so that I could hang on to the hoist cables without getting my palms ripped off on the way up. He also put two lads to work unscrewing the emergency exit and portions of the suspended ceiling.

'Douse those interior lights, too,' I said. 'Let's make it as tough for him as possible.'

While they were removing the fluorescent tubes, I asked, 'How far a jump is it to the floor?'

Sandy shrugged. 'Maybe nine feet.'

'Any idea what kind of weapons he's got up there?'

Sandy scratched his head. It looked as if it needed scratching. 'The boss says he was in combat gear. I guess he could have anything.'

That was comforting. 'OK,' I said. 'Send me up.'

He punched the combination and I jerked upward. Sandy watched me go with the tranquil look of a pipe smoker.

As I neared the top, I shook off the right glove and grabbed Cugat's pistol. I would make the son of a bitch eat the gun if he had hurt the girl. If he hadn't hurt the girl, I would make him eat the gun. If he didn't kill me first, I would make him eat the gun.

The elevator jerked to its final stop, with my head about two feet shy of the top of the cement shaft. I stared down into the dark, empty elevator and waited for its doors to open. Then I perched for as long as it took Grady to realize that I wasn't where he was expecting me.

A few very long seconds dragged by. I heard him shout my name. I wasn't even mildly inclined to answer. The gun in my fist was dripping with my sweat. I began to worry that Cugat might have given me a lemon. Suppose it didn't fire. Suppose the girl was dead. Suppose I broke my leg jumping . . .

Then I heard Sarah's voice and it sounded shaky. 'Maybe he's coming up the outside of the building . . .'

Grady shouted at her, and then there was the noise of a struggle in the room. It was time. I jumped down into the elevator, gun drawn. My eyes were accustomed enough to the darkness to pick them out immediately, especially outlined in the window with the bright flaring lights in the sky behind them.

The kid was on the floor. Her neck was bloody. The bastard Grady had his knife raised. I emptied the contents of the gun into him without even a second's thought.

He bounced back against the console, and as he slid down it, he turned on every light in that whole goddamn, festering park.

*

2. 'That's kind of you to offer, Mr Bloodworth,' Edith Van Dine said. 'But I'll take care of Faith's funeral arrangements myself.'

She sat across from me in the damp night air, her cast resting on the arm of her wheelchair. She had been crying. She asked, 'Could you get her body away from the police?'

I nodded that I could.

We were sitting on the patio to her agent's home in Laurel Canyon. Cugat and the agent, Lacey Dubin, were inside the house, downing drinks and chatting like old cronies.

'You found her in the – trunk of his vehicle?' Mrs Van Dine wanted to know.

'Lieutenant Cugat found her,' I said, 'and Danny Gutierrez. Once the crowd dispersed, there weren't many cars left. Grady was driving a new van. The windows were tinted so dark you couldn't see through them. The cops think he may have murdered them right there, in the van.'

'Poor Faith . . . I wonder what I could have done . . . ?'

'It's no good blaming yourself,' I said.

'How was she mixed up with this Grady?'

I shrugged. 'The Hermosa police think he was a psycho.'

'Could he have been the one who tried to hurt me and Mr Lorenzo? He was on the same lot . . .'

I nodded. 'Maybe. The day I visited his office, he'd scraped his arm. Maybe by pushing over a wall.'

She arched an eyebrow. 'Why would he have done that, do you suppose? I never even met the man.'

She was a tricky one. I smiled at her, sorting out the fact and fiction in my head. 'If he was fixated on your daughter, maybe he saw you two together on the lot. Or maybe it was Lorenzo he was after. He could have known him from New York –'

She cut me off. 'But he seems to have followed Faith and that

Gutierrez man, slaughtering people right and left. Why? What obsessed him?'

I couldn't think of a lie that would work, so I changed the subject. 'Serendipity's asleep upstairs. The paramedic said the cut wasn't much. They didn't even have to put a clamp on it.'

She eyed me warily.

'But they want her to rest for a few days, just to play safe,' I added.

'What are you keeping from me?' she asked sternly.

'Nothing that would improve things. Nothing that anybody should be interested in. Not you. Not Sarah. And definitely not the newspapers.'

She nodded. 'You're right, of course. We've been through enough. Would you take me inside now? It's very late.'

I helped her navigate the wheelchair into the house. A slightly bandaged Cugat and the agent, Lacey, were clinking glasses and talking movies in a comfortable, country-looking den. Lacey wanted to sign him up as both adviser and actor and he wasn't saying no. They stopped talking and watched us as we passed by.

Once Mrs Van Dine was situated comfortably in a soft chair in the guest room, next to a pile of scripts and books, I hopped up the stairs to the bedroom where Sarah was sawing wood. The pennants on the wall and the photos of sports greats made the sleeping, scrubbed pug face look wan and helpless. I knew better, of course.

I wondered where Lacey's son, Clarence, had been hiding since we arrived. Probably out terrorizing some other young girl by a swimming pool. Assuming that Sarah hadn't made up that episode.

I stood at the side of the bed and looked down at her. If Grady had killed her, would I have held together? I wondered.

This business of caring for somebody, especially a kid, took a little getting used to.

3. 'That Dubin woman has an eye for talent, Hound,' Rudy said on the drive back to his place. 'She thinks I could be the new Ricardo Montalban.'

'You're not that much younger than the old Ricardo Montalban.'

'You don't understand,' he said, paying too little attention to the road. I wondered if the paramedics had been wrong about his not having a concussion.

'I don't understand much of anything,' I said. 'Is there gonna be any problem with the gun?'

He fingered the adhesive that the medic had stuck to his forehead to stop the bleeding. 'Naw. As long as you remember that you picked it up off the floor up there, that it was Grady's gun.'

'I heard you talking to some of those cops. How many people did that son of a bitch dust, anyway?'

'Quite a few.' He held up a tan hand and began lowering fingers. 'In addition to the ones we mentioned – Kaspar, Dotrice, the brothers Soto, and the plastic surgeon – we got Gutierrez, the kid's mom, and the two youngsters who were trampled to death at Rock City.'

'And he probably killed the real Gary Grady in Vietnam,' I said.

'Huh?'

'Never mind. Forget I mentioned it.'

'Forget, hell. That guy wasn't even Grady?'

I had to tell somebody. 'I could have stopped him,' I said.

'Don't lay that bullshit on me, Hound. You're beginning to sound like some goddamn martyr with the sins of the world on your back.'

'I could have put a tag on him sixteen years ago.'

He turned and stared at me. The car swerved. He forced his eyes back on the road and pulled over to the curb, cut the engine and the lights, and sat back. 'You're not gonna tell me that Grady was –'

'His real name was Frank Dahlquist.'

'But according to the army records you asked for, Dahlquist is six feet under some rice paddy.'

I took the sheets he'd given me earlier from my pocket. 'Check it out. He and Grady were assigned to the same unit.'

He waved the sheets away, so I redeposited them in my pocket.

'Tell me about sixteen years ago,' he said.

'Dahlquist and his girlfriend, Faith Van Dine, broke into Golden Pacific Bank's Silverlake branch that night. They grabbed a folder from the desk of a junior official, your buddy Charlie Dotrice. Guess what was in it?'

Cugat blinked. 'The material he was using in his scam.'

'The letter and list of suckers. That's what set Dotrice off. That's why he tried to shoot 'em. Not that they knew what they had. They stuck the stuff away and eventually it turned up in their daughter Serendipity's memory box.'

Cugat looked at me anxiously. 'Well?' he asked.

'Well what?'

'The rest of it.'

'Not stone sober,' I told the new Ricardo Montalban. 'You and Lacey Dubin were swilling down booze like water while Mrs Van Dine and I were sipping tea. I want my share now.'

He looked at his watch. It was nearly 4:00 A.M. He sighed and started the car's engine.

4. At that hour of the morning, your choice of drinking spots is severely limited. Cugat took me to a dive named Lulu's, on Gower just off Sunset. The bar was in a crowded room with

grease-stained gray walls decorated with woozy pink elephants. At the rear was the hint of a kitchen where, in desperation, one might buy a Grade Z hamburger or a specialty of the house, Cajun jambalaya, which consisted of highly seasoned odds and ends from a short-order house that Lulu also owned down the block.

The noisy, always crowded bar was a favorite of pimps, hookers, pushers, junkies, college kids, and at least one cop, apparently. Lulu, a big transvestite in red tutu with black bangs sweeping her forehead and half of her makeup worn away, leaned across the bar to give Cugie a hug, clucking sympathetically over his bandaged forehead.

He looked at me sheepishly, slipping from Lulu's hairy, muscled arms. 'What'll you have, Hound?'

'The same as you, Ricardo.'

'Two Cuervo Golds,' he told Lulu.

I wandered over to the jukebox and removed the junkie who was wrapped around it. It was the last nickel jukebox in the world, and it was stocked with my favorites. I fed in fifty cents and punched the buttons.

June Christy began to sing 'Whee, Baby' and I suddenly felt better about life in general.

Cugat carried our drinks to an empty table off the kitchen. A pretty but dipsy blonde asked me if I believed in the rights of animals and I said sure. Cugat was impatient. 'So tell me the story, *amigo*.'

I downed the shot of smooth tequila and went back to the bar for a refill. Cugat shook his head. 'Goddammit, Hound!' he shouted.

'Better make it fast,' I told Lulu.

'Oh, you men are so impatient,' she pouted.

I suggested she give me the bottle, and she was glad to. 'On your tab, handsome.'

Cugat waited until I was seated and another shot was poured. 'Now,' he said, 'please continue to educate this curious Latin who has been wounded risking death and the madness of crowds in your service.'

'Where was I?' I asked.

'You know damn well. You were talking about the girl's parents.'

'Yeah. Right,' I said, downing another shot. 'Well, as you know, I let them take that walk at the bank. Faith got knocked up. They married and lived off her mother's dough for a while. Then the kid arrived. And Dahlquist, so his service files say, enlisted and ended up in Vietnam.'

'The guy was a goddamn hippie,' Cugat said. 'He enlisted?'

'Mrs Van Dine told me he was quirky, had personality shifts. He probably saw a John Wayne movie. Anyway, he wound up over there with Special Services. Entertaining the frontline troops, along with a comic named Gary Grady. They caught some action and Grady was among those who bought the farm.

'Dahlquist suffered damage himself, to his face and hands. He saw it as an opportunity to step into the shoes of a guy – a loner, by all accounts – who was at least one rung higher on the show-biz ladder than he was. And it was a way to ditch the family and start out fresh.'

The Cuervo was working very nicely and I was beginning to float a little. Christy was now singing 'Midnight Sun' with her smoky voice and perfect phrasing. Cugat said, 'Hound, please. I want to get home soon.'

'Well, we don't always get what we want, *amigo*. I wanted to be a policeman.'

'And that was my fault, huh?'

'Not at all, Cugie. Not at all.'

'You know how these things work, *amigo*. They wouldn't have taken you back. Even if Dotrice had changed his mind . . .'

I gave him a long look. 'Anybody who could find a legit bank for the Gutierrez Family to launder their cash, could probably have worked a minor miracle like getting a little badge back.'

The blood rose to his face and he leaned in close. 'Lemme tell you something, you son of a bitch. When Dotrice bounced you, you went around telling everybody that it didn't matter, that you were happy to be off the goddamn force, that you didn't need the goddamn force. You were free and your own boss, and you didn't have to put up with any departmental bullshit any longer. You remember that?'

I didn't answer.

'I went to grammar school with Carlotta Gutierrez. She had a thing for my sister, Teresa, the one who got sick. I don't know if Teresa thought about Carlotta in that way, but if it made her happy, then I hope she did.

'Anyway, I had no dealings with the Gutierrez Family until after El Jefe went a little nuts and Carlotta took over. I bumped into her one day and we had lunch and she told me about this little cash problem she had and asked me if I could help.'

I poured another shot. My hand wasn't too steady. I paused to see if I could tell if my heart was beating properly. It felt fine to me. 'So you laundered some black money for her,' I said, 'and picked up a few bucks doing it.'

'Aw, you begin to disgust me, Hound. You don't get it, do you?'

The music stopped, then picked up again. Ella Fitzgerald was singing about her little yellow basket. I leaned forward. 'Maybe you can spell it out for me.'

'I guess I have to. Carlotta Gutierrez asked me to help her, so I did. She was a friend. I made a few bucks, sure, but the thing is: You help your friends if they ask. You never once asked for my help. You never asked for anything.'

'I didn't figure there was any point.'

'You were too fucking proud and you know it. And now

you're trying to lay the guilt on me, but it ain't sticking. I put in a lot of time with you tonight, Hound. And I took risks. Not for any goddamn money. I don't think I want to sit here and take any more crap from you now.'

He started to get up, but I put a hand on his arm. 'You're dead right, *amigo*. I've been behaving like a donkey. Have another hit.' I poured more amber fluid into his glass. 'You still want to hear the story?'

He nodded. I leaned back in the chair. While Lulu arm-wrestled a black guy in a silver jumpsuit, I told Cugat how Dahlquist went back to New York as Grady and became a radio favorite doing his Vietnam-vet comedy. 'The new face helped. It was boyish and friendly. It was the work of Dr Devon Helmdale, who was then an officer attached to a hospital in Saigon.' I tapped my pocket where I was keeping the biographical material he'd gathered for me. 'Helmdale began practicing in Manhattan about the same time the new Gary Grady started his brilliant career.

'The doc came west last year and Dahlquist/Grady made the same trip about a month ago. Somewhere out here he bumped into Faith. Maybe it was on the UBC lot, with her visiting Mrs Van Dine. Or it could have been in Helmdale's office building. It's full of plastic surgeons. She'd had some work done recently and he probably was getting a nip or tuck himself before starting the new show. He wanted to appeal to the youth audience.'

Cugat scratched his head. 'He must have known she'd recognize him sooner or later, once he was on TV.'

'He didn't look anything like the guy who was in that bank. The nose, the chin, the cheeks. Nothing's the same. Of course, a wife would be harder to fool. Especially if she saw him coming out of a plastic surgeon's office.

'Maybe she approached him, friendly like, and he gave her

the brush. Maybe she and Gutierrez went straight for the blackmail bit. As I've been told, there is still some scandal that can deep-six a career these days. The abandoning of a family, not to mention the use . . . usurping – that's tough to say at this time of night – usurping of a war hero's identity, could fill the bill.

'Faith and Gutierrez got a little too cute. Just before shipping out to Saigon, Dahlquist gave his baby daughter a dog that he'd trained himself. I'm guessing that Faith Dahlquist grabbed the dog and brought it to Grady's office at UBC to see his reaction to the dog and maybe to see the dog's reaction to Grady. What the mutt did was to piss on Grady's new rug. There's a white stain on it that looks like the stains on the rug in Sarah's room.'

'The dog isn't house-trained after fifteen years?' Cugat asked.

'The kid says it's got a nerve problem. The dog's name was Groucho, by the way.'

'So?' I was boring Cugat.

'It suggests that Dahlquist was a Groucho Marx fan. When Grady attacked me on the roof of the apartment building, he used a Groucho mask as a disguise. And there's a picture of the Marx Brothers in his office.'

'Hell, lots of folks like Groucho. Get to the part that matters.'

'It all matters. Take your contribution. The kid's pet is stolen. She goes to the cops, and what does my old buddy Cugat do? He sends her to me.'

'Ah. So this whole thing is my fault, too? Jesus!'

'Hell, no. Now you're not getting the point. What made you send her to me?'

He frowned, ground the cigarette into the sole of his shoe, and dropped the mess on the floor, where it blended right in. 'It was just a joke.'

'Why me? What made you suddenly think of me? Wasn't it because she reminded you of somebody? That blond hippie girl I gave a free pass to at Golden Pacific?'

'Hey, come on . . .' He stopped. His mind was working. 'Maybe. I dunno if I even remember what that girl looked like. Nothing like what we found in the back of that van. That's for sure.'

'OK, let's say you were just making a joke.' He nodded as if he wanted to believe it. 'She came to me and wound up with Kaspar. He spotted the bank stuff in her memory box and figured out fast what it was. Only he didn't know how to make money from it, so he hunted down Faith and Gutierrez. Faith supplied the name of banker Dotrice, and they must've decided to use Roy to put pressure on her husband.

'Kaspar visited both Grady and Dotrice the day he was killed. He called on the plastic surgeon, too, now that I think of it. Hell, if I only had a goddamn brain, I'd have put the pieces together long ago.'

'I would never call you slow-witted, *amigo*.'

'Anyway, Kaspar pushed Grady past his limit and became just so much wet work. That was enough to scare Faith and Gutierrez away from the city. Gutierrez had to make his collections for the Family anyway. Dotrice, meanwhile, found out that I shared an office with Kaspar and naturally assumed I was part of the shakedown. He sent his young Turks to get the list and the scam letter from me, but I didn't know from Century Lists.'

'The Hermosa cops found the list in Faith Dahlquist's purse, by the way,' Cugat said, 'tucked in the kid's bankbook. It meant nothing to them. They were more interested in her lady gun that she didn't get a chance to use.'

He gestured toward Lulu, who was opening a beer bottle with her teeth.

'How does she do that?' I asked.

'It's all in the gums,' he said. 'In another hour, she'll be chewing broken glass. But please continue your story, *amigo*.'

'OK. The kid's grandmother had her "accident" and started worrying about Faith. She hired me, and I took off with the kid after Faith and Gutierrez. We weren't the only ones. Grady was too involved with his new show and was too recognizable to hunt the couple down, so he hired two expendable stooges, the Sotos, to follow us to the blackmailers.'

'How did he know to do this?'

'He knew me. Maybe thought I was part of the blackmail gang. Maybe I was just taking care of the kid. Either way, I was his ticket to Faith. He trailed me and the kid to the airport, and put in a call to the Sotos to be waiting when we landed.'

Cugat grinned. 'He hired the Sotos, and Dotrice hired the lady P.I. That must have been some parade, the bunch of you.'

'It was the Tournament of Roses all the way.' I had another hit of Cuervo, and breathed deep. The air smelled sweeter. I yawned.

'And Gutierrez kept collecting for the Family at the dogfights.'

I nodded, feeling suddenly bone-weary. 'The Sotos ran him and Faith down in San Jose and relayed the info to Grady in L.A. He flew there to terrorize the couple a little. By then, he had killed Helmdale and probably thought there was a whole conspiracy out to get him. He wanted to panic Faith and Gutierrez into leading him to the rest. So he left the kid's pooch in their hotel room with its head cut off.'

Cugat winced. 'How did he know they'd have the animal with them?'

'I don't think they had the dog. My guess is, they left it with Grady and he brought it with him, probably in a private plane. Which is something we could check. Anyway, he smeared the room with the animal's blood. The Viet Cong used to slaughter domestic animals to show the locals they meant business. Just something a G.I. would probably know.

'Faith and Gutierrez took flight from the motel and Grady stuck with them. In Oceanside, one of the Sotos must have spotted him. And that was that for the Sotos.'

'Why didn't Grady kill Faith and Danny G. in Oceanside?' Cugie asked.

'I'm not sure. From all that crap he was saying at Rock City, the guy thought there was a plan to destroy him. He could have been following Faith and Gutierrez to see who else was trying to get him. By then, they'd figured out he was the one who'd killed Kaspar and was stalking them. That meant Dotrice was still a viable source of cash, which they sorely needed.

'Grady trailed the couple back to L.A. When they went to Dotrice at the bank, he assumed that another character out of his past was part of the plot against him. Goodbye, Dotrice.'

'That's some story, Hound,' Cugat said. 'Some story. Now, personally, I find it too complicated. I prefer the Hermosa Homicide version: Grady was a psycho, and why look for reasons when you're dealing with a psycho?'

'There's a certain logic to that,' I agreed, polishing off my last drink of the evening. The room was starting to spin. Not too much. Just right.

'That way, your little chickie's mom was killed senselessly, as they say on TV, and it remains that her dad died honorably in the, ah, Conflict. And you don't have to worry about having police for breakfast tomorrow.'

'And UBC will try to throw a blanket over it all. The one time they don't sensationalize the news is when they're involved.'

He nodded. 'And the newspapers will go crazy trying to fill in the blanks. And nobody will think of working back to a dumb act of youthful rebellion that took place long ago in the Sixties.'

I nodded, yawning.

'Better to let sleeping dogs snore,' Cugat said.

And, on that note, with Cab Calloway singing 'Minnie the Moocher' on the jukebox and Lulu playing liar's poker at the bar with four guys in leopard-skin leotards, I fell asleep. My pal Cugie says I had a smile on my face as he hauled me out to his car.

35

On the evening of my fifteenth birthday, I was leaving the grounds of Bay High with a boy named Jean (pronounced the French way, *s'il vous plait*, and not the feminine American way) when I spotted a familiar tree trunk of a man half sitting on the fender of a fine old Chevy that was parked directly in front of the school gate.

I hadn't heard from him since that terrible night, though I'd left countless messages on his answering machine. His yellow eyes flashed my way and he waved. Immediately, I sensed jealousy stirring within Jean. He'd been in this country for only a year; his father is a semi-famous film director who was trying to complete a personal epic about Joan of Arc at Warners'.

'It's an old friend,' I told him.

'I can see the old part,' he said with his charming accent.

'Would you mind if we didn't walk home now, but just met later at the party?'

'Mind? Of course I mind. But if it is what you wish . . .'

I nodded and he wandered off, reluctantly, as I headed toward the big man.

'Hiya, kid,' Mr Bloodworth called to me, displaying that famous grin of his. 'Long time no see.'

'Not my fault,' I said. 'You never return your calls.'

'Work and such,' he said. 'Is that pale, good-looking fella with the droopy sweater your beau?'

'Jean? Oh, just a friend. Nothing serious.'

'And how's your grandmother?'

'Her shoulder and hip are knitting nicely and she's back at work. She's giving me a party tonight.'

'Yeah. I got your invite. I'd love to make it, but there's some business out in Duarte.'

'I don't suppose you need any help?'

He shook his head. 'Besides, you wouldn't want to miss your party just to stake out a dusty old warehouse.'

'I think of you all the time,' I rather blurted out.

'Yeah? That's good, Sarah, 'cause I think about you, too.'

'I'm sure,' I said. 'Probably when you're with those drunks in that terrible bar.'

'Sometimes then,' he said. 'And sometimes when I'm driving around listening to the radio. Anyway, I wanted to talk with you.'

'About what?' I asked, daring to hope.

'About our little, uh, adventure.'

'Oh.'

'There were certain things that – ah, certain facts that – never surfaced.'

'I know that,' I said.

'You do, huh? Well, I wanted . . . Look, remember that guy we met, Jerry Flaherty, from the *Post*? Well, he sort of helped me write this book and – ah, part of the book is fact, but part is – well, not exactly fact. That is to say, Flaherty felt that we had to put stuff into it that didn't come out in any of the police investigations.'

'Like what?' I asked.

'Like – why your mom was – well . . .'

'I think it only fair to tell you, Mr Bloodworth, that I, too, have written a book about the murders.'

'Oh?' He gave me a funny little smile.

'Some of it has already been published in the *Guardian*. The *Bay High Guardian*.'

'Oh?' he repeated.

'Gran's agent saw it and sold the book to a New York publisher for quite a lot of money.'

'Oh?' he said again, and seemed to pale a bit.

'In any case, in writing about what happened, it became quite apparent to me that Gary Grady did not pick my mother as a random victim. I think she did something to cause her own death, something prompted by her sociopathic tendencies.'

'Uh, you wouldn't be studying criminology, by any chance?'

'Indeed I am. And all the clues indicate that Faith was blackmailing Gary Grady. Maybe she had a right. I don't know. He did abandon her. But they both abandoned me, did they not?'

'Then you knew who Grady was?'

'Could any daughter not know?' I asked.

'Jesus, kid, I'm sorry.'

I put my hand on his. 'It took me quite a while to get over it. I didn't think it would bother me all that much. It wasn't like I'd grown up with them. But they were my parents. And it was such a terrible thing, such a heart-wrenching thing. But I don't know what else anybody can throw at me, after that.'

'There may be a few tough ones still to come, kid, but I'd bet on you to handle 'em.'

We both grinned at each other for a few seconds, then he pushed away from his car and said, 'I almost forgot. I got something for your birthday.' He reached into his car and came out with a lovely little bullterrier, just like Groucho, only a puppy, and maybe a few shades darker.

'He's beautiful,' I said.

'He's got more papers on him than Prince Charlie. I thought you could call him Groucho II.'

I hugged the dear little dog and fussed over it. Gran had given me another just that morning, but maybe we could find a home for that one. I might even persuade her to let me keep them both.

'Well,' I said, 'the Bloodhound delivers, once again.'

He nodded and his yellow eyes hooded a bit. 'So, I just dropped by to give you the puppy and tell you about my book. I wanted to let you know about it myself, rather than have you read . . . It's pretty cold in black and white and –'

'Could I have another gift, Mr Bloodworth?'

'Huh? Sure, kid. Anything within reason.'

'A kiss.'

He frowned and looked around the area at the other students as they wandered on their way home. 'Uh, maybe some other time, huh?'

'You kissed me that last night.'

'What last night?'

'After my – after Gary Grady tried to kill us. I was in bed at Lacey's and you stood over me and bent down and kissed me.'

'I didn't.'

'You most certainly did.'

'You were asleep,' he said.

'If I had been, that would have wakened me.'

'It was just a peck on the cheek,' he said.

'That's all I'm asking for now.'

Looking more nervous than even that day when he first met Gran, he bent over and kissed my cheek. When he drew back, he stared at me. 'You're getting to be quite a grown-up young lady.'

'You know, you're barely three times my age now,' I told him. 'I'm catching up to you all the time, Mr Bloodworth.'

He grinned and got into his Chevy, which I was pleased to see was just as dusty and trash-filled as ever. 'Well, Miss

Dahlquist,' he replied over the growl of the engine, 'as the years start to pile up, you'd better be careful you don't get too old for me.'

Then he was away.

I watched until his car turned the corner. Groucho II wriggled in my arms. I took him home to meet Gran.